WHERE DO YOU GO
AFTER YOU'VE GONE
TO THE STARS?

Lt. Nicole Shea was once a top space pilot. She crushed a marauding Wolfpack—and established first contact with an extraterrestrial civilization.

Now they've taken away her flight rating and reassigned her to a diplomatic post on Earth. Shea is supposed to disappear into the footnotes of history.

But the defeated raiders have not forgotten her—and neither have the alien Halyan't'a.

Soon Shea is enmeshed in intrigue more deadly than any outer-space battle. Still, even without wings, a true pilot can never be . . .

GROUNDED!

Praise for *FirstFlight* by Chris Claremont:

"A lean, tense storyline, a graphic visual sense, and a talent for action."
—*Publishers Weekly*

"An excellent first novel."

—*New York Newsday*

"Chris Claremont, well-known writer in another medium, makes an impressive debut in novel-length with *FirstFlight*—solid with plausible technical detail and excellent in story—a writer definitely able to sustain a strong start right to the end. I'm really impressed."

—C. J. Cherryh

Ace Books by Chris Claremont

**FIRSTFLIGHT
GROUNDED!**

GROUNDED!

CHRIS CLAREMONT

ACE BOOKS, NEW YORK

This book is an Ace original edition,
and has never been previously published.

GROUNDED!

An Ace Book/published by arrangement with
the author

PRINTING HISTORY
Ace edition/August 1991

ISBN: 0-441-30416-8

Ace Books are published by The Berkley Publishing Group,
200 Madison Avenue, New York, New York 10016.
The name "ACE" and the "A" logo are trademarks belonging to Charter
Communications, Inc.

PRINTED IN THE UNITED STATES OF AMERICA

10   9   8   7   6   5   4   3   2   1

To Beth

GROUNDED!

United States of America
National Aeronautics & Space Administration
Department of Manned Spaceflight
Office of the Chief Astronaut

After reviewing the opinion of the Medical Evaluations Board, together with all other pertinent data, it is the judgment of this office that Second Lieutenant Nicole Shea, United States Air Force, is currently unfit to hold an astronaut's rating and is therefore removed from Flight Status, pending further evaluation and review.

(Signed)
David Elias
Chief Astronaut

one

"BARON THREE-SIX Sierra, Las Vegas Center."

"Las Vegas, Three-Six Sierra," she replied.

"Departing our range," the controller said in its perfectly modulated, computer-generated voice. "Terminating direct route radar coverage. Squawk transponder code one-two-zero-zero until further advised by LA Center." There was a small *beep* from the display screen that filled the right side of the control panel as an electronic signal from the ground initiated the frequency change, but Nicole took a look anyway to confirm it visually, then pressed the transmit button on her control yoke. Manual backup for what the electronics should have done automatically. Another beep and a flashing light on the display indicated the controller's acknowledgment of her transmission. "Contact them directly," she was told, "on frequency one-one-nine-point-seven-five."

"One-one-niner-seven-five," she echoed, entering the numbers on the secondary transceiver channel.

"Have a nice day, Three-Six Sierra."

"You, too, Center."

Nicole Shea shifted in her seat, rolling her shoulders to ease a slight stiffness. There were few things she loved more than flying, and few things about it she found more annoying than not being able to get up and stroll about the cabin when the mood struck. A problem she wouldn't have in a bigger, more modern aircraft than this antique that rolled off the Beechcraft assembly line in her grandmother's day. But then, the actual flying wouldn't be anywhere near as much fun.

She'd taken the flight cross-country in easy stages, four days to cover what she could have done in one—although, she told herself with a grin, spending the weekend with friends in Durango didn't really count—rarely airborne for more than a couple or three hours at a stretch. The Baron was good for five—she as well—but traveling alone it was always better to play things safe. There was far more of a margin for error down here in the atmosphere than out along the High Frontier, but a stupid mistake could kill you just as dead.

Automatically, she scanned the dials—checking altitude, course, engine stats—the pilot's side of the panel crammed with analog instruments that any airman worth the name since the Wright Brothers could easily have understood, while the right-hand side was an ultra-modern flat crystal display. At the moment it was illuminated with an overhead schematic of her course—a smaller, localized version of the display available to the Air Traffic Control network. The autopilot was running things—quite nicely, as usual—but that didn't mean she had to take that for granted.

It hadn't been a pleasant scene at Sutherland Station after the shuttle's arrival. There were some outraged noises from the corporate rep, demanding to know precisely how Nicole had discovered the violations she'd reported, intimating that she'd been poking her nose into restricted data bases and was therefore potentially in far more trouble than the pilots. Simone Deschanel put a fast stop to that. "How Lieutenant Shea developed this information is irrelevant," the Secret Service agent said with an icy outrage that was no act.

"The point, gentlemen," she continued, while Nicole squirmed uncomfortably in her own chair, partly wishing she'd kept her mouth shut even though she knew she'd done the right thing, "is that your actions put the President at risk."

"Bullshit," one of the crew protested, "there was never the slightest danger. Even Lieutenant Shea can't say there was!"

"Not this trip, perhaps," Simone shot back, "but what about next time? Ten–twelve months down the line? What to my mind *is* established, beyond doubt, is a pattern of slipshod disregard for procedures that shouldn't be tolerated on *any* flight, much less a presidential one. And which had damn-all better be fixed before the Boss leaves atmosphere again!"

The crew got reprimands. In a sense, they lucked out, since they weren't fired—the need was too great and qualified personnel still too hard to come by—but they'd probably end their careers flying bottom-of-the-barrel shitloads. Total loss of seniority as well, plus the pay and perks that went with it.

"You jealous, Shea, that it?" the co-pilot snarled at her after the hearing. "You figure, you lost your rating, you want to make sure to drag some other poor slobs into the garbage dump with you?"

She didn't have an answer—then or now—and anything she said wouldn't have mattered much of a damn.

And her mind put her back on the Moon, in the office of NASA's Chief Astronaut, meeting David Elias's gaze but not really seeing him, barely aware of anything in the room at all. His desk was abnormally clean, its clutter piled away on sideboards and cabinets. This was a formal moment, it deserved an appropriate setting.

The letter lay in front of her, where he'd placed it.

"No comment?" Elias asked softly, with the faintest of Georgia drawls.

"Doesn't this say it all?" she asked back, her own voice equally quiet and surprisingly steady.

"Actually, it does—but I think more than you realize. The operative phrase in your case is 'pending further evaluation and review.' The file isn't closed, the decision's not final."

"Yet."

"That sounds a mite cynical."

"Physically, I'm fit—fully recovered from my injuries."

"No argument. Indeed, the medical staff was quite impressed; in some ways, they count you as better than before. But your 'First Flight' was an ordeal that would have put experienced command officers to the test. You went up against a Wolfpack, got your spacecraft shot out from under you, half your crew killed, and then pulled off a First Contact encounter with an extraterrestrial civilization. Most people don't see that much excitement in a career. And you did well." The way he said that last line made it clear this was, for him, the supreme compliment, more so even than the Solar Cross she'd been awarded.

"But I'm grounded." There was a flat, bitter edge to the words, as though they were a living, breathing enemy she could vanquish simply by speaking them.

"Yes."

"I feel *fit*, Dr. Elias, I can handle the job!"

"Do you, Lieutenant? Can you? I'll be blunt, the vote was as close as it can get, and *none* of the Board members were certain; I've never read more dissension in one of their opinions. Empirically, you're quite correct; you aced the recertification exams, as well or better than you did when you first came up here. You have an excellent case for reinstatement, because in the final analysis, my decision came down to instinct. I choose the fliers in my shop."

"I should have guessed. You tried your damnedest to get me thrown out of space from the moment I arrived."

"Because I thought you were cocky and arrogant, too good to be true, so good that you were guaranteed certain to make the kind of stupid, careless, overconfident mistake that would get you killed and cost the taxpayers a multibillion-dollar spacecraft. Goes to show, I'm not infallible."

"If that holds true for then, why not for now?"

"This is different. I know you now, Nicole. As much, I think, as you do yourself. You won't even need Canfield's intercession this time. You want to challenge my decision, all you have to do is request an Appeal. I'll lay odds you're flying within the month." He pulled another sheet of paper from inside the desk, slid it across to her. She spared a glance, saw a standard form. "You're entitled, everyone is, and more'n a few take the chance."

"How many successfully?"

"There's always hope. We invest considerable money and time and effort training you people, makes no sense to throw it all away. We *are* only human, we *do* make mistakes. In both directions. This could indeed be one. Hell, maybe you're right—perhaps I am erring on the side of a personal bias, that's been suggested already." She looked up, surprised, wondering who had stood up for her. "This is as close to certain as things come, Lieutenant," he finished, indicating the paper.

She touched it, wanting more than anything to sign; then she shook her head and pushed it away.

She rose to her feet, unconsciously, automatically, standing to attention; Elias was civilian, but she wasn't, and seven years in a blue suit had left its mark.

"Will that be all, sir?" she asked.

"We're done, Ms. Shea, you can go."

She saluted, did an about-face more suited to the parade quad of the Air Force Academy—a quarter million miles away, in the shadow of the Colorado Rockies—and strode out of the office.

"LA Center," she tried, deliberately breaking herself out of her reverie. "Baron November-One-Eight-Three-Six Sierra, with you at ten thousand five hundred, on a two-eight-zero radial, thirty miles outbound from Dagget VOR, westbound VFR to Mojave, over?"

Barely a mile below, desert stretched to the horizon in all directions, broken here and there by small mountain clusters and the occasional solitary butte. A sea of dull yellow, scattershot with darker strains of brown or red-orange. Nothing green. Precious little evidence that the land was any different today than when the first Indians found it aeons ago. A satellite doing a local flyby might understandably conclude that the world was fundamentally uninhabited, or possessed of only the most minimal technology. *Until, of course,* she thought, *they conducted an atmospheric analysis.* A half century of increasingly serious and enforced environmental legislation had made a substantial difference—the air far fitter to breathe and the seas mostly safe to swim in—but there was still a ways to go.

She repeated her call to Los Angeles Center, and this time was rewarded by a reply.

"Transmission acknowledged, Three-Six Sierra," another computer-generated voice, as pleasant and featureless as the one she'd heard from Vegas, and indeed every other controller from one end of the country to the other. Actual human beings only came on-line when there was trouble; otherwise, it was an entirely computer-run system. "Your current position is beyond our direct radar coverage"—to be expected, given Nicole's altitude, in this rugged, randomly mountainous terrain—"but be advised that your course will take you through restricted airspace, a Military Operating Area."

"Understood, LA," she said, "I have authorization for transit through the MOA to Mojave Airport"—outside the town of the same name, just north of the sprawling Air Force base, it billed itself as the Civilian Flight Test Center—"and will be contacting Edwards TRACON for specific vectors, over." She stifled a yawn—more the effects of flying at altitude than actual fatigue—looked suddenly out the right-hand window as a distant flash caught her eye, down low on the deck. Probably nothing, she decided when she didn't spot anything, somebody hot-rodding across the dunes, sunlight bouncing off his windshield.

"Acknowledged, Three-Six Sierra. Contact Edwards Traffic Control on frequency one-two-four-point-eight."

"One-two-four-point-eight, LA, roger."

"Three-Six Sierra, LA, over?" New voice, a person this time. She sat a little straighter in her seat, took a quick glance across the sky around her.

"Three-Six Sierra, go ahead."

"Say again your aircraft type."

That prompted a smile. No major crisis then, but a question she heard most often from mainline hub facilities, where the personnel dealt more with state-of-the-art commercial equipment than the smaller fields she preferred, where they still remembered the old days and older planes.

"Beechcraft," she told the woman, "Baron, Model B for Bravo, five-eight. Over."

"Baron?" the controller repeated, voice rising slightly into a query of disbelief.

"Twin-engine, propellor-driven, six-seater, circa 1985."

"And it still flies?"

"Very well, thank you." Which prompted a low whistle of admiration.

"More power to you, then, Three-Six Sierra. However, we recommend you exercise a heightened degree of discretion. You're in a sort of no-man's-land between Vegas Center, us, and Edwards airspace. At your altitude, we cannot provide comprehensive radar coverage."

"Acknowledged, LA, and appreciated." She switched the main display over to RADAR, refined the scan to give her a clear picture of the route ahead. Looked clear. For all she knew, might actually *be* clear.

Four years since she last walked the high desert. She'd been assigned to Edwards after graduation from the Air Force Academy, which had been a major shock, since her career profile had her on track for NASA and astronaut training. Turned out the Commander of the Flight Test Center, Harry Macon, had asked for her specifically, and for the better part of the year she spent there she functioned as his shadow, pulling all the scutwork duty that went with being an aide but getting as well invaluable training and hands-on experience in the art of flying. The tour culminated in her being tapped to be his co-pilot for what turned out to be the first successful test of the XSR-5 Controlled ReEntry Vehicle. A week later she'd been part of the memorial overflight for Harry's funeral. And within a month after that, she was on her way to NASA.

Now, full circle, she was coming back. Step up, step down, she didn't really care. Part of her was still numb and she was beginning to wonder if it'd ever thaw.

She blinked, looking off to the right again, tilting the wheel slightly to tip the Baron starboard side down as she eyeballed the desolate landscape. Pulled off her RayBans to see if there was any difference without her sunglasses. Something had registered out of the corner of her eyes, more as an afterimage than anything else; truth to tell, she wasn't sure it was anything at all but she felt better making certain. Another small smile, but this with a lot less humor. One of the more hellish realities of flying was how infernally hard it was to actually *see* anything. More times than she'd care to remember, she'd gotten a call about another contact in her vicinity, been told where to look and how far away, searched the sky with diligent ferocity, only to come up empty. Amazing how aircraft that looked so big close-up could disappear so completely once they got off the ground.

She keyed the transmit button, to give Edwards TRACON a call.

And her plane seemed to run into a wall.

No sound, no warning, a dart-winged shape blurring past her nose, trailing twin spikes of flame as afterburners hurled it for the stars, had to have been transitioning through Mach, sonic booms creating the jet wake of a plane ten times its size, waves of solid air punching the Baron's nose down with brutal force, throwing it one way, Nicole snapping the other, crying out as her head bounced off the wall. Alarms and telltales were flashing all across her control panel, mixing with the light show inside her skull, while some insistently heavy hand tried to shove her out of her seat and squash her flat on the ceiling.

Opened her eyes, found her glasses twisted crookedly over
her nose, her body wedged in the corner formed by her seat and
the left-hand side of the fuselage. World was spinning like a
top, left to right, so fast she couldn't bear to look for more than
a millisecond. Knew instantly what was happening, a state all
fliers feared, the flat spin. Think of that top, spinning 'round
and 'round on its central axis; now think of a plane doing
the same thing, corkscrewing into the ground, in such a tight
circle the wings can't pull decent lift from the air or the control
surfaces sufficient to maneuver. And if you're not careful,
when you apply power, all you do is spin faster and faster.

No noise, silence where she should have heard the comforting *thrum* of the engines. Simple reason for it, both propellors
were standing stock-still. Again, realizations flashing faster
than conscious thought, so that by the time she verbalized them
to herself her body was already reacting—flying at altitude,
and to reduce both fuel consumption and engine wear, she'd
been running the fans lean. Meant riding a very fine line, but
ordinarily that was no problem. When she ran into the jet
wake, she didn't just have turbulence to cope with, but also
the residue from its engines—which, on afterburners, with
raw fuel being injected into the ignition chamber to intensify
combustion, meant a foul soup of heavy hydrocarbons. For
her engines, like flying into mud. Ruined the mixture, fouled
the combustion cycle within her cylinders, starving them of
the oxygen they needed to fire. Instant shutdown.

The Baron was shuddering so hard, she couldn't focus on
the instruments, no notion of her altitude, didn't matter anyway, wasn't sure enough of her position to know how much
clear air she had below her. Charts listed the ground as topping
out at about five-six, but some of the ridge lines and attendant
peaks didn't go much above four thousand feet. In this kind
of madcap descent, the rate-of-climb indicator was virtually
useless; if she wasted time determining how much time she
had, she'd be dead before she got around to actually trying to
save herself. Again, while these thoughts were popping like
fireworks across the panorama of her awareness, her hands
were moving of their own accord, one shifting the mixture
to full rich while the other worked the fuel pump to get fresh
gas into the engine. Twin fans complicated the problem, the
counterclockwise spin created a centrifugal effect that pushed
fuel away from the port engine, but into the starboard one.

What was sufficient to start one would either be too much or too little for the other, and she had no way of knowing which except her instincts.

Turned the key, nothing happened. Hissed a curse, gritting her teeth as a burping hiccough pumped a mouthful of bile to the top of her throat. Repeated the process, concentrating on one engine, winced as a couple of popping explosions shook the aircraft, but thankful as well because the backfires meant there was combustion occurring in the cylinders. The propellor began to turn and she played with throttle and mixture, trying for the ideal combination to get it running, was surprised by the sound of her own voice crying, "Yes *yes yes*," as the triple blades spun faster and faster, the sonofabitch was running rough, more backfires with accompanying gouts of black smoke out the exhausts, but it was running. She opened the throttle wide, shoving the yoke forward, the wheel hard over, rudder pedals as well. The Baron was falling tail down—tended to happen in flat spins—now, she had to get air flowing over the wings, generate lift so the control surfaces could do their job. Of course, if she'd lost too much altitude, she'd simply be diving herself the last stretch into the desert. Not that she had any choice. The plane shuddered violently—so much so she thought it would tear apart around her—but this was a design that had stood the test of time, the private aviation equivalent of the legendary Mack truck, and as the engine roar became a shriek, matched by one of defiant fury from Nicole herself, the flight profile stabilized, the horizon settled, and with breathtaking suddenness she was once more straight and level.

For a moment all she could do was sit and stare in wonderment, while the Baron ripped through the sky a few hundred feet above the scrub rock and Joshua trees. Her breath came in the shallowest of gasps, the desperate, automatic gulps of air that a marathoner makes as he hits the "wall"—that part of the race where mind and body face their ultimate test. She didn't move, wasn't sure she could, tension had turned her into a living statue. Finally managed to reach out to the throttle and back it off from the firewall. Immediately, though, she felt a response from the controls, a dangerous sluggishness accompanied by a quiver from the altimeter; so far, she was holding her own but any less power and she'd once more be on her way down.

Belatedly, she realized no sounds were coming through her headset, discovering when she reached up that it wasn't there anymore. Her hand came away scarlet and sticky; she decided to leave well enough alone and not go exploring. So long as she could function, she didn't care how badly she was hurt; and if she couldn't function, knowing the extent of the damage wouldn't really matter. The headset and boom mike must have been torn loose when she hit the hull; she took off her glasses, stared at the mangled frame, one lens splintered by the impact. She was lucky she still had her eye.

A check of the radio display told her it was functional— *thank God,* she thought, *for small favors*—and she switched it over to the cabin speakers, taking up the hand mike from its cradle between the two front seats.

"Baron . . ." she began, then had to stop in amazement at how calmly matter-of-fact she sounded. No shakes, no quavers, nothing but a little dryness to differentiate this from a normal call on a normal flight.

"Baron One-Eight-Three-Six Sierra," she said, "calling any station. Mayday, I repeat, Mayday. Position . . . *uh,* somewhere north of Barstow, within the Edwards MOA, altitude around six thousand. On one engine, pilot injured. Any station, please respond. Over."

The reply was instantaneous but growly with static, and she wondered if the spin had damaged her aerials.

"Baron Three-Six Sierra, Edwards TRACON, receiving you, acknowledging your declaration of emergency. Identify yourself, please."

"Nicole Shea, Lieutenant, USAF. En route to duty assignment at Edwards. Cleared through MOA to Mojave. Something"—a pause, to gather and sort out recollections—"almost hit me. Very small, very fast, exhaust fouled my fans, lost both engines, got thrown into a flat spin." Her forehead furled as she put some more pieces together, she'd fallen almost a mile in a matter of seconds; if she'd hesitated in the slightest, or made a wrong move, if the engine hadn't fired that second time, there wouldn't have been a third. Too damn close. "I'm out of it now, stable flight, maybe a hundred-ten knots by three hundred feet. I'd appreciate a vector direct to Edwards, over."

"Three-Six Sierra . . ."

"Say again, Edwards, your transmission's breaking up." She fiddled with the squelch and gain controls, trying to clean up

the reception, the thought striking simultaneously that perhaps it wasn't the hardware glitching but she herself. Hearing
wrong, or scrambling the input between ears and brain.

"Barstow is closer, Three-Six Sierra." The controller was
speaking slowing, overenunciating the words to make sure she
got it. "Suggest you divert . . ."

"Understood, Edwards," she interrupted, "but there's high
ground between me and Barstow, I don't know if I can get
over the hump. It's pretty much downhill to you."

"How about your other engine?"

"Next item on the agenda."

"Roger, Three-Six Sierra. We have a helo scrambled and en
route. If possible, squawk five-five-zero-zero—double-five,
double-oh—on your transponder." The auto-sequencer was
out, so she entered the code manually.

"Transmitting, Edwards," she told them.

"Received, Three-Six Sierra, we got you. At this time, turn
left to a heading of two-six-zero."

She made it a wide, slow, gentle turn, putting as little pressure as possible on her single engine. Once she'd settled back
to the straight and level, she primed the other fan and turned
the key.

The explosion nearly blew her out of the sky. A sharp *bang*,
accompanied by a hole the size of a softball erupting from the
cowling, hardly any smoke, too much flame. She slapped the
throttle closed, cut off all the fuel, pulled the fire bottle to
flood the engine with foam, at the same time fighting to regain
control of an aircraft that was wallowing like a dory in heavy
swell. A buzzer announced what she already knew, that she
was slipping down again at the tail, coming dangerously close
to a stall. More power then to the good fan, all it would take,
the hell with the consequences, shove the nose down, trade off
altitude for control and gamble the price wouldn't be too high.
Turned out to cost a hundred feet and change. But too many
red lights on the status telltales meant she didn't dare try to get
it back. The only way she'd grab herself some more sky was
to stay where she was while the land dropped away beneath
her. Automatically, she swept the locality for a place to set
down, if worst came to worst. Though she knew if she did,
that was the end of her plane. Nasty country, though, nowhere
viable.

"Three-Six Sierra, we mark a drop in altitude."

"My engine, she broke bad. Looks like, blew a cylinder. Had a fire, but that's under control. So's the aircraft. But it is not a happy puppy, Edwards."

"Treat it right, Three-Six Sierra, Baron's sure to do right by you."

, Man knew his aircraft. Good for him. And maybe for her. "So far, so good," she told him. She craned forward for a better look through her windshield. "I believe, Edwards, I have your helo."

"Affirmative, Three-Six Sierra, and vice versa."

"Big sucker," she said, mostly to herself, "very impressive." Understatement actually, the Sikorsky dwarfed her Baron, each of its five rotor blades longer than the Beech's wingspan, with a cargo bay that could have easily fitted the entire fuselage. It took up station off her left side, maintaining a respectful distance, not wanting the wash of its own propellors to slap her down.

She'd been about fifty miles out—usually a fifteen-minute flight, unless the winds were totally rotten—but the better part of an hour passed before the sprawling expanse of Rogers Dry Lake, and Edwards itself, swam into view in the distance. A couple of times on the flight, between regular calls from TRACON, to see how she was faring, she'd been startled by a strange sound in the cockpit, realizing with a chagrined shake of the head that it was herself, making a noise that was more than a hum, less than outright singing, an absently subvocalized rendition of one of her favorite Lila Cheney songs. And remembered Paolo DaCuhna laughingly telling her—the remains of a ceviche and paella dinner and a bottle of prime tequila littering the table between them—it was what she did when she was pushed right to the edge, with everything riding on her next move and how well she performed it. Sharp pang inside—*Damn*, she thought, *the timing of some things, absolutely* no *sense of place*—and she wondered if she'd ever stop missing him. Wondered if this was her time to join him, and Harry Macon. No effort at all to auger in.

"Three-Six Sierra, Edwards."

"Go ahead, Edwards," she acknowledged, grateful to have that train of thought broken, "Three-Six Sierra."

"You have field in sight?"

"Affirmative."

"Okay then, we're handing you over. Contact the tower on one-two-zero-point-seven."

"One-two-zero-point-seven," she repeated, "thanks for all the help, TRACON."

"Our pleasure, Three-Six. You've come this far just fine, take it home."

"Do my best." She entered the frequency on the secondary com channel, then switched it to the primary; that way, if there was any mistake, she could always reverse back to TRACON. The Tower was waiting for her.

"Altimeter zero-eight, Three-Six Sierra," they told her and she adjusted the pressure setting on her altimeter accordingly. Backup to a backup to a backup, because the same information was displayed—far more precisely—by an inertial radar altimeter and another one slave-linked through the transponder with ground control. If she wanted, she could see her height charted to the millimeter. As it was, without making any effort, she'd managed to give herself a good twenty-five hundred feet of grace, thanks to the ground's downward slope from the high country at five thousand to the dry lakebed's twenty-two hundred. Unfortunately, as the flight progressed, her remaining engine had begun growling ever more vehement protests. The compression readings refused to settle down and she was virtually certain at least one of the cylinders was misfiring, the head possibly—strike that, probably—cracked.

"Winds bearing three-one-one . . ."

"Damn," she said with quiet vehemence. Nearly a broadside crosswind.

" . . . at fifteen, gusting to twenty-five."

Worse and worse. And she began to consider the option of ignoring the runways and putting the Baron down on the dry lake itself. No major problem with that, Rogers Dry Lake was one of Edwards' reasons for being. A flat, hard pancake surface that went on for miles, an ideal place to land an aircraft. And she made the suggestion to the Tower.

"We concur, Three-Six Sierra. If you're flying that close to the edge, that might be the best approach."

Terrific. Now all she had to do was pull it off.

She backed off a little on the throttle, nudging the yoke forward into a nose-down attitude, initiating a cautious hundred-feet-per-minute descent. Next move on her dance card was turning closer into the wind, using its force both to slow her further and give her more stability while doing so. In a single-engine aircraft, lose the engine you were essentially in a big, ugly, not ferociously aerodynamic glider. Flying a twin, though, with one fan gone, the operative engine tended to torque the aircraft in the opposite direction—in this case, the starboard engine pulling the plane perpetually to the left. You countered that by going full right rudder, engine going one way, control surfaces the other, resulting in a reasonable facsimile of stable flight. Turning left was no hassle, since that was the direction the plane tended to naturally; right meant backing off on engine power, to give the rudder ascendancy. She gave it a try, saw the compass begin to pivot.

The airframe trembled about her—could have been the passage through a rough patch of air, the equivalent on the ground of bouncing over cobblestones or a stretch of classic Manhattan potholes—but she knew instantly that wasn't the case. A glance at the panel, then at the engine, confirmed it. There was a significant falling off of RPM, even to the naked eye the propellor was spinning markedly more slowly. She restored the throttle to its initial setting, heard more dyspeptic growl than roar from her right, and saw no significant change in revs.

"Edwards Tower," she called, "I have a problem. I think I'm losing my good fan. Going for the deck, down and dirty."

"Three-Six Sierra, this is One-One Bravo"—the helo—"we'll follow you down. We have fire suppression and rescue personnel aboard if needed."

"Hopefully not, One-One Bravo," she said, "but I appreciate the consideration."

She shoved the yoke forward, tripling her rate of descent, putting the Baron as close as she dared into a dive. Approaching five hundred, she leveled out, took a second to steady the aircraft, then dropped gear and flaps together. The plane bucked as the suddenly messy silhouette disrupted the smooth passage of air around the airframe, but she managed to settle it, maintaining airspeed while her speed over the ground dropped to a virtual crawl. Nothing about her was at rest, body attuned to every nuance in the plane's motion, both hands on the wheel, staying a beat ahead of every wayward move, eyes flicking ceaselessly from the ground ahead to the panel before her and back again. Unaware she was chanting a singsong mantra, interweaving another Lila song with a soft exhortation to her plane: "C'mon, Baron, that's my big babe, you can do it, almost there, c'mon c'mon c'mon, there we go, no problem, almost there, that's a fella, c'mon, Baron."

Less than a hundred feet to go, at a speed most highway-configured cars could top with ease, but which to Nicole seemed far too fast. Goosed the nose up a tad, final flare to touchdown, cursing as a sudden gust combined with ground effect—the cushion of air formed by the compression of air between the wings and the ground below—to bounce the plane too high, send it skidding sideways. No more time to be gentle or worry about the consequences, shut down the fan completely, push full forward on the yoke. Instantly turning the Baron from aircraft to a brick with wheels, dropping it the last dozen to twenty feet so hard on its gear that her teeth snapped together, body hammered into its seat. Plane made a halfhearted bounce—*Christ knows*, she thought, *what this impact's doing to my shocks, minor miracle the struts haven't smashed, aren't smashing, all the way up through the wing, thank God Beech built this beast so well*—and rolled a few hundred desultory feet before coming to a stop.

She knew she should get out, put as much space between her and the aircraft as possible, just in case something decided to blow. But she felt gripped by a weird certainty that nothing would. The plane had done its best to save her, somehow seemed like a betrayal to run away now that it had. She turned off the switches, listened to the master power system whine down to silence as the avionics display went dark, then gave the panel a gentle pat of appreciation and a murmured "Thank you, little plane," before releasing her safety harness, wincing as she flexed her shoulders. The heavy straps had scraped the skin over her collarbones raw as the plane's motion had bounced her violently back and forth. She was glad for the four-point restraints, though; standard seat belts would have made it a lot more difficult, perhaps impossible, to reach the controls on the far side of the cabin.

She didn't stand to step onto the wing after opening the door, but slid out onto the walkway, pausing to pull her flight jacket around her shoulders against the surprisingly chilly air before pivoting on her backside to stretch her legs full length, semicollapsing her forehead to her knees to ease the kinks from her back. Off in the distance came the whooping sound of sirens as rescue vehicles sped towards her across the desert

hardpan, mostly drowned by the ear-busting shriek of the
Sikorsky's monster jets as it settled downwind of her.

She dropped to the ground herself as the first of the
"Hot Papas"—firemen in gleaming, flameproof bodysuits
that allowed them to plunge safely into the heart of the
most fearsome inferno—lumbered over, lugging bulky foam
extinguishers. They weren't needed, the medic was.

She winced as the other woman gently touched a gauze to
her scalp, along the hairline by her ear where the headset boom
had made a ragged slash.

"I thought that plastic was supposed to be unbreakable,"
Nicole grumbled.

"Write the manufacturer," the medic replied matter-of-factly.
"Helluva bump." She held up a finger. "What do you see?"

"One finger, in focus."

"Follow it," and Nicole did so, tracking her eyes right, left,
up, down, in concert with the medic's movements. "How do
you feel?"

"Wrung out. Achy. Sore."

"Tired?"

"It was a long flight, even before the emergency."

"Might be concussed. We'll take you into the hospital, do
a preliminary workup."

"Terrific."

"Hey, Lieutenant, ain't my fault."

"Ain't mine, either."

Brass with the vehicles, a brace of MP's and one of the duty
officers, a Major who raised his eyebrows in silently obvious
astonishment at the sight of Nicole's jacket. Few of the senior
pilots had one, much less any baby blue shirts. Nicole handed
over her CardEx and orders, which he inserted into a portable
Reader slung over his shoulder.

"Certainly have a knack for making an entrance, Lieutenant," he said, handing back her document cards.

"Not my intention, sir, believe me."

"Colonel Sallinger"—boss of the Flight Test Center—
"wants to see you." *Probably*, she thought sourly, *after
a stunt like this, to throw me out on my ass*. He hadn't
been that fond of her last tour here, when he was Harry
Macon's Vice-Commander, vocally and vehemently protest-
ing what he perceived as the special treatment his friend was
giving her.

"I have first dibs on her, Major," the medic said. "Boss'll have to wait 'til we make sure she's okay."

"What about my Baron?" Nicole asked, and the Major turned to a stocky weather-beaten man with Top Sergeant stripes on his fatigues.

"Your call, Castaneda."

"Came down hard, Major," the Boss LineTech said, looking up from where he was crouched by one of the engines, his words softened by a mild Spanish accent, "but these old brutes were built to take worse. No problem to roll it up onto a flatbed and take it over to the maintenance ramp, give it a proper once over."

"Thanks, Ray," Nicole said. He shrugged and smiled, came with the territory, the fun that made the job worth having.

"Major," the medic said, "you got nothing more here, the Loot an' I're gonna roll."

"Take her, Adani. But soon as you're cleaned up, Lieutenant, Colonel Sallinger's office, full burner, copy?"

She pushed herself erect and gave him a sharp salute, which he returned in kind, waiting 'til he was back in his car and speeding away before muttering, "What's the bug up *his* ass?"

Medic laughed. "Midlevel on the totem pole, worked hard to get where he is . . ."

"And resents hotshot junior officers on what appears to be a faster track?"

"You said it."

Nicole shook her head. "If he only knew."

two

IT WASN'T UNTIL much later, when shock gave way to pain only marginally dulled by basic pills, that she began relating to what had actually happened, pulling the pieces together, cohering random imagery into a complete, sequential whole.

And got angry.

She'd been where she was supposed to be, on track, on schedule, following a flight plan filed and approved over a week before, certainly listed on the Master Regional Plot if not on the screens of the local Route Centers. And some pudknocker sonofabitch had zipped up from below and behind—where even her on-board radar hadn't a prayer of spotting him—out of the mountains, where he was blind to everyone else's ground-based scans, to bounce her. And damn near buy her the farm.

By the time she hit headquarters, after a shower and a change into a fresh uniform, anger had become white-hot fury, a flame as piercingly intense as any from an acetylene welding torch. Only to discover that Colonel Sallinger was off-base, not expected back 'til sometime much later that evening. Hunger got the better of her then, and after leaving word with the receptionist, she flagged a lift up Rosamond—the main drag in from the small desert town of the same name—to Hap Arnold Park, named for arguably the greatest Chief of

Staff in Air Force history, who'd commanded through World War II and up until the Air Force became a separate service in 1946.

Not much in the way of greenery, there was a perverse pride on the base about keeping true to the environment's prehistoric desolation. Paths led away from the road, between twin rows of parked aircraft, representing the benchmark test flights made off the high desert, going all the way back to the Bell X-1. From the most primitive to designs too outrageous to be credible, some looking like they'd never get off the ground, others like they couldn't wait. So many she'd read about, videoed, more than a few she'd seen, and a rare couple or three she'd actually flown herself. If Eagle Landing was her favorite place on the Moon, this was it on Earth. Where she lost herself in memories of a time when Edwards was mostly make-believe, Mad Monk nutcases perched on the edge of nowhere, teasing the impossible out of machines that were state-of-the-art one morning, obsolete the next, the cutting edge so sharp it more often than not killed those who tried to ride it. When the Unknown truly was that.

She looked over the ridge lines where they rose and fell like waves curling across the ocean swell, perched chock-a-block with houses and trees and even lawns for God's sake, all the hallmarks of a fair-sized company town, complete with schools and stores and a minimall. And tried to imagine what it had been like for Yeager and Ridley and Crossfield and Kincheloe in those first crazy years when they were pretty much all by themselves, hanging out on the outside of the envelope, and then thought of the time not much later when it seemed like a pilot a week was being buried and some started wondering if the price of knowledge was too high.

The sun had gone while she was in her reverie, hardly anything left of day but a wild palette of colors streaked in layers up a small ways from the horizon, where they faded into the deepening twilight. A couple of stars flickered over the east, a chill breeze making her turn up the collar of her jacket and wish for something warmer than shirtsleeves underneath. She'd left her gear aboard the Baron, God knew where it was now. Made a disgusted noise and strode through the park, across a grassy knoll to a sloppily haphazard building set off by itself in the middle distance. There was a driveway, but that was really supposed to be restricted to delivery vehicles.

The right and proper way to approach Hotshots was through the park. Past the planes. So you entered with a true sense of place and perspective.

The club was nothing really special to look at, inside or out. Weather-beaten because most of the materials had fallen off the back of somebody's truck. Scrounged. Stolen. The pilots did it, no one knew whose idea it was or who'd set things in motion, it seemed to be one of those synergistic moments that just . . . *happened*. Fliers started hanging out here, on this little rise overlooking the park and the huge dry lake beyond, chugging beers and doing their best with barbecue grills and hibachis of steak or burgers while they talked and boasted and argued about their work. Then the picnic ground sort of grew some walls and became a type of lean-to, shelter from the elements when they turned nasty. And one thing led to another. Until there was a real, honest-to-by-God restaurant. With one tradition carried over from the oldest days, when the pilot's hangout had been a rumpled, tumble-down paradise called Pancho's: the wall behind the bar was crammed with pictures, men and women and the planes that killed them.

"Hail the conquering hero," cried the woman behind the bar as Nicole crossed the threshold, rolling her eyes in dismay as she took herself a stool and ordered a seltzer.

"Don't like the limelight?" Sue asked while Nicole nursed the drink and scanned the shadows for anyone else she knew.

"Gimme a break."

"I'm only busting chops, Nicole, 'cause I care. And I'm damn proud."

Nicole lifted her glass in an acknowledging toast. Sue barely touched five feet and life for her seemed a perpetual battle with a figure that would never be as svelte as fashion demanded. Scuttlebutt cast her past in terms of exotic mystery, which everyone knew was a crock because there was no way anyone got on base, especially to work, without being checked out every which way by Air Force Security and the FBI. Some even wondered if she was a spook herself. She'd come west ages back, casting off a career as an accountant to cook and tend bar, and gradually made Hotshots her own, eventually becoming its manager. The Air Force had no complaint with that because she made a tidy profit; the customers loved it because she ran the place like her own home, dispensing superb eats, advice offered whether it was asked for or not, and very occasionally help with taxes and budgeting.

"Hungry?" Nicole was asked.

Sue got a shrug in return, and gave a short, barking laugh. "I thought you blue-suit zoomies were trained to be decisive."

"It's been a long day, what can I say?"

Arms came around her from behind and a beery voice growled, "Booga booga booga," in her ear.

"Seductive as ever, *eh*, Ramsey."

"Where you're concerned, L'il Loot, I can't help myself." A Major, with a lazy smile and classic features that got him more than his share of second looks when ladies passed him by, wearing a leather flight jacket that matched Nicole's own. The name came from a WASP father, the looks and natural grace from a Tuscan mom, Ramsey Sheridan bringing to social occasions the same easy, relaxed, seemingly unflappable manner that made him one of the Center's premier test pilots.

"You're the proverbial lifesaver," he continued, draping an arm across her shoulders and accepting the Anchor Steam Sue poured for him.

"My cue to rabbit."

"No, seriously, Nicole, we got a game going, we're a bod short."

"Rain check, Ramsey?"

"Hey, would I be asking if I could take no for an answer?" And he gently bumped her off her stool and towards a back table, where the usual gang of ruffians had gathered for the weekly game.

Stakes were moderate, which suited Nicole fine. She wasn't that thrilled with the idea of playing—the more time passed, the more the effects of this afternoon's landing made themselves felt—but Ramsey left no courteous way to back out. She was in an odd state where she felt consumed by weariness—there was an ache across her shoulders that reminded her of her first ride in the centrifuge—yet was far too jazzed to sleep. Dangerous combination, guaranteed to make her sloppy, but she didn't care enough to focus out of it. Couldn't be bothered, what was the point? She stayed for two cards the first hand, then folded when the bet to her hit ten bucks.

Second hand went pretty much the same way. Third, she stuck out with two pair, only to be nailed by a trip, three of a kind. By the time the deck came 'round to her, she'd won some, lost some more, was down about twenty dollars and

thinking some seriously hostile thoughts in Ramsey's direction, of which the son of a bitch seemed serenely oblivious.

"Room for another?"

A young man, within two or three years of Nicole's age,
tall and lean with a Byron-esque cast to his heartbreaker features. Good bones over naturally hollowed cheeks, creating
a splendid frame for his wide-spaced, dark eyes, though the
total effect was perhaps a tad too delicate. Full lips, quirked
in the slightest of smiles that carried an edge of mockery, the
sense that this was a person used to getting his own way, bound
by only the most minimal of limits. There was a sleek, almost
designer athleticism to his form, coupled with a self-awareness
of the body Nicole was most used to seeing in her youngest
brother and his fellow dancers.

"Your game, Ramsey," Nicole said, masking her pleasure
at the flash of discomfiture across the Major's face; here, she
decided, was appropriate payback for putting her on the spot
earlier. "Your call."

"He can have my seat," groaned Stu Hanneford with a
glance at his watch, "I gotta be over at Ops for my shift
in an hour. 'Sides, the cards have not been kind tonight, no
sense prolonging the agony."

"Stakes?" the newcomer asked, pulling a handful of bills
from his wallet. He wore civvies but it was the way he carried himself that told Nicole he wasn't military. Even in the
most casual and informal of settings, every rank had a way
of relating to each other that told you subconsciously where
they stood on the totem pole. This guy's attitude was that he
topped them all.

"Dollar, five, ten bets," Ramsey replied in too even a voice.
"Three raise max. Dealer antes and calls the game."

"A hundred dollars worth of chips, please?"

"It's a friendly game, Alex," Ramsey said, "and some of
us work for a living."

"No problem." Alex flashed perfect teeth in a perfect and
pro forma smile, and took fifty instead. "I'm Alex Cobri," he
said to Nicole.

"Ah," she said, as all became clear. She knew the name; there
wasn't an astronaut flying who didn't. Since Cobri, Associates
built the starships they flew. Manuel Cobri—Alex's father, she
assumed—being the man who, virtually single-handedly, had
turned Jean-Claude Baumier's conceptions into reality and

thereby booted humanity out of the Earth-Moon system and into the galaxy. Hailed by media commentators as the modern equivalent of Da Vinci. Not to mention Croesus.

"Nicole Shea," was her reply.

"I know."

She called seven-card stud, and proceeded to deal herself aces, a pair down. That got her attention.

"Rumor has it," one of the other pilots noted, continuing the political discussion from the previous hand and opening with a dollar bet, "Mansfield's going to challenge for the nomination."

"He feels betrayed," said Alex, and Nicole heard a faint intake of breath as he saw the dollar and bumped it ten.

"He was," this came from Nicole's right. "President Russell said he'd bow out in his favor after one term. That's why the man backed down last election and came aboard as Veep."

"What the hell," Ramsey said, "six years in the White House oughtta be enough for any man. Almost half Lee's term, after the President died, and one in his own right, what more does he want? You'd think he'd be glad to get out."

"Circumstances change," Nicole noted, calling the cards as she dealt another round, "four years ago, there were no Halyan't'a."

"You had something to do with that"—Alex turned a side-long glance towards Nicole—"am I right?"

"A very small something, in point of fact," she replied noncommittally.

"You took a fair beating, Lieutenant, as I recall," he continued.

"The better part of a year in hospital and therapy," this from Ramsey, answering for Nicole, "but quite fit now, I understand."

"Physically, at any rate," Nicole acknowledged.

"I wonder, what's it matter who grabs the Oval Office," mused Alex, "Mansfield or Russell, or whoever the Democrats toss into the ring?"

"Smart money," Ramsey noted sotto voce, "pegs the Democratic nominee as Senator Ishida."

"Good choice," another agreed, "she'll give either of 'em a fair run for their money."

But Nicole wasn't paying attention to their exchange, she was focused on the younger Cobri.

"It matters," she said, "because of the Halyan't'a."

"How so?" Alex demanded.

"They came to us as equals. One civilization—one *species*—to another. They've no interest in dealing with a balkanized political structure. They want one government to deal with, that speaks not simply for the Earth but for the Colonies as well."

"I can't wait to see how the Afrikaaners on *Nieuwhome* react to that," he countered with a sneer, "they made it plain when they left they want nothing more to do with Earth."

"They may have no choice," Nicole said softly.

"I'm an *American*," Alex said, leaning forward on the table, his eyes on Nicole, and suddenly she had a wild sense that things were spinning out of hand, a roller-coaster ride down a set of open-ended tracks, "and as an American, I'm not terribly thrilled with the idea of ceding national sovereignty to the United Nations."

"You think the Russians like it any better," she heard from across the table, "or the Europeans or the Chinese or the Japanese or the Brazilians or the Iranians?"

"Not to mention the Belters," added Ramsey.

"Consider the alternative," Nicole said.

"Which is," this from Alex.

"We're *not* the Halyan't'a's equals, militarily or technologically. If they'd wanted, they could have moved in on us just like the Great Powers did on Africa and China—and tried to with Japan—two centuries ago. Playing one country off against another, divide and conquer, until we woke up one bright morning to discover we worked for them. You don't think there are factions on s'N'dare advocating just that? Why share when you can dominate, it's a seductive argument."

"You ever consider, Lieutenant, we might try that ourselves?"

"Hardly the way, Mr. Cobri, to build trust between two peoples."

"Since when does trust have anything to do with national interest?"

"The minute the national interest left the atmosphere. Trust is the only thing that keeps us alive up here."

"Are we playing cards here, or what?"

"Sorry, Ramsey," and she dealt the last up card.

"Forget I said anything," he muttered after taking a look, "the way this hand went we were better off with politics."

"You missed your calling, Ms. Shea," Alex told her, "Russell ought to have you on his payroll, writing speeches."

"I already have a job, thank you," thinking, *Such as it is these days*.

The game was down to her and Alex. Ramsey had three to a straight flush until this last card busted it; that was why he'd stayed in so long, in the face of Alex's succession of five- and ten-dollar raises each round. This was the biggest pot of the night, the one that had done the most damage along the way; she was fairly certain it would also be the last. The game was as much about companionship as winnings and no one seemed to have much interest in the former with Alex. She hadn't a clue how to read him, either; with the others, after an hour and more of play, she had a sense of how they thought, what moves were strategy and what emotion, when they were bluffing and how they could be bluffed—just as she was sure they were trying to do the same with her.

Based on what she could see, he potentially had anything from two pair to a full house, pushing the bet to the limit every time. Half the table had dropped, not because they had bad hands—a couple appeared quite formidable—but because the cost of losing was getting way too bloody. From what she'd seen on the table, though, plus in her own hand, she was pretty much certain she had him beat, even if he wasn't bluffing.

"Ten to you, Ms. Shea," he said, adding one more bill to the pile. Still one more card to go, with its own betting round. Twenty bucks more, absolute minimum. Anything she raised, Cobri looked ready to match without a second thought, with all the gambling finesse of a sledgehammer.

She turned her cards face down, the game was over.

"Sorry about that," Ramsey said as she excused herself to the bar for another seltzer.

"You shoulda stayed," Sue chided her.

She shrugged. "Wasn't worth the effort."

"If not for the money, sweetheart, the pride. You let him chase you."

I've already fallen, Suze, she thought, *I got no need for this kind of pride, thank you very much*.

In the background, Alex had gotten involved in a heated exchange at another booth with a couple of pilots.

"It registered on the sensor package as the target drone," he said, "of *course* the remote executed the intercept, that's what it's programmed to *do*!" Upset as he clearly was, he still managed to convey the contemptuous impression of a bored grown-up explaining the blindingly obvious to a hopelessly backward child.

"Mr. Cobri," an officer said patiently, "your jinxing through the passes swung you into the wrong pattern, the target was twenty klicks the other direction."

"You saying it's *my* fault, Captain?"

"What's he talking about?" Nicole asked Ramsey.

"Don't you know?"

She shook her head.

"Oh, jeez, Nicole, I'm sorry."

"For what?"

"The remote . . ." Ramsey's voice trailed off.

"*Him?*"

"If you'd followed flight profile," the pilot was saying.

"Straight and level at a safe altitude, we'd have learned nothing. The remote coped with low-level, max-speed maneuvers as well and better than most of your manned beasts, it proved itself beyond all shadow of a doubt!"

"Except," Nicole said quietly, moving into view, "its operator couldn't tell the difference between a target and a civilian aircraft."

"If that were true, Ms. Shea, the accident investigation team would be picking tiny pieces of you and your plane off the desert."

"So sorry. My error."

"You had no business being in an MOA."

"Excuse me, mister, *I* was on profile, on track. If anyone had business there, it was me!"

"You should have been under TRACON direction."

"And what good would it have done? They'd have told me then what my uplink did this morning, that you were operating twenty klicks away, on the other side of the damn mountains."

"It's only a plane, for God's sake."

She leaned over the table, staring him down, the two officers not quite sure which way to jump, whether to pull her off or enjoy the show. Cobri certainly seemed amused.

"It's my *life*, chum." And even as she spoke, she felt the suspicion that he didn't understand a word she was saying, not

in any way that mattered. "Not the one I almost lost, the years
I spent putting that Baron back together, the joy it's given me.
Those moments have meaning, mister, you don't dismiss them
with a airy wave of the hand."

"Please, Lieutenant, the *moments*—as you call them—hav-
en't been touched. Only the machine that helped provide them.
And it can be repaired. Or replaced. You did it yourself." He
grinned, a disturbingly disarming grin for what she decided
was such an enthusiastically royal prick. "I probably did you
a favor, actually. More work, more ultimate satisfaction, more
joy." Without thinking about it—again, that dangerous lag
between physical response and rational decision—she'd balled
her right hand into a fist. *Screw it*, she decided, *time for the
boy to lose some teeth*.

"I believe, Lieutenant Shea," Colonel Sallinger said from
behind her, "*I* have sole claim on your attentions this evening."

With a curt turn of the head—as much acknowledgment to
the others in the room as summons to her—Sallinger motioned
Nicole to follow him to a corner around the bar, as far from
everyone else as it was possible to get. Not bothering to look
back to make sure she followed, as though daring her to try
anything else, Cobri nattering derisively on while his companions exchanged looks of true amazement, silently asking how
any even marginally aware person could have been oblivious
to what had very nearly happened. Alex knew though, Nicole
accepted that like she did the morning sunrise. He was the
kind who lived perpetually on the edge of the abyss; what was
the point, where was the thrill, in anything less, especially
when you never had to face the consequences of your actions.
Always more money to cover a bet, always someone to step in
the way—and why care what happens to your vehicle, you're
not really aboard to share its fate.

The table was already set and as Nicole followed the Colonel's lead and sat down, Sue appeared with salad.

"I took the liberty of ordering," Sallinger said, "we've both
had a hard day and there didn't seem any profit in delay."

"Thank you, sir." The lettuce was fresh and crisp, the dressing delicious—nothing terribly fancy about the cuisine, Sue
did simple things here supremely well—and with the first bites
Nicole decided she wasn't hungry at all, but starving.

"Feel better?" Sallinger asked, partway into the main course.

She answered with a sigh and a smile.

"Amazing what a full stomach will do to your sense of perspective," he noted.

"I still want to kill him, sir," she said, thinking, *The arrogant little shit.*

"An hour ago, Lieutenant, you were ready to give it a shot. Understandable. But unprofessional." She didn't have an answer for that, he was right. "Most new arrivals," he continued in that same infuriatingly relaxed tone, changing the subject without missing a beat, "fly into LAX and drive up."

"What's the point of having wings if you don't use 'em?"

"Fair enough. Nice bit of flying, by the way. Castaneda says you cracked the piston chamber on the left, a couple of cylinders on the right, gonna be a bear finding replacements."

"I know a place." Thinking, *Sonofabitch, he checked before coming here.* Surprisingly pleased that he cared.

Sallinger smiled. "So does he." Seated, they looked each other in the eye; standing, she had the edge by about a head. His was the classic high-G fighter pilot's bod—short and stocky— with a stevedore's broad, muscular chest that came to him from a Russian peasant ancestor along with a slight epicanthic tilt to the eyes that bespoke some Tartar blood from even further back. Lot more grey in his close-cropped hair than last time, deeper lines gouged in his craggy features. He was the kind of man who somehow didn't look comfortable in uniform, the ideal for him was a flight suit. Yet for all the supposed casualness of his attire, there was no mistaking the aura of command and it was a rare, foolish individual who didn't recognize right off the bat that you crossed him at your own (considerable) risk.

"Dave Elias thinks a lot of you," he said suddenly.

For all the good that does me, she thought and the look Sallinger gave her made her wonder—with a small flash of panic—if she'd somehow spoken aloud.

"To be honest, sir, while I'm glad to be here, Edwards is the last place I expected to be assigned."

"Why?"

"You know."

"Yes"—a small smile—"I do. I thought Harry was out of line. But sometimes, for the right people, exceptions can be justified. He proved me wrong. That's why I asked for you back. Insisted upon it, actually. Even without this medical decertification, I was prepared to move Heaven and earth to get you."

"Why?"

"Let's take a walk."

Full panoply of stars tonight, notwithstanding some midlevel cirrus speckled silver by the rising crescent moon, and it would only take a short drive—to get clear of the base and out where the desert was still properly and completely dark—to reveal a view of the heavens that was truly spectacular. Next best thing to being there. To anyone who hadn't actually been.

But there was no more hinting about the chill Nicole had felt earlier, the air was cool enough to send a stream of condensation from mouth and nose with every breath; she zipped her jacket, turned up the collar, and shoved her hands deep into its pockets while Sallinger led her back through the park.

"Don't tell me this bothers you?" he asked. "Girl like you, grew up in Nantucket, all that open-water sailing?" *Terrific*, she thought sourly, *he's read my dossier*.

"You deal with cold by preparing properly for it. And I was better at it then."

"What changed?"

She paused by the X-15, amazed at how small the rocket plane was, but also admiring its sleek, slab-sided lines. "That first day," she said, "after the raiders ambushed us, before we jury-rigged the systems back on-line, *Wanderer* had no power. Couple or three billion klicks out from the Sun, the local temperature isn't that much above absolute zero. Spacecraft's insulation helped, but as time passed, it got colder." Such a calm and matter-of-fact word for a sensation unlike any she'd ever experienced. She shrugged, "Even after we jump-started the Carousel"—the habitat module—"back to life, we didn't dare put too much pressure on the systems. Set the heaters on a very slow and gradual warming curve. That was the worst, when the cold was still close to unendurable and you knew the heaters were on and that things would get better—didn't dare consider anything else—it was just a matter of hanging on 'til they did. Only seemed to take forever."

"And then you found the Halyan't'a." Sallinger pronounced it the way most people did, the way its English transliteration was spelt, without the subvocal resonances indicated by the apostrophes. Human throats didn't appear to be constructed for those kinds of sounds, or ears to hear them.

"The dumbest of luck, sir."

"Discovery, perhaps. What came after, no way." Off in the distance, a sudden flash caught Nicole's attention; as she turned her head, the sound caught up to her, a thunderous roar cresting like a wave over a bar as the pilot waiting at the end of the runway keyed in his afterburners. Takeoff was almost too fast to be believed, the plane had barely started moving before it was off the ground, canting into an impossibly steep angle of attack atop a cone of blue flame half as long as the aircraft itself. In another twinkling, it was gone, navigation strobes lost among the myriad of natural stars, its exit announced by a soft *boom* as it went supersonic.

Overlooking the park, and the dry lake beyond—a vantage point that gave a surprisingly comprehensive view of the entire working area of the base—was a memorial. Severe cenotaph, dignified plaque bearing the names of every pilot who'd lost his or her life here from Glenn Edwards—who'd given the base its name—on up. This was for the tourists; the real memorial, as far as the test pilots were concerned, was on the wall in Hotshots.

"You have any idea, Lieutenant," Sallinger asked conversationally, "how many people are currently conversant in Halyan't'a?"

Puzzle began locking into place and she felt a sudden icy-electric thrill up her spine, but as she started to reply, he interrupted, "On Earth, that is."

"Three," she said, hazarding a guess because her information was reasonably out-of-date.

"Main delegation goes to New York, to deal with the United Nations—those lucky devils"—this in a tone that really meant, *those poor bastards*—"but three of the Hal get spun off our way." She looked questioningly.

"Evidently, we face similar problems in our space programs—namely, the difficulty in getting from orbit to the surface and back again. Pity matter transmission didn't come to us as easily as star flight. Anyway, the suggestion's been made that we pool our resources, see if together we can't find a solution that evades us individually."

"Won't this strike some as favoritism, sir, the Halyan't'a working with us?"

Sallinger laughed and shook his head. "How the hell do you make that little noise, Nicole? I mean, I've heard it in the tapes—from you and that Marshal, Ciari—but I can't even come close. Gives me a helluva sore throat."

"Me, too, sir, and it only sounds right to our ears. Heaven knows what the Hal make of it."

"The fact that you can make it at all—rough and rude approximation or not—is why I asked for you. And to answer your question, they won't be working with just us. We've spent the last six months culling the best and the brightest from all over—we've got Russians coming and Brits and French and Israelis and, God help us, Iraqis and Japanese, it's going to be a goddamn zoo. In which the ones who look to us the most like animals will probably turn out to be the most civilized. Your job's to make sure there's as little trouble as possible."

"Colonel, my knowledge of their language—not to mention their culture—is rudimentary at best."

"My understanding is Marshal Ciari's been sending you regular updates from their homeworld." She was shaken, he *did* know her dossier.

She made a semihelpless gesture, started another protest, "Ranjamaryam and Szilard . . ."

"A, will be busy as hell in New York with the President. And, B, are not pilots."

"The Halyan't'a'll probably have a Speaker with them, their own translator, who'll be a lot more familiar with us than I can possibly be with them."

"Granted. I want one of my own. You're it."

"I'm not qualified."

"Nicole, I understand the premise behind this Speaker of theirs, someone who's been genetically engineered to comprehend not simply our language but the cultural and societal context. Great. All for it. Wish to hell we could do that with one of our own. But he still comes with a bias. He still sees through their eyes, comprehends through their thought processes. The same words don't necessarily have the same meaning. No matter how clumsily—and I suspect you're selling yourself short—you can do that same service for me. Give them a sense of *our* perceptions. And maybe give their Commander and me the extreme parameters between which we can find a viable middle ground."

"Christ on a crutch," was all she could say.

"And, of course, help them deal with the media."

"Of course. What fun."

"We'll still hold to your cover story, that you were a participant in the *Wanderer* First Contact but not a major player. That's one of the nicer things about this still being a military installation, we can restrict access. There'll be some obligatory dog and pony show-and-tells, but we will most definitely keep the bullshit to an absolute minimum. Again, fortunately, they're coming to work."

They'd been walking some more, paralleling Rosamond Boulevard past the athletic fields and on towards another cluster of single-family houses.

"You'll be part of their test program, primarily responsible for liaising between them and our own people."

"Will I be flying?"

"Probably. Another major point in your favor was your familiarity with our own ReEntry Vehicle project. You know the territory."

"As of three years ago."

"Not to worry. Everything we've done since has been uploaded into your house memory. I expect you up to speed within the week."

" 'House'?"

"Assignment has a few perks. We don't know what they'd like, so we'll be quartering them here on G Street. They have the residence at the end, you'll be in the one next door. We're light on personnel this season, so the rest of Golf, and Hotel beyond, are empty."

"All by ourselves."

"Being so close to the main road creates a potential problem, so we'll be increasing security along this stretch."

"You worried about someone getting in or them busting out?"

"You tell me, you're the closest I got to an expert. We have a century and change of bad video and worse books describing what it'll be like when the aliens land. Well now, they're here. And to one degree or another, everybody is scared shitless."

"This is nuts."

"Absolutely. But this is one pooch, Lieutenant, that can't be screwed, 'cause we got no way to bail out. All of a sudden, the best of us are just pudknockers again, hardly know which way is effing up, 'cept we're expected to fly the hottest bird built. With the whole world watching."

"Yes, sir," she said, because there was nothing else *to* say.

He nodded. "Your vitals are all logged in off your CardEx. I wish I could say this'll be easy. I'm afraid, probably anything but. And it is not an altogether good thing to have an officer with such critical responsibilities be the subject of a psychological decertification. Matter of fact, in the State Department's eyes, that was a major strike against you.

"But the Hal spoke quite emphatically on your behalf. That made a difference, their being prepared to accept the risk.

"And of course," he said with a half smile, "there's the fact that there's no one else to turn to.

"You'll have to initialize the door and the interior systems. Gear's already inside, anything else you need, log it into the housekeeping systems. You can have tomorrow to get organized, day after I want you on the line, interfacing with the XSR team."

"Yes, sir."

"Watch your ass, Lieutenant. I got too many friends on Hotshots's wall already."

"Do my best, sir. Thanks for caring."

"Comes with the territory. *Oh*, one more thing"—this as he turned to go—"the Halyan't'a . . ."

"Yessir?"

"They'll be here Friday."

three

"SHIT!"

You'd think, as she hunched on the edge of the bed, contemplating the ruin of yet another pair, *after all this time, someone, somewhere, would be able to design stockings that wouldn't bloody* run!

And she hated the "Powers-That-Be" for allowing men slacks and socks while mandating that women, especially in formal situations, wear skirts and hose. It was one of the things she'd never gotten used to, try as she had ever since high school, when she'd discovered that there really were places and occasions where pants simply were not permissible for Proper Young Ladies. Didn't matter to her that there were male officers who hated this just as much; uncomfortable as they might feel, it was still infinitely harder for them to do fatal damage to their wardrobe simply through the act of getting dressed. Adding insult to injury, the sons of bitches didn't have to wear makeup.

She put her forehead on her hands, tried a couple of slow, deep breaths, then relaxed the rest of the way, stretching her torso along the length of her thighs, trying not to look at the dark blue fabric clutched in one fist. She hadn't even gotten the damn things on, she'd been gently snaking a hand down

the inside to open them up when she'd somehow snagged a
nail and come up with a beaut of a run. That was one of
the things she loved about the Moon; the farther out you
went from Earth, the less "Mickey Mouse" you had to deal
with. Uniforms—casual and dress—were a blend of comfort
and functionality; yes, looking your best meant conforming to
an arbitrary standard, but there it seemed a somehow saner and
more livable one.

This is silly, she told herself, *it's only one party, one night,
stop acting like an effing baby!*

She tossed the pantyhose towards the bedroom trash, decided she needed a drink before trying again. Strange feeling,
having a house, pretty much unheard of for a single officer—
especially one as junior as she—pretty small compared to her
parents' places, but more raw space than she'd ever had in
the military. Certainly more than she felt she needed. Two
bedrooms, a living room, combo dining room/kitchen, bath
and a half, the lap of luxury. Halyan't'a had a bigger one,
with two levels, but there were more of them.

In her underwear, Nicole padded over to the fridge and
grabbed a bottle of seltzer. Shadows were long outside, day
was officially over, a glance towards the clock told her she
had barely an hour before transport was due to pick up her
and her Alien charges. She wondered how they were doing,
whether the Hal went through such hell for their equivalent of
tonight's reception. Smiled as she imagined what the primary
delegation must be facing in New York.

"Main video," she announced, returning to the living room,
"please replay Halyan't'a arrival." And the display wall did
precisely that, first generating a spectacular panorama of the
morning sky from one of the interceptors sent aloft to escort the
shuttle down the Edwards range. A data overlay in the bottom
right corner informed her of the time, position, and altitude of
the camera aircraft. That early in the morning, over a hundred
thousand feet, the curve of the Earth was clearly visible, sweeping from bright sun in the east past the terminator and on into
predawn shadow, out over the Pacific. The sked called for a
midmorning touchdown; that way, the sunrise winds would
have died down but the air itself would still be on the cool
side, allowing for more effective maneuvering. This would
be a gliding descent, same as with the original generations
of NASA shuttles—before the shift over to hydrogen-fueled,

suborbital RamScoops—and no one, on either side, wanted to
see it end in a crash.

Long-range lenses caught the Halyan't'a craft first, computer-
generated graphics isolating and enhancing the image until it
filled the huge screen. At that extreme distance and the speed
it was traveling, still wreathed in its corona of atmospheric
friction, it was difficult to make out any details; even so,
Nicole's heart leapt at the sight. Same as it had two years
ago, when she'd seen Hana Murai's pictures of *Range Guide*,
the Halyan't'a starship. Which reminded her . . .

"Secondary window, please," she asked, and the house
computer complied, sectioning off a nonessential segment of
the wall and displaying a blank data field. "Mail, personal."

Two entries in the buffer. Ben Ciari's letter, as always, was
in Halyan't'a, "to help my own fluency as much as yours,"
he'd written that first time—and she had to smile as she imagined the wicked glint in his eyes while he did it, the rank,
unregenerate bastard. Hana used English, but scrambled and
encrypted in a computer-keyed, multilevel transposition algo-
rithm that she assured Nicole was virtually unbreakable. While
Nicole had been in the hospital, recovering from the injuries
she'd suffered in that last battle with the Raiders, there'd
been a couple of attempts to get into her personal files. Hana
was gifted, borderline brilliant, and her deep-space long hauls
served to hone those talents to an ever-keener edge; she gleefully determined to deny the intruders access and thereby guarantee her friend's privacy. Nicole couldn't help having doubts.
The hackers—whoever they were—had to be top-notch just to
penetrate the DaVinci Net; among that class, the greater the
challenge, the more fiercely determined the response.

She asked for Hana's letter. One had come every week since
Hana's departure on a nine-month research mission—Nicole
herself hadn't been anywhere near as conscientious in her
replies, she'd always found it hard to set her thoughts down on
paper for someone else—but Nicole hadn't scanned any in over
two months. On the Moon, she'd been too busy preparing for,
and then taking, her Recertification Exams, always figuring
she'd get to them in a lump when she was done. After she'd
been grounded, she simply hadn't felt like it, retreating into a
shell for the flight home and the three weeks following, spent
on Nantucket waiting for her new orders to come through. The
last few days at Edwards had been her first chance to catch up.

Opening grin from Hana brought one in return from Nicole. And as always, the other woman's striking beauty made Nicole feel like her Baron next to the Hal shuttle. Attractive in her own way but built more for strength and sturdiness, versus a machine that was as much a work of art.

Hana's height and crystal-blue eyes she got from her grandfather, a man-mountain Minneapolis Swede who, as Hana had told Nicole when they first met, "swept my gran off her feet like a tsunami." Trans-Pacific—like many these days—born in Japan but with major family across the water in the States, educated in both countries, able to slip with ease from one culture to the other. She had a couple of centimeters on Nicole, cut from the same long and lean mold, yet Nicole always felt Hana was the finished product, where Nicole herself was more the rough-hewn outline, with a delicacy of feature and grace of movement Nicole could only envy. Nicole had been a fighter from the moment she could make her body do what she wanted, if not with her schoolmates than with the elements, at sea or in the air. Problem was, that left its mark.

Hana's hair was black—on the rare occasions when she wore it natural—close-cropped from the necessity in deep space of being able to quickly don a pressure suit; anything beyond collar length presented too great a risk of fouling the helmet seal. She'd taken to slicking it straight back from her face and forehead, fitting the line of her head like a gleaming skullcap.

Nicole's—a deep autumnal russet that appeared more like black with flaming highlights—was a brush-cut barely two centimeters long, which served to focus the eye on the strong, definitive planes of her own face. She wasn't beautiful—in a classic or contemporary sense—but she could be striking and was always memorable. People had the sense looking at her that she was one of a kind.

She'd known from the start she and Hana were virtually the same size—to the extent that they could even switch custom-fitted pressure suits—and when they moved in together they spent a memorable evening, surrounded by the day's leftover chaos, working their way through each other's wardrobe, comments and stories flying over glasses of wine that never had a chance to stay empty, horrorshows from their past that left both women gasping with laughter. Nicole was as predictable as Hana was adventurous, she'd decided years ago what made her look good and felt no need to stroll further afield. Hana set out to change that perception with a vengeance, producing outfits that left Nicole stunned, even before she found herself trying them on. And discovered a side of herself she'd never suspected—or, as Hana sagely noted, either three or four bottles along into the evening, had been busy denying—which she had to admit was pretty damn impressively spectacular. Knowing she'd never have the courage to try it sober and in public.

On the master screen, the Halyan't'a shuttle was taking a long slow turn leftward off base leg, lining up for the final stage of its descent to Edwards. All sleek, smooth curves, moving with breathtakingly natural grace through the air, as much a part of it as any bird. Touching down without a bump, right on the mark, rolling swiftly and smoothly to a stop.

Alarm chimed. "Nicole," the house said in its neutral voice, "you now have a half hour to finish dressing."

"Fine," she said, "thanks." Sighed, eyes blinking away from the wall, around the room lit solely by the giant screen. "Thirty percent interior illumination, please, and can the video. Hold mail in the buffer, full security." The house computer obligingly blanked the wall, while activating the lights to the level of twilight. More than enough for her to see, without being blindingly bright.

She managed to get her tights on successfully this time, half-slip over that, then a starched white dress shirt with a stand-up collar and French cuffs. Getting her skirt on was no problem, walking was the bitch.

The latest uniform aesthetic called for the establishment of a "sleek, aerodynamic silhouette"—a nightmare concept even if you happened to be built like a jet—that hugged the figure all the way down. Which for women meant a pencil skirt that allowed at best a half-meter stride. The jacket was derived from English Edwardian-era dress uniforms: broad-shouldered, slim-waisted, accented by discrete frogs and flourishes, the cut of the heavy material locking her into a fully erect posture. Like it or not, she would spend the evening at perpetual attention. She had to admit, it looked spectacular, especially in cobalt black-blue. If she were a mannequin, she'd be in Heaven. Breathing, she could manage. Even moving, within limits. Bending over—she made a rude noise. The only consolation being that every other officer present would be in equivalent torment. Designed, she felt sure, by someone who'd never had to wear his creations. *Amazing*, she thought as she cast about for her shoes, *how the more unproductive and redundant a service starts to feel, the more extravagant its uniforms*. The contrast between where she'd been and where she was—the Air Force of the future versus the Air Force of the past—couldn't, in her own mind, be more marked.

The wings on her left breast only added insult to injury, those of a pilot-astronaut: the supreme irony being that she'd won them, not on her first orbital mission for NASA, but here at Edwards, aboard the XSR-5, when she and Harry Macon topped sixty miles, clearing fifty being the necessary requirement. And underneath, hanging from a scarlet and silver ribbon, a silver cross with a flaming golden sun at its intersection. The Solar Cross, highest award given by Space Command, save for the Congressional Medal of Honor. Only six others like it. Didn't make her feel proud, more like she was wearing a brand.

"Medals," Judith Canfield had said, "are won. These"—and the General had tapped the Command Astronaut wings on her own tunic—"are earned."

Any fool could be a hero. Nicole wanted to fly.

At five to seven, she strode up the path to the house next door, doing better on the concrete walk than she had a few meters earlier on a stretch that was still gravel, wishing with all her heart for the chance to take the person responsible for high heels up for a joy ride the sad, sorry son of a bitch would *never* forget.

The door opened as she reached it.

"Welcome," the Halyan't'a *Speaker* said, standing a step aside to usher her in.

But she paused in the doorway, steepling her hands before her, breast high—almost in an attitude of prayer, except that only the fingertips touched—and offering a small bow, the slightest of inclinations forward, more with the head than the body, a deliberately awkward stance that left her momentarily vulnerable.

"R'ch'ai," was the ritual response, a husky noise from the base of the throat with the barest hint of a growl, one equal's greeting to another—in the oldest days, this was between warriors—a statement of trust. By entering into your habitat, I do you honor by placing my life in your care.

The Hal let Nicole see the barest flash of a smile before holding out his own hands, palms upward, with a bow of his own, accepting both life and trust.

She completed the exchange by lightly touching her palms to his, her fingertips brushing the inside of his wrists just as his did hers. Mattered more on his part, since his nails—legacies of an overtly predatory past—were capable of tearing through flesh with frightening ease.

"I am Kymri," he said as they stepped through the foyer to the living room beyond. "Tscadi and Matai will be with us"—paused a moment, scanning for the right word—"directly?"

"I'm . . ."

"Shea," he said. And as if responding to a cue, her holographic image materialized in the center of the room, projected upward from a small globular crystal on the coffee table. A computer-generated voice began speaking Halyan't'a and scanlines of written data appeared beside the figure, automatically orienting in their direction. Kymri snarled and the image popped like a soap bubble.

"Apologies," he said. "That was not supposed to happen."

"A fair likeness," she said conversationally, masking an almost-irresistible desire to find out how much they had on her, wondering irrationally if any had come from Ciari.

"It does not do you"—again that flash-search for a word—"justice. I would crossload the crystal into your data bank, but our computer systems are fundamentally incompatible."

"I know," remembering a yelp of surprise the first, and only, time aboard *Range Guide* they'd tried interfacing a NASA PortaComp with the Halyan't'a Core. Damn thing had nearly blown up in her hand, hadn't even been aware she'd moved until she slammed into the opposite wall, having reflex-kicked herself backward through the zero-G air. Watching in amazement as what was left of the tiny computer floated after her, reduced by the overload surge to so much high-tech slag. "I believe that's one of the problems we're all here to address."

"You are welcome to access it on any occasion."

"It isn't necessary. I suppose you have a briefing file on everyone you're likely to meet here."

"Your Seniors were courteous enough to provide us with an appropriate orientation network. A great many names and likenesses, but precious little meat on the bone."

"The VideoWall can interface you with just about any network on the planet. Or off, for that matter, within limits. You'd be amazed at what you can pick up from the public links. And, of course, you're cleared into certain classified systems. Pardon my asking, but have we met before? There's something about your pattern . . ."

The most fundamental way to tell people apart is by skin color; then there's the shade and texture of the hair—in a man's case, whether he has any or not—and, finally, the actual features themselves.

That held with surprising similarity for the Halyan't'a as well. Their bodies—on the whole a head shorter than Terrestrial norms—were covered with a fine down that faded towards the extremities, leaving most of the hands and feet bare. Hair was much thicker, forming a natural pompadour—almost like a leonine mane—that Kymri, being a spacer, wore as short as Nicole did her own. The fur came in a staggering diversity of colors, though Nicole had come to realize from Ciari's tapes that they derived from roughly a half-dozen primaries. And that, as with humankind, each "race" had physical traits in common. Broader cheeks for one, a leaner look for another. But there was another element as well, a natural patterning that occurred in the fur—so that you might have someone whose basic coloration was gold, highlighted perhaps by streaks of bronze flaring down the back and out around the rib cage. Some Halyan't'a took this a step further, by adding designs of their own, in much the same way a Terran might have themselves tattooed.

Kymri was mostly bronze, his supplementary markings unusually subtle. The surprise for Nicole—what struck the chord in her memory—were his eyes, a deep gold-flecked blue that reminded her of Hana.

"On *Range Guide*," he told her, "I stood as Shavrin's First." Second in command. "To her went the tribute of the Contact."

"While you stood in the background and took notes."

"Copious." He growled something to the empty air—Nicole haltingly able to follow, sighing to herself in frustration at the difference between coping with Ciari's tapes and the real thing. To follow Kymri's colloquial use of the language, she had to be able to think in it as well. She was still translating Halyan't'a to English and back again inside her head and praying she'd chosen the proper turn of phrase. In this instance, though, she didn't need the details to get the gist and had no trouble at all with the response from the next room. A thump that shook the wall.

"Some people," she said with a smile, "don't appreciate being hurried."

"It is important to make a positive impression."

"You don't seem to have any worries."

He made a small movement with his hand, the Hal equivalent of a shrug, and Nicole had an even stronger flash of recognition that had nothing whatsoever to do with having met Kymri himself, and everything with the type of man he was. Confirmed, with his next words. "I made my impression," he said, "this morning." Landing the spacecraft, she realized, thinking, *Sonofabitch, a pilot is a pilot is a pilot.*

An instinct, more than any noise, prompted a half turn towards the hall as Kymri's two companions emerged. Both females, but one was a match and more for his physique. He was built broad for his height and, given the natural compactness of the Halyan't'a form, was easily half again Nicole's mass, despite her being taller. Superb body form for withstanding the stresses of high-gravity maneuvering.

If anything, though, the first female was larger, wider in the shoulders, without a gram of excess fat anywhere on her superbly muscled body. She was the engineer, Tscadi, with the knowledge to take the Halyan't'a spacecraft apart and whang it back together again combined with the raw strength to do it pretty much on her own. Matai was the designer, mission specialist primarily in cybernetics. All three were, like Nicole, in uniform, though she'd have given anything by that point (the evening barely begun) to trade. Soft boots and comfortable slacks for all, in a soft khaki cream, snug-fitting shirt and jacket completing the ensemble. Mission patch on one sleeve, intricate swirls of braid down the other, practical pockets at the hip. Like everything else about the Halyan't'a, the clothes were as much for function as show.

Nicole led the way out to the waiting car; they went in the back while she shared the front seat with the driver. Ten minutes later they were at the Officer's Club. An impressive turnout—senior brass from Fifteenth Air Force (who had jurisdiction over the Pacific Coast) and Air Force Systems Command out of Wright-Patterson Air Force Base in Ohio (who actually ran Edwards), a whole host of foreign military, everybody who was anybody out of NASA plus the usual clutch of folks who *thought* they were. Taking a quick eyeball sweep of the room, Nicole figured she was the only one present who wasn't at least field grade, and all the Majors she spotted looked like hat-holders for some General or other.

Of course, the moment the Hal entered, they became the focus of attention. Those first seconds, the four of them grouped in the doorway facing a phalanx of uniforms and suits and gowns, imagery scattershot across Nicole's mind: *Christ*, she thought, *do we as a species really look this dumb?* And in that flash, she was floating in her pressure suit, on *Range Guide*'s Command Bridge, staring over Ben Ciari's head at a combat string of Halyan't'a, her breath coming in deliberate huffs, gripped body and soul by an eerie calm that was the smallest step removed from shrill, shrieking terror. A series of moves to make, instantaneous choices which had so little time for deliberation, the knowledge that right or wrong her actions would have untold consequences. Never imagining, in her wildest, this might be one of them.

"Good to see you, Nicole," said Colonel Sallinger, breaking the ice.

"What, boss, you think we got lost en route?"

"Never can tell. Happens to my daughter all the time."

A seemingly endless round of introductions began, with Nicole and Kymri alternating the translations, Nicole omitting any gratuitous background comments. She thought Kymri was doing the same, nothing in what he said indicated any different, but there were looks to the two females' eyes, the barest flicks of the head in the direction of an offending voice, that made her suspect otherwise.

Someone reached out, flicked the metal cross on her breast. Nicole found herself face-to-face with another woman, maybe ten years older and wearing them very well, prime condition, shoulder-length hair hanging loose in a feminine wave that was well within regs but managed quite nicely to soften the formal lines of the uniform. Not, though, the commanding arrogance to her features.

"Lot of medal, for such a little girl," Grace Kinsella said, looking Nicole in the eye as she took another sip of bourbon. Nicole was on seltzer for the duration, her choice even before Sallinger's orders.

"So I'm told, Colonel." Only a light, actually—Lieutenant-Colonel—top of her class at the Test Pilot's School midway through her first tour at the Center. On track for the rank, so said the word along the flight line, skating the high end of the career curve, with a better than fair shot at a General's stars. Senior pilot wings—but only in air-breathers. She may have trained as an astronaut, but she hadn't yet flown.

"You figure Pussy's your ticket to glory, Lieutenant?"

"Colonel, with all due respect, you're out of line."

"You think? Bright, shiny, gold-bar shavetail like yourself?"

"Excuse me, ma'am, I have duties to attend to."

"Very touchy. Line I heard on you said you gave as good as you got."

Nicole knew the type, barn-burning fighter jocks, always hot to push the outside of the envelope, *any* envelope, with what seemed like only the most minimal awareness of the consequences. Game was, they push, you push back.

"You heard wrong."

"Poor dear. Must've broken Canfield's heart to see her prime protégée dropped down the Well right out of the box."

She walked away with deliberate speed, daring Kinsella to make a scene, well aware there were an infinite number of ways the Colonel could make her life miserable over the course of her tour, not to mention her career, and surprising herself to discover she didn't give a damn. She felt Kinsella's eyes on her every step, though when she finally turned for a look back, the older woman was engrossed in conversation with Alex Cobri. His eyes flashed her way once and he said something while they were on her that made Kinsella laugh. But beyond them stood Kymri, watching with an expression Nicole remembered only too well from the firefight on *Range Guide*—until Matai alerted him to Nicole. And suddenly he was offering only the most professionally bland of smiles, so complete a shift of mood, accomplished with such ease, that Nicole found herself doubting what she'd seen, wondering if she'd somehow misread him, realizing in the same instant that was precisely how he wanted her to feel.

"There are words that apply to Grace," a youngish voice commented, "and my brother, but I'm not supposed to use them." A slender powerhouse of a girl, on the leading crest of puberty, one smooth line from top to bottom, impeccably dressed in a way that didn't deny her age yet carrying herself with a gravity that belied it. Helped by a clearly evident muscularity that bespoke natural gifts in the process of being superbly honed. The shape of the jaw, the lustrous dark hair, and Catalan eyes—and, most especially, the way she stood and surveyed the room—marked her immediately as a Cobri.

"Quite right, too."

"She's a bully."

"No comment."

"Are you afraid of her?"

"First thing I learned was never fly into a thunderstorm. If you can avoid it."

"So you'd call it common sense," the girl sneered in a tone that made plain she considered it something else.

Nicole shrugged. "If you like."

"That's terribly discreet."

"State of being for Second Lieutenants."

"Even heroes?"

"Especially heroes. How fortunate then that doesn't apply in my case."

"I'm Amelia," the girl said, plain, unadorned statement of fact, forthright and direct.

"Nicole," was the reply. "Come here often?" she asked, and got a ghost of a grin in return.

"Meaning, am I crashing?"

"No one else your age about."

"No one else my age is a Cobri."

"Which cuts you all manner of slack."

"It has advantages." Bland words, with a pose to match.

"How lucky for you. Still"—Nicole took a look towards Sallinger, but he was engrossed with a brace of Generals, while the Halyan't'a appeared to be doing fine on their own, and neither had any need for her—"this can't be the most exciting of ways to spend an evening."

"I always check out the new arrivals, see if there's anyone interesting."

"I suppose the Halyan't'a qualify on both counts."

Another bored shrug. "Old news really. I mean, it's been over a year since the Contact. I met my first batch in Washington, right after their landing."

"Crash that party, too?"

Again, the ghost smile, showing just the smallest amount of pride, and Nicole thought it was perhaps the first real emotion she'd seen from the girl. "Got the Secret Service major upset. Papa, too. Tried to ground me for an age. President thought it was a total goof. Persuaded Papa to ease off."

"Old man have a temper?" Amelia made a dismissive face, a tiny, reflexive warding gesture with her hands that spoke volumes. Made sense to Nicole, actually; Manuel Cobri was a physical man, who'd grown up doing the most physical of work, stood to reason those ways of dealing with things would carry over to his personal life. "With me," she said, "it was my mom. I had a knack of always crossing her the worst way, at the worst time."

"So what happened in the end?" Hint of genuine interest.

"I grew up, went my own way."

"Some people have all the luck."

"Hang in there, kiddo, you'll get your turn."

"The way she keeps pushing," her brother interrupted, "I wouldn't make book on it."

"So, who asked you?" Nicole challenged, shifting a half step to place herself between Amelia and Alex.

"No skin off my backside, L'il Loot"—Nicole's eyes narrowing at his appropriation of Ramsey's nickname for her— "if the baby chooses to break the rules."

"And there I thought that was a Cobri trademark."

"We can afford it."

"Or anything else, for that matter."

"I just don't want to see you burn with her."

"I'm surprised you care."

Alex threw up his hands, chest high, a dismissive-defensive gesture. "Tell you the truth, so am I." He looked down at his sister. "Old man's circulating this way, you won't have crowd cover for long. You don't want a fight, pull a fade." And he snagged the arm of a passing woman, sidling her onto the dance floor.

"Man has moves," Nicole noted, mostly to herself.

"If it wears a skirt," Amelia groused, "it's fair game."

"Including Scotsmen?"

Took a second for the deadpanned reference to click, and Amelia couldn't repress a giggle at the concept. *Second time tonight*, Nicole thought, *a real emotion's slipped out from behind the mask. Must be a helluva life at the top of the pyramid that forces you to endure it in such a straitjacket.*

"Alex is right, Amelia, there's your father. You got a way out or do you need a diversion?"

"You'd do that?"

Nicole shrugged.

But Amelia shook her head. Different order of smile on her face this time, akin to her look earlier surveying the room: no less real, a lot less girlish.

"I own the place," she said with a kid's fierce delight at having put something over on the adults. "Isn't a corner of this base I can't get into. Or out of. Be seeing you, Nicole."

"Hope so." Thinking, *It's been a pleasure, kiddo.*

"We meet at last, young Lieutenant," Manuel Cobri boomed, clasping her hand in both of his, before gathering her in close with an arm about her waist—and Nicole had a flash of where Alex inherited his technique. There couldn't be a more absolute contrast between father and son, the one rough-hewn where the other was sleek, his broad-shouldered laborer's body built low to the ground. There was something almost gnomish about the man, as though whoever crafted him chose to do so in broad, sweeping strokes, creating an essential being, without any sort of smoothing or finishing. Far more suited at first glance to workingman's clothes rather than the custom-fitted tuxedo he was wearing. His wasn't a particularly handsome face; it held only the barest promise of the idealized perfection of his son, with surprisingly more in common with his daughter, yet there was a strength of feature that matched the rest of him. He wore his silver hair cropped short, which suited him, and Nicole could see looking down at him that it was thinning at the temples.

"The honor is mine, sir." She tried to sidestep but found no way to do so gracefully and settled instead for edging him in the direction of Sallinger and the Halyan't'a.

"Did I perhaps notice you talking with one of my children?" There was an ease to his manner that took Nicole almost completely aback; he was totally relaxed, unaffected in the slightest by this assemblage of the so-called great and powerful. *Small wonder,* she thought with an inner smile, *he could probably buy and sell the lot for chump change.*

"Your son? Briefly."

"You know very well who I mean." She said nothing, and he sighed heavily, shaking his head. *Disappointment in Amy,* Nicole asked herself, *or me?* And looked about for either escape or rescue. "One of these days . . ."

"It's a rebellious age, sir. You're desperate for structure yet starting to feel the need to make your own mark."

"By kicking that structure down?"

"You never did?"

"Not I, the perfect paragon."

Nicole spoke before she could stop herself: "Forgive me, sir," she said, "but that kind of remark seems more your son's profile."

"Alex"—he thought a moment, eyes taking on a slight glaze while he considered some distant memory before focusing back to her—"is a bit too much his mother's child."

"And you thought you'd rectified that error with Amelia."

A sudden sharp look—she wondered what she'd said to prompt it, alarmed that she'd put a major foot wrong and somehow offended him—masked as quickly by a smile she recognized as twin to Amelia's, just as false but far more deliberately charming. She had the sense she'd just tripped over a major joke but that Cobri was the only one privy to it. And Cobris didn't share.

"That's why one has more than one, didn't you know," he said with sage good humor, "to keep trying 'til you get it right."

Practice makes perfect, Nicole thought. And said, "I'm not trying to be rude, sir, I really wish we could continue, but my time this evening isn't my own and I believe I'm needed."

"You don't much like my son, do you, Lieutenant?"

"I hardly know him, sir."

"He'll be handling some of the primary cybernetics work on the proposed Hybrid Shuttle, so you'll be working quite extensively together. I just want to ensure there'll be no problem."

"I understand he has quite a considerable professional reputation, Mr. Cobri. I'm sure everything'll be fine. I'm sorry, sir, I really must go. If you'll excuse me . . ."

"Colonel Kinsella will be a project officer, as well." *Why*, she thought, wondering what disaster was coming next, *am I not surprised?* Wondering more why Cobri was telling her this?

Alex and Kinsella were watching, she saw that as she turned towards Sallinger and the Halyan't'a, Kinsella smiling, cat to cornered mouse. Surprisingly, though, Alex was glaring towards his father with barely disguised fury. Was he angry at what the old man had just done, or simply that he'd wanted to drop the boom on Nicole himself and Manuel had stolen his thunder? And Nicole found herself starting a step forward, gripped from deep within by something fierce and predatory that refused to allow Kinsella's challenge to go unanswered.

The MicroCom beeped, gave voice to a basso rumble so low it was basically subvocal requesting her immediate presence. Kymri. He hadn't missed a thing and he was calling her away before events got out of hand. And she turned to obey, forcing herself to take a deep breath. It came with the quavery shudder, echoed by a slight tremble to the body that she'd felt all too often of late. Fear, she knew. Of what was about to happen. But was it what would happen to her, or what she was afraid she'd do?

She looked up, found Kymri's eyes, favored him with the blandest and most accommodating of subordinate smiles. Before hurrying to his side to help him through the rest of the evening.

four

ALONG ABOUT THE seventh hill, pride gave way to common sense and she stopped dead in her tracks. Hunched over, knees slightly bent, letting hands resting on her thighs take the weight of her upper body. She was breathing in a steady, deliberate rhythm, with a fair way to go before she was winded. But enough, she decided, was enough.

She'd reached the crest of a ridge overlooking the vast expanse of Rogers Dry Lake. A line of heights marked this southern "shore," dotted with a random scattering of various bunkers—some active, most left over from the rash of esoteric weapons testing that marked the end of the last century. What passed for roads were actually tracks worn in the desert earth by long usage, there was never sufficient traffic to have them properly graded and paved; most of the operational systems were completely automatic, requiring technicians only to install and remove the equipment, and service the rare malfunctions. It was Harry Macon who first brought Nicole up here, the week she arrived at Edwards. He liked running, said that getting his blood pumping—then roaring—through his veins helped him think. It was also one of the few opportunities he had to escape on a more-or-less regular basis the pressures and responsibilities of his job. To regain at least a partial sense of perspective and, when necessary, vent the

more than occasional frustration. "Out in the boonies," he told
her, "no one can hear you scream." Except Nicole, of course,
huffing along a dozen or so steps behind, wearing MicroCorder
and PortaComp in case he had a flash of inspiration.

Not much sign of use in the years since his death. The other
pilots and staff personnel preferred covering their klicks on the
high-school track, or the ParCours exercise circuit that snaked
through the base proper. This terrain was a little too wild, with
too much chance of turning an ankle on a wayward rock, or
worse. Hurt yourself, you didn't fly. And if you couldn't fly,
why else come to Edwards?

"You okay?" a voice called from a small ways up the trail,
and Nicole was surprised to see Amy Cobri chugging towards
her. She was all gangly legs and arms, mismatched bits just
starting the spurt out of childhood with only the barest promise
of the adult to be, tucked into the latest in designer sports-
wear. By contrast, Nicole wore sweats—long-legged, long-
sleeved—against the predawn chill, unadorned plain greys.

"Done for today," she replied, absently kneading her right
thigh, keeping as wary an awareness of what was behind her
as in front.

"What's the matter, you hurt?"

"No," she told her, which was true, "habit, I guess, from
the memory of pain," of which there had been a lot. With a
small groan, she straightened up, glancing over her shoulder
towards the east, where the sky had almost completely paled
in prelude to the sunrise. There was a preternatural stillness to
the air, a small sense of the way things might have been in ages
past, and she wondered if there were places—and moments—
like this on s'N'dare. And, with a flash of bitterness, if Ben
Ciari had enjoyed them.

"Musta been a righteous mess, huh? For it still to bother
you? I mean, it was ages ago, right?"

"What are you doing up here, Amy? This is restricted turf."

The girl shrugged, face twisting dismissively as she dug a
toe into the dirt and looked down towards the base. The shoes
were at odds with the rest of her outfit. Top of the line trainers,
but well worn, indicating hard and frequent use. "Wanted a
place to run," she said finally.

"Plenty down there."

"You run up here."

"I'm allowed."

"No one said I couldn't," with a bit of defiance.

"Yeah, right," Nicole scoffed, "as if you asked." And Amy, caught, allowed herself a gleefully elfin grin.

"Track's boring," she said, "I mean, all you do is run 'round in circles, major thrill. And you see one PC circuit"—meaning the ParCours—"you've seen 'em all. 'Sides, I hate crowds."

"Why?"

Another shrug.

"We should get back," Nicole said.

"Where's the hurry? Big Bitch . . ."

"I beg your pardon?"

"Colonel Kinsella."

"I know who you meant, young lady."

"Hey, I call 'em as I see 'em, that a crime?"

"There are crimes and crimes, Amelia."

She cocked an eyebrow full of practiced cynicism, striking an attitude that would have had Nicole in stitches were it not for the fact it wasn't at all an affectation. "You telling me, Nicole, after the way she's been riding you, you haven't thought a lot worse?"

"What I think, and choose to say, kiddo, is *my* business."

"So why can't I claim the same privilege?"

"Just be a little more tactful, okay?"

"No prob. Didn't figure you for such a total flatline, though."

"What, brain dead?"

"Not quite. Just lacking in interesting spikes."

"Sorry about that."

"But then, the more people you come to know, the more the curve flattens out. Real depresso. I mean, what's the point in playing if there's no one in your league?"

"So I've heard your brother say."

Amelia blew a Bronx cheer in the direction of the airfield. "Major disappointment. All he does is crawl into his box and fake it."

"What do you mean?"

"He's a master of simulations. Has such a good time inside his own head you have to drag him kicking and screaming into the world. I mean, why fly for real when a remote can do it for you? All the sensations, none of the risk."

"You prefer the risk?"

A grin. "Where's the fun, winning, if you rate the game?

"Anyway," she continued, looking upward and stepping into a more than respectable pirouette, "Colonel Kinsella"—smile and a bob of the head Nicole's way to make sure she noticed— "is flying her HOTOL evaluation this morning, first reentry from orbit. Even if she touches down on schedule—which she won't because there was a one-hour hold on her departure from Sutherland—she'll be in debriefing for the better part of the day. Plenty of time for you to beat her to the job. Assuming she even shows, which is doubtful—'cause if it's a *primo* approach she'll be out celebrating and if she augers . . ."

"Don't say that," Nicole snapped with an edge she hadn't meant to be there, "about anybody."

"Well," Amy finished offhandedly, "if it's less than *primo*, she'll probably drown her sorrows." She didn't bother hiding her unspoken subtext, *and maybe herself along with 'em!*

"You two have a problem?"

"Perish the thought."

"Where'd you hear about the hold?"

"I heard."

"You weren't kidding, were you, at the reception—you really do have this place wired."

"No big deal, trust me. It's a whole lot easier than it looks."

"That what passes for fun, punching buttons in the hierarchy to see it jump?"

"Has its attractions. 'Sides, how're you s'posed to know your limits if you don't push 'em? Isn't that what Edwards is all about?"

All depends on the consequences, Nicole thought, knitting her fingers together and reaching both arms high overhead, stretching the full length of her body and making a small face at the twists and pops she felt along the way. *Is that a word—is it even a* concept—*that has any meaning to you Cobris?* And then, follow-up thought: *Cut her some slack, Nicole, she's just a kid, doing pretty much what you did at her age.*

"So, you gonna run some more, or what?"

Nicole shook her head. "With or without the Colonel," she told Amy, "I got work. Sun's up. Air's already warming. If you're not careful, it can get pretty brutal out here. A lot faster than you think."

"The base is right over there, Nicole, how hairy could it get?"

"You'd be surprised, kiddo."

There was no conscious recognition of the attack, a multitude of things seemed to happen simultaneously, plastering themselves across her awareness like splashes of paint thrown randomly against a wall, each color individual and distinct when it struck, but blurring into an amorphous whole as they ran together on their way down to the ground. Sensation of movement combined with a flash of something on the periphery of her vision combined with perhaps the faintest scrabble of bare feet on dirt combined with Amy's squeak of surprise— all triggering an instinctive, instantaneous response.

She spun on the ball of one foot, dropping as she turned on her pivot leg, registering Kymri charging her—deeper awareness, not even considered until much later, of how the brilliant glow of sunrise lit up the tips of his fur, so that he seemed to be edged in a corona of light—slitting her eyes to protect them, because he was coming out of the sun and a careless glance would dazzle-blind her. Kicking off the pivot leg the instant she landed in her crouch, using the other leg for even more speed, hugging the ground as she went for his ankles, forcing him to spring awkwardly over her or be tripped.

She made him leap, but there was nothing awkward about it. And by the time she reached her feet, rolling with smooth, desperate speed into a martial-arts stance that had nothing to do with the manual and everything with what Ben Ciari had taught her about close-combat grunt fighting, he was gone.

She didn't waste time looking, but grabbed Amy by the wrist and headed off the trail, climbing—in a fair imitation of a mountain goat—from rock to rock.

"That," the girl gasped, "that was one of the Halyan't'a."

"Yup. Kymri, the Commander-Pilot."

"He tried to kill us!"

"Hardly. If he were serious, he'd have used a weapon."

Amy broke Nicole's grip with a violent tug that nearly overbalanced the pair of them.

"You mean this is a stupid *game*," she shrieked.

"Tag," Nicole said calmly, "he's it. Sanctuary's my bike."

"That's crazy!" Amy's voice was shaking, a mixture of adrenaline-laced terror and exertion. She was in superb shape— private trainer saw to that—but even the finest tournament muscles were put to the test by this open-field terrain.

Nicole put her hands to her side and looked back the way they'd come. A couple of hundred meters, easy, flat out, up a steep grade of jumbled, broken scree—a nasty stretch, no wonder everything ached. No sign of Kymri. Wouldn't be, though. She'd learned, the hard way over the past weeks as they played together, how good he was at camouflage. He had a way about him, an inner stillness, that somehow made your eye glance right past him, as though he wasn't there or had somehow become transmuted into a natural part of the local landscape. So, she'd stopped trying to spot him by actively searching; instead, turning over the job to her back-brain. A matter of watching with all her senses, sort of taking inventory of the setting about her, waiting for the one anomaly to show itself. Ciari'd taught her that.

There was a shallow depression, running along the backside of the ridge, nothing much to speak of, save that it would mask them briefly from sight. Likewise, they wouldn't be able to see Kymri, and if he caught up to them while they were in it, the game would be all but over.

Two long steps took them into the arroyo—she figured a couple of seconds grace while Kymri considered the options, before he made his move—and the moment they were under cover, Nicole whipped off her sweatshirt and tossed it at Amy, telling her to put it on.

"Wha' for," was the indignant reply, the girl holding the shirt as though it had a bad smell, which, considering the morning's activities, probably wasn't that far off the mark.

"A glance at your leotard'll tell him who you are," Nicole told her, "in my shirt, he'll need a second look. If there was time, I'd give you the pants as well. Now, quit arguing, put it on, and *go!* Out the other end, fast!"

Now, the sun was in Nicole's favor. That was partly why she'd headed uphill in the first place. If Kymri angled to intercept them anywhere near the end of the arroyo, he'd have it right in his eyes. Especially now that the few minutes since sunrise had lifted it at least three solar diameters above the horizon.

Amy was a quick study, donning the shirt without breaking stride and bursting out of the arroyo like an Olympic sprinter going for the gold. Kymri made a move, realizing almost immediately—and quite a bit faster than Nicole had anticipated—his mistake. But by then, she'd rolled out of her own hiding place, into position behind him. She wore a regulation T-shirt underneath her sweatshirt, painfully aware of how bright the white cloth was, but that couldn't be helped. In this direct sun, she wasn't about to strip down to bare skin. Especially when the move would give her away.

He hunkered down on his haunches, head cocked a fraction to one side, and Nicole allowed herself the smallest of smiles. *Not that easy, buster,* she thought, *up-sun and downwind, it can't get much better than this.* The barest breeze tickled her body from one direction, while the sun warmed her from the other. A stone was digging into her side, mostly an annoyance at this stage, and off in the distance she heard a birdsong. It was a sinfully peaceful moment and she knew that if she surrendered to it, she'd probably broil before she woke. And yet, she couldn't help taking a long moment to simply look at the Hal. At rest or in motion, she found them a constant delight; the more she learned, simply from being with them, the more she wanted to know.

Amy broke the stalemate, heaving a baseball-sized rock in Kymri's direction. He caught it with a casual ease that would have broken the heart of any baseball manager, and in the same fluid motion, without even a glance in her direction, tossed it right at Nicole.

"Son of a *bitch,*" she muttered, rising slowly to her feet, shaking her head at the sharp, throaty noises that passed in him for laughter. He was a joy to watch, blessed with a slinky, insolent grace that made Nicole feel like a slug. It was as though the rule of gravity didn't apply, save as a convenience that kept them tethered lightly to the ground. Not so much that they were especially fast or strong—though Kymri was both—but in the way one movement flowed seamlessly into the next, like a piece of perpetual, instinctive choreography. Kymri, like Shavrin, was *centered* in a way Nicole felt she could only dream of; physically, nothing seemed to faze him. Like the Terrestrial felines they remotely—disconcertingly—resembled, the Hal had the knack of always landing on their feet and looking like that was their intent all along.

"You had me," she said.

He made a deprecating tilt of the head. "My range of awareness is sharper, Shea-Pilot. And when a diversion is cast in one direction, common sense dictates intensified vigilance in the other."

He was breathing more easily than she, but Nicole noted a sheen to his skin and allowed herself a hint of a smile that today's game had at least raised a sweat.

"We're done," she told him, and this time meant it. He nodded, sudden instinct prompting the pair of them to simultaneously look straight upward in time to catch a flash of sunlight on metal high overhead a split second before a faint *boom*—that was felt more than heard—shivered the air around them.

"A flight coming off the Frontier," she noted, "downshifting through transonic. Be on the ground soon."

"Kinsella-Colonel?"

"Far as I can recall, she's the only mission due this morning."

"Am I in error, Shea-Pilot, or are you not assigned to me and mine as liaison?"

"No mistake."

"Then do I not have primary access to your person? Save perhaps for Sallinger Colonel-Commander?"

She shook her head, adding a small, reflexive shrug. "Kymri," she said, "I'm a Second Lieutenant, and thanks to the time I spent in hospital, I'm behind the curve for my promotion to First. The more the Air Force orients itself towards space, the less people it'll need down here in the atmosphere. They can pick and choose, competition for slots is already fierce as a dogfight. I got more enemies now, I think, than most make in a career; I'd rather not add to the list."

"And you suspect that possibility where the Kinsella-Colonel is concerned?"

"Why push my luck?" A heartier sigh, more to close the thought than as an expression of frustration or despair. "She certainly rides me hard enough." And she made a face at how childishly whiny she sounded.

From Kymri came a noise that mingled disgust and contempt, and Nicole wondered if it was for her, until he said, "I do not wish to see you so troubled."

"Makes two of us." She smiled, starting along the trail to where Amy was waiting, keeping a respectful distance from the Halyan't'a. But his hand on her arm stopped her.

"I was not referring entirely to Kinsella-Colonel," he continued, staying uphill of her so that they were at eye level. "Questions have been raised about what happened on the Moon. Concern has been expressed." She didn't need to be told by whom, and wondered how the news had made the round-trip to s'N'dare so quickly.

"I appreciate it, Kymri. But it isn't necessary."

"You do not understand. You are of Shavrin's House, bonded by Oath and Blood."

"Please tell her then not to worry. I can take care of myself. And I have friends. We look after our own."

"So do we, Shea-Pilot. That is all I wished to say."

She mulled that one over as she returned to where she'd stashed her mountain bike, at the bottom of the hill, noting that Amy had arrived on one of her own. One of the last things the Hal Commander had done, before her departure home from the Moon, was adopt Nicole. The moment had come out of nowhere, they were at the top of the boarding ramp to the shuttle that would take the newly established Terran Embassy up to the starship waiting in Lunar orbit, for the trip outbound to s'N'dare. The final call had just sounded, when Shavrin took a silver and fireheart necklace from her own neck and placed it around Nicole's.

" 'Of my House,' " Nicole breathed, surprised at how readily the words popped from memory, " 'art thou become, of my flesh art thou made; thou art to me as a kit from mine own womb, bearing rights, titles, honors, and assigns as do pertain thereof. Blood hast thou shed on my behalf, blood have we shared to bind our spirits forever.' " At the time, she hadn't given a thought for the consequences, probably wouldn't have mattered if she had, she owed Shavrin far too much to back away from such a gesture. That was all she figured it really had been, a gesture. An impulse formality with no meaning or resonance beyond the moment. But now she thought about it, she knew that was wrong. On occasion, Shavrin acted from instinct—partly, that's what prompted her to accept and trust the Terrans when she encountered Nicole and the *Wanderer* survivors—but those actions were never casual. What she said, she meant. And obligations were taken seriously. Clearly, Shavrin considered herself at least partially responsible for Nicole's welfare, which left Nicole wondering how she was obligated in return.

She wasn't sure she liked that, either way. She preferred
standing alone. It was how she sailed, and why she flew. To
define and dictate her own destiny. Of course, objectively, she
knew that was a crock. Nobody, especially pilots, *especially*
spacers, was an island unto themselves. Your life depended on
a small army, starting with the team that designed the vehicle
and its attendant systems, moving on through the ones who
built it to those who maintained it, ending with the crew
who shared its operation. You trusted everybody to do their
job, so you could do yours. Your life depended on that. A
failure anywhere along that line, the consequences could be
catastrophic. But there always came a point where you could
take matters into your own hands, meld your skill and smarts
and whatever else went into the mix with the moment to win
or lose, survive or die.

Now, suddenly, her life felt cut to pieces and scattered
across the floor. And even though she felt ready and willing
to gather them up and fit them together into a new mosaic,
there were all these people trying to help. And while she
was grateful, because she knew she needed it—and flattered
beyond words to know as well that they cared—it hurt to
realize that they might not only be able to do a better job
than Nicole herself, but that without them she might not even
succeed.

Kymri had no use for transport; he considered the run out
across the flight line his warm-up and the return, a fair cool-
down. Twice, he broke out in sprints that forced Nicole and
Amy to pedal for all they were worth just to keep up—hard
enough on a decent road surface, absolute murder on open
country. *Your way of demonstrating Hal superiority, you fuzzy
son of a bitch,* she snarled grimly to herself, *or maybe determining what I'm capable of?* Whichever, she hated him for it,
shards of fire sizzling up and down the long muscles of her
thighs, with equivalent aches at the knees and hips. *Keep it up,
buster,* she cried silently, *and I guarantee you'll find out!* And
then chanting a privately profane mantra to goad herself to an
even greater effort, one word to a breath: "Helluva. Fucking.
Way. To. Start. The. Goddamn. Fucking. *Morning!*"

Dirt became asphalt as they crossed onto one of the taxi-
ways leading from the South Complex to the field proper, and
almost immediately a light flashed on the com unit clipped to
her handlebars. She pulled up, calling to Amy and Kymri to

do the same, while she slipped a headset over one ear and acknowledged the transmission.

"Remote Nine"—that was the ident tag given them by the Tower when they'd originally crossed the field—"hold position for arriving aircraft. HighJump inbound, direct approach off the Curve. ETA, less than five."

"Shit," she muttered, pulling a pair of full-size headsets from her saddlebags, shading her eyes with her free hand while she swept the horizon for any sign of the approaching aircraft.

"A problem," Kymri asked.

"Took us longer to get off that ridge than I thought," she told him, "we're stuck here 'til Kinsella lands. And for a few minutes after, to allow any toxics off her exhaust to dissipate. Better take one of these"—handing him a 'set and Amy the other—"coming straight in off its suborbital trajectory, the pig's a screamer."

The headsets had built-in transceivers, so everyone could still converse—with each other and the Tower. Nicole had only brought two, so when the time came, she'd have to improvise. But she didn't see that as being much of a problem. The flight wasn't supposed to touch down anywhere near them, this hold was simply a standard precaution.

"As well as being the fastest way of getting from point to point on the globe," she explained to Kymri, "the hypersonic ScramJets are our primary transportation system up to low orbit. Which means, since they fly above the eighty-kilometer line—the official boundary between atmosphere and true space—their flight crews have to be rated astronauts. Public and private sector both. NASA handles Ground School in Texas, then the crews come here for flight training. Cost and expertise being what they are, Edwards also happens to be the only place on Earth equipped to do the job." She smiled, but not altogether with humor. "Of course, we charge the commercial carriers for the privilege, helps NASA and Systems Command write off some operating expenses—no small consideration these days, seems like the whole government's semiprivatized, one way and another. Trouble is, too many bods, on both sides of the desk, seem to have problems remembering who we blue suits are supposed to be working for. That's what I like about space, those lines are still clearly drawn."

"There," Amy cried excitedly, "just above the sun, and to the right."

"Got it. Good eyes, kiddo, gold star for you." Out of the corner of her eye, Nicole caught a grin of shy delight, and answered it with one of her own. "Downwind leg, about to turn onto base. Nominal profile."

"A magnificent sight," Kymri commented.

"Boeing-seven, state of the art. Only two companies produce commercial ScramJets, Boeing and the Europeans. They're not ferociously profitable, less than a half-dozen airlines operate 'em. And not that many more airports can handle the traffic—New York, Los Angeles, London, Tokyo, Singapore, Sydney. Most everybody else still loafs along in the wide-bodies, same as they have for the better part of a century."

"The eternal, inescapable paradox—we fly to the stars with an ease that beggars the imagination, yet find it infinitely harder to traverse our local system, or the world of our birth."

"You have the same problem?"

She heard the scratchy, subvocalized rumble of Kymri's laughter. "Is it not the hope that we two species are more alike than apart? We are all bound by the same laws of physics."

"In entertainment, it's so much easier. Teleportation beams, or power systems that allow a vessel of any mass and configuration to make planet-fall, and boost with ease back to vacuum."

"Still, Nicole, in your own literature, this very conversation would be considered total fiction barely a generation ago."

Now it was her turn to grin, which turned into a yawn as she absently scratched a bit of dry skin by her elbow. "Good point."

"I believe Kinsella-Colonel's work in the simulator was exemplary," noted in a tone of voice so dry it was positively arid.

"Yup," she nodded.

"You have no faith?" he asked. "In the simulator?"

"Love the beast. Finest toy ever invented. Probably saved my ass, more'n once, certainly damn near cost me my career."

"I recall, from your dossier. Elias-Doctor—the Chief Astronaut—almost separated you from the astronaut program after you failed a simulation flight."

She looked at him, wondering what he didn't know about her.

"Got cocky," she said, "got careless, made a stupid mistake. Learned, I hope, my lesson. But that's the thing about a simulator, Kym, you can make mistakes. It's also the greatest danger. Because there's a different feel to reality. Not the sense of the vehicle, or the flight conditions—they can duplicate that so perfectly now, it beggars belief. But nothing's at risk there. You screw the pooch, the operator simply recycles the simulation and starts again. Not an option on a live approach. Here, *bang,* you're mortal. And very aware of it. Some folks can't make the adjustment. By the same token, some magnificent natural fliers can't hack the simulator; they can't surrender to the illusion, they don't take the moment seriously. They'll never make a mistake outside, but in the box, they simply don't care, it's all a game." Off to the side, Amy was nodding sagely, probably because Nicole's feelings echoed her own about her brother. Nicole had always faced a healthy rivalry with her younger siblings, especially the twins, but there was something in Amy's undertone—the faintest yet sharpest of edges—that bothered her.

"How was it with you?"

"Little of both." She stiffened, eyes narrowing fractionally. "Edwards Ground, Remote Nine."

"Nine, go."

"Reference one-one-Delta-Bravo, am I wrong or didn't the Master Plot sked the flight out on the dirt, over?"

Fractional pause, while the duty controller called up the file. "Ay-firm, Remote Nine," he told her, "Aircraft Commander made an in-flight request to change over to a runway approach, three-five left. That's why you gotta hold. Sorry about that. We tried to alert you, but you didn't have your 'ears' on, over."

"Appreciate the thought. We'll know better next time. Nine, out."

"Is something wrong with that?" Kymri asked.

Nicole shrugged. "First approach, you generally come down on the lake. Kilometers of flat hardpan, plenty of room to correct any mistakes. Runway, even with the overrun beyond, isn't as forgiving. Which is probably precisely why a hotshot fast-tracker like Grace chose the option. Couldn't be satisfied with simply executing a manual proficiency reentry, the lady just has to strut her stuff."

"Nicole . . ."

"Shit!"

" . . . the approach is off."

"I see it. She cut the corner too tight turning onto base, that doesn't leave her a whole helluva lot of margin to set down. Not a major problem, though, especially since the Scrammer's maneuvering under power; she simply hangs a right, goes out a few klicks at altitude before pulling a one-eighty and resuming the approach. Wouldn't be the first time—had to do it myself, once—matter of fact, the maneuver's programmed into the flight control system." Nicole's mouth twisted slightly. "Probably piss Grace off no end, though."

"She is turning towards us," Kymri noted quietly.

"Oboy. Time to pray, Colonel, you're as good as you like to think you are, and dump some sky." And the ScramJet did precisely that, going into a dive that resembled the kamikaze approaches used by the first-generation Rockwell shuttles in the previous century. In what seemed like an eyeblink, the dot in the distance took on discernible shape and size.

"*Shit,*" Nicole breathed, and her body was taut with sympathetic tension, "she's *way* off-line."

"Is there danger?" Kymri asked.

"On the lake, you can land pretty much along any vector. Although generally it's safer—certainly easier—to touch down where there are marked-off runways. That isn't an option here. Got no choice now, she'll have to abort and go around for a second try. Grace, *don't!*" she cried as the hypersonic transport suddenly slipped sideways through the air.

By slicing across the line of attack, the smooth flow of air over the wings was instantly and violently disrupted. Deprived of the lift that kept it airborne, the plane dropped like a stone. Behind her, in the distance, in the direction of the main field, Nicole registered the hooting of the alarm klaxon, scrambling the crash crews. But her attention was focused on the ScramJet.

"C'mon, Gracie, quit screwing around, you're almost out of sky, let's see some smarts, slap those throttles, Kinsella, boost it boost it what're you waiting for a bloody invitation *boost it! Yes!*" Her voice building to a yell even as a distant rumble swelled past them to crash against the hillsides like a cresting wave. The great needle of an aircraft, impossibly long and slender, with wings that seemed hardly able to support the fuselage, much less the monster engines slung beneath, flattened out its descent, skimming the desert at barely a hundred meters while Kinsella dropped both flaps and gear. Then it flashed off the lake and over the concrete of the base's main runway, the banshee shriek of its engines stabbing through the hands she'd cupped over her ears. Nicole saw smoke as the main gear touched, contact friction burning off the wheels' outer layer in the split second before they started spinning; then a second roar—louder and more impossibly punishing than the first—shook the air around them as the thrust reversers kicked in, gateways opening in the engine nacelles to direct the airflow forward instead of back and slow the ScramJet almost to a stop.

"Edwards Ground," Nicole called, watching the distant aircraft clear onto the taxiway with surprising daintiness, perched atop its stalklike landing gear. In this instance, that appearance was mightily deceptive, because those struts were thicker in diameter than she was. "Remote Nine requesting clearance to cross the active, over."

"Nine, Tower," came the immediate reply, "you take it slow for about five minutes, you should have no problem. Next scheduled traffic in fifteen, over."

"No prob, we're rolling."

"You would prefer to run, I think," Kymri said as they started on their way. She didn't trust herself to reply. "A successful landing makes you so angry?"

"She should have known better." His turn to play the mute, forcing her to fill the silence. Her rage allowed her no alternative. "That's a stunt you pull—Christ, you think twice about it in a piston plane, something like my Baron. Rupture positive airflow on a jet—any jet, but *especially* that beauty—and you're flying a brick."

"She succeeded."

"She got lucky."

"You do not allow for her obvious skills? Are you so sure of yourself, Nicole?"

"No, I'm not sure, and maybe she is God's Gift, I dunno. But that was pudknocker flying"—throwing out an arm for emphasis in the general direction of the ScramJet—"she was showing off. She made a mistake—hey, it happens, that's why Edwards exists—but she didn't acknowledge it. She fought it. Sod, the buggers only cost upward of a bil apiece, who cares if you splatter one? 'Course, there is the small matter of her crew."

"Are you jealous, Nicole . . ."

"Gimme a *break*!"

" . . . that she took a gamble, that perhaps to her was a calculated risk, and won? What would you have done in her position?"

"Gone around, of course. I'm not paid to be a hero, Kymri, just to fly airplanes. And that doesn't include turning them into wrecks."

"Perhaps then, you see her as someone who is what you no longer dare to be."

She swung her leg over the bike, and settled herself on the seat, face set as she glared at him, belatedly aware of Amelia on her own bike a little beyond him. "My apologies, sir, but I think it's past time we got back to where we're supposed to be. We've a full day's work ahead and standing here won't get it done. Sir."

She rode hard, pushing herself past the aircraft parked on the flight line and out the main gate, almost daring the sentries to challenge her as she flashed her ID at them on the way past. That they didn't was more due to the sight of Kymri pacing along a couple of short steps right behind her than any recognition of who she was. Up Popson Avenue, along the bike path out to Housing Sector Bravo, she hung a louie at Kincheloe, didn't stop, didn't slow, until she pulled into her own driveway. And then, without a word, or even a backward glance, she hefted the bike onto her shoulder and strode inside.

Her heart was hammering as she climbed into the tub, setting off an icy trembling that reached from the base of her throat down to deep within her belly. For a moment, she just stood, resting hands on the cool tile, mind off-line in a soft fugue—aware of where she was and what she should be doing, she knew what came next, it's that she found herself unable to bring it into being. A flash of total inertia, here I stand, here I'll stay. She was panting, but it had nothing to do with physical exertion. Kymri's words kept bouncing in her head, like a squash ball in perpetual motion, coming at her from every conceivable dimension, with her always reacting a split second out of phase, turning as it ripped past. She thrust an arm blindly towards the tap, slapping the shower full on,

gasping at the shock of the first burst of spray, intensely cold
from sitting in the pipes all night. Warmed up fast, though,
and she let it cascade off her head, down her back, hoping it
would soothe her out of her panic.

Panic, it was. A tidal wall of primal terror that she hadn't
felt since her first deep-space EVA, in those first, fateful,
make-or-break seconds after stepping out of the spacecraft,
when she realized there was nothing around her in any direction but empty space for as far as the eye could see. Which
was forever. And the ancient animal in the bottom of her brain,
conditioned by millions of years of evolution, reared up and
shrieked its fear—because as far as it was concerned, if there
was nothing (like the ground) to hold you up, then you fell.

It wasn't a common response in local Earth space, because
astronauts had the Earth and the Moon as reference points,
subconscious reassurance that there was indeed something to
hold on to. A top and bottom to the Universe. No such luck
in the Beyond.

But she'd worked her way through it. Training, common
sense, her rational intelligence and the character mated to it
ganged up on the animal, put it back where it belonged.

Here, though, none of that seemed to help. Kymri's voice
became Elias's and suddenly her head was crowding with the
trio that formed the Flight Review Board; it wasn't so much
an examination, not that part of her evaluation, the traditional
tests were behind her and she knew she'd aced them. There
was no sense even of it being a formal interrogation. They
met five times, which she knew now was way out of line.
Standard procedure was two sessions, three max, and each of
her last two ran longer than the first three combined. They
sat and talked, pilot to pilot, every one a spacer as well as a
shrink.

And when they were done, so was she. And she wasn't even
sure why. That was the most awful part, sensing instinctively
that something was wrong, but unable to lock it down.

Is this it, she wondered, folding at the knees and hips into
a corner of the tub, face twisting with pain even though every
part of her was numb, telling herself that all the water on her
face came from the showerhead and that the taste of salt was
just sweat. *A loss of nerve?*

But a pilot had to be careful—playing the flash-ass was the
surest way to getting your picture mounted on the Hotshots's

memorial wall. *No*, she told herself, resting her head forward on her hands as though it had become a weight too intolerable to bear. "No," and this time, she spoke aloud, with a flat, rough finality that wouldn't be denied. *A pilot has to know the capabilities of her craft, when to push, when to back off, what's the gamble, what's the calculated risk.* And the ultimate craft of course, the core key without which all the rest was essentially bullshit, was the pilot herself.

Somewhere along the way, Nicole had changed. She lost a layer of self, and what was underneath was raw and prickly, too tender by half until the elements toughened it into shape. Raw steel that had gone through a single tempering but which, at heart, was still mostly malleable metal.

And suddenly, for the first time in her life, Nicole didn't have the slightest idea how it would come out.

five

"R!T'SYJAN!"

"I'm bloody *trying*," she snapped back into her boom microphone, twisting the right-hand yoke as the cabin bucked around her. A sudden pitch drove her body forward against her shoulder harness, the violent compression of her diaphragm turning her words (thankfully) into an inarticulate bellow. There was so much rain hitting the windscreen even the shuttle velocity couldn't keep it clear, and the matching turbulence made it almost impossible to get a stable fix on the panel displays. Bad enough she kept bouncing about in her seat, hard enough to snap her teeth together with an audible *clack*, but every so often the video images themselves would destabilize, either disintegrating into a field of incoherent static or losing V/H hold, rolling wildly through the vertical or horizontal or both. Red warning lights were lit beside all the main RNAV displays, indicating critical ionization conditions, telling the flight crew that the atmospheric conditions were wreaking havoc on the navigational electronics and that consequently none of the data being displayed could be trusted.

The final straw, of course, was that none of that data was written in English, nor were the control surfaces designed for the human form. This was a reproduction of the Hal shuttle and the simulation scenario—designed, she was sure, by Alex Cobri, with the most maliciously sadistic delight, in concert with Matai—an approach to Edwards through the worst storm imaginable.

An alarm went off. She couldn't place it immediately— either in her mind or on the panel—and it took precious seconds to sort things out (cursing all the while because in one of her own ships she was sure she'd have known the answer instinctively, raging as well at the part of her self that was saying quite sagely and sanely, but in Alex Cobri's voice— *damn* his eyes and face and soul—*Well, L'il Loot, isn't this what simulators are for?*), found it was the sink rate. She was way below the glide path, losing too much altitude too fast.

"Wing configuration three," Kinsella told her from the left-hand seat. Nicole reached for the control, but a sudden swerve sent her hand flying the wrong direction and she snapped it back for fear she'd hit something else by mistake and only make matters worse. Got a second chance, did as she was told.

"Anshdryl halach'n m'nai," came over her headphones, Kymri acting as ground controller, telling them they were too low, which Nicole could see for herself whenever the main displays settled down. No English was being spoken on the uplink, nothing but going the other way, to get the flight crews used to coping in both languages.

"Throttles to sixty percent," Kinsella said, moving the four sticks herself, the cabin shakes and shudders taking on a different quality as the main engines made their presence felt.

"Reports of major wind shear," Nicole said, as an updraft emphasized the point by giving them an additional hundred meters altitude in what seemed like barely a heartbeat.

"You don't sound happy."

She tossed a fast glance Kinsella's way. The Colonel's teeth were bared in a tight, wild grin that lit up her whole face. This wasn't a landing, it was one-on-one personal combat between her and the environment, a duel she was determined to win.

"Colonel, the weather's way beyond specs. Recommend we abort the approach and retrieve orbital status."

"I thought you were a fighter, Shea."

"Only when I have to, ma'am."

"Sounds eminently—*huhnhnf*—relax, I still have the vehicle, no need to worry!" So easily said, but they fought a downdraft mixed with a massive broadside gust that was like trying to crest a wave only to find yourself without enough momentum to go over the top. Nose bouncing high, tail low, the whole vehicle threatening to turtle onto its back, stall warnings wailing like banshees, Kinsella reacting faster than conscious thought, playing hand and foot controls to slew the shuttle around so they were once more nose down, with air rolling over the wings to provide them lift, yet taking care at the same time not to push things too far, lest the stall turn into a spin they had neither height nor raw power to recover from.

"Of course," Kinsella continued breathily, exertion and excitement making her lungs pump like a bellows, "the beauty of such a position is that it allows one an almost unlimited latitude of rationalization. So that no situation provides sufficient justification."

The wind was on their quarter, made worse by random killer gusts, forcing them to crab sideways towards the field. Full power landing as well, with the great wings configured for takeoff, Kinsella holding tight to her options until they were actually on the ground. Only then did she throttle back and let the shuttle coast to a final stop.

She held up a hand for a high-five, and Nicole obliged.

"That, youngster," the Colonel said with satisfaction, "is how it's done."

Nicole wondered, staying where she was in the co-pilot's seat after the other woman's departure, staring at the luminescent screen beyond the canopy as the projection system shut down, its computer-generated representation of the base fading to formless, featureless opalescence.

"A thoughtful countenance," Kymri rumbled behind her, and she shrugged, not all that eager for company.

"You called for an abort," he continued, leaning on the back of Kinsella's seat.

"It was a standard approach. No imperative reason for us to be down. Nothing dirtside, no in-flight emergency. With the weather scans on the board, reentry shouldn't have even been initiated."

"No imperative, Shea-Pilot, to complete what you have started?"

She took a deep breath—rather, as deep as her harness allowed, which reminded her to pull the tabs to give herself sufficient slack to wriggle loose, rolling her shoulders as she

did to ease the tension in them—then said, "To my mind,
Kymri, it wasn't necessary. And if not, why proceed?"

"Someday, you may face such a situation."

"Excuse me, maybe I'm missing something, but that didn't
strike me as the purpose of the exercise. We started from orbit,
were given the specs and told to take things from there."

"At that point, you had acceptable minimums."

"I can read a weather fax, Kymri. The potential was there
for a marked deterioration. Which is precisely what happened.
We could have afforded another orbit to make sure, and if
necessary diverted to our alternate. We shouldn't have started,
and once started, shouldn't have finished. It's just like her
landing the other day, she couldn't resist the opportunity to
show off."

"And yet, Shea-Pilot, Kinsella-Colonel got you down."

"She's very good," Nicole conceded. "In a simulator."

"You still believe she was wrong."

"What does it matter? She's the Colonel, I'm the Second
Loot; as far as our opinions go, there shouldn't even have to
be a contest as to which of us is right."

"In point of fact"—the Hal pilot held out a hand, which
Nicole was surprised to discover she needed to climb out of
her chair, grunting at the stiffness in her joints as she hobbled
after him off the flight deck—"there is not."

"When do we try this for real?" Kinsella asked as they emerged
from the jetway. With the crew aboard the simulator, this access
tunnel was withdrawn, leaving the cabin atop a hydraulic stalk
some ten meters off the floor, in the center of a huge cube of
a room some twenty meters square, allowing for a significant
range of motion through any flight dimension. About the only
regime that couldn't be duplicated was inverted flight; those it
could accomplish, however, more than made up for the lack.

"When you are ready," was the reply. "We have but the one
vehicle here." Kymri went on to explain, "We cannot afford
to hazard it. Any more than you can yours."

The conversation stayed with Nicole as she strode from
the simulator to the Experimental Surface ReEntry Vehicle
Project offices, all housed in the Edwards South Complex,
a massive agglomeration of hangars and test facilities initially built in the 1980s for the B-2 "Stealth" project and
used ever since for anything that required a major degree of
secrecy.

Sound and motion caught her attention in the middle distance, and she paused, shading her sunglasses against the fierce midday glare for a better look. Out on the field, a jet pivoted onto the main runway, the piercing banshee shriek of its engines downshifting suddenly to a basso profundo roar, twin cones of blue flame spiking from the narrowed exhaust nozzles as the pilot kicked in the afterburners, injecting raw fuel into the combustion chamber to maximize its power. He was running on full military power, every kilo of thrust his torches were capable of producing, and was off the ground seemingly before he'd started a decent takeoff roll, arrowing straight up into a vertical climb that took him into five figures and past the sound barrier within a matter of heartbeats. Gone from sight before the echoes of its departure had faded. Nicole hoped it was fun. Had to be better than sitting at a desk, playing junior-grade flunky.

Running the simulation proved to be the most sublime joy compared to writing up her evaluation of it: a full-range assessment of mission, vehicle, and flight crew, combining a subjective narrative recitation of the events with as objective as possible critique of every element's performance. The further Nicole got into the report the more ambivalent she became, on the one hand more certain than ever her response had been the proper one—this was an approach that should never have been tried—yet as increasingly suspicious of the judgment behind it. Fear of failure? Jealousy over Kinsella's continued success? Not for the first time she found herself hating composing on a display screen, yearning atavistically for the luxury of pages of scratch paper to crumple and toss to burn off some frustration. Kinsella loved risks, she was never more *there* physically and mentally than when she was pushing her limits to the max, possessed of a mad certainty that nothing could beat her. Much of the friction that existed between her and Nicole came from both their realizations that Nicole wasn't cut from that mold, and refused to be fit into it.

Yet, for all of that, Nicole had something Kinsella desperately craved, believed passionately she deserved.

Nicole unpinned the astronaut wings from her blouse, twirled them in her fingers. Swiveled her chair around to stare out the windows at the whitewashed expanse of desert and the mountains that shimmered in the distance from the heat wash off the blistering sand. Switched images in her mind's eye with the view from the DaVinci surface dome. Different levels of desolation, the ultimate difference being that here she could go for a stroll outside dressed as she was. She might be uncomfortable, but unless she was ferociously stupid she wouldn't die. Whereas on the Moon, all other elements notwithstanding, she was good for as long as she could hold a single breath.

Here, she had the world. There—a succession of boxes, be they the main starport at DaVinci or Ceres Base out in the Belt, or the ships that journeyed from one to the other. With the possibility that someday, she might have been lucky enough to crew a starship—another warren of boxes, oh, joy—off to another system, for a stroll on another world. But no matter where she went, it would only be for visits. Home would become the ships. Life forever in a box, a cage, a cell.

She wondered if Kinsella ever thought about it in those terms, ever truly let herself imagine a fifty-week round-trip to Cocytus Station on Pluto, the "milk run" of a mission Nicole had been on aboard *Wanderer* before their encounter with the Wolfpack raiders and then the Halyan't'a.

Any more than Nicole herself thought about life without it.

She took a swallow of tea, grimaced in dismay at the realization that her drink had grown cold, wondered in alarm how long she'd been sitting wrapped up in thought. The door suddenly banged open, startle-spasming her to her feet with a curse as tea sloshed over the rim of her mug, doing a final awkward flinch-step backward as it splashed off her desk.

Amy Cobri stuck her head into the office, holding back a laugh as Nicole belatedly tried to recover herself.

"Interrupting something important?" she asked with that small, special touch of malice kids have when they catch adults looking silly.

Nicole hunted for an appropriate retort, then let it go with a resigned sigh. Amy grabbed a handful of paper towels off the coffee maker and handed them over, Nicole nodding her thanks while mopping up the mess.

Staying on one knee, she reached up to the CardEx clipped to Amy's denim overalls; it wasn't a visitor's tag, but one of those issued to base personnel, allowing her unrestricted access to the facilities. The only other one she'd seen like it was Colonel Sallinger's.

"It's real," Amy said.

"I'm impressed."

The girl shook her head as she plonked herself down in Stu Hanneford's chair and twirled herself around—Kinsella rated two assistants, Hanneford being a Captain Kinsella had brought with her from her old squadron. He was an ace with a word processor, so while Nicole got her fair share of the scutwork, he usually ended up handling the bulk of the correspondence. Didn't seem to mind so much. Flying wasn't the passion for him it was for his boss; he took his place in the standard rotation, did what was asked of him, got his jazz from the motorcycle he took off across the desert every weekend.

"Lot less to it than meets the eye," Amy sniffed. "Having the right to go anywhere doesn't mean people'll let you in."

"And the key to privilege is knowing when not to push your luck, *hmnh*?"

"Yup." Amy looked around, making a face, and said, "Seriously sterile environment."

"Not as bleak as some I've seen."

"Up there," pointing skyward.

Nicole laughed. "Not hardly. I was thinking of some of the pits we got bounced through back at the Academy. Actually, spacer quarters are anything but bleak."

"I thought they were all boxes."

"Standard design, yes. But you're free to do with it what you like. I remember, when I was a kid . . ."

"My age, right?"

"Maybe a little shorter. Anyway, my uncle Rob is a skiffy buff—seriously into science fiction videos—has a collection that goes all the way back to Méliès."

"George's Méliès, right, Frenchman, silent film called *A Trip to the Moon*?"

"Full marks for you."

"Your uncle, my dad, they're a pair."

"Anyway, all these films and TV shows, they picture life in space as modular components, designer uniforms, everything neat as the proverbial pin. No allowance for the human capacity for clutter. Or self-expression. Just because you can't bring much with you doesn't mean you can't do all you can with what you've got."

"Sounds like Japan."

"Not far wrong. So what brings you down here?"

The question got her a mischievous grin. "You said you'd teach me to play ball."

"I thought tennis was your game."

Another face, more disgusted than the one before. "In Papa's bracket, it's *everybody's* game. Either *très* terribly social—*wack wack wack* but not so hard you sweat, have a drink and some munchies, and moan your brains out, seriously ash—or you obsesso your way to Wimbledon."

"No middle ground?"

She sighed. "Not there. Not for me. 'Sides, I can play tennis. Ball's something new."

"We'll have to see. My time's not my own."

"I can change that." •

I'll bet you can, Nicole thought, but said, casually, "Don't. Please. Someone told me you ski?"

"Working on it." And here, Nicole saw what she'd come to recognize was that rarest of smiles in Amy, an actual expression of delight. She wanted to tell the girl how good it made her look, that it was something she should try more often, but knew how patronizing it would sound.

"Downhill or cross-country?"

"Downhill. Giant slalom."

"You any good?"

"Yeah," Amy said quietly with the matter-of-fact, taken-for-granted pride of someone who meant exactly what was said. "Thing with people, there's always a way to slice 'em. Can't do that with a mountain. You got the slope and the snow and your skis."

"Figure that makes it an even fight?"

"Yeah," she said again, the same way, with such an edge of surprise that Nicole didn't tell her she was making a small joke.

And looked around suddenly as a sharp voice from outside heralded Kinsella's arrival.

Nicole met her at the door, coffee as freshly brewed as it was poured, Kinsella taking it with barely a nod of acknowledgment as she strode past to her office. The Colonel took it black, in a mug emblazoned with the crest of her former command— a squadron of F-31 fighter-bombers, the 101st Interdictors of the Third Aggressor Wing, called themselves the "Berserkers," because (or so they claimed) you'd never know they were

about until they dropped the hammer—and Kinsella took the
nickname to heart.

She loved to wander, poking her nose wherever the fancy
took her, and Heaven help the person responsible if what
she found wasn't on profile. Nicole still didn't much like the
woman, but over the past weeks she'd learned to respect the
officer; Kinsella took the measure of her people right off the
bat, more often than not with surprising accuracy. She had an
arrogant self-confidence that was part and parcel of being a
fighter jock but also the smarts not to pretend to be something
she wasn't. If Kinsella didn't know anything, she wasn't afraid
to ask. By the same token, she had no tolerance for bullshit.
And anyone who tried invariably got their head handed back
on a silver platter.

For all the skill and talent, though, she'd arrived at the most
dangerous stage of her career. Young enough to still hack
combat flying but reaching the rank where the responsibilities
of command allowed her less and less time for it. A situation
made worse, in her case, by trying simultaneously to make the
transition from atmosphere to vacuum, and carve a place for
herself along the High Frontier.

Nicole knocked, got the briefest flicker of a glance in
acknowledgment, placed a full file folder on her desk.

"Halyan't'a status updates are in your buffer, ma'am," she
said, "and here's a hardcopy of the XSR evaluation for your
review. It's uploaded as well, ready for processing."

"Very good, Lieutenant," was Kinsella's reply, without even
a glance upward from her own work. "I have Flight Review this
afternoon, so I probably won't be back after lunch 'til near close
of business."

"Excuse me, ma'am, but the initial test sequence for Mr.
Cobri's Virtual system is scheduled for two."

Kinsella gave her that look seniors have for subordinates
whenever they're about to pull rank. "Tell Captain Hanneford
to have a nice time. I'll expect a full report. Damned if I can
see the sense of it."

"Mr. Cobri feels it has extraordinary potential," Nicole
began, only to be almost immediately stopped.

"I read his proposal, Lieutenant. And you know as well as
I that if there had been any name on it but Cobri, if he weren't
our best hope for establishing a direct interface between the
Hal cybernetics systems and our own . . ." Kinsella let her

words trail off with a shake of the head. "He wants to play, he can afford his own toys, why not humor him? A decision, as always, made by those who don't have to deal with the consequences."

Nicole saluted and was starting to leave when Kinsella's voice turned her back.

"I noticed Miss Cobri outside."

"Just dropped in, ma'am. Shall I ask her to leave?"

There was a strange, ambiguously torn expression on Kinsella's face, as though the thought was tempting but the risk too great. "If she's no distraction," the Colonel said with a perfunctory wave of the hand, "she can stay."

Nicole couldn't help a inner, bitter smile at how neatly her boss had dumped the burden onto her shoulders.

Stu didn't look thrilled when Nicole gave him the news.

"I'll be hours in that damn harness," he groused, slouching in his chair and drumming his fingers on the desktop, "and most of the night finishing the report."

"Comes with the territory, Stu."

"It's Friday."

"These things happen."

"You don't understand, Nicole." He was on his feet, pacing from the outer doorway to Kinsella's, with half an eye cocked in case she decided to emerge. "Carla called me, my new bike's finally in and ready to roll."

"Cut yourself some slack, Stu, you've got the whole weekend."

"Hey," he snapped. "I had things arranged, today was light duty, just so I could cut loose early and get in some off-road time. Check out the wheels, do whatever mods were necessary tomorrow morning, run it hard in the afternoon, same deal on Sunday. This way, I bookend the weekend with a run. And it's not as though there's time to spare. I mean, the race is next month! *And* all my personal time's tied up with that," he explained further, anticipating Nicole's question, "I can't ask for any more full days to practice."

Nicole said nothing. She'd come to learn that Stu loved schedules—part of what made him such an efficient paper-pusher—a structure for his day to match the structure of his files. But when the real world threw a curve, he found himself boxed, unable to bend. In fact, it surprised her that he was a fighter jock, since they generally thrived on the rush of the unexpected. Stu hated it.

"Unless . . ." He also could have the subtlety of a brick. It wasn't much fun playing poker with him; he was as achingly predictable as he was conservative.

"Stu!" she protested.

"A favor."

"That'll get both our butts in a royal sling when Kinsella sees my name on the report."

"I'll finesse things with the boss, you got my word. We go back, she and I, you got no worries."

Famous last words, she thought. *Like Colonel, like Captain.*

And, against her better judgment, nodded.

"All *right*," he cheered, then held up his hands in a placating gesture. "Look, I'll be back this evening, shouldn't be long after sundown, we'll work on the report together, howzzat?"

"I'd appreciate it. What is this miracle machine, anyway, aren't you satisfied with what you've got?"

"Oh, Nicole, you've got no idea. I mean, my old bike's a piece of work, but this—! Totally blew my credit line and worth every penny."

"All for Baja."

"I can win it with this."

"To each his own, sport. Have a nice time."

"How's it feel," Alex asked as she settled the helmet a little more comfortably on her shoulders.

"Disconcerting," Nicole replied, rolling her eyes in every direction, trying to find the smallest pinpoint of light in the absolute darkness, "as always."

"State-of-the-art CyberSpace," he told her, "I thought you'd've become used to it ages ago."

"There's them that do, pal, an' them that don't." She didn't need the image in her mind's eye to tell her how silly she looked, lying on a contour chair in Alex Cobri's lab, wearing a helmet that looked like nothing so much as a giant, opaque goldfish bowl.

"Sealed?"

"Tight," and she felt the rubber gasket that fit snug around her neck. Normally, of course, the helmet would seat into the locking ring of a pressure suit, but for this test that wasn't necessary; she was wearing just a regular flight suit over a body-hugging skinsnug that literally wrapped her in the sensor web that would key her into the Virtual Reality field.

"You sound a bit edgy. Scared of the dark?"

"I just like to see where I am and where I'm going."

"Oh, well. If that's all."

She couldn't help a gasp of surprise as daylight burst all around her. There was a moment of disorientation while her mind struggled to accept the new input and then, with an almost physical shock, she realized where she was. Or rather, she told herself desperately, where she appeared to be. Ten thousand meters, maybe fifteen, over Tehachapi, in air so brilliantly clear she could pick out the Los Angeles skyline off to the south. Looked left and down, aware of her head moving, but no sense of any shift in her globular helmet—indeed, disconcertingly, no sense of any external physicality at all—saw intermittent flashes from the giant NOAA windmills at the foot of the pass, Mojave Airport almost right beneath her, Edwards itself a comparatively small ways beyond. The other direction, across the San Rafael Mountains to the Pacific beyond. An impossibly perfect flying day, classic CAVU— Clear Air Visibility Unlimited.

"Eat your heart out," she heard Alex Cobri say, and she started—ever so slightly—as his disembodied head appeared in midair before her, "Man of Steel."

"Not too shabby," she conceded. "No live input, everything here's computer-generated?"

"Synthesized, the lot. What, you think weather this clear comes naturally? That bother you, L'il Loot?"

"I'm not looking at the real world," she said. "All I know about what is, and what's going on, is what your interface chooses to tell me. And I'd appreciate it if you'd stop calling me that, *Mister* Cobri."

"You've got all you need to know and more. Anything you like, any way you want it. For example, how 'bout a Fox-two-niner, standard air supremacy package—that's six air-to-airs and a gatling, conformal fuel tanks to top you out at roughly thirty minutes hang time." Before Nicole, but slightly off-center, appeared a miniature down-view silhouette of the teardrop-shaped F-29 interceptor, with weapons clearly marked. Straight on was a gun-sight targeting grid. "Let's throw in a solo bad guy," the Alex-head continued with a

chuckle, "at Mach three closure." No gasp this time, but a
snarled "*Jesus*" as Nicole suddenly found herself barreling
through the sky at one and a half times the speed of sound.

"God's-Eye," she snapped automatically, and a tactical
schematic overlay of the situation materialized before her.
A single bogey, as promised, her altitude, thirty klicks out.
At this speed, approaching head-on, she had all of seconds
to act.

"Data, hostile," she said, and a data window opened off
to one side, zooming in for a close-up of the other aircraft,
displaying all its relevant statistics. F-31, dual-role fighter-
bomber, with capabilities on a par with her own. She had
the edge in raw speed, it in maneuverability; it carried more
hardpoints for ordnance—in this case, missiles—while she had
the higher gun load.

And yet—while mind and body kicked instinctively into
combat mode, the one racing through a score of possible
options to get the jump on her opposition, the other preparing to execute them and deal with the physical consequences—something, a wrongness, kept burring at the base
of her consciousness. More and more information was flashing
at her from the floating displays, so much that she deliberately
ignored most of it, focusing solely on what was necessary
for the fight, letting the rest pass on through to storage in
her back-brain, accessible when needed but otherwise out of
the way. This had been the major problem with air combat
since before the turn of the century, vehicles that far surpassed
the physical capabilities of their operators, combined with an
ever-more bewilderingly comprehensive volume of data. A
multitude of critical elements to keep track of, requiring split-
second responses, in a regime of acute physical and mental
stress. It had gotten to the point where it wasn't possible
to *think* your way through a dogfight anymore—it was like
playing an entire Grand Master chess match in five seconds
or less—everything had to be left to instinct. Which essentially made any decent fight a match between flash responses;
if a body took time to take a breath, that was pretty much
guaranteed to be its last. The antithesis of how she'd learned
to behave in space.

She shook her head angrily to clear the hair from her eyes,
squinted against the sting of the wind across her face, sheer
speed cooling her skin while the raw sun high overhead tried

to roast her bare back. And came to a dead stop in midair, just by thinking about it, as the realization crashed home that she wasn't in an aircraft any longer, simulated or otherwise. She was stark naked, a Valkyrie figure with hair sweeping most of the way down her back, staring in dumb astonishment at the equally naked, dauntingly impressive figure of Grace Kinsella diving towards her at better than fifteen hundred klicks per hour. The impact sent Nicole tumbling head over heels, and as she tried desperately to recover herself, she sensed rather than saw Grace sending a right cross towards her jaw.

The punch was about to connect when Nicole tore at the helmet, yanking it off with desperate force and an almost incoherent cry of rage to find Alex standing safely out of reach—*very* sensible boy—by the monitor console with a shit-eating grin plastered over his face.

"What the *hell*," she snarled, and would have thrown the helmet at him, cheerfully used it to pulp his matinee-idol features bloody, if not for the minimal play of the data and power umbilicals linking it to her couch. Not to mention the fact that the helmet alone represented an expenditure of perhaps ten times her current annual salary. She was panting, as much from physical exertion as anger—a part of her felt as if she herself had actually provided the motive force to propel her through the air, as though it had suddenly somehow become physically possible for the human body to fly at Mach one and a half, with the equivalent drain on her inner resources, and there were equally real aches as well from where the Kinsella avatar had slammed her. She half expected to find bruises running down her side, but wasn't about to give Alex the satisfaction of looking. Amy didn't help matters from her perch in a corner, wearing an I-told-you-so smirk.

"Had you fooled," he said with bland delight, as though he scored this sort of triumph every day.

"Very fucking funny, sport."

"You're missing the point," and she made a rude noise. "Nicole"—he paused, hunting for words that wouldn't make things worse than they already were (a forlorn hope, from her perspective)—"look, if I hadn't gotten carried away"—and she gave him a glare to match her vocal comment—"you had no differentiation"—he hammered each word, to give it emphasis—"between doing and being. Until I let the

Virtual Reality get too silly to support, *you* were flying. All the characteristics of the aircraft, all its capabilities, but *you* were doing it. And you didn't know. It seemed like the most natural thing in the world."

To buy herself some time before responding (because a response was clearly what he wanted, and applause, too, but also because she was damned if she would show him how truly shaken she was, she'd *never* been sucked so quickly and completely into an illusion before) she reached up with both hands to set the helmet back on its pedestal at the head of the couch. She was moving slowly, as though pummeled, growly stomach and light-headedness combining to tell her she needed some food, quickly. A shower, too, her skinsnug was plastered to her by sweat that the room's air-conditioning was turning to clammy ice.

"It wasn't me, though," she said, taking refuge in the trivial. "Not my shape. And in my whole life I've never had hair that long."

"Artistic license," he replied, trying for the joke.

She wanted to thump him, he was so blissfully dense; instead, she said simply, "I'm not your canvas, sport."

"I didn't mean it that way," he protested, starting belatedly to relate to her anger—but only by turning sulky, as if she were ruining a perfectly great and triumphant moment.

"Standard VR is limited," he went on hurriedly, "there's always a sense of being removed from the event, an observer rather than a participant."

"Strikes me that's not an altogether bad thing."

"I'm working on a way to integrate all the elements of the system—biological and cybernetic—into a true synthesis. A software linkage that allows wetware and hardware to function as one. A true cyborg."

"Is that an altogether good thing?"

"You're the astronaut, Nicole, you tell me. If I can give you a chance to experience through a remote a walkabout on the Venusian surface, or a swim through the Jovian atmosphere. To *be* outside a ship on EVA, without actually going. To be the ship itself. You gonna say no?"

She honestly wasn't sure. The only thing she'd encountered that came close to matching this was the Halyan't'a Environmental Sensorium aboard *Range Guide*, that managed to create not simply the look of a place but all the physical sensations

that went with it. Sights, sounds, scents, everything but the
raw texture of the materials. At least there, though, she had
the protection of knowing she was in a room aboard a starship,
and that all around her was illusion. Alex was talking about
erasing that "fourth wall" and making the subject one with the
illusion. Taking the "Virtual" out of Virtual Reality. *But what*,
she thought, *if you got lost?*

Her hands were trembling and she tried to cover it by shaking
out her arms, flexing her cramped shoulders.

"This isn't playtime, Alex," she said in a tone she'd learned
as Spacecraft Commander aboard *Wanderer*. "We're here for
a purpose. If you can't relate to that, stop wasting my, and the
Air Force's, time."

"My apologies," strangely sounding like he meant it.

"Let's just get on with business," she responded flatly,
returning to the couch, Alex helping fit the helmet once more
into place.

Most of the base was in bed by the time she made her way
home, the desert touched with a special sort of stillness that
she wished she had the energy to enjoy. That first session
with Alex's VR system had been the merest harbinger of what
was to come, a run of scenarios that proved as grueling and
physically exhausting as the real thing. Just what she needed
after this morning's ride in the simulator.

It didn't help that every so often, he'd throw her a curve—
like the naked Kinsella—just to see if she'd notice. Nor that a
couple of times, especially towards the end when fatigue was
wearing her down, she almost didn't. The whole point of the
exercise was to evaluate the system, and then fine-tune how
well it resonated to the operator.

In the end, as at the beginning, it was Nicole who'd called
it quits. She was totally wired, crackling with a nervous energy
that wouldn't let her stay still, either on the couch or her feet.
She spoke in quick, staccato bursts, with moves to match, and
a barely concealed fury towards Cobri that she didn't bother
to hide. Alex's reaction only made things worse, as though
this was an extension of the test sequence and her actions
more grist for his notebooks. She couldn't wait to strip off
the skinsnug, but for a long while after that she just sat on the
bench in the pilot's locker room, clothes in hand, undisturbed,
unmotivated by the slightest conscious thought.

She shook her head when the fugue finally broke, smiling in wry dismay at how she must look, just like one of her parents' cats whose favorite activity was to snuggle face-first into the corner seam of a sofa, where the back met the arm, staring at nothing and seeing who-knows-what.

She moved like an old woman, exercising joints that had forgotten how to move, slowly donning her uniform, and returning past Alex's lab to the project offices. The lights were out, the doors locked, a post-it on the door from Alex telling her she could return the skinsnug Monday morning since he had plans for the weekend.

"Lucky you," she murmured without even the energy to muster some appropriate profanity, hoping the 'snug would be safe in her locker with her flight gear.

The sky was still light, the sun just gone, as she slumped at her desk over a mug of leftover tea, freshly nuked in the office microwave, and tried to collect her thoughts for Kinsella's report. No sign of Stu, but she wasn't surprised; when he was playing with his toys, it was always better to give him some serious latitude. She was glad of that, in fact, grateful for a chance to sort out her reactions—thoughts and feelings— while she was still by herself.

So much of what she'd seen was so seductively tempting, Alex's reputation didn't even begin to do him justice. He'd been as good as his word, integrating himself into the field to take her for a sunlit stroll on the Moon and then kicking them both off the surface as though they were classic superheroes soaring down the Terrestrial gravity well, passing a couple of HeavyLifter shuttles en route and taking her for a loop around Sutherland Station before plunging at last into Earth's atmosphere, sailing blissfully through the air to a landing on a flower-covered mountain meadow. He'd given her a smile she'd never seen from him before, that mingled delight at his accomplishment with the sheer pleasure of sharing it with someone who appreciated what he'd done. And she'd smiled back.

The possibilities were as endless as the risks.

How to put that into words, she asked herself at the keyboard, staring at the glowing cursor on her flatscreen display, *or rather, how to put it into words that are safe?*

She was still struggling hours later when she called it quits here, as she had in the VR field, and put the office to bed. A call to the Provost Marshal's office brought one of his cars to carry her across to the North Field, she went the rest of the way on foot.

She almost kept on going down Rosamond when she came abreast of her house, it wasn't all that much farther to the park and Hotshots and despite the hour she was sure of at least a beer and some food from Sue. Being Friday, there'd probably be the usual gang of suspects, possibly a poker game, someone to stand her a round of eight-ball at the pool table. But she didn't want company, wasn't sure she'd know quite how to handle it. She felt scrambled up inside, as though what seemed like solid earth beneath her feet was really ice, ready to trip her up at any step. And she still wasn't sure why. The Virtual experience itself or the emotions it pulled from her? It all seemed so real, except that was the point. The damn thing called into question the very concept of reality. And if she couldn't trust what was real, how could she trust any reaction derived from it. Christ, for all she knew, she could still *be* there, sprawled on the couch in Alex's lab, cycling through a VR scenario of herself walking home, considering the day's events.

She let her head loll forward, clasping her hands behind her neck, and groaned. She'd been wrestling with those questions the whole evening and all she had to show for it was a killer headache.

Her legs decided they didn't want to go any farther and she plopped herself down on the shallow slope, halfway between the road and the houses. She knew it was too chilly to stay here for any length of time but couldn't find the resource to get herself moving. It was the strangest sensation; she knew what was needed, but also found the effort of making the decision, much less carrying it out, quite beyond her. Almost as though, despite the fact that her eyes were open and she seemed fully aware of the world around her, she was actually deep in REM sleep and this nothing but a dream.

If only, she thought, and started slightly as a shape materialized behind her, hunkering down on its heels to rest hands gently on her shoulders.

"An impressive view, Shea-Pilot," Kymri noted quietly.

She couldn't help relaxing back against him. Hal blood ran hotter than human, a warmth that rose through the skin, and his fur held the cinnamon tang she'd come to associate with them.

"One among many," she replied.

"Come here often?"

"Every chance." And marveled that she could still produce coherent speech.

"You are cold."

"We are as a species," she told him sagely, "compared to you." And hoped this was a dream, refusing to accept that she could act so stupidly in reality.

He rumbled laughter and tweaked his claws under her arms, a rude tickle that made her jump with a sharp cry of protest.

"Don't you *dare* do that," she cried, sprawled on her back and feeling totally foolish.

He held out a hand. "It served its purpose, you are now fully cognizant."

"I suppose you never get tired," she grumbled, scrambling up on her own and not caring how awkward she looked, pausing a moment to brush dust from her uniform.

"Of course," he said in a laughing tone, "have you not yet learned that in all ways we are superior to you?"

She muttered something foul and it wasn't until he burst out loud with laughter that she realized she'd spoken in Hal.

"You look awful," he said.

"Been a bitch of a day." She decided that if she narrowed her concentration to its tightest possible focus and took things a step at a time, she could reach her back door. After that, first soft surface she came across, sofa or bed, it could have her.

"Come," he said to her, taking her by one hand with his other across her back, "join us."

"Another time, Kymri, please," she protested, "I really can't!"

"You have not visited since we finished the renovations to our habitat."

"It'll make a better impression when I'm awake."

"Perhaps. But do you more good now."

"It's late."

"No matter. We have been waiting for you."

The ground floor was still fundamentally as the Air Force Housing Office had furnished it, on a par with what Colonel Sallinger was entitled to as Base Commander. Kymri led her upstairs though, to the bedrooms, where some substantial changes had been made. The style, and indeed some of the individual pieces, Nicole recognized from her time aboard

Range Guide—plus one of the early articles submitted by
Ben Ciari to the *National Geographic*—and she sank down
into a corner piled high with plush pillows with a groan of
sybaritic delight. She'd left her shoes at the base of the stairs
and wished she could ditch her pantyhose as well, the better
to rub her bare feet in the luxuriously thick rug the Hal had
brought down from orbit. The lighting was indirect and much
softer than was comfortable for most human eyes, since the Hal
functioned better across a wider range of visual perception; one
of the odd discoveries that had been made early on was that both
races had need of sunglasses. And spectacles as well. Nicole
had no problem with the twilight. As a matter of fact, her own
acuity seemed to have improved with her return from space;
her eyes were markedly sharper, both in terms of what they
they could see and how well she saw it.

"Try this," Kymri suggested.

It was a bowl of steaming liquid, slightly more than drink
but less than soup, bouillon with a bite that had most in
common with the spices that gave Cajun panfry its taste.
She drained the contents cautiously, the first sip telling her
that not only was this potent stuff, its temperature as well
was worthy of respect. Even so, she gave her tongue a minor
burn. Kymri brought her a glass of ice water and she fished
out a cube, laving it over the sore spot to ease the pain.

"Shea-Pilot," Kymri asked, "would you care to refresh yourself?"

She looked up at him, gathering herself with a breath and a
shudder, shaking her head while she looked about for somewhere to set her empty bowl.

"Wha'ssat mean?" she asked more sleepily than she really
felt. "Why are you always so formal with my name, Kymri?
I'm Nicole to my friends."

"You are freer with your names. Among the People, we have
House names, which are tied to our various tasks and responsibilities. There are names, such as my own and Shavrin's, which
are honors."

"You mean, like titles?" She leaned forward, holding out
her mug for a refill, hoping the broth would clear her inner
cobwebs even more. "The way the British King, say, appoints
someone a Lord or Lady or Knight?"

Kymri gave that some thought and asked the CyberCrystal
standing on a tabletop off to one side for clarification; it came

in a rapid-fire burst of Hal that Nicole couldn't begin to follow.

"A very rough analog," he told her. "And then are the names shared between friends." He spoke a Hal word first, one different from what Nicole was used to hearing as a translation. She didn't have a crystal to help and her PortaComp was in her shoulder bag, which had gotten away from her sometime after coming in the downstairs door, but some serious thought popped up a possible answer, culled from one of Ciari's tapes. The term generally used referred to acquaintances, professional associations mostly with only shallow personal resonances. This though was something altogether different. The friendship implied a bond, rarely entered into and never taken lightly. A commitment as meaningful, and in some ways more demanding, than a marriage.

"I understand, I think, the distinctions. But, Shea-Pilot, all the time." She shrugged, then brightened with an inspiration. "Can't you consider Nicole my honor name?"

"To single you out from your comrades, that would be a mistake. But among ourselves, it would be a privilege. The question, however, remains unanswered."

She looked, uncomprehending for a moment while sorting through the files of short-term memory.

"I should be going," she said, and made semicoherent excuses about home and bed.

"You will sleep as well here," he replied, "and better."

"I don't think so."

"Are you afraid to try?"

"What do you want from me?"

"There is a ceremony, the *chn'chywa*. For want of a better term, it is a sort of consecration of what is for us the heart of the house. You have a place in it because you are both of Shavrin's Hearth, as we are of her Family, and of this range, in which we make our home during our stay."

"Hearth and Family," she asked, "what's the difference?"

"The latter encompasses all who serve her. Clan is a word used much the same way among your kind. Hearth"—and he paused for a slow, steady, single breath, as though weighing for a final, irrevocable time what he was about to say—"betokens those of her blood, who reside in the household of her heart."

"Kymri," Nicole said with helpless desperation, words coming in a madcap babble that proved her point, "I can't. I'm totally wrecked, I'll make a muck of it."

He smiled lazily, showing teeth, and she thought of Sher Khan, the great tiger of Kipling's *Jungle Book*. "You are, you know," he said, "assigned to me and mine as liaison."

She laughed without anger, responding in the same playful manner. But to her surprise, he was gently serious.

"You cannot assist, Nicole," using her name for the first time, "those who you do not know."

Nicole was so tired, she couldn't see a way out. She doubted she'd have been able to do any better even at her peak. And she didn't really want to.

Matai was the celebrant, stepping into view at Kymri's quiet summons. She came up to Nicole's breast, which placed her close to Terran norms for a woman's height, with a frame that bespoke a wiry, almost alley-cat strength rather than the massive tigerish power reflected in Kymri and Tscadi. She had a sable primary coat that made her almost invisible in the room's shadows; she'd been there almost from the start, Nicole realized, and chuckled at her earlier thoughts about her own eyesight. Better perhaps but still nowhere near a match for her hosts. As the Hal cyber tech steepled her fingers and made the slight bow of greeting, Nicole saw that she was wearing a dress, a sleeveless sheath design from the co-op boutique that showed off her athletic figure to good advantage. Her voice was low like Nicole's but without the husky resonance, and she spoke with a shy diffidence that echoed her manner, so quietly Nicole had to strain to hear, much less understand, what was said.

"Do not be alarmed," Kymri told her as she looked to him in confusion. "Matai's focus is more the written speech of your cybernetics systems than of your spoken word. She is much the same with her own people." And he quickly repeated the line—or so Nicole deduced from the few scattered words she caught—in rapid-fire Hal to his crewmate, who bared teeth in a snarl of irritation that seemed so human a reaction to Nicole that she couldn't help but giggle.

"I don't know what's expected of me," Nicole said.

"Matai will lead. You observe and follow. Trust me, Nicole. It is necessary for you to know this. A time will come when you must take your rightful place among the People. The less you are ignorant of, the easier that will be."

An extension had been tacked on the side of the house and the ground-floor bathroom expanded to create a space that was perhaps half the size of the living room. Thanks to a superbly artful arrangement of lights and mirrors, it actually seemed much larger, with almost no sense at all of being an artificial construct.

The heat was a palpable force, sweat bursting from Nicole's pores within moments of her entrance as her body tried to cope. She couldn't take her eyes off Matai as the Hal moved through the room, laying out towels and robes and checking the toiletries set by the tub, any more than she could off Kymri during their morning runs together, unaware that her own movements were an unconscious attempt to follow. When Matai caught her though and made a *chirrup* noise, as if to ask what was up, Nicole flushed and looked away, trying to cover herself by focusing on the extraordinary variety of foliage around her.

The room was thick with plants, mostly broad-leaf tropicals interspersed with a multitude of fiery blossoms that cast an intoxicating fragrance. Standard quarantine forbade the importation of any off-world fauna so she knew all that lay around her was of Terrestrial origin, yet the choice and arrangement was such that the overall effect was disconcertingly alien. She had an eerie feeling that she was no longer on her world, nothing that she saw was familiar to any of her physical senses, and wondered if this was a further residue of her Virtual session, that it somehow made her more susceptible to external stimulus?

Matai peeled off the sheath and then the leotard worn beneath it, sinking gracefully down onto her knees beside the tub with a gesture that indicated Nicole should join her. Shaking her head, with a flash glance towards the door and the thought, *This is nuts I can't go through with it I gotta get out of here*, Nicole turned her back and began unbuttoning her shirt. She knew she wasn't going to do anything of the sort, it would be too direct and great an insult to the Hal. She simply had to trust that they would be as considerate of her. *Way to go, girl*, she told herself, *all your life you dream of contacting whatever's out there and now it's in your face, you got your wish, you can't hack it? Terrific.* Fact was, and she didn't bother denying it, she was as scandalized as excited, with fear in equal measure on both sides of the line.

Even on her knees, she seemed to tower over Matai, and the surface contrast between them couldn't be more marked, the Hal at one with the shadows that seemed to swirl about them while Nicole gleamed like alabaster, pale as a ghost, with a painfully sharp demarcation line down from her shoulders to

the top of her cleavage marking the boundary between what
was tanned and what wasn't. *Bilaterally symmetrical, bipedal
homonid*, she noted, seeking refuge in the analytical as Matai
mixed oils from various jars while crooning to herself, much as
Nicole did when nervous or stressed. *Warm-blooded, carbon-
based, mammalian*, she continued, *opposable thumbs. Evolved
from creatures who bear a superficial resemblance to Terrestrial cats*. And therein, she knew, lay the greatest danger.
Because the Hal appeared so much like Earthly felines, there
was an unconscious, automatic tendency to ascribe to them
similar traits of attitude and behavior. Rather than broaden the
knowledge base between the species a slow, careful step at a
time, with judgments grounded only on that experience, and
abandoning any prejudicial assumptions. Much like walking
across a frozen lake without the slightest clue where the ice
was safe and where it was thin as paper.

A pendant crystal, smaller variant of the CyberCrystals that
were the Hal's organic computers and a mark of her office
and status, dangled from Matai's right ear, somehow catching
even the diffuse twilight and focusing it deep within itself into
a glowing sapphire radiance. Matai opened a gleaming wood
box and removed a second earring lying on a silken cloth, a
crystal bound with silver that at first glance seemed as clear
as the one she already wore. But this wasn't for her. She
took the jewel in both hands and, with a bow of the head,
held it towards Nicole. Looked up quizzically a moment later
when nothing happened, to realize that Nicole hadn't hardly a
clue what came next. She replaced the earring in its case and
arranged Nicole's hands palms upward, as hers had been, then
lay her own atop them, so that whatever was being held was
totally enclosed. And held out the earring once more.

Nicole looked at her hands, then into the Hal's eyes, then
did as she was silently bid. Only to gasp in astonishment as
her fingers lit with a fiery glow. From Matai came a noise of
approval as they broke their hands apart to reveal the crystal
gleaming from deep within, as though a fire had been lit in
its heart. Matai took the earring and the luminescence faded
almost to nothing, but the moment she lay it on Nicole's
still-outheld palm it blazed brighter than before. This was the
fireheart, one of the rarest and most prized gems known to
the Hal, valued mostly for the ability of the virgin, untouched
crystals to imprint with their initial wearer and manifest a

unique inner radiance. In accordance, so the Hal believed, with the essential character of that person.

Matai took the jewel and hung it from Nicole's right ear. And then bowed until her forehead touched the floor, an obeisance deeper than any Nicole had before from a Hal. As she straightened, and without caring whether the response was appropriate or not, Nicole did the same, as deeply, as formally. To the uninitiated, Matai's face remained an expressionless mask throughout but as Nicole straightened—taking a quick moment en route to flex her feet in a vain attempt to relieve the growing ache in her ankles—she caught some quirks of motion at the corners of the Hal's mouth that she recognized as a barely repressed smile.

An acrid, though not at all unpleasant, burr tickled the base of her throat and Nicole cocked her head in recognition of the scent; it was a much milder concentration of the atmospheric hallucinogen she'd experienced aboard *Range Guide*, during the Memorial Service for the Hal and human dead. A heady time, and she closed her eyes at the memory of Ben Ciari's form blurring in her perceptions between the human reality and an illusory facade that made him one of the Hal. *A tiger*, she'd thought with fierce pride, *my tiger!* Although she'd known even then that was a lie, for he was no one's but his own. Her eyes closed tighter at a pang of loss twisted tight around a skein of jealousy that refused to get out of her heart, that he was apart from her and worse where she herself so yearned to be. And another memory image swirled into focus, of her own transformation, no facade it seemed in her case but a perfectly natural evolution of self that made her one with the Hal crew and especially their Captain.

Matai's fingers on her arm made Nicole jump, eyes wide with shock for a wildly disoriented moment until she regained her inner bearings. Very gently, because humans tended to get understandably nervous when Hal claws came too close to their eyes, Matai stroked her fingers across Nicole's face, dipping them after each into a bowl of clear ointment, repeating the process down her neck and torso, along her arms, shifting position to continue on her back. Almost immediately, Nicole realized Matai was crafting a pattern and as she looked down at herself, unsure whether it was a trick of the light or some facet of the hallucinogen or a synthesis of the two, she saw her body glow with an exotic display of Hal striping. She wanted Matai to stop, there was a ball of panic in her throat choking off her air, a terror that each brushstroke was casting her more and more adrift. She was trembling, as she never had her whole life, body in total rebellion from a mind that had abdicated all authority.

Stop it, she screamed silently, hating the way her inner voice cracked into the upper register, just like a girl's *stop it*!

Matai paused, Nicole assumed to admire her handiwork, then poured some of another potion she'd been mixing into Nicole's palm, followed by a clear indication of what Nicole was to do with it. So, Nicole began applying it to Matai's arm, working it into the Hal's downy fur and skin beneath with a gentle massage as she made her way up to the shoulders. Sense memory here as well, of Hana describing the family communal bath back home in Japan and how hard it was because the family was bi-hemispherical shifting between there and the States—where folks weren't anywhere near so relaxed about their bodies—and then back again.

"Perhaps it's context," she murmured, realizing only belatedly she'd spoken aloud. Didn't much matter, she decided, since Matai didn't understand. The Hal was still singing softly to herself, probably wasn't even aware of it—Nicole certainly wasn't most of the time when she did the same—though the tenor of the tune seemed far more at ease than earlier. Nicole kept on talking, her voice low and reflective, the sound of it a refreshing anchor to the familiar, countering the shrieking cacophony inside her head. "I don't seem to be so . . . inhibited in space. But then it's hard to be shy when your job's to stuff your partner into a pressure suit, and make sure everything fits where it's supposed to, including the plumbing. Hard to tell who was more embarrassed back in training the first time that chore came along, us or the men. Maybe it is like Hana's transitions from Japan to America—the attitudes accepted as commonplace in one country make you feel totally ashamed in the other."

She'd reached Matai's back, feeling the play of the Hal's muscles beneath her hands, gathering a gradual, physical awareness of her body to complement the remote observations and descriptions. At first, she knew she was being incredibly clumsy, but as time passed, she began to find the patterns that lay beneath the skin, the sense of where the elements fit and where they were ever so slightly ajar, managing once or twice to bring a small sigh of pleasure from the

Hal as she smoothed the kinks out of a wayward muscle. The texture of fur was markedly different down Matai's left side and a gentle touch told Nicole the flesh itself had the pucker of old scar tissue. A wound, covered by a graft.

"Where'd that come from?" Nicole asked in English, although she could have in Hal. The question was rhetorical, not because she wasn't interested—quite the opposite, she was intensely curious—but this wasn't the time or place. She was losing herself in the mindless flow of the exercise, a simple task that she was doing well. There was a tempting luxury in this act of service, release from the demands and pressures she'd have to face once more outside. To be told what to do, to have a place unassailably her own, no more need to take risks or to fear the consequences.

And then it was her turn, and Nicole found herself in the grip of a strength that matched her own and to which she surrendered, with an immediate enthusiasm that would have frightened her had she the energy to care. Until Matai started work, she hadn't known she was so tense, her own muscles stretched taut as steel cords, and the groans the Hal massage pulled from her were as much weary pain as pleasure.

Finally, Matai slipped into the water with barely a stir, Nicole following with what she was sure was the grace of a boulder, letting the raw warmth of the bath saturate her body as she sank neck deep. It was a luxurious lassitude that made her want to stay where she was until she shriveled like a prune. She dimly registered voices, a conversation that casually mixed Hal and English, but she paid it little mind. She was thinking of herself in a way and to a degree she usually didn't allow, head chock-a-block with hopes and dreams and too many fears, so much so that she broke from Matai's grasp—the Hal had been giving Nicole's skull a second lather, with fingers that seemed to have a direct line to the young woman's pleasure centers—and dunked her head underwater. Finding no place at that end of the tub shallow enough to stand, Nicole levered herself out of the water, pausing in midmotion to remain poised at the full extension of her arms, legs still immersed before letting herself sink back. As though the water had become her native environment, the world of the air having no more place for her. She didn't turn back to Matai though, but held herself on the lip of the tub with chin resting on crossed arms, each hand to the opposite shoulder.

Again, with scarcely a ripple, Matai climbed out of the tub. When Nicole looked up, she saw the Hal wrapped in a white robe that vaguely resembled a cross between the ancient Roman toga and the Indian sari, gathered snugly about the body with one end tossed over a shoulder, leaving the other attractively bare.

Matai reached out both hands, Nicole instinctively taking them, and with an ease that left her breathless was pulled out of the water. She looked for a towel, but Matai held out another robe, arranging it about Nicole with a brusque, no-nonsense efficiency that seemed more in keeping with the engineer, Tscadi. Nicole's head was swimming, the fatigue she'd felt earlier crashing back with a vengeance, hammering at her with the same inexorable force of Atlantic breakers on the Nantucket shore. She knew she hadn't a prayer of making it through any sort of meal, much less to her own doorstep, and prayed the Hal wouldn't think the less of her for collapsing at their feet. She wasn't even sure she'd make it out of the bathroom. Matai seemed to sense that, because she stayed close at hand, one arm about Nicole's waist, to prop her up.

As they stepped towards the door, however, Nicole caught sight of their reflection in a mirror. And was seized by an unaccountable sadness when she saw only Matai and herself, as herself. The stripes the Hal had added weren't there, in reality or imagination, only a tall, slim form that was a shade too thin than was good for her, who seemed as out of place here as she felt in the world outside. Even the earring had faded, magic all gone, leaving only a magnificently styled piece of jewelry.

Her knees started to buckle, Kymri looming in the doorway before the sound of Matai's call had faded, scooping Nicole up as though she weighed nothing, carrying her to a sleeping alcove and tucking her snugly abed. Left to her own devices, Nicole would have collapsed where she was. There was nothing within her to drive her on. Better instead to cast her fate to other hands.

She wasn't sure if those were thoughts or words and tried to tell herself it was no concern of hers that there was a sudden sadness in Kymri's eyes, a twist of disappointment—swiftly masked when he saw her watching—to his features. It was as though she'd just faced some test.

And failed.

six

SHE WAS STARING at the vending machines, with no interest in anything they had to offer but even less in making the effort of heading over to the commissary, when Ray Castaneda called out to her, his richly accented voice echoing hollowly across the hangar. As always, the dark grease stains highlighting the Line Sergeant's hands belied his spotless uniform, eloquent testimony that no matter how gleamingly high tech the world became, there would always be a need for someone to get down and dirty with the hardware.

"Got some time, Nicole?" he asked.

"Breakfast, at least," she replied, punching out a teapak for herself, a can of juice for him.

"Figured you'd want a look-see at your pride-and-joy the moment she was ready."

"The Baron?"

"Signed off first thing this morning, full FAA inspection, certified fit to fly."

"Hot-diggety-*damn*!" And she swept the shorter, stockier man off the ground in a twirling embrace that left him laughing and her a little breathless. Working for Kinsella and taking care of the Halyan't'a team had kept her running five-ways-from-Sunday pretty much ever since her arrival, so she hadn't had anywhere near the time or energy to put into repairing her plane that she wanted. Fortunately, though, Ray Castaneda hadn't minded picking up the slack.

As Maintenance's Boss NonCom, there was virtually nothing he didn't know about aircraft and he pretty much defined his schedule according to need. Mostly, these days, that meant working with Tscadi, comparing notes on the respective shuttles, but he always seemed to find time for Nicole's Baron.

"Everybody wears digital these days," he told her after they'd pulled one of the engines and taken it to bits, the pair of them slumped against the hangar wall on their fannies, nursing a six-pack, Nicole staring in mute despair at the slagged ruin of the blown cylinders, wondering (and not for the first time, either) why the force of the explosion hadn't torn the whole assembly completely off its mountings, and the wing along with it, "it breaks, you toss it and buy a new one. Practical, cheap, useful, I got no quarrel with that. But that still doesn't deny the beauty of a fine, old, mechanical Swiss watch. The craft that went into making it, that goes into keeping it running. Same applies here. These brutes"—and he waved an arm to encompass not simply the shuttles but just about every major aircraft on the Edwards line—"they need an army. And every component's modularized. You got a bust, you pull it, you slug in a new one. Takes a lot of skill, but not much craft. This, though"—and he stabbed a thumb towards her plane, suspended on jacks so the landing gear was off the floor—"whole other thing entirely. One person can hack it all. Requires not simply the skill to know what to do, but the craft to make it work."

He'd done both—skill and craft—proud, the old bus looked factory-fresh. In fact, she'd lay any odds and any amount that Beechcraft itself in Wichita couldn't have done a better job.

"Pulled the main panel," he explained as he paced her through the walk-around inspection, Nicole checking every inch of the plane's exterior, "took the opportunity to upgrade all your electronics hardware."

"Ray, you're kidding," she rounded on him from the open cowling of the bad engine, where she'd been examining the repairs, "I pretty much gutted my bank balance paying for this, I've got nowhere near enough left to cover anything more."

"That's not your concern, actually," Alex said from the other side of the fuselage, where he'd approached unseen. "Consider it my way of apologizing for what happened."

She wasn't sure she liked that, but wasn't sure why.

"Jesus, Nicole, cut me some slack," he protested, picking up on her thought. "I'm not trying to buy you off, just balance the scales. Even if only a little."

"There was no need."

"Actually, there was. I was out of line in what I did, and in what I said that night at Hotshots. So I'm sorry. It is a nice piece of work," he conceded, patting the Baron's nose, "if you like antiques."

She smiled thinly and wiped a chamois over the metal where he'd touched it. "Same goes for flying it," she said, "as maintaining it. Needs skill *and* craft."

"Care to show me? After all, no sense having the silly thing if you never use it, am I right?"

"Well, it'll need some exercise. I suppose I can clear a quickie slot later today."

"Actually, I had something else in mind."

"I'll just bet."

"Seriously. You sail, yes?" She nodded, that was no secret. "I have a boat, moored down in San Diego. Who needs her workout as much as your wings here. What say we take next weekend to do both? C'mon, Nicole"—she was reflexively shaking her head—"you can't bullshit me that you've got work, 'cause I've got the clout to make it go away. Not, of course, that I'd ever use that influence on your behalf"—she was giving him a dangerous look—"nosiree, not a chance, be more'n my life was worth." His tone made plain how little he thought of that attitude; power for him, she realized, was like the plane for her, what sense having it if it was never to be used?

"Compromise? A day sail, okay?" he was saying. "We've both been working ourselves stupid, we could use the break. A sail, some sandwiches, maybe a nice dinner in town, fly home after."

She let him stew while she finished going over the engine, locking down the cowling, wiping her hands on a work towel handed over by Ray, whose poker-faced expression was totally undercut by the puckish gleam in his eyes.

"Off the ground at first light," she said.

"I'll be here," was Alex's reply. "Give yourself half a chance, L'il Loot," he called as he sauntered off towards his lab, "you might even have fun."

"Yeah, right," she muttered, thinking, *What have I done?*

"Yeah," Ray agreed good-humoredly, her basilisk glare having not the slightest effect, "right."

There was no sign of Stu Hanneford in the office, no message from him in her buffer, no answer when she rang his quarters.

"Oh, Stuart," she muttered at her desk, rubbing her palms together in a nervous up and down motion, then tapping them a few times, rubbing then tapping, "oh, Stuart." This was totally out of his profile. No way was he the type to go AWOL, and if something had happened, he would have contacted the base. Which left only the possibility Nicole didn't want to think about.

She grabbed the flatscreen display off its cradle and lit up the system, tapping a sequence of commands into her keyboard.

"What's doing?" Amy Cobri said. "I was waiting where we always meet. Kymri was out and running but you never showed."

"Pardon me, Miss Amelia, but aren't you supposed to be in school or something?"

"And good morning to you, too, Miz Lieutenant Shea," Amy retorted as she plonked herself down in a chair.

"Sorry. I . . ." *didn't want to see Kymri*, she thought, but said, "wasn't feeling up to it this morning."

Amy shrugged. "I don't do school, any more'n big bro. Partly the Pops worrying about security, mostly 'cause no curriculum can keep up with me."

"Congratulations. But don't you miss the social side of things?"

The expression Amy made told Nicole how eloquently little the young girl thought of that.

"So what," Amy prompted, "is doing?" She rolled her chair over and craned a look at the screen. "You're accessing Sig-Net?"

"To see if Stu Hanneford's bike is listed."

"Oooo. He been a bad boy. That's right," she said, "he's always the first one in, very proper little flunkoid."

"Amelia," Nicole said with a quiet but noticeable warning edge to her voice.

The girl shrunk ever so slightly into her seat.

"He was all hot to take his new wheels out onto the desert," she said as Nicole's display resolved into a local schematic of Rosamond, with a transponder flash just off the main highway.

Nicole nodded, keying in another query to confirm what she already suspected. "He was entered in the Baja Enduro motocross next month."

The location was Paul's Two-Cycle, the best place on the high desert for bikes—and, to many, one of the best in California—owned and operated by Ray Castaneda's daughter Carla. A phone call determined that Stu had left his old bike there Friday while going off on a shakedown run aboard the new one. Because it was brand-new and undergoing constant tune-ups and modifications, it hadn't been listed on the Net, so there was no way to track him. At least, not directly.

A quick command produced the last month's tracking telemetry on Stu's bike. Most modes of transportation were tagged these days; even though there were more than a few grumbles about the "Big Brother" aspect of having vehicles constantly monitored from orbit, there was also no denying the effect it had on theft, or the way it speeded assistance to accidents, especially out in the boondocks. Or, ultimately, how the satellite tracking—combined with on-board inertial guidance microprocessors—made it virtually impossible to get lost. Tap in the right commands, your dashboard display would not only show you the best route from A to B, but places to stay and eat, local points of interest, things to do along the way. Essentially, the same technology and features that kept aircraft and ships on course brought down to earth in every respect.

In Stu's case, the request got Nicole a whole, tangled cat's cradle of trails, branching off California 14 into the Sequoia National Forest, with a few heading the other direction, out onto the raw desert.

"Son of a bitch does like to travel," Nicole muttered.

"Lot more to the mountains than the desert," Amy noted.

"Baja route runs mostly through rough terrain. Desert stretches are hot and dusty but no great challenge. Or so Stu said. It's the high-country heart of the race that's the backbreaker." She leaned back in her chair, one arm wrapped around her waist while she absently slid the three middle fingers of the other back and forth across her lower lip, considering data and options and liking neither.

"Lemme guess, this is one of those where it's supposedly real impressive just to finish, right? Instead of win?"

"Yup. Same basic challenge as you and your mountain. Man, machine, the road, the clock. Problem is, Stu could probably do that with his old bike. New toy was his bid for the gold."

"You think something happened, Nicole?"

"He isn't in his quarters, Amy, hasn't logged back on base since he left Friday. His old wheels are still at Carla's shop, and she hasn't seen hide nor hair of him, either. He isn't the kind to go AWOL."

"Alert the Chippies, then?"

She reached for her phone. "Highway Patrol's always stretched pretty thin out here, chances are they won't have any assets available for a full-bore search, especially through wilderness land, unless we declare a full emergency. And even then, they'd probably tap our people to handle the bulk of the work. Sorting through that kind of mess could take an age."

"There's another way, Nicole," Amy's brother said with a grin from the other side of the desk, craning his head over for an upside-down look at Nicole's display. "You can run a whole search pattern without leaving my lab."

Nicole looked a silent question at him, hating the way both Cobris seemed to pop out of nowhere.

"We have regular MilSat overflights, all the telemetry downloading automatically into the base mainframe nexus. I can access it, easy, plug it through to my Virtual CyberSpace System, make it almost as good as being there. Probably better. All the thrills, none of the aggro. Least you should be able to do is eliminate a fair chunk of the possibilities. And, best of all, it even fits in with what we're supposed to be doing here."

"And there I thought it was just an excuse for you to play with *your* toys."

"Better make sure, Nicole," Amy said waspishly, "he understands you mean the hardware."

Alex made a face, as though trying to reduce the exchange to normal sibling banter, but Nicole caught a flash of something behind the eyes that made her wonder.

• • •

Same opening as before, same unreal crystalline sky, same infuriatingly disembodied face floating before her. And—best, or worst, of all, she wasn't sure—the same sense of *being*, but without form or physicality. She was here, she existed, she had substance, if only in her own awareness; everything beyond that was totally subject to change. And she felt a thrill of temptation she prayed wouldn't register on any of Alex's sensors.

"I've screened the scud out of the atmosphere," he told her. "What you're perceiving is a real-time construct, ideal conditions, no sense in making things any more difficult than they have to be. Remember, this isn't things as they are now; it's a synthesis of all the available data from the time of Hanneford's departure up to the current download."

"Understood."

"Okay," he said, "integrating Hanneford's routes." And brightly colored trails appeared below, a thick trunk of them heading down Rosamond Boulevard and out the main gate, turning north at the town along Highway 14, out across the high desert. Beyond Mojave, the next town along, it started branching into smaller threads, inertial tracks of every previous ride taken by Stu Hanneford aboard his old bike.

"Shifting to infrared," Alex said, and the scene turned crimson, the Earth below an abstract patchwork of colors—some bright, mostly muted—representing the heat patterns of the terrain. No indication of anything on the desert, which meant he hadn't ridden out there in a while, precious little more towards the mountains.

"Any chance of spotting him? When he left the base, I mean, or perhaps Carla's place?"

"I've been wondering. Depends on whether his departure coincided with a satellite overflight. Tracking his old bike, that'll probably be no problem because of the SigNet transponder. The new one, though, with all the traffic on the highway." He didn't sound hopeful.

"Worth a try?" Nicole prompted.

"Certainly that. An interesting technical problem, actually. Take some time, though. To gather the raw data and then run a screening evaluation."

"How do I move?" she asked.

"Same as you would in a standard simulator, using the sidesticks built into your chair." She heard the grin in his voice. "Just 'cause you can't see it doesn't mean it isn't there. If you don't mind, I'd like to see how direct induction works."

"Come again?"

"Just think how you want to move. Electrodes in the helmet and your skinsnug should pick it up and respond accordingly."

"Terrific. It reads my mind."

"Fortunately for me, I suspect, only in the most limited sense."

"Touché. I wondered why you were so insistent on my changing."

She thought about moving forward and to her amazement did precisely that, until she came to a stop over the Kiavah Range. Alex had shifted the view back to normal vision, once more overlaying the ground with Hanneford's multiple trails.

"Too many, Nicole," he said disgustedly, "too scattered, no real pattern to them. Didn't seem to play any favorites."

"Maybe. Lemme see a schematic of the Baja course, can you do that?"

"Compressed, yeah. Otherwise, it'd stretch over three hundred klicks." And it appeared before her in the air.

"Focus on the mountains," she said, and when the Baja display did, she sat and pondered awhile, unaware that her body had manifested itself, clad in a flight suit, floating in the middle of nothing, humming a Lila Cheney tune as she tapped her lip again.

"Looking for a physical match?" Alex asked.

"That was the idea. I figure he was trying to approximate the conditions of the race."

"Logical. I had the same idea. A bust, though. Terrain's similar but that's about as close as it gets."

She looked more closely at the Baja projection. "Some seriously gnarly stretches in there," she said.

"A fact. That's where the boys like to push. If you like, I can give you a taste . . ."

And before Nicole could object, she was on the deck, straddling a top-line mountain racer, struggling to maintain control as she rocketed along a track that was more path than road, sheer wall on one side, equally sheer drop on the other, at a speed that courted suicide.

Another bike pulled up beside her, Alex, in boots and leathers, sun-streaked hair blowing straight back from his forehead. Shades but no helmet. She had no chance to worry about her own appearance, corner came fast, too fast, kick down two gears, touch of brake, careful not to lose it as the back wheel spun sideways, use the offside leg for the quickest of pivots (snag the heel and you risk pitching off, or a broken bone), then open the throttle to keep pace with Alex, who managed the same maneuver with insouciant ease. Instead, though, she pulled to a stop and swung off the bike, unzipping her flight suit and pulling it off her shoulders, wishing there was a T-shirt underneath instead of the skinsnug so she would have softer material than her sleeves to wipe the grit from her eyes.

"Didn't think you were the kind to give up so easy," he called, turning back towards her.

"And I didn't think you were such a consummate asshole," she shouted back, hearing a ghost giggle deep in the distance that she figured was Amy, off in Standard Reality, enjoying the scrap.

She strode to the edge of the precipice, automatically tying her loose sleeves around her waist to get them out of the way, part of her marveling at how completely she was relating to this reality. Nasty drop. With nothing really to stop a fall but the bottom. The center of the track was hardpan, worn by a lot of use and baked by the merciless sun, but the shoulders were dangerously soft. Stay in the groove, there was no problem. But that groove was frighteningly narrow, with an equally small margin for error.

"This is it," she asked Alex, "Baja, no bullshit?"

He shrugged. "What you see is what should be, as good as my data can make it."

"GIGO, chum."

He bridled, but reined in his anger before he could lash out at her. "No garbage, L'il Loot, in or out. My sources include LandSat geo-scans, topographical surveys, orbital video. It's as real as it's humanly possible to make. Be *better* than real," he muttered, "once I rig an interface to the Halyan't'a crystals."

"Pull the plug, Alex, I'm outta here."

At first, all she did was lie on the couch, amazed at how exhausted she felt, especially since this withdrawal lacked the adrenaline surge that triggered the last one. Then, she groped

for the desk phone, tapped in the code—it took two tries—
and the handsome features of Ray's youngest appeared on
screen.

"I'll need a bike, Carla," Nicole told her.

"No problem. Gassed and ready when you get here."

"Figure a half hour, tops. I'll need to borrow some gear as
well."

The other woman shrugged. "You want, Nicole, we got."

"You're an angel."

"You're going out," Alex asked.

"If Stu's in the mountains, it's the only way we're going to
find him. Certainly the only way we're going to help him.
That country's too rough to depend wholly on airborne recon-
naissance."

She stopped by her desk to gather some things from her
desk, including keys to the jeep assigned to the project, and
leave a brief note in Kinsella's buffer, both Cobris pacing
beside her.

"You don't need to go on the ground," he said. "Put a drone
in the air—one of the long-duration Boeings—with a real-time
livelink to my system. Guaranteed, faster and easier."

"Alex," Amy said with exaggerated patience, as though to
a child, "some people like to get their faces dirty."

"At least my way," speaking to Nicole, deliberately ignoring
his sister, "you're available if Kinsella comes calling. You've
no authorization to leave the base."

"You know your system, Alex," Nicole said. "You try it
your way, I'll go mine. We'll backstop each other, all right?
One way or the other, someone's got to go in there. Might as
well be me."

They reached the jeep and Amy hopped into the passenger
seat.

"I haven't time for this, kiddo," Nicole snapped, "out."

"Then don't waste it," Amy snapped back, matching tone
for tone, "drive."

Effing Cobris, she thought—only the pronunciation got jumbled in her mind and it came out "Cobras." Apt.

"C'mon, Nicole, you figure on doing this yourself? Alex
helps his way"—said in a way that made plain how little she
thought of that—"I can in mine."

"Better be careful," Alex noted with some acid of his own,
Nicole looking from one to the other in astonishment. "Kid's

not under warranty anymore. Papa won't like it if she's broke."

Amy's reaction was an unprintable so foul it made Nicole stare in amazement. The girl leapt from the jeep and dashed back towards the hangar. Nicole found her just inside the door, deep in the shadows where no one could see unless they were really looking, face to the wall as she hammered her left fist again and again against the cinder block. Nicole reached out, but Amy turned violently and strode away, with a stiff-legged, herky-jerky motion that told eloquently how furious she was. Whatever Alex had meant, he'd struck a nerve that was about as raw as it could be. Nicole wasn't at all sure she wanted to be around when Amy got even. Because she was sure that's what was in the cards.

"He didn't mean it," she said lamely.

"What d'*you* know?"

"Not a damn thing, except that it's the nature of brothers and sisters to needle the living hell out of each other and that even among the most loving siblings, that can occasionally get out of hand. That's all."

"Spare the homilies, okay."

"And spoil the child?"

Nicole didn't need to see Amy's expression as the girl looked back over a shoulder towards her to know she'd made a very rude face.

"That was *so* bad," she said.

"The nature of test piloting," Nicole said, "you try this, you try that, you try anything and everything, in hopes that eventually you'll score."

"Or crash."

"Well, there is that. He's right, though"—and pressed on despite the shadow of anger from Amy—"it could be a rough ride and I'll have enough to worry about without adding you to the mix. Pass on this, Amy. Please."

There was a moment when Nicole thought the girl was going to make a fight of it but then she gave a shrug and a nod. And that was that.

At Carla's, Nicole stuck her head under the cold-water tap, wishing she could just do a slow tumble forward until her whole body was immersed. The landscape shimmered in the midday heat and the simple act of breathing turned the mouth into a baking oven. Sunlight bounced off the faded sand with a brilliance Nicole thought reserved for arctic snowfields, so intense she was forced to narrow her eyes to slits even behind sunglasses and she grimaced at the first warnings of a headache deep inside her skull. Nicole kept her flight suit and added a padded leather jacket, gloves, helmet, and a pair of racing boots that clipped snug 'round her legs all the way to the knee. A radio transceiver was built into the helmet, and her PortaComp was duck-taped to the handlebars along with a reserve walkie-talkie. A seat-pack went on the pillion, water and medical supplies. Lastly, Nicole checked the transponder, both with Carla's terminal and Alex back at the base. Whatever happened to Stu, she wasn't about to take any chances.

She didn't push things along the eighteen-odd miles into Mojave, using the time to get reacquainted and comfortable with Stu's bike. She'd ridden it before, quick runs into town for Stu when he had duty; that was why Carla had suggested she take it today. She didn't own a car, hadn't seen the sense of it since she figured on spending most of her career off-planet.

"What are you looking for?" Alex asked over their com link.

Part of the answer was a reflexive shrug. "I'm not really sure," she said aloud.

"He could've gone anywhere."

"That's a fact. The key is trying to think like him, figure what he wanted and hope that'll lead us down the same path."

"Nicole, remember the terrain schematics, this is nothing like Baja."

"Not form, Alex, content. You don't replicate the details, you try for the sense of things. Where are you?" she asked.

"Ten kay, in a counterclockwise racetrack pattern paralleling the highway. Off to your left, roughly ten klicks ahead, rolling into my first turn."

She looked, but the air was too hazy, the target too small and far away, couldn't see a thing.

"Nice try, Shea. Pretty much on the button with vectors and angles. Next time, use binoculars."

"You *saw* that?"

"Best optics money can buy."

"Such as?"

"Baby Boeing, like I said. Condor. Twin-fan remote drone."

"Impressed."

"Only if it does its job. Want to compare notes?"

She pulled off the highway, unfolded the computer's display plate, blocking the sun with her back to put the screen in shade so the data would show better. A tight-scale map appeared, illuminating their position, the drone up in the corner heading "down" the race course towards them, and all Stu's myriad routes into the mountains.

"Alex," Nicole called, "paint the tracks in three-D, willya?"

"Go you one better, take 'em in sequence, north to south as the drone flies by, livetime video—I assume your screen can handle that," he added, as an afterthought.

"I'll let you know." And the display turned from computer schematic to a crystal-clear video picture of the Sequoia National Forest, towards the southern end of the Kiavah Mountains. It was a midrange image, neither too close nor too far away, and threading their way west off the highway were all the trails they'd pulled from Stu's file.

She took a salt tablet as she watched, a swallow of water from her canteen to wash it down. There was no breeze to speak of, the air stirred only by the occasional passing car, and then only to coat her and the bike with another layer of dust.

"I told you," Alex said.

She made an interrogative noise.

"Shoulda stayed with me, L'il Loot. Could be doing the job in air-conditioned luxury on a nice comfy couch, cool drinks at hand . . ."

"Give it a rest, Cobri. And how the hell?" But even as she voiced the question, the answer popped into mind.

"You're still wearing the skinsnug," he told her. "I'm pulling in a full range of telemetry. What you feel, I'm recording. Actually, I'm really grateful. I've never had so comprehensive a physical data base from anyone other than myself. The more information I have of my subject, the more completely I can configure the Virtual environment. I guarantee, Nicole, what you've been through here is *nothing* compared to what I'll be able to do."

"Oh, joy," she said. "Any residual images that look promising?"

"Only what we saw before. Hardly anything, I'm afraid, worth speaking of. Here, here, here . . ." And tags appeared behind each appropriate trail.

"No sign of anything?"

"Well"—thoughtful but a little miffed—"I hate to concede any limitations, but there are a couple or three routes where I can't get decent imagery. At least not with this bird."

"Lemme see." And he did.

"Windy little bugger," Nicole muttered, "where does it intersect Fourteen?" About a half-dozen kilometers ahead, no name on the road, hardly any road—in the accepted sense of the word—to speak of when Nicole reached it a few minutes later. Hardpan dirt, demarcated by use.

"I'm going in," she told Alex.

"What makes this one so interesting?"

"Content. Twisty switchbacks, a lot of tight, total-reverse turns matched with some equally extreme verticals. If you can run this at speed, Baja'll be a piece of cake."

"For what it's worth," he noted, "analysis indicates other sets of tracks, comparatively fresh."

"Pity we don't have a record of his tire tread."

"I could access the manufacturer's data base. New equipment, recently purchased; with enhancement I could probably get you a decent determination on whether or not it's a match."

"Through channels? You're allowed to do this?"

"Hardly, on either count. That way'd take too long. Actually, so might this. But it's something to file away for future reference."

"No such thing as a locked door for you, *eh,* chum?"

"To each according to his ability, my dear."

"Ah, what the hell, worse comes to worst, you could always buy the stupid company to get the information, same as you did that drone."

"Don't think it hasn't been done."

She took a turn a little faster than she should have, skidding out a touch, braking too hard, a tight call that she almost got away with but something flashed from her offside peripheral vision, worst possible moment for a distraction, and she yelled a futile protest as the bike seemed to collapse under her. She wrenched her leg free and lay sprawled on her back, helmet off, catching her breath and feeling like an absolute fool. With an effort, she got to her feet, checking to see that arms and legs still worked fine, no cuts, no bad bruises. Then came time to make the far greater effort needed to haul the bike up on its wheels, but once she'd succeeded and was trying to lever it onto its stand, she discovered the ground was too soft. That

was why she'd spun out, there was a thick layer of sand that
made the solid ground underneath slick as ice. So she settled
for leaning the damn thing against the near-vertical wall the
trail ran along.

She was panting from exertion and heat, took some more
water from her canteen in a vain attempt to counter it, made
her way to the edge of the road. The slope was steep, but not
impossible.

"Something's down there, Alex," she told him over the
walkie-talkie, "in the ravine. I think I saw sunlight on metal."

"Can't say either way, Nicole," he replied, no more banter
in his tone, "I have no visual access to that location. Terrain's
too messy."

Told you, she thought, and said, "Lord'a mercy, the man
has limits."

"You okay? I saw some nasty spikes on my telemetry when
you took that spill."

"Worried about my warranty, too."

"You never heard of sibling rivalry?"

"That was a shitty thing you said, Alex."

"I give as good as I get." Making clear that this was none of
her business. *Fine*, she thought, *suit yourself, chum. I couldn't
be happier*.

She shook her head and, after shouldering a carryall and taking her walkie-talkie, made her way over the edge. Started out
on her feet, made most of the trip bouncing off her backside,
with one nasty spill that made her wonder if she was done for
as she slid sideways, starting to tumble and roll out of control,
desperately throwing arms and legs out wide as far as they'd go
as she came over onto her face, same as she would skydiving,
to stabilize herself. Spent a good minute panting, regretting the
impulse that had prompted her to leave her crash helmet by the
bike. Her nose was bleeding, but the air was so dry it stopped
almost immediately. Was a lot more careful on the last stretch,
to where the land flattened out and she could, albeit carefully,
regain her feet.

"Alex," she said into the radio, spitting sand out of her
mouth, but got no reply. No sound from the speaker, not even
the susurrus of static. The fall had put the walkie-talkie out of
commission. Looking up the slope, she was amazed she hadn't
landed just as badly broken. And she began to give serious
consideration to finding another way out of the ravine.

First things first, she decided, and made her way towards the wreck. Stu lay about a half-dozen meters beyond his cycle, body twisted up like a boneless rag doll. The sun hadn't been kind to him, nor had the local scavengers, but at least he hadn't suffered. Probably was dead before he came to rest.

"Name?"

"Mine or his," she asked back, offering the CHP officer a bleary gaze as she took another sip from her water bottle.

"His first, please."

"Hanneford, Stuart, unless the autopsy says different."

"You have reason to believe it will, miss?"

She shook her head. "Not a one. On the other hand, he doesn't look a whole helluva lot like the man I remember."

"Damn coyotes. Them an' the buzzards, got no respect for the dead."

"Just another of the basic food groups, that's us."

Even with Alex's alarm, sounded the moment he lost contact—her tumble had severed the telemetry links with her skinsnug as well—it was the better part of an hour before anyone arrived. Nicole was taking things in stride, treating this like a variation on Academy and NASA survival tours. She made one try at the slope, but a small slide that started before she'd gone a half-dozen body lengths persuaded her of the folly of that course. She decided instead to take things easy until the sun slipped out of direct sight and then, in the comparative cool of late afternoon and dusk, make her way along the ravine until she was out of the hills. At one point, fairly early on, she thought she saw movement up on the road, called out as loudly as she could. But there was no reply and she concluded she was either seeing things or it had been some animal. Which started her thinking about the ruin of Stu's face and when whoever did that might get interested in her, taking small comfort in the sound and occasional sight of Alex's drone, which had taken up a tight station a mile overhead. She found a piece of chrome bodywork lying loose and used it as a heliograph to signal the aircraft, grinned as she saw it waggle its wings in response. It made her feel better to tell him she was all right.

A U.S. Forest Ranger was the first to arrive, on horseback along the road from farther up into the mountains, with a highway patrolman out of Mojave a little while later, bouncing along the gully in a borrowed all-terrain vehicle—essentially, a fat-wheeled motorized tricycle.

"Know him well?" the officer asked.

Some scrub brush threw up scant shade, but Nicole took it for all it was worth, telling herself anything that blunted the sun was worth the effort. She'd long ago peeled her flight suit to the waist, trying the sleeves about her as a belt. The Ranger was an old hand at this kind of weather, applying some Bedouin adaptations to his uniform, the better to cope. The cop, spending most of his time cruising the highways, had no such leeway, his own uniform looking less impressive by the minute.

"Well enough, I suppose," she replied, then shrugged, "we served together."

"Why'd you come look for him?"

"I was worried." The look he gave her was full of suspicions, mostly centering about the possibility of a relationship between her and Stu, but she didn't have the energy to explain herself. Spaceflight was a communal enterprise, you learned very quickly to watch out for your mates, whether you liked them or not, the same way you knew they would after you. The person who violated that unspoken covenant was one who generally didn't last long.

The cop had shifted his attention up towards the road, looking back and forth along it with an assessing gaze.

"He must have been going like a bomb," Nicole observed.

"Uh-huh," the officer replied. "There's a downhill stretch just before that last dog-leg turn, trick's to find the right speed so you can spit around it without having to do more'n touch your brakes. No downshift at all."

"You've done this before?"

"Everybody's young, miss. For him—too much speed, too much turn, too much bike. Had the right notion, just couldn't strike the balance. I checked, there's a broadside skid trail where he went over, but no sign of brakes. He probably didn't even realize he was in trouble 'til he was airborne."

She was nodding. "I almost went the same way myself. Totally treacherous footing. But Stu wasn't that kind of guy."

"Call 'em as I see 'em. He bounced off the other slope—see how high up—and still momentum ran him another hundred meters or so along before he hit bottom. He that good?"

She bit back the smart-ass reply, *obviously not,* said instead, "What do you mean?"

"Ms. Castaneda, she said the Captain was training for the
Baja Enduro. Maybe for a shot at the gold."

"Yeah."

"I ask again, was he that good?"

"Not my area of expertise. I guess Stu must've thought so,
why else the investment in the new bike? He pushed his credit
to the wall to get it."

"'S'a champion set of wheels all right."

"What are you getting at?"

"Nothing I can say officially. I mean, the coronor'll run a
full-spectrum toxicology but I doubt we'll find anything. In the
open sun like this, with all the scavengers have done . . ." His
voice trailed off.

"*What*, dammit?!"

"You know Dust?"

"Oh, shit no."

"Fits the pattern. Body has skill but not enough skill, and
way too much hunger. Figures Dust'll provide the edge. Problem is, whatever value the drug gives is tempered by the
instrument it's forced to work with. The knowledge and skills
of a world-class biker don't matter beans if the body ain't up
to the load. Figure that's how it was with your boy. Probably
took his hit out on the highway, allow time for it to burn into
his system, wire itself into all the circuits, then tore right into
the hardest trail he could find. No danger. In his own mind
he knew he could hack it."

"Until he went over."

"Yup."

"Same temptation in the air"—*and in space*, she thought—
"same dangers. Stupid, *stupid* sonofabitch!"

"And that's a fact."

She said as much again, mostly to herself, at Hotshots
over her third beer. The officer had cut her loose as soon
as he'd taken her statement, telling her he'd be in touch if
any follow-up was needed. A line had been rigged to the road
and after hauling herself up the ravine, Nicole had made her
way back to Edwards in style, blowing the throttle wide open
and ripping down the highway as fast as Stu's wheels'd take
her. More reports then, without any more than the most perfunctory pitstop, a seemingly endless succession, to Kinsella,
then Colonel Sallinger's office, Base CID, the works, the day

all but gone by the time she was through. Kinsella claimed the bike, with an icy bitterness that made plain what she'd implied during the interrogation, that she considered Nicole responsible for what had happened. If she hadn't covered for him . . .

"It was a goddamn fool pudknocker stunt," Nicole heard from a neighboring booth, where Alex Cobri was in a passionate argument with a couple of flight officers.

"Dust is a legitimate means of enhancing your capabilities," Alex countered.

"No," the other pilot, Ramsey Sheridan, said. "It's a delusion, Cobri, a mask that allows you to *think* you can do things. And maybe in some people, thought and reality are the same, bully for them, they're still relying on a crutch. But most, I suspect, get hoodwinked. And ultimately, screwed."

"I want to pretend I'm Chuck Yeager," the first one followed up, "I'll pull his simulator program. But no way do I want that illusion when I'm in the air. I'm not him, I can never *be* him, I start reacting like him in a mind and body that are used to a completely different set of signal structures, guarantee I'll spaz. And auger in. Seriously bad profile, no thank you very much."

"It's a way of tapping your instrument—mental and physical, Moss—to its fullest."

"And when you run out of gas, Alex," Nicole asked from where she sat, pitching her voice over the top of the booth, "what then?"

"*Et tu*, Shea?"

"Bullshit," she sighed. "You ain't Caesar, I ain't Antony."

"Brutus. Wanna bet there's a Dust configuration that'll make you a top-notch Shakespearean scholar?"

"Fine. I'd rather read the plays myself. Or better yet, see 'em. Or not. My choice, my consequences. But if I pop a vial full of RNA-impregnated crystal up my nose and presto-changeo become God's Gift to theater or academe or whatever, what happens when it wears off? The effect's transitory, Alex, right? It lays a veneer over your own primary programming, a temporary enhancement." From the way she deliberately spaced the words, she knew she was looped, a surprise on three beers, but understandable given the day. *Finish this off,* she thought, *and scramble for the barn. Hell, probably shouldn't have come in the first place.* "But if you're used to having it around—if you become *dependent*—how happy you gonna be when it's not there anymore?"

"Surgeon has an emergency," Alex countered, abandoning his two companions—much, it seemed to Nicole's peripheral awareness, to their relief, always a danger inherent in bucking a Cobri—and taking a chair opposite Nicole. She remained tucked into her corner of the booth, not even bothering to keep her eyes all the way open. "Hasn't time to learn the procedure," he continued, as bright-eyed intense as Nicole was totally blitzed, "life's hanging in the balance. Dust can give him that knowledge, where and when and as it's needed. Which is how the stuff came into being, for use in combat emergency situations."

"Stu's dead, Alex, because . . ."

"You don't know that!" he snapped, and she bit off her viciously instinctive reply.

"Stu's dead," she repeated with emphasis, "because he was deluded into believing he possessed a level of skill and ability that he most patently did not."

"You don't know that, Nicole," Alex repeated, "he could just as easily have cracked up on his own. And if there was as much a danger as you say, the stuff'd be banned, am I right?"

"That's not the point. It doesn't just change your ability to cope with a given situation, it also affects your ability to assess that capability. You think all the factors add up, you figure everything's locked tight; the problem is, the very analysis you're making is flawed, because the analysis is just as affected by the Dust as the abilities it's supposedly passing judgment on. So Stu Hanneford—who in his right mind probably wouldn't have even considered running that track, much less at speed—roars into it like a bat out of hell. Because the biker whose profile went into the Dust's RNA matrix did. Except"—and she hammered her fist lightly on the table with each word—"Stu ain't him."

Alex had no snappy comeback, which was something of a surprise, and she nibbled on some cold french fries to pass the silence that followed.

"Another beer?" he asked at last.

She still had better than half the bottle left, so she shook her head.

"Such a fucking waste," he said.

"And that's a fact."

"Why? I don't understand why."

"He liked to race. He wanted to win."

"You saw my VR simulator. I offered it to him. All the thrills, all the excitement, the ride of a lifetime if he wanted against the best that ever were."

"It's not the same."

"No heat, no bugs, no sand, no grit, no risk—some fucking trade-off."

"That's the point. The heat, the bugs, the sand, the grit, the risk, they're all *part* of the mix. The simulation is limited by the imagination of the programmer."

"Pardon my French, Nicole, but that's a crock. My system's cutting edge, so much so it damn near had you fooled; imagine the possibilities once I interface my capabilities with the Halyan't'a environmental generator. Full-range direct sensoral input, replicating any situation, any reality, better than 'being there.' I could give Stu the race of his life, with all those precious elements, the only difference being I'd guarantee to bring him home every damn time. The only thing he'd lose— that any one of you would—is your death wish."

"Is that what you think it is?"

"You going to tell me different?"

"So if you had your way, nobody'd actually *do* anything. We'd just strap ourselves into your VR cubicles or helmets or whatever and kick into whatever fantasy we please."

"Precisely. Instead of watching a game, you could actually play."

"Actually have the illusion of playing, you mean. No matter how you rationalize, it'll always be a counterfeit."

"You don't approve."

She nursed her beer through its last two swallows before replying, giving her words weight with a slow, sad shake of the head. "No, I don't. Not the way I think you envision it. As a learning tool, that's one thing. And even as a means of entertainment. But there'll always have to be things that need physical accomplishment. My being, my strength, my skill, my smarts—my fate—all weighed in the balance."

"It could put you back into space, whether you regained your astronaut's rating or not."

"Call me old-fashioned then," she said flatly, pushing herself to her feet and ending the conversation, Alex realizing too late the moment he spoke he was lashing a raw nerve, "some things I need to feel for myself. Sometimes, Alex, reality needs to *be* reality."

"Why? When the capability exists to make it better?"

She didn't have an answer he'd understand, so she simply said, "Be seeing you," and left.

She was so zoned she was halfway through the front door of her house before she realized someone was waiting for her in the porch settee.

"I heard," Amy said. "I'm sorry."

"Me, too, kiddo."

"Polls say President Russell's in major trouble," she continued, offering refuge in banal current events chit-chat as Nicole sank down beside her. "Both Mansfield and Ishida are taking off like they're solid-fuel boosters. Republican nomination's turned into a real bear fight and that's only the prelude to the main event."

"How nice," stifling a yawn.

"That all you got to say? Boy, some informed citizen you are."

"You on the warpath today, kiddo, getting even for this morning? How 'bout showing some mercy and backing off a touch? It's late, it's been a bear of a day, the whole rest of the week's waiting."

Amy held up her hands in a placating gesture. "Seriously, Nicole, you have any idea what it means if your Prexy loses? *Total* mess. A huge chunk of his own party figure he's the next best thing to a traitor . . ."

"Typical bloody grounders," Nicole muttered, slumping onto the space Amy made for her on the settee. "If they change the rules at this stage . . ."

"Why shouldn't they? It doesn't seem to you that Russell's giving away the store? Thanks to our off-planet assets, the United States is back where it was a century ago, where we should be, right? In the driver's seat, setting the political and economic agenda of the world. And is that such an awful thing? It was an American spacecraft that made First Contact, an American crew that saved the Pussies . . ."

"Amy!" Nicole interrupted with a snap to her voice. "I don't like that term, I won't have it used in my presence. Understood." The last word wasn't a question but a command and Amy seemed taken a trifle aback at being spoken to in such a tone.

"It's totally popular," she said in a lame attempt at justification, once more the kid who hung out behind the jaded
sophisticate facade.

"It's wrong. And you should know better."

"Anyway," Amy returned to her original tack, "it was our
guys did all the work, why shouldn't we claim the benefits?"

"Maybe some things should be shared?"

Amy didn't think much of that.

"Maybe, kiddo, the Hal don't see us as Americans. Calling
folks 'grounders' is a lot like saying 'Pussies,' and *I* should
know better. But it also describes a mind-set that differentiates
people down here from the ones up there. You put on a
pressure suit, Amy, you can't tell men from women, much
less skin color or national origin.

"Those distinctions don't matter. Survival's a joint exercise,
everyone pulling together, cooperating, trusting each other,
regardless of where they came from. Earth has only one race,
homo sapiens, and that's who the Hal want to deal with. The
subdivisions we've grown among ourselves over the course of
time, they're complications they'd rather do without."

"Suppose that becomes unavoidable?"

"Oh, they'll adapt. They're neither stupid nor unsophisti-
cated."

"So they're just cutting us this really great deal out of the
magnanimous kindness of their collective hearts? Gimme a
break!"

"Self-interest, kiddo. Joining our two species as equal part-
ners may sacrifice short-term gain for long-term advantage.
Ultimately less strain on the relationship."

"I still think we're being screwed. If they're nice to us, it's
for a reason, and we're fools not to use that to our advantage.
Especially if the cost involves the U.S. sacrificing its national
sovereignty. I mean, you blue suits swore an oath, right, to
preserve and protect and defend the Constitution."

"I don't think it's in jeopardy."

"But if it was, you'd have to do something about it."

"Me personally, or the military as a whole?"

"Whichever."

"I don't like the scenario, Amy. I'm not going to play."

"I don't either, Nicole. And who said you'll get a choice?
Geez, listen to me, willya? Spend the afternoon plugged into
a political theory tutor and, presto, one instant agitator."

"How far ahead of your grade do you work?"

"Undergraduate level for some, graduate for others. I stopped doing formal school when I started reading. Free-form tutorials seem to work best. But that wasn't why I came over. They've had first snow up at Cinnamon Ridge, totally rip powder, there's a pickup downhill set for the weekend, sort of an unofficial tune-up for the World Cup Team. I got a slot."

"Congratulations."

"I think those boys are in for some rude surprises. But even better, as an extra, added attraction, there's a Rathbone concert that night, totally killer brainfry-bodyshok dance music, for which I have backstage passes."

"That sounds really great, Amy."

"Then you'll come?"

"I'm afraid I have other plans."

"Nicole, my bro's so lame, a total spud, dump him."

"Nice talk."

"The voice of experience, trust me. The boy lives in a state of perpetual terror."

"Could'a fooled me."

"That's what we Cobris do best, don't'cha know? I mean, Nicole, his idea of Heaven is to create the perfect facsimile of reality. Basically because he can't hack the alternative. He ain't worth the effort, he's a flaw."

"Aren't we all."

"C'mon, please, this gang's fundamentally zip, puts your sweetie Lila into total eclipse. And I'd really like for you to see me ski. Whaddo I gotta do for a yes?"

"I know it means a lot, Amy, but I can't just blow him off."

"Sure you can, he'll get over it."

"So will you."

"After what he said this morning? After what *you* said? I thought we were friends."

"We are. But I won't be pushed, by you any more than him."

"Sure doesn't look that way to me."

"Amelia, this isn't proper behavior. It's rude and very cruel, and I won't have it. I made a commitment, I'm standing by it."

"Hey, no sweat, your loss. No need to make it a federal case or anything, geez! Look, it's late, you're blasted, I'm sorry.

I'd better burn, Nicole, see ya later."

She danced across the yard as she spoke and in the background a car moved away from its parking space up by the corner. A man slipped out of the front seat passenger door and around the car to open the back door for her. From the way he moved, a particular economy of grace, Nicole assumed him to be professional muscle, probably ex-military. As the car moved off, its headlights caught a figure standing shadowed down the deserted street, Matai. She was dressed for running and from her looks had been pushing hard. Nicole gave her a wave, but she wasn't really paying attention to the Hal.

Against her better judgment and for what seemed like diametrically opposed reasons she found herself liking both Alex and Amy, even though they did their best (intentionally and otherwise) to drive her bugfuck crazy. This being one of those moments.

She couldn't shake the suspicion that Amy'd given no thought to match or concert until she somehow got wind of Nicole's plans with her brother. And wondered, were the situation reversed, would Alex be pushing as hard the other direction? What the hell was this, a contest?

Was she the prize?

seven

AMY KEPT HER distance throughout the week and the few times their paths had crossed was coolly formal to the point of insulting. Nicole knew the pattern, she'd seen it in her own brothers and their friends at that age, had probably gone through the same stage herself though she refused to admit it. She figured either the girl would come out of it or she wouldn't. Alex's temper was like a flash fire, it burned bright and hot when it was set off but it also quickly passed, its very intensity limiting the amount of damage. Amy tended to bury things deep, as though an overt emotional reaction was somehow beneath her. Alex got mad, she got even.

Nicole listened to the news while she did the preflight, radio tucked into one of the pockets of her flight vest, letting out a cheer and staging a small victory dance to hear that Cassie Monahan's Red Sox had swept the Yankees and thereby clinched first place. Politics wasn't anywhere near as much fun, the presidential election going pretty much as Amy had said, with the U.N. negotiations grinding pretty much to a halt while the delegates waited to see who'd come out on top.

All well and good, assuming the Halyan't'a had the same agenda. From Ciari's letters, Nicole knew there were as many factions as here, as deeply heartfelt an opposition to the proposed union, with Shavrin pushing her own people just like Russell. Nothing was settled, beyond the fact that the two races had been formally introduced. And probably wouldn't be for generations yet to come. The trick was getting off on the right foot.

Alex stowed his bag in the back of the Baron, closed and locked the double "barn doors" to the passenger compartment, joined her up front. She didn't greet him with much of a welcome.

"Am I going to need a bloody manual to figure all this out?" she grumbled with an exasperation she felt was more than justified, slapping the back of a hand lightly against the electronics displays that filled most of the panel.

"Hey, I thought you were a hotshot pilot," he retorted, his infuriatingly good cheer not exactly doing wonders for her mood, " 'skill and craft' and all that."

He held up his hands in a placating gesture. "Really, it's not a problem. You've got all your standard systems—COM, RNAV, LORAN, radar with, I might add, greatly enhanced range and sensitivity, and, the pièce de résistance, and APOD-HUD generator." On cue, an iridescent display popped into view, seemingly in midair, filling the center of the windshield. "Same capabilities as you'd find on the latest state-of-the-art military wing job, and maybe a little more."

"Trifle excessive, don't you think? That gizmo alone probably cost more than the whole flamin' aircraft!"

He shrugged. "Never thought about it, to be honest. I use 'em in the Virtual modules, so I have a whole storeroom full to play with. Don't give me that look, Nicole, being who I am isn't my fault."

"Maybe not, but on occasion it do boggle the mind. I mean, Alex—chump change for you is what most folks won't earn in a lifetime!"

"It's not my fault! What, am I supposed to walk away, change my name, crawl into some hole somewhere and spend the rest of my life apologizing for the fact my old man's a certifiable genius?"

"Certified," she said automatically, correcting him.

"*Certifiable*, goddammit, I pick the words I use. Shit," he hissed with a raw vehemence that turned her head, "if you wanted to cancel, why didn't you just say so? Christ, go with

Amy to her precious fucking downhill and her precious fucking concert, who the fuck cares?"

"What is the matter with you?"

"Amy invited you out."

"So what? I didn't cancel on you, chum. Want to make that a mistake?"

"Too late for that, where she's concerned." His mood changed as suddenly, and wildly, as it had begun. "Memory's positively elephantine when it comes to . . . disappointments."

"You guys. Are a pair."

"Question is, of what? Look, I'm sorry, okay." He looked with some exasperation of his own at the mostly dark sky outside, the eastern horizon just beginning to hint at the approaching sunrise. "I'm not a morning person. Could never understand for the life of me why something whose only function is to make travel more convenient seems to require that every trip start at the crack of flipping dawn!"

She snorted, set throttle and mixture, turned the ignition key. She took her time taxiing out to the runway, listening to the sound of both engines, eyeballing the cowlings to make sure nothing was leaking, checking the panel—forced to concede the usefulness of Alex's displays, which projected a far more detailed analysis of the engine's status than the old analog gauges—used the APOD to 'scope out their course south to San Diego. Fans ran good as new, better in fact than they had before the accident.

"Makes a difference, doesn't it," he said, "being able to actually see the routes, instead of simply visualize 'em in your head. The APOD can not only show our position along the way, it can tap into the ATC grid and show us our context with other traffic."

"So each pilot in effect becomes their own flight controller."

"They'll have access to the same information, yeah."

"Sometimes, chum, there can be too much of a good thing."

"Baron One-Eight-Three-Six Sierra, Edwards Tower, how do you read?"

"Five-by, Edwards. Three-Six Sierra," she replied, telling them she was receiving them perfectly.

"Cleared for takeoff. Routing approved as per filed flight plan. Maintain runway heading after departure until further advised by LA Center. We have a four-engine Boeing heavy setting up on the main, so watch out for wake turbulence as he passes you."

"Affirmative, Tower."

"Is that dangerous," Alex asked as she pivoted into position, "that turbulence?" Got a small shake of the head in return.

"Shouldn't be." She pushed the throttles forward, smiling to herself at the full-bodied growl of her engines as they picked up speed and the Baron started to roll. In a matter of heartbeats, they were off the ground and pulling hard into the thin, clear air over the high desert.

"Look over your right shoulder, Alex," she told him, "lemme know when that heavy starts its roll."

"I think I got his lights—here he comes."

There were a thousand meters between the Baron and the ground when the transport passed them, gaining rapidly in height as it swung into a climbing turn that took it right across their course.

"Hang on," Nicole cautioned, "this may prove a trifle bumpy."

Like boats casting a wake across the water, planes do much the same in the air. The larger and more powerful the vehicle, the more intense the atmospheric turbulence caused by its passage. Here, they were getting intersecting wave forms—from the front and the side—complicated by the spinning, whirling dervish vortices thrown off by the transport's jet engines. It was like running into potholes in the sky. The Baron shuddered at first, as though bouncing over small ripples in the road surface. Then, suddenly, all pretense of a road vanished and they were bouncing across sharply rutted open country in a rude, violently sway-backed motion that almost tore the control yoke from Nicole's hands.

"And wasn't that a treat." Nicole grinned as they moved into calmer air, still climbing towards their assigned altitude. Hearing no reply, she looked over at Alex. He was ramrod-straight in his seat, stretched taut, eyes closed, teeth clenched tight. She reached out to his hand, but he didn't respond.

"Alex," she called softly, "it's all right. We're fine. There's no danger."

"So *you* say."

"I'm the pilot, I know whereof I speak."

He took a deep, shuddery breath, posture seeming to melt before Nicole's eyes as he slumped back into his seat, still refusing to open his eyes.

"Hey," she said, "you worked on the flamin' aircraft, you should know how well it's put together."

"Yeah."

"Alex"—adding a bit of steel to her tone, hoping that would get through to him—"we're all right."

"I believe you." Subtext, he meant no such thing.

"You scared of flying?"

"Among many other things."

"Pardon my asking, but if it bothers you so much, why the hell take my plane on this jaunt?"

"Haven't you ever heard of beating your fear by confronting it?"

"There are limits to every indulgence, chum."

Now, at last, he looked. "What's that supposed to mean?"

"You going to flip into a panic every time we hit some bumps? You know the flight regime down the coast—mountains right to the shoreline, plus an approach to Lindbergh in San Diego that takes us off a desert, over hills, and down to the seafront—no such thing here as a smooth ride. I have enough to do worrying about the aircraft, Alex, I won't add you to the mix." He said nothing, but turned his eyes straight ahead. An impressive profile, Nicole found herself noting with an appreciation—and she had to admit an attraction—that took her a trifle aback, when it wasn't acting so heartstruck sorry for itself.

"Look," she went on, "the day's still young. I can amend our flight plan, drop us into LAX, we can grab the shuttle the rest of the way. Don't even need to fly. Amtrak runs their Coastal MagLev on the hour." She knew she was pushing but somehow she felt it important to follow all the way through on their plans. Which was another surprise. Wasn't all that long ago, she didn't even *like* the man.

"I'm okay."

"We have options. You don't need to feel boxed by anything."

The chuckle he gave seemed to indicate otherwise, but she decided not to press the point.

"Too damn much imagination, that's my problem." A laugh this time, not much of one, but of genuine amusement, as he looked towards the ground. "A wing can snap, the plane can be tossed into a flat spin, anything can happen. Be made to happen."

"Anytime, anywhere, so what? Clichéd as it sounds, nobody lives forever."

"So they say. Is it so wrong not to want to be hurt?"

"Depends, I suppose, on the extremes you're willing to go to keep yourself safe. But every moment, every action, has its own element of risk. And if you end up locking yourself in a house, going nowhere, doing nothing, because you're terrified of the consequences, what's the point of anything?"

"I can live as fully, experience as much, as anyone. More importantly, I'm in control."

"VR? Plug into a Virtual dreamscape where you call the shots? Masturbation for the mind."

"What's the old saying, 'At least it's sex with someone you love.' "

"Very clever. The other old saying is, of course, 'Nothing ventured, nothing gained.' Besides, if you believed as fully as you make out, what are you doing here with me? Humans are social animals, Alex, we thrive on interaction with others and our environment. Make up all the elements, you lose the spice of variety. The challenge of the unexpected."

"You sound like my shrink."

"Sheer common sense."

"Fine. What's your excuse?"

"Hmnh?"

"At least I admit I'm scared, Nicole. Every so often, I even try to confront it." A pause, the next line coming in a fractionally softer tone as though Alex was admitting something to himself. "Though it gets harder and harder. And the end result less and less worth the effort." His voice picked up again. "If you had faith in your own words, you'd still be on the Moon. And those wings you wear wouldn't be for show."

The boat was a beauty, a classic Maine DownEast design, unchanged through the decades, made the same today as it had been for more than the past century—much like her Baron in that respect, although Beech had phased the line out of production a generation ago. Built for speed and comfort, the Bermuda Forty had a single tall mast, able to fly jibs or spinnaker to complement the huge, triangular mainsail.

Ideally, she needed a racing crew of at least six, but two could handle her, with a lot of work and skill to match plus the odd mechanical backup. This wasn't a show boat either, some billionaire's toy purchased solely to impress, that never left the dock; she'd been exquisitely kept—an absolute necessity—but all the gear showed the worn patina that comes with use.

As she looked up from the cockpit, she saw Alex grinning above her on the dock.

"What?" she demanded.

"The look on your face just now, never a damn camera or even a *paparazzo* around when you really need one."

Thank God for small favors, she thought with no small sigh of relief, while saying, "She's a lovely boat."

"And then some. First thing I ever bought," he said, handing down their gear.

"I find that hard to believe."

"Sorry. First thing I ever bought with money that I earned."

"Must've been some little job."

"Not really, the boat was in piss-poor shape. I was sixteen, spent all summer working at a boatyard."

"Why?"

"Make my Old Man crazy. And prove that I could. I was out of college, accelerated scholar program, fast-tracked like you wouldn't believe and bored blind by the whole stinking ratrace. I'd learned pretty much all they could teach me, didn't see any sense hanging about grad school just for the initials. Most of the areas I was interested in, I was already on the cutting edge, so a DSc or a PhD wouldn't add to my credibility. And being a Cobri, they sure wouldn't make a difference about getting a job. I wanted to try something new. Where maybe I wasn't necessarily God's Gift. And where maybe being who I was didn't matter so much. So I found a place in Maine, walked in like any other high-school kid looking for some seasonal bread, became a BN. What's so funny?"

"Just thinking how some terms never die, no matter how ticky-tacky. Best time of your life, right?"

"You kidding"—he laughed—"it was hell. Most totally scorched people I've ever seen—world-class poseurs summer-cruising up the coast from Beantown and the Apple, using their hulls to flash their status—ran my ass ragged morning to night, seven days a week, sunburn, muscle strain, blisters. Guy who

owned the place, though, he taught me to sail. Figured I had
'potential.' Let me hook up with one of the locals, do a few
regattas. Started as rail meat. Then I graduated to grinder—
Jesus, that first afternoon I knew I was dead. Arms popping out
of my sockets from working the crank, getting the sails up and
down, figured I'd never stand up straight again, either, 'cause
I spent most of the day hunched over."

"I know. I've been there."

"Last couple of races, though, I got to steer. Even got
myself a bullet. Came back next spring, crewed on Newport
to Bermuda. Had dreams of a TransPac. Maybe even the
Whitbread Cup. Then Amy came along."

"So much changed, just because of your sister?"

He ignored her question as though she hadn't spoken a
word. "Anyway, I had the money I'd earned, I saw this boat
in the yard, made an offer. Me an' Toby—he's the fella
owned the place—put her back in shape." Rueful chuckle.
"Actually, that isn't quite true, he did the work, I did what
he told me; same pretty much as with me and Ray, working
on your plane."

"You should be proud, this is a beautiful job."

"Yeah. Given half a chance, I don't do half-bad work.
Finish stowing the gear, okay, I just have to touch base with
the dockmaster, then we'll shove off."

The sun was just clearing the downtown skyscrapers and
beginning to make its presence felt, reminding everyone that
for all the glories of San Diego's natural harbor the land
around was reclaimed desert. Nicole ducked into the cabin
and stripped out of her clothes, pulling on what was for her
normal sailing attire: a one-piece swimsuit under baggy shorts,
a loose T-shirt to keep her shoulders and back from frying,
and a pair of boating sneakers, plus a Red Sox baseball cap and
shades. The ensemble was brand-new—the suit the only one
left at the Edwards co-op in her size, a slikskin racer that was
a bit too tight and daringly cut for her taste—her old sailing
clothes she'd worn out before leaving for the Moon better than
two years ago. Didn't worry about replacing them then because
she hadn't thought she'd be back soon enough to matter. She
shook her head angrily. Every day she seemed to find some
way of reminding herself of what she'd lost, as though what
happened was something she needed to be punished for, over
and over, without even hope of a reprieve.

The boat stirred against the dock as someone stepped aboard and she poked her head up through the hatch, assuming it was Alex.

"Looks tasty," a stranger said, poking through the picnic basket she and Alex had found waiting for them—together with a Range-Rover for transportation out to the San Diego Yacht Club, where his boat was berthed—at Lindbergh Field's private aircraft facility.

Couple of young buckos starting to seriously edge past their prime and refusing to admit it, dressing flash with the air of folks who can't conceive of being refused anything. As she climbed up to the deck, the man's buddy struck a pose on the dock, eager to impress. Strangely, these were a type Nicole found more often around yacht clubs than airports; there was something about the act of flying—perhaps the subconscious realization that you literally took your life in your hands every time you took to the air—that seemed to strip away a major layer of artifice. Also, you went out to the airport to fly, whereas at marinas a lot of folks just hung out, either in the club proper or aboard vessels that wouldn't know the open ocean if it bit them on the ass. Nicole was surprised at their interest, she'd have thought she wasn't their type— too tall, too rangy a form on what these guys would no doubt class as a nonexistent figure, as little for show as the boat she stood on. But evidently that didn't seem to make much difference.

"Can I help you?" she asked.

"Heading out?" the other asked with a charming smile, brimful of designer teeth. He helped himself to a beer, tossed another up to his friend.

"Yup," she replied as laconically as she could, taking her cue from the high-country wranglers who looked after the cadets during zoomie summer camp back at the Air Force Academy. Their job being to help teach kids all of two months removed from civilian high school, still trying to get their bearings on military life, how to handle themselves in the wild.

Ben Ciari was like that, too, not a word or gesture that wasn't called for, as though the Marshal's entire being had been pared down to barest essentials, and those as dangerous as they come. He'd done his best, during their *Wanderer* flight together, to hone her in that image. And even though she'd fought him all the way—it wasn't why she'd joined the Air Force, and most definitely not what she wanted from space— she'd also responded.

The guys didn't even catch the hint, much less take it. And she wondered about her next move.

"I'm Phil," said the one beside her. "Donny," pointing to his companion, who—not quite as practiced—returned a halfhearted wave. "Pretty old boat for a young girl." Another flash of his back molars.

"Not my boat. Not your beer, either, for that matter," she continued pleasantly. "But now you've got some, enjoy by all means. Somewhere else, if you don't mind."

"Excuse my frankness, but you strike me as the kind of lady who enjoys speed, and the finer things in life."

She didn't know whether to laugh out loud or simply deck the man, and wondered why she was hesitating with either?

"That's ours, four slips down," and impressive it was, too, a gleaming cigarette, long and low and sleek, with an engine-to-hull/horsepower-to-mass ratio guaranteed to break world records. Where Nicole came from, a sure sign of a huge ego and small . . . and she had to stifle an irreverent giggle. "I know the best little place for brunch over on Catalina, we could be there in next to no time."

"You're really too kind, but I can't."

"I know you, right?" said the man on the dock.

"Not to my recollection, no, we've never met."

"Wait a minute." Donny was rummaging in his belt pouch, Nicole's heart sinking as he came up with a micro-terminal that he immediately clipped to his headband. As standard a businessman's accessory these days as a cellular phone used to be, on a perpetual link with the national data nets. The orientation to the eye was such that, even though the screen was all of an inch square, the visual perception was the same as that of a standard full-size display. Before she could turn away, he'd pointed a pencil camera at her and entered the query.

Without realizing she'd moved, Nicole found herself on the dock, ignoring Donny's reflexive protest as she swept the terminal off his head. She took a step back, balanced on the balls of her feet, free hand a little behind her, ready to block or strike, whichever was needed.

"What the hell?" the man cried.

"I don't want any trouble," she said, "but this isn't your boat and you're no longer welcome."

"Look, missy," Phil, the bigger of the two, poised to haul himself up from the boat.

"Some problem here?" Alex called jauntily as he strode towards them from the shore.

"None at all," she replied quietly, not taking her eyes off the other men.

"How're ya doin'," Phil said, holding out a hand as he clambered out of the sloop. Alex took it without breaking stride, a gesture so perfunctory that it became more of a deliberate slap than ignoring him completely would have been.

"Nicole," Alex said, "want to stow the lunch?"

She dropped down the hatch to the floor below, taking the basket and ducking into the shadowed cabin, ignoring the voices of the men talking, Donny excitedly demanding the return of his headband display, Phil wanting more than ever to tag her as a trophy, Alex responding with remarkable poise while she worked on automatic, filling the icebox and a couple of lockers.

She held the tiny terminal up to her eye, saw an archive still photo of herself, taken up on the Moon when she was awarded her Solar Cross. The screen automatically scrolled to the next entry in the data file, some video caught of her when she returned to Earth, with a later scene on her way to the family homestead on Nantucket. There was a period—thankfully brief—when seemingly every time she looked up it was into a camera lens, and every other line spoken at her was an inane question. She didn't need audio to remind her of how she must have sounded, achingly formal, her only refuge the clipped, perfunctory speech and manner of her Academy days. The journalists saw her as nothing but a cipher, she gave that prejudice right back at them, deciding that if they were bound and determined to steal pieces of her life, she'd make sure what they came away with wasn't worth much.

All she really wanted to do, though, then as now, was run away. So she could be left alone.

Her hands were steady, but there was ice inside her, a thrill of mixed confusion and fear. *Only two guys,* she thought, *making as clumsy a pass as ever I've seen, no big deal. So why couldn't I handle it, handle them?* She'd reacted as training and practice had taught her, only they hadn't

responded according to program, because they'd realized
that the moves were hollow, a dumb-show bluff without
strength—of will, not body—to back it up. This was new
for her. In her whole life, the thing she'd come to take for
granted was that she could handle any situation. Caution
was one thing, this flinching hesitation scared her. What
one of those old Colorado wranglers would call a "hoo-
doo." She wasn't reacting to the moment anymore, when
those moments involved a potentially violent confrontation,
but to her anticipation of it. Not what was, but what
might be. Jinxing herself, crippling herself, before she even
began.

Was this what it came down to, bottom line, final analysis?
Everything was fine so long as nothing was at risk?

Small wonder Elias bounced her.

She closed her eyes, faces rolling into view out of the darkness of memory, slain friends and foes, hard to tell which hurt
worse, the losses already endured or those yet to come.

A grinding whine from outside, the clatter of gear across
the roof of the cabin, shocked her out of her reverie, to find
herself on a bunk, curled tight into a corner. She snapped
to her feet and was up the companionway in three quick
steps, ducking back down a split second later as the mainsail topped out and the boom stirred right above her head.
Donny had already freed the bowline from its cleat and he
gave the sloop a hearty shove with his foot to push the bow
away from the dock. Aft, they were still secured, Phil holding
that line.

"Alex," she started to say, but her interrogative became a
cry of protest, "what the *hell*," as Alex heaved the boom
off to the side, forcing her to duck again. Overhead, the
sail rippled with whip-crack sounds as it was stirred by the
fresh morning breeze. Procedure called for sailboats to use
their engines to clear the marina, raising sail only when they
were free of the mooring fields. Alex clearly had other ideas.
Phil let go the stern line, tossed it aboard, the sail belling full
as it caught the wind. With a surprisingly emphatic surge, they
were away.

"Raise the jib," Alex told her, and she scrambled forward.
Everything was set, the turtle laid out on the deck. She broke
open the bag and grabbed the sail packed tight inside, tossing
a quick glare over her shoulder as Alex exhorted her in no

uncertain terms to hurry, as though split seconds were crucial. The boat was already building a fair amount of headway, the jib was needed to give that force control. One point of the triangular sail got attached to the very front of the bow, another to the halyard that stretched up the forestay to the top of the mast, and the sheets were attached to the third corner.

She found the bill of her Red Sox hat in the way, so she reversed it, threading the jib sheet through the port and starboard tracks, then hauling on the jib halyard to raise the sail. There was a small chop across the harbor and as they turned across the wind, she caught a splatter of spray, just like standing at a corner when a car wheel pops through a water-filled pothole on the way past, that left her shirt moderately drenched.

She ducked back into the cockpit, preparatory to stripping off the shirt and tossing it below, when a faint tremble to the deck beneath her warned her he had other ideas. She'd already dropped to her knees as he yelled his command and pushed the wheel hard over, throwing the boat into a sharp tack. Speed was of the essence here, she had to release the jib from the old leeward side and switch it over to the other as the boat came about, cleating it in place before the wind filled the sail without losing any headway. This was pure muscle work—usually, on a boat this size, the job of three—as she pulled on the sheet for all she was worth, ignoring the pain from her lower leg where she'd barked it on an offensive piece of gear. Murphy's Law of Sailing: If there's anything aboard that can possibly do you injury, you're sure to run into it. Hard.

Her effort, though, wasn't quite enough, as the jib luffed a moment or two before filling taut with air, the boat staggering a little, its forward progress slowed. She tossed the tail aft to Alex, then used the winch to grind it in a little tighter. Her back and shoulders burned, and this time the sun had nothing to do with it, or with the sweat that soaked her top to toe. She was fit, in as good a shape as she ever was, but this was specialized work, taxing a specific set of muscles that hadn't been pushed in such a way for quite a while and didn't like it one bit. She didn't understand the need for the tack, there was plenty of sea room—not too much in the way of sail traffic and even less in terms of the big ships porting at the naval base—she'd figured one, two max, to sail them out the harbor mouth. But even as she posed herself those thoughts, she heard Alex's shouts of "Tack" and sprang for the sheets with a curse as he reversed course. The boat protested, even as it came about. He was sailing right at the edge, pulling moves where fractions make the difference, and the crew wasn't up to it.

A buoy marked the channel edge, at the head of Coronado Island, and he took it with less than a meter to spare, on the latest of a half-dozen fast tacks, as though bent on clearing to the ocean in record time. A couple of front-line aircraft carriers were parked on the eastern side of the island, a line of grey steel cliffs fifty meters high and almost a thousand long. The wind got squirrely coming over their decks and then across the flat open space of the Naval Air Station's runways, dying momentarily before coming back stronger than ever, the sudden header catching Nicole by surprise.

She was too stroppy with fatigue to quite register what was happening, so pissed off she tuned out Alex bellowing at her from the helm, and hesitated a moment to get some bearings. The jib filled fast and full, and she cried out as the sheet burned through her bare hands; there'd been so much work, coming in such a fast and never-ending stream, she'd never had the chance to put on sailing gloves. Now she paid the price, as she made a frantic grab for the runaway line to give it a turn around the winch, before collapsing into the cockpit, blinking back tears as she held up both hands before her until the initial burst of pain passed. The left had caught the brunt of the damage, she'd actually broken the skin, while the right was just rubbed raw.

"Nicole," Alex was calling, "I'm getting headed, pull the line taut and make ready to come about!"

She craned her head up a fraction, saw open ocean to one side, the Del Coronado Hotel off the other, not all that far away, and seriously contemplated rolling off the deck and making a swim for shore. Sensibly realized she didn't have the energy and lay where she was, figuring that if Alex was stupid enough to come any closer, she'd happily give him a foot in the face for his troubles.

But he kept his distance, holding out some salve as a peace offering. The cool ointment at least took the pain away but the fingers were still claw-hooked stiff.

"You okay?" he asked.

She didn't bother with words, letting her eyes say it all.

He held out a pair of worn sailing gloves, but at the look she gave him silently pulled them back.

"Head us in," she said.

"Nicole . . ."

"You hear me, Cobri, head us *in*!"

"Suppose I say no."

"Is this your bloody idea of a bloody good time, chum? You mind telling me what the hell we were doing back there? This was supposed to be a day sail—for the *pleasure* of it, Alex—not the goddamn America's Cup!"

"I got a little carried away."

"Keep pushing and you sure will. On a stretcher!"

"I just wanted to show you what she could do."

"Bullshit. That stunt show had nothing whatsoever to do with this boat. You ask me, based on your performance, you haven't a bloody clue how to sail her properly."

"We were going like a champion!"

"Why?"

"What d'you mean?"

"Simple question. Why the need to sail like a champion?"

"Because I can."

"Fine. Get a boat that doesn't need anyone else and have yourself a ball. I'll crew if the need arises but I'm not *your* crew, Alex. Remember the distinction."

"Second chance? C'mon, Nicole, you're here, we're on the water, it's a glorious day. Let's not waste it." He grinned. "Besides, I know this really great little place over on Coronado for brunch."

"Sod," she said, unable to help the small smile and shake of the head that took the sting from the word. "I was wondering what you guys were talking about."

"I'm going to come about, clear us some more sea room."

"Gimme a minute to get ready." She wrapped some gauze around her wounded hand, gingerly pulled the fingerless sailing glove over it, thankful for the padded palm. Belatedly, she became aware that Alex was sailing closer and closer to the wind, building up ever more speed through the water. As they peaked, he spun the wheel into a tight racing turn, trying to spin the boat on the proverbial dime. She didn't even bother with the jib, letting it flap uselessly as the boat wallowed in the easy swell, she simply stayed where she was, her face an expressionless mask as he hurled commands and curses with equal enthusiasm, until he and the boat finally ran down. Then she turned to confront him.

"I'm taking the wheel," she said flatly.

"I'm sorry."

"I believe that. As much as I do it's not you at the wheel." And without warning, her control slipped, her anger flaring, "God *damn* it, Alex, you're a good sailor in your own right, you don't need a snort of Dust to turn you into the second coming of Dennis Connor!"

"You think that's what . . ." he began, anger and amusement mixing like a riptide, tangling each other so tightly he couldn't choose between them.

"Did it make a difference? Sure, you burned through the harbor like a raving hell-for-wheels nutcase, but so what? It was a wasted effort if it was to impress me, and pardon my arrogance who the hell else was there that mattered? You can't mean to tell me it made the act of sailing more fun?"

"I wouldn't know, I haven't tried."

"What?"

"You heard. She's a good boat and I'm a damn good sailor. I wanted you to see that. I set up the port in Virtual, I've been running scenarios all week. Yeah, I was showing off. Sue me."

"It wasn't necessary."

He shrugged. "Who cares, it's done. You take the wheel, I'll lower the sails. Shouldn't take the engine more'n a half hour to get us back to the mooring."

"Shame to waste this lovely a day."

"I don't want to fight, Nicole. I mean, I got my sister for that."

"Let's head farther out, Alex. See what develops."

They were sailing fast, close to the wind to give them every ounce of speed, Nicole piloting with one hand on the wheel. The sky was mostly clear, patched here and there by clumps of cotton-ball cumulus up around two kay, a little over six thousand feet, just about ideal weather for flying or sailing. Alex sat slumped diagonally opposite her in the cockpit, feet up, a can of beer resting on his belly, looking down at the deck, out at the water, off towards the climbing sun, everywhere but at her.

"You're really angry about Dust," he said, holding his can out to her.

"I don't like it," she replied, taking a long swallow, using the inside of her wrist to wipe foam from her lips before handing it back.

"Because of Hanneford?"

"That isn't reason enough?"

"In the right circumstances, you don't think it can be an asset?"

"Alex, look what happened to you in the harbor."

"I told you—!"

"Don't get so steamed, I'm not busting chops. But think about it a minute, as a scientist, as the system's creator. You trained yourself in Virtual, honed your skills to a peak of perfection."

"Hardly, I've been away too long. But yeah, I got myself back on track."

"But look what happened. You weren't relating to the realities of the moment—not the capabilities of your craft, nor those of your crew—only to the desire to win. Everything else was subordinate to that, even your own damn wishes. The moment you touched the helm, you snapped into race mode, the hell with every other consideration. You weren't sailing, you were replaying the Virtual scenario.

"I haven't sailed in an age, either, chum; the difference is I know it. I know where I'm rusty and where I'm not. My instincts, my skills, my talents, I know are my own. I put the pieces together, I know how they work, same as you do this boat under ordinary circumstances.

"*My* capabilities, Alex, when to push, where to back off, how to bet. Virtual, the way you use it—and Dust as well, in this instance they're flip sides of the same coin—takes all that and coats it in ways I can't predict. It makes my analysis of myself flawed and suspect.

"Perhaps there are situations where it's necessary, I'll grant you that, but I can't help thinking it's a cheat. And call me the product of a retro-traditionalist household, I also can't help a belief that the wheel turns and the cheats are eventually caught out."

"You wish."

"Yeah. I do, really."

"Well, I hate to burst so pristine a bubble, L'il Loot, but the only place you're likely to find so perfect a world is in a Virtual configuration. In this venue"—he waved his arms wide to encompass the horizon—"you're doomed to perpetual disappointment."

"That's clever."

"That's me. Isn't that what you hate about traveling? I know I do."

"What?"

"How some folks turn into assholes before your eyes and there's precious little you can do about it."

"Nice talk."

"I wasn't referring to you."

"I know. I can't figure which is worse, Cobri, the attitude you've got with the world or the one you use to hammer on yourself."

He made a chiding noise between his teeth. "Tell me, that happens in space, what do you do?"

"Work it out, so I'm told."

"That's right, you only flew the one mission."

"And that for only a fraction of the rated trip time. We had a good crew, though, everybody synched."

"You must've heard stories."

"What're you looking for, Alex, that accidents happen and the rough edgers who won't smooth out end up strolling without a suit? Or maybe inside one that isn't quite as functional as it should be? You heard 'em, so did I, hang about the right crowd long enough you can't help it. Whether any of 'em are true or not, damned if I know. Satisfied?"

"Why does it hurt so much? Being grounded?"

She didn't have a ready answer and just sat in silence for a little while, listening to the hiss of the Pacific as it rushed past, letting the sun bake her bare arms. Once or twice her mouth opened, as though to say something, but no words came, and finally she pushed up to her feet and stepped towards the hatch, pausing momentarily as Alex's outstretched hand touched her hip, before brushing past and into the floorbelow.

He started to apologize but she wasn't listening.

"Because I only had a taste," she said, overrunning him, taking refuge in the act of preparing lunch as she had in descending to the cabin. "Ever since I can remember, I've looked up at the sky day and night and wondered what's out there. I wanted it more than anything. I worked, I *fought*, to get my wings. I barely got to take my first step and now I'm lame. Damnation!" She snarled as the sail shuddered, he'd let the boat fall off a fraction too far, lost the wind, had to struggle to get it back.

"When was the last time you came aboard?" she asked, after another while, the pair of them sharing sandwiches.

"Haven't given it any thought."

"That long?"

"What does it matter?"

"Just curious."

He sipped some coffee. "Must be a year, at least," he said finally. He tried a smile. "But you wouldn't believe the places I've sailed."

"In Virtual."

"All the thrills of Fastnet or the Whitbread, only you get out alive and unhurt at the end."

"Nothing ventured, nothing gained."

"That's absolute. Not everybody has the means or the opportunity, you know, to do it for real. Who are you to judge?"

"The satisfaction of accomplishment?"

"Fine, sweetheart. But the terms of 'accomplishment' aren't the same for everyone. You and I can actually participate in those races, what about a paraplegic, or a quad, or a geriatric? Leave aside the field of entertainment—though it might make life a whole lot more bearable for someone who's bedridden— Virtual slave-linked remotes allow them to access their environment, personal and professional, in much the same way as they did when they were fully physically capable."

"I'm not denying any of that. But they have no choice, Alex, you do."

"A matter of opinion."

"Stop."

"Just because this 'reality' doesn't have 'virtual' in front of it doesn't make it any less mutable."

"You think?"

"You're at the bottom of your professional ladder, Nicole, I've lived my whole life up top."

"What is it between you and Amy?"

"Don't change the subject."

"Ask me, they're all bound together."

"You consider yourself part of that 'all'?"

She nodded. "Dragged in, I suspect, kicking and screaming."

"Welcome to the club."

"I'm serious."

He took a distancing breath, and said, "We compete."

"She's a kid, Alex."

"Try telling her that."

"Point taken. It's as if that pass she has giving her access to every facility on the base applies to people's lives as well. You'd think, if she wanted anybody to see her ski, to be proud of her, it'd be family. You, or her father at least."

"Where's the accomplishment in that?"

"So it all comes down to making people do what you want?"

"Isn't that the essence of life?" And when she vehemently disagreed, "Controlling your environment? Forgive me, but I beg to differ."

"What is it with you guys? I mean, it's like the pair of you are part of a zero sum equation, one of you can't be up without the other being down. Everything between you is reduced to gamesmanship, and nothing's more important than keeping score."

"It's how you know who's winning."

"You're not taking this seriously."

"My privilege, I have to live with it. Besides, you're wrong. It's just you can't, won't, accept what you're hearing."

"Does she have any friends?" And then, a quirk of expression on Alex's face telling her how that must sound to him, "Do you?"

"Nicole, we're marked, all of us, by birth and circumstance. You in your way, we Cobris in ours. Expectations. Demands. Resentments. In the end, it comes down to being a target. Better we do, more eager it makes folks to cut us down. At least, in my Virtual nest, I define the terms of engagement."

"This isn't Virtual. I'm real, Alex. Flesh and blood. *Body* and soul. I am as I stand here, you can't change that with a mod to the primary program."

"On the other hand, if this were Virtual, I could dial us somewhere far more appropriate. Sailing two-handed on the open ocean can be a real pain."

"Live with it. Not everything's meant to come easy. Wishes aren't always commands."

"Want to sit by me?"

"Not yet."

"You ever thought about walking away? Kick yourself off the loop, out of the flat spin of your life, find something new? Maybe better?"

"I still have hope, I guess."

"Sure it isn't fear? I mean, how many of you throttle jocks ride into the deck and splatter when one good tug on the ejection ring is all it'd take to save you? When ground control's telling you to do it, when you *know* it's your only salvation? Because pride—this 'right stuff' obsession that if you only try hard enough, think fast enough, you'll come up with the solution that'll save both you and the aircraft—won't even allow you to consider that alternative?"

"My career heading for that kind of crash-and-burn?"

"You're the one who's grounded, sweetheart."

She didn't like the turn the conversation was taking and said so. Alex's response was to grab her hand, tight enough to hurt even without the abrasions she'd already suffered, his eyes burning into hers.

"Fuck this, Nicole, fuck *them*, bail out now while you still got air enough beneath you. The dockyard on Catalina can give us all the supplies we need, we got an ocean out there waiting for us. You want to explore, let's start with your homeworld, whaddya say?"

Her eyes stung and reflexively she brought up the heel of her free hand to wipe away the beginning of tears.

"Tempting," she said, mostly to herself.

"Be daring, then. Yield. I won't go back if you won't."

Why d'you need me, she thought, and supplied the answer herself, *because we're of a pair. And in his own way Alex is just as scared. Because I think we both know that if we do walk away there won't be any turning back. Whatever it was drove me down to Earth'll keep me here, it'll've won, can I live with that? No guarantee, though, that bird'll fly any better, for all I know I'll just be exchanging one crash-and-burn for another.* She shivered, from a chill that had nothing to do with the wind.

"It isn't that easy," she said.

"Sure it is."

"And every night, Alex, when I look up at the stars . . ."

"It'll remind you of what you walked away from," he finished bitterly, letting go of her hand but still staying close. "That's right. You saying you can't deal with that? Nicole, would it be any different if you'd broken your back or gone blind?"

"Yes, it would."

"You figure, 'cause your glitch is mental, you can recover?"

"My body got better, Alex, so can my mind."

"Suppose you fight for reinstatement and lose?"

"Then, if I decide to, I'll walk away."

"What's left of you will, anyway. Tahiti's still a paradise, Nicole. Bora-Bora. Slide past the Great Barrier Reef and on to Bali. You've got the body for a sarong." *So do you*, she thought. "Live for ourselves, not the world's expectations."

He reached to her face, stroking fingers along the line of her jaw, and she couldn't help turning her cheek into his palm, feeling newly raised calluses that were the price of too long a time off the water. He tilted her head ever so slightly and shifted his fingers to touch the *fireheart* and silver stud that came as part of the set, to be worn in place of the more formal earring. She leaned forward and their lips touched, very slightly. He was the one to pull away.

"Don't *you* understand, Alex," she said, searching his eyes, his expression, for a sign that he did but pressing on regardless, "*my* self, it belongs up there! This is glorious, it's fun, I love it, but *that*"—and flashed a look towards the sky—"God help me, is where I belong.

"My mom used to say, when she was talking about writing, there were many things in her life that she loved, but words, her stories, the act of creation that went with them, that was like breathing. Beyond emotion, but absolutely fundamental, even necessary, to the fact of her being.

"Space is that for me. And if that ends, it has to be because there really and truly is no alternative. Everything's been tried, nothing's left. Maybe I have to auger in, and just pray this is the crash I walk away from. But I have to know. Here"— she pointed to her head—"here"—to her heart—"*here*"—to her gut. "No second thoughts, no 'what ifs.' "

"Just like Canfield."

"There are worse role models."

"It's getting late."

"Come about then, pop the chute?" she asked. "Head her back in?"

He looked at her, and handed over the wheel, clambering over the cabin to the foredeck.

"Your call, sweetheart."

eight

ALEX WAS OUT of the Baron even before she cut the engines, hopping off the wing and striding away without a word— which was pretty much the way they'd spent the whole trip back to the yacht club and then the flight north from Lindbergh to Edwards, a silence so strained it was almost palpable. She watched him until he rounded the corner of the hangar, then turned back to the panel before her, automatically following through the shutdown procedures, until she was left sitting in shadows and silence.

They were a lot later than they'd originally planned—a weather hold had kept them on the ground at San Diego until well after sundown—and the sprawling flight line was mostly deserted, save for a Boeing ScramJet being prepped for takeoff all the way across the base at the North Field Complex. Nothing unusual about that; depending on the orbital configuration of their destination, and the importance of their cargo, HighJumpers went anytime, day or night.

She clambered onto the wing, stepped stiffly to the ground, shaking her legs one after the other to clear the kinks from joints and muscles, then finished the job of putting her plane to bed. She'd just slung her bag over a shoulder and locked the doors, wondering without enthusiasm or energy if she was going to make it the couple of miles left to her own doorstep or if she'd be better served simply crashing in the Ready Room over here, when a Range-Rover pulled up, Colonel Sallinger ordering her into the back.

There was someone already there, and Nicole offered up a tired smile of greeting at the sight of Simone Deschanel.

"A ways off your turf, aren't you?" Nicole asked as the wagon pulled away from the hangar.

"That's the joy of the Secret Service," was the amused reply, "every day its own little adventure."

Sallinger half leaned over the seat, held out a personal flight bag. "All your ID, Lieutenant," he said, "in here, please."

"May I ask, sir"—even as she complied with the order—"what's going on?"

"You may ask." And he handed a second bag over to her. She snuck a peek, found a CardEx with her face on a totally different name, toiletries, and change of clothes, civilian and uniform.

"You're flying jump seat on tonight's run up to Sutherland," he continued. "Essentially, a dead-head. You're not on any manifest; officially, you won't even be aboard the vehicle."

"I don't understand."

"That makes us pretty much even. First I heard of this caper was when Ms. Deschanel walked into my office late this afternoon with a sealed, handwritten order from the White House. In my whole professional life, young lady"—this was to Simone, who took it in stride, making Nicole wonder on what other occasions she'd played a similar scene—"I have never seen one of those and I'll be quite happy never to again."

Nicole looked to Simone for an explanation.

"Report came down to the Boss"—meaning, Nicole assumed, President Russell—"by hand from Althea Maguire," who was Deputy Chief United States Marshal at DaVinci. "She wants to see you, in person and immediate. Boss agrees. She's been Lunar too long, Terrestrial gravity's too much of a strain for her. More importantly, her presence Earthside would be noticed. Sutherland's a different matter, it's within her jurisdiction."

"So the mountain goes to Mohammed?"

"Depending on your point of view, child, precisely."

"Won't I be missed?"

"You're about to come down with a bug," the Colonel said. "Very nasty. Confined to quarters, bedridden, that sort of thing. As far as the world's concerned, for the duration of your absence, Agent Deschanel will be you. She'll have your CardEx, and we'll put a Mask filter over your phone to screen her appearance."

"Seems like an awful lot of trouble."

"Boss figures you're worth it," Simone replied.

"I don't know whether to be flattered or scared stiff."

"Try both. But here's something else to chew on," Simone said while Nicole lay on her back in the cargo space, struggling into a flight suit.

"I'm listening," but she wasn't really, a trouser leg had gotten twisted under her and she snarled as she fought it the right way around. Regs required that at least one flight-qualified member of any ScramJet crew wear a full pressure suit, so that—in case of any environmental emergency, such as a loss of atmosphere—someone would be left capable of handling the vehicle. And while current designs were an impossibly vast improvement over their first- and second-generation counterparts, they still weren't meant to be donned in the back of a moving station wagon.

"You remember what happened on the Moon, prior to your departure?"

"Environmental systems malfunction that damn near killed me." A pause, Nicole breathing in small pants, taking a moment to wipe her face—and any other part of her she could reach—with the towel Simone handed her. Then she reached over, switched on the PortaPak air conditioner, and plugged it into the suit's main input valve. Wouldn't do a ferocious amount of good until she was finished and fully sealed, but it was at least better than nothing. Problem with a closed system, it got real hot, real fast; she was already slick with sweat all over, with a fair ways to go before she was done. "So what about it?"

"It wasn't an accident."

Nicole peered up over the back of the seat as she shoved one arm up a sleeve. "Come again?"

"Not an accident. Deliberate sabotage, keyed to your CardEx."

"How?"

"Maguire didn't go into specifics, I gather her people are

still figuring things out. Sounds as if someone's infiltrated the
Lunar computer networks. That's why we're playing with your
identity. Using a Tripwire program, she's managed to uncover
three separate sniper sequences, designed not so much to kill
but incapacitate and cripple."

"What about the others," Nicole interrupted, "the rest of
the surviving *Wanderer* crew, Hana and Ben and Andrei
Zhimyanov?"

"Null response thus far to any provocation, and believe me
Maguire's troops have been trying. Their consensus is, you're
the sole target."

"Hence, Lieutenant," from Colonel Sallinger, "the need for
prudence."

"You realize the implications, Nicole?" Simone asked.

Second arm now, a couple of shrugs of the shoulders to
settle it comfortably about her before she pulled the helmet's
seal ring over her head and around her neck and zipped the
entire mess closed.

"Nicole," Simone said again, a fraction louder, "you understand what this means."

"Someone knows," she said flatly, gripped suddenly by an
eerie duality she'd felt before, that this wasn't really a moment
and event happening to *her* but to someone else who bore an
uncanny resemblance, while she—Nicole—watched safe and
secure from a distance that seemed to get farther and farther
away all the time. "That it was me commanding *Wanderer*, not
Ben Ciari."

"More, I'm afraid. Al's assessment, and I agree with it,
is that whoever's responsible for this is brilliant, viciously
inventive like no one I've ever seen. This person doesn't want
you dead so much as hurt, he wants you—and those around
you—to know what's happened and live with it a long time.
That isn't the mark of a professional."

"Cold comfort, Simone."

"Damn it, woman, will you *listen*? It could be that this isn't
business for whoever's after you, it's *personal*! And if that's
the case, it isn't going to end—they aren't going to quit—until
they nail you. Or you get them."

New flight boots. Like the suit, her size but not even marginally broken in. And she prayed for a quick, uneventful
flight. Sooner they were up to Sutherland, sooner she could
turn into something civilized.

"Apologies, Lieutenant," Sallinger said. "But someone might notice if we pulled your personal gear. These are from basic stores."

"I'll manage, sir. What's my brief when I get up there?"

"Listen to what the Marshal has to say, do as you're told, come back safe."

"Yes, sir."

He pulled the Range-Rover to a stop on the ramp and turned to Simone. "I'm afraid we may have something of a problem. Next month, the Lieutenant's scheduled to participate in the International Aerospace Conference in New York, to accept their Gold Medal on behalf of the *Wanderer* crew. She'll also be participating in a symposium about the mission and the contact with the Halyan't'a. There's an address to the Wings Club, and a reception they'll be hosting afterward. I believe the President . . ."

"He's especially looking forward to it," Simone said with a nod of dismay. "Even under normal circumstances, I don't think we could talk him out of it, and with the political situation being what it is . . ." She didn't need to finish. The race had grown so tight, with Vice President Mansfield bolting to stage a third-party candidacy, that Russell was cashing every marker he had. "Fortunately," Simone continued, "in this instance, I'm naught but a spear-carrier. Time for higher echelons to earn the big bucks that come with the big titles."

Sallinger looked to Nicole. "In your bag are the latest performance specs on the combined vehicles, from Thursday's flight," he meant the Hybrid Shuttles, mating Terrestrial systems to the Hal spacecraft and vice versa. "I want to expand the envelope another five points, especially as regards comparable maneuvering regimes in mid-atmosphere."

"Shouldn't I run these by Colonel Kinsella?"

"Nicole, you've been structuring the program since it started, working with the Halyan't'a team. I know Grace has been signing off on the reports, I also know who's been crawling around in the guts of both ships. I have her assessment, I want yours. Is that a problem?"

"Nossir. A day and a downlink from Sutherland and I should have it for you."

"Good. The launch is in a standard crew hold"—he glanced at his watch—"gives you a ten-minute window to get aboard. Have a safe flight."

"I wish I had happier news," Simone said as she walked Nicole towards the crew access ladder that led upward to the Scram's forward hatch. Nicole took a moment to run her eyes over the entire spaceplane, flash-carding it back and forth in her mind with the Hal shuttle tucked away in its South Field hangar. As Kymri had said, the laws of aerodynamics apply the same to everyone, so given the similar physiognomy of human and Halyan't'a, it stood to reason there'd be a commonality of design as well. And superficially, there was. The same sleek lines blending fuselage to wing form, allowing for the optimum mix of speed and maneuverability. Yet she had to concede here as with their pure spacecraft, the Hal designs possessed an inherent quality of beauty that made their Terran counterparts pale in comparison.

Condensation from the liquid hydrogen fuel sheathed the belly of the spaceplane, creating a translucent cloud of ice-steam that diffused the work lights, casting the whole scene in an eerie fairy-tale atmosphere. Even at the opposite end of the plane, the chill was enough to raise clouds of steam from both women with every breath as they talked.

"I'm still not sure how to take it," Nicole said.

"That's partly what this meet with Maguire's all about, to give you some ideas."

"Seems like a lot of trouble."

"She thinks you're worth it. She isn't alone."

As Nicole turned to go, Simone called out, "You're looking good, Red. Whatever you've been doing down here, it's made a difference."

Nicole shook her head in disbelief. "Look, if there's anything you need . . ." she started to say.

"Already worked out between me and your boss. And I can always query the house itself. If it's standard military housing, it has a standard military household computer, right? I'll be fine. You do the same."

"For what it's worth, Simone," she said, "I think the President's right, about the Treaty and the Hal."

"Hold that thought. Like I said, he needs the help. Safe journey, Nicole!"

She settled the helmet on the collar of her pressure suit and locked the seal ring. This was a standard model, padded to fit snug about the head (to protect against violent impacts), with the communications gear built in—as opposed to the "vacuum bubbles" used in open space, which required a separate head-set. Moreover, this design allowed the faceplate to be unsealed and left open. Which is how she wore it now.

She worked her jaw—up, down, and sideways, stretching it to the limit—to make the fit a trifle more comfortable, well aware that it pouched even her long cheeks like a chipmunk's. Then, with a last wave to Simone, she gathered the PortaPak air conditioner and her flight bag in her left hand. Using her right hand to pull her along the rail—in addition to weighing the proverbial ton, the bulky pressure suit did wonders for her balance—she climbed the ladder to the hatch and stepped aboard.

She passed over her CardEx to the pilot, who slugged it into the scanner slot and gave the display a perfunctory glance before handing it back, motioning her to the jump seat right behind his. Somebody'd left a pile of gear there and after asking twice for help and getting no response, she moved it herself. With a smile of apology, the flight systems engineer gathered it up and started filing the logs and manuals in their proper cubbyholes. Even a century into the computer age, flight crews still carried hardcopy backups for all their electronics.

While the crew continued with their checklist, she followed through her own, settling herself as comfortably as possible in her chair and running status diagnostics on the emergency air bottles racked along the wall beside her. Essentially, she had her own system, totally isolated from the mainline environment that supported the rest of the spaceplane—the idea being that despite any disruption or even total failure of the plane's atmosphere, she'd have these to rely on. Of course, the down side was that—assuming the problem was terminal—it simply meant she'd survive that much longer than the crew, and be aware of what was happening while they were either blissfully unconscious or dead.

When she was satisfied, she transferred her external environment lines from the PortaPak to their on-board junctions, and plugged in the communications links. Immediately, she could hear the crew and the Tower. To her right, the FSE—nicknamed "Fuzzy"—monitored the co-pilot as she entered the navigational data by hand into the guidance computers. The information had already been uploaded electronically, this served as yet another layer of cross-checks; a query from any element along the chain and they'd start again. Nicole pulled her gloves from her flight bag, locked them to the wrist couplings at the end of her suit sleeves. All that was required now for full integrity was that she close her faceplate. Finally, she pulled the four-point restraints over her shoulders and locked them in place, tightening the straps until they were snug about her. Couldn't move worth a damn, but that was the point.

"Major," the pilot called over the intercom, and Nicole had to remind herself that he meant her, "you all set?"

"Systems clear on my board, all readings nominal," she acknowledged, and got a backup confirmation from the FSE. These were strangers to her, which she assumed was no coincidence.

"Edwards Mission Control," the pilot said, "this is HighFlight Zero-Two, prestart checks complete, all on-boards in the green, awaiting Activation Clearance. We are in receipt of Information Hotel." Which was a recorded announcement of the basic conditions of the airfield, updated every hour.

"Roger, HighFlight Zero-Two," replied Mission, which shared jurisdiction for the Scrams with the Tower, "cleared for start. Flight plan approved as filed."

One after the other, the great engines were fired and spun up to idling while the crew—this time, with Nicole included—went through yet another checklist. There was a relaxed ease to the exchanges that bespoke long familiarity, both with the procedures and the personnel, but just because they'd done this before—probably more times than they cared to count—didn't mean they were going to take anything for granted. The crew that got careless was begging to get dead.

Just like any ordinary air-breather, the Boeing taxied out to the runway, Nicole closing her visor as they turned into place. The pilot advanced the central throttles, co-pilot calling off the numbers, velocity and distance, as they picked up speed. Nicole felt a faint rise beneath her, less of a sensation from the nose gear far below as thrust pushed the body of the spaceplane down on the mains, while lift took ever more pressure off the nose, stretching the oleo strut shock absorber to the limit of its extension.

"V_2," the co-pilot called, announcing that they'd reached the minimum speed necessary to get them into the air. Next, a few moments later, came, "V_1." Decision speed. Should they lose an engine, they still had sufficient velocity to complete the takeoff, or runway enough to stop if the pilot chose to abort. They were racing along now, the runway lights starting to blur into a single yellow streak while G-forces gently, firmly pressed Nicole into her chair. She couldn't see the pilot's console—his body blocked her view—but didn't need to; her station had its own, albeit limited, heads-up display, capable of projecting basic flight and navigation data. Moreover, she had her own experience and instincts, so far telling her this was a prime takeoff, every element optimum.

"Rotate," the pilot said quietly, both he and the co-pilot pulling back on their yokes, the nose rising immediately to what seemed like so steep an angle of attack that the instinctive, instantaneous reaction was that the spaceplane was sure to stall. But the Boeing had power to burn, an extraordinary thrust-to-mass ratio, and it left the ground with a tremendous rush, leaping skyward as easily as a fighter plane a fraction of its size. Little more G now, though nowhere near what Nicole had experienced in vertical rocket lift-offs.

The pilot keyed their assigned cruise altitude and course into the autopilot—again, a manual confirmation of what was automatically uploaded into the navigational computer—then settled back in his chair. They were flying a standard profile, taking them up to twenty kay and five hundred klicks offshore, where they'd make their turnaround and begin the eastward run to orbit. This was the fundamental disadvantage of a West Coast launch. Orbital tracks ran west to east, following the rotation of the Earth, which was fine for anything lifting from New York or Canaveral, or even down along the Gulf. But environmental regs, and hotly debated safety restrictions, mandated that anything boosting out of the atmosphere do so primarily over unoccupied territory. Ideally, the ocean. An east-west frontal intercept was considered prohibitively difficult—hardly surprising, since that meant the two objects, spaceplane and space station, would be hurtling towards each other at a combined closure speed of better than fifty thousand kilometers per hour—so the Scrams were forced to fly an hour out to sea, climbing to the top of the stratosphere in the process, and then begin their orbital insertion. By the time they crossed land once more, they'd be pretty much in space.

"Hear talk of Cobri, Associates financing an equatorial needle," the co-pilot noted.

"That'll be a treat," the pilot replied with a chuckle, "take an elevator out of this world."

"It's been hypothesized for years," Nicole said. "In theory, it does seem a far more efficient means of moving goods and people up and down the primary gravity well."

"I dunno," the co-pilot shook her head. "The thought of a forty-thousand-klick elevator ride up to synchronous orbit makes me just a tad nervous. Even assuming you could overcome the construction difficulties. I mean you've got all manner of torque to contend with. No land mass is *that* stable. I mean, how do you *anchor* the damn thing?"

"Not that many places to put it, either," offered the Fuzzy. "Ecuador, I suppose, that'll give you a head start in terms of ground-level altitude. Maybe the Kenyan highlands. Otherwise you're talking Zaire, Sumatra, and Borneo. And the Galapagos Islands."

"If anyone could pull it off, though," the pilot said, "you've got to admit, Cobri's the one. Think how many people thought he was nuts when he set out to turn Baumier's FTL theories into reality."

"Man should've left well enough alone, y'ask me."

The pilot cocked a querying eyebrow towards the woman in the right-hand seat, who shrugged emphatically and pressed on with what she was saying: "Some blue suits get to play Captain Kirk, zooming hell-for-leather around the galaxy, big deal. What's that do for the rest of us who get left behind?"

"Probably heard the same opinion, Ruthie"—the Fuzzy chuckled—"about Columbus."

"And maybe, Lou"—she half turned in her seat to face him—"with good reason. The arrival of the Europeans wasn't exactly a blessing for the Indians who met 'em on the beach. Who's to say we won't be the same?"

"Depends on your point of view, Ruth," the pilot said, "who's to say we're the 'Indians' in this scenario. The Hal could be just as leery of us. But all the wishing in the world won't make a whit of difference, this is the way things are, we simply have to learn to live with them."

"Thank you, Mr. Cobri."

"Better say that with a smile, Ruthie," Lou said, "the man, I hear, has a long reach."

"You have to be impressed, regardless of what you think of Cobri personally," the pilot was talking more to Nicole now.

"In his lifetime, he's pretty much single-handedly transformed the world even more than the Wright Brothers did in 1903, with the first powered flight. Or Henry Ford, with the first mass-produced automobile. Still"—he thought a moment, before returning the conversation to its original topic—"the 'needle' would take a lot of the romance out of the business."

"That's what folks want," the co-pilot said, "to go from point to point with as little hassle, and especially 'adventure,' as possible."

"Who'd've thought, though? I mean, my gramps can remember when every launch of the shuttle had folks' hearts in their mouths, praying it wasn't *Challenger* all over again. Look at us now, flying the same route as easily as driving to the office."

"The times," Nicole said musingly, "they're always a'changing."

"That, Major, is a fact."

"You ever met one," Ruth asked her. "Of the Aliens," she finished when Nicole looked confused.

"I work full-time at Edwards, hard not to these days."

"We flew with one the other week." Nicole knew that, had helped Kymri prep for the flight. The other woman was shaking her head. "I mean, was it weird."

"Didn't know his job?"

"Not that. Just . . . *him*, I guess. He isn't human, except we're supposed to treat him like one of us."

"Hey, Ruthie," this from Lou in a gently chiding tone, "you were a lot more vehement about those guys from the Gulf."

"Don't get me started, Lou."

"There was a problem?"

"Don't get me wrong, Major, I have nothing against individuals of that national or ethnic heritage . . ."

"Oh, Ruth," the pilot said with amused approval, laying it on thick in the way that only old working buddies are allowed to get away with, "that's *very* diplomatic."

"In your ear, Clark," Ruth retorted in the same vein. "And that's a whole lot more than could be said for those . . . gentlemen, thank you all *very* much. Clark and I"—she faced Nicole—"we're professional flight officers, both qualified left seat and fully rated command pilots to boot, and as far as I'm concerned you don't bring *any* attitudes onto my flight

deck. Political or social. I don't care how you live at home or
what you believe, this vehicle has its own rules and operating
realities and when you're flying, they get paramount respect.
I mean, the *nerve* of that son of a bitch!"

"I'm at a loss, I'm afraid . . ."

"It was a qualifying flight," Lou explained, "with Ruth as
check pilot. Not a problem, it's part of her job, she and Clark
rotate. Only our trainee didn't like working with a woman,
especially one in short sleeves. Made some rather uncharitable
comments."

"Lou, he called me a bloody whore!"

"In Arabic," the Fuzzy said, "you've got to give him that."

"What, I'm supposed to cut him slack because he cusses me
in a language I don't understand? Far as I'm concerned, it's
the thought that counts."

"Let me guess," Nicole said, "you had a translation program
linked with the com system?"

"Did indeed. Standard procedure. But," Ruth said with grim
pride, "I'm a professional. I behaved professionally. I passed
him, in terms of flight proficiency. And the minute we touched
down, I ripped his lungs out."

"Right there on the flight line"—Lou grinned—"it was a
sight to behold."

"I think I heard about that one. Formal grievances filed, the
whole works."

"Total toad," Ruth grumbled. "And that moron Russell wants
to hand us over to the likes of him?"

"Hardly."

"Hey, Major, you trying to tell me the United States is going
to end up first among equals in a world government consisting
mostly of scumbarge little nations who'd like nothing better
than to screw us blind and piss on what's left? Gimme a
break!"

"Sometimes, you've got to give a little to get. A little less
clout on Earth for a lot more possibilities in space."

"Great, for the vacuum riders. Which most of us ain't, aren't
likely to be, and have no interest being. And for some folks,
you give that little, they figure it's 'cause you're weak, so they
demand more. And more. And more. Not the most equitable
of trade-offs, understand what I'm saying?"

"Ten minutes to turnaround," the pilot said quietly, deliberately breaking the thread of the conversation and reminding

everyone of why they were here, "pull the ascension checklist, please."

"We have a hold," Ruth said, "coupled with"—she paused while the information flashed onto her display—"a lateral shift in our approach. Absolutely brilliant," she muttered with a shake of the head, "we've got a 'smudged window.' Initial vectors bring us too close to Patriot. The mods should give us decent clearance."

"What a mess," the pilot agreed, his tone a match for hers. "Damn thing's been up there my whole lifetime, been a derelict Lord knows how long, you'd think somebody'd get off their butt and do something about it."

Patriot was the first American permanent space station, launched at the turn of the century. State-of-the-art at conception, rendered totally irrelevant within a decade as the Baumier StarDrive turned the world's attention from near-Earth space to the far reaches of the galaxy. It was simply too small to be practicable for the facilities required by the starships, and not really designed to be expanded to accommodate them. Those same deficits prevented its use as anything more than the most preliminary of staging areas for the Lunar and out-planet habitats that were suddenly being yanked from archival memory banks. Its heyday was during the construction phase of Sutherland, where Patriot served as the orbital base camp for the work crews, and then a few years later—when all concerned had thought such conflicts behind them—as an eye-in-the-sky strategic observation platform during the Second Gulf War.

After that, with Sutherland fully operational, giving birth not only to DaVinci StarPort on the Moon but the two L-5 stations, Hightower and Hawking, as well, Patriot became more and more the redundant backwater until it was finally abandoned altogether. Unfortunately, when it had been touted as a "permanent" installation, the NASA flacks spoke far better than they suspected (in their wildest dreams); it had somehow found the ideal orbital niche, with an absolute minimum of the atmospheric drag that had doomed such earlier attempts as SkyLab and Mir. Even untended, the station would stay up—it was now acknowledged—easily through the next century. And nobody wanted to knock it down en masse, because its size— although a fraction of Sutherland—guaranteed that enough would survive the incinerating heat of reentry to strike the ground with significant force. The obvious solution was to cut it into more manageable bits and either recycle them elsewhere or drop them where they'd do the least harm. Trouble was, any and all proposals along those lines appeared perpetually bogged down in the natural maze of the Space Administration's bureaucracy.

"Has there been any trouble with flaking?" Nicole meant debris tumble-flying off the main body of the derelict, bound to happen from time to time.

The pilot shook his head. "Surprisingly little. Who'd've thought the 'lowest bidder' could've built so well." He grinned. "You know, of course, Major, the place is reputed to be haunted."

Nicole smiled. "That I've heard. The occasional ghost transmissions, vaguely coherent reports of activity aboard . . ."

"Yup. Been looked in to, too, a bunch of times. No joy, of course. Place is dead as can be, stripped pretty much clean of everything movable."

"Mission's on-line, Clark," this from Ruth, after a verbal acknowledgment of the transmission, "window's open, we're released from the hold, cleared to lift. Parameters on-screen."

Second stage of the ascent required cycling the engines from air-breathing jets to fully self-contained hydrogen-fueled rockets, then boosting out of the atmosphere along a slightly shallower ascent curve that more resembled a standard aircraft climb than a rocket's lift-off. The mission profile was to match track and velocity with Sutherland Station, at the three-hundred-kilometer level, so that when the station finally caught up with them (it was now about a third of the way around the planet to their rear), the two vehicles would be almost perfectly in sync, thereby making docking a proverbial piece of cake. Worked fine in theory. Of course, a glitch anywhere along the way meant either a stern chase to catch up with Sutherland, or a long wait to try again the next time it rolled 'round. Neither of which looked too terribly good on any crew's flight record.

"Black sky," Ruth announced quietly as the soft blue of the atmosphere faded below them, then she switched over to the cabin PA to inform the paying passengers. "As some of you may have noticed," she said calmly with the relaxed ease of someone for whom this was no more a big deal than a stroll around the corner for a magazine, "we've just made the transition from Earth's atmosphere to the lower regions of outer space. In a few more minutes, we'll be in zero gravity, which for those making their first trip should be quite an experience. For your own safety, however, and that of your fellow passengers, please keep your seat belts securely fastened. If assistance is needed"—and Nicole grinned at the memory of an unwary traveler, during one of her first high flights, lunging after a pen that had decided to go drifting off across the cabin, only to find himself overshooting the mark in a moderately mean somersault that bounced him from the ceiling upside down into her lap—"please use your call buttons to summon one of the crew, who'll be more than happy to assist you."

Nicole scanned through the menu of her HUD, a quick review of ship systems, their progress from launch, their position in relation to target, their approach to docking. Satisfied that all was well, she craned forward as far as her restraints would allow for a view through the canopy. They were still in a nose-up attitude, the Earth a bright splash of light and color beneath them. The sun dominated the way ahead, a small, blinding golden dollar of fire so intense the crew wore sunglasses. Not much to see at the moment in the way of stars, that would come with more altitude and the turn to nightside.

"Like the view?" the Fuzzy asked.

"Always."

"You one of *those*, then?" That was from Ruth.

" 'Those'?"

"SkyBoys, we call 'em."

"I know the term." Didn't much like it, either. Went into the same dump for her as calling the Hal Pussies.

"Well?"

"I got the rating, Ruth, same as you."

"That's what I thought," and the other woman's mouth turned down in a dismissive sneer.

"You make it sound like it's a crime to be an astronaut."

"Some dreams maybe should stay nothing but dreams. I ask you, Major, is it any more of a crime to be afraid of the consequences? Space isn't a fantasy any longer, it's in our face. I'm sorry, I don't like it." She sighed, thought a moment. "Destiny isn't ours to control anymore."

"Was it ever, Ruth?"

"Yeah, Clark. I think. Maybe because there was no alternative. Our world, love it or else, 'cause we got nowhere else to go. Now, we do. The pressure's off, who cares how badly we shit where we live, we can always zip off somewhere else. Only problem is, someone else may be out there first. Jesus Mary and Joseph, guys, we can hardly live together on *this* dirtball an' we're at least all the same species! Now we're expected to act sane, to play well"—she put a viciously mocking twist to the words—"with others? Too much, my friends, too fast."

"You're probably right," Nicole said and the woman flashed a glance of angry suspicion that she was being patronized, "but that choice was made the moment the first starship completed its first successful round-trip."

"Nah," Lou said, "for me it was when they found the Pussies."

"I'll tell you," Ruth agreed, "I'd be a whole lot happier if that rendezvous had never taken place."

Sutherland was a wheel, a giant torus taking two-hour turns around the world below, at the same time spinning on its own axis about the core spoke with sufficient velocity to create a one-G environment on the outermost ring, the effect weakening as a body progressed towards that central axle until it became weightless. The core itself was so huge, the entire Patriot Station could be accommodated with room to spare. It was here that passengers and cargo made the transition from the spaceplanes that brought them up from the Terrestrial surface to the short-haul HeavyLifters, pure space vehicles that would carry them the rest of the two-day journey to either the Moon or the two L-5's.

There was no reservation for Nicole in the housekeeping system and she was directed to wait in a nearby anteroom while the glitch was dealt with. The room was a standard module, bare walls and ceiling, chairs and worktables, sockets for power cords and data/com links. Nicole dimmed the lights, then keyed in the display code, and one of the main walls seemingly dissolved into a real-time presentation of space outside, the view away from Earth. Panoramic ebony, liberally splashed with pinpoint dots of light.

Stepping clear of the furniture, Nicole pulled her feet free of the deck and kicked herself into a forward roll. She straightened her body as she somersaulted so that she was spinning face-forward, like a propellor, and flexed her shoulders to give her a lateral rotation as well. Technically, a miserable motion, guaranteed to make most sick just to watch, much less give it their own try. Then, as she neared the center point of the room, she twisted her shoulders the opposite direction, arching her body backward, sweeping her arms down almost as though she were swimming. The spin, she stopped; the roll, not quite.

"Impressive," Althea Maguire said.

"Hardly," Nicole replied, flushing at the spectacle she must have presented, instinctively stiffening to attention, ignoring the absurdity of doing so while her momentum gradually spun her forward and down, out of reach of any surface and unable to reorient herself without making an even greater fool of herself. But Maguire didn't seem to notice or mind as she stepped confidently towards her and held out a hand.

"You're looking well, Lieutenant," she said, gently restoring Nicole's contact with the floor. "Gravity suits you."

"Way things seem to be going, I guess I'd better get used to it."

"I'm afraid you may be right."

The Marshal stood average height, her body built more for power than fashion. Hair cut shorter than Nicole's, a red-shaded sand liberally sprinkled with gray, styled to emphasize the strength of her features. A square face, severity seriously undermined by a dusting of freckles from cheekbones across the bridge of her nose. The eyes, surprisingly, were a cobalt blue that Nicole wasn't used to seeing in a redhead, with a level, assessing gaze that gave the sure and deliberate impression that the woman didn't miss a thing. Uniform was a black jumpsuit, and over the left breast pocket she wore the crested shield of a Senior Marshal. As First Deputy Chief, she was operations boss for the entire spaceside command.

She held out a small bag. "Before I forget," she said, although Nicole seriously doubted the Marshal ever "forgot" anything, "all your ID's, please. For our security as much as your own. Officially, you'll be logged out on the next departure. In reality, you're my shadow, your identity a reflection of mine. You'll go home as someone brand-new and completely different."

"Is this really necessary?"

"I assume Simone told you what we found."

"Precious little. I thought that was why I was sent up here, for you to tell me the rest. Basically, I seem to be a primary target."

"Quite correct. And I think you should take a step back to consider the full implications."

"I know, this is some kind of personal vendetta."

"That's the least of it. These attacks, Lieutenant, came through the computer systems that are the heart and soul of our very existence up here. They appear to be confined to the Moon but they also appear to be the work of a software designer of the first order. An algorithmic Mozart, if you will. I've had two of my best people—lone-wolf solos on Out-System patrol and, believe me, you can't get more wild-and-wooly, idiosyncratically brilliant than that—trying to crack the infiltration codes and they're not even close. It may well be, even if they succeed, that we'll never be able to guarantee the integrity of *any* data system you're involved with. Which poses an unacceptable risk, not simply to you but anyone dependent on the same system."

"So even if I were somehow to regain flight status . . ."

"I don't think, under these circumstances, we dare let you out of the atmosphere."

"You tell that to Elias?"

"And General Canfield, yes. They both concur."

"So this is what, my last trip?"

"May well be."

Nicole gave herself a small push, and floated over to the window wall, switching scenes to a starfield display, standing right up against it as though by sheer force of will she could pass through and become one with the Universe beyond. And found herself once more remembering the first time she'd gone strolling out in The Deep, where even the Sun wasn't much bigger than the background stars. Simplest of maneuvers, one she'd done a hundred times in training and reality, step off the spacecraft's hatch and out into the dark. No problem, she thought, piece of cake. After all, the EVA—Extra-Vehicular Activity—was one of the base realities of a working astronaut's life.

Unfortunately, that step took Nicole into absolute emptiness, a *vastness* stretching distances beyond comprehension in every direction. Her forebrain—the analytical intellect— told her, over and over and over again, shrieking it as loud as possible towards the end, this was fine and natural, she was in no danger. Zero gravity, weightlessness—just like now, aboard Sutherland—she'd only move by her own action. But the mindless primitive lurking in the basement, all it recognized was that she was floating and that was a prelude to falling, and from what it could see, once she began she'd never stop. She'd pissed herself, she was so scared, and allowed herself a small smile at the memory.

Still, she got better. She learned to cope. Some didn't, she knew. In every class, there were those who hacked the exams and the Earthbound training, only to discover once they left the atmosphere that they couldn't adapt to the reality. That's why the medical strictures were so exacting; if NASA erred, the decision had long ago been made, it would always be on the side of caution. Calculated risks were one thing, stupidity was tantamount to suicide.

She flinched a tad, the reflex floating her slowly away from the wall as the starfield image shifted to a new scene.

"We've been evaluating the data you brought back with you aboard *Range Guide*," Maguire said while Nicole touched the back of a chair to brake her drift and come to a full stop.

"This," she continued, and a moderately small dot relatively center screen was tagged with a brightly colored circle, "is the Wolfpack asteroid. One of the things that bothered us from the start was how something so big and well equipped could operate illegitimately for so long with nobody noticing."

"Let me guess, we blew a totally legit operation."

"Not quite. The problem we Marshals face, same as you blue suits when it comes to keeping the peace, is that there's simply too much raw space. Even with the technology to cover every cubic centimeter of volume—what the hell, just in the Sol System alone—we don't have the human capacity to evaluate the data. So we key the system to respond to anomalies. In that sector, over the past few years, we haven't had any. Totally nominal activity curve. Now we think we know why."

"That computer genius bollixing your mainframe?"

"Fair guess, but in actuality far more simple. And brutal." Course tracks appeared on the display, fanning out from the asteroid like the anchor lines of a spiderweb, arcing across the Belt to other appropriately labeled dots, other asteroids. "We ran the location through our master plot, to backtrack the traffic, see where it was coming from. In each and every case we had on file, we discovered a claim that had been abandoned as unprofitable, or sold, or made void by the accidental death of the occupant miners. Perfectly legitimate and aboveboard transfers of title. So we went a step further, trying to contact any of the surviving original claimants."

"There weren't any?"

"Not a living soul. We have transit records showing their return In-System, complete electronic evidence of their existence right down through Terrestrial Immigration. But no physical substantiation. Been cross-checking through Interpol and the FBI for any evidence of them dirtside. No joy. Either they went and disappeared completely after reaching the ground—"

"Or they never were to begin with," Nicole finished.

"Precisely. We diverted three patrol missions for physical eyeballs of as many of those rocks as we could cover. All gutted. Moreover, in each case, residual evidence revealed that the claims were significantly more impressive than the assay reports on file indicate."

"So what you're theorizing is that the raiders jumped these claims, killed everyone on the rock, and proceeded to mine it for themselves, while presenting a totally legitimate front to the rest of the System?"

"That about sums it up."

"How many?"

"Fifty-seven. In excess of seven hundred people." Maguire shook her head. "As for the monetary value of the jobs themselves, incalculable. But presumably sufficient to justify the investment in resources and capital that went into that main base. It was an ideal scam. Blitz an isolated rock, dupe its commo signature so that there's no significant disruption in housekeeping traffic, then either stage an accident, or falsify a perfectly plausible reason for the folks involved to vacate the premises. In the process, transfer title to your own holding corporation and proceed to work the claim yourself. Bring the valuables in as perfectly legit imports."

"Uh-uh. Marshal, I can't buy it. There are supposed to be code phrases, key word encryptions, backups upon backups to prevent that sort of thing. Ceres Security *prides* itself on guaranteeing the sanctity of any claim filed with it."

"The company is in for a seriously rude shock. I think you were partly right before, I think our software wizard probably has compromised more than a few data nets both down home and in the Belt."

"That would have to be, wouldn't it? When the Wolfpack's

chief raider, Morgan, came after *Wanderer*, his own ship had
the complete IFF/ID signature for the cruiser *Von Braun*.
We didn't have a clue they were hostile until they started
shooting."

"So tell me, Nicole, know anybody who's God's Gift to
software?"

Nicole took a long, slow look towards the Marshal. "You're
talking like I should know the answer."

"You're certainly a target. There has to be a reason."

"After a year?"

"We wonder about that, too."

Terrific, Nicole raged to herself, *how 'bout coming up with
some damn answers, you're the professionals, this is supposed
to be your job!* And said, "Forgive me, Marshal, but Ben Ciari
was always preaching the innate superiority of Out-System
talent, including criminal. Shouldn't you be asking yourself
about the most likely candidates among that crowd?"

"I did. I have. Came up dry. Nobody wants to talk. Which
struck me as unusual because, this type of operation, everybody pitches in to shut it down, for their own survival. Strange
as it seems, we have a code of conduct even among the
criminal element. There are lines you simply do not cross.
Because essentially, it comes under the heading of shitting
where you live."

"I know. It's one of the things I admire most about space.
What about the people behind the Wolfpack?"

"Whole other question entirely. Think about it, Nicole. Consider the raw resources required to mount that kind of operation. We tagged upward of a dozen ships moored around that
rock."

"And close to a thousand people within, I know, I scanned
the data, too."

Now it was Maguire's turn to look, a level appraisal. "Still
bothers you?" she asked.

"It isn't"—and Nicole clenched her fist, choking a cry of
fury deep in her throat as the sudden movement stirred her
from her place and she had to flip-flounder gracelessly to keep
from tumbling—"an easy thing to get over," she finished,
meeting Maguire's eyes defiantly.

It wasn't Morgan who woke her in the middle of the night,
shaking and sweating, eyes staring for a target while her hand
grabbed for a pistol that thankfully wasn't there. Daniel Morgan,

decorated hero turned renegade, leader of the raider Wolfpack
that blew *Wanderer* out of space. The gauntlet had gone down
between them the moment they met, and when they finally faced
off—in the shadowed corridors of the raiders' base asteroid, she
armed with a crossbow, he with a rifle blaster—she was the
one who walked away. But that had been a fair fight—*Hell*,
she thought fiercely, *if anything the odds were stacked in* his
favor—and the only scars left from it had been physical.

But there'd been another man, earlier in the day, aboard the
Halyan't'a starship. Nicole and Hana Murai and a team of Hal
warriors ambushed a cadre of raider technos and their escort.
She'd nailed one of the combat troopers in the back, wasn't
even a pretense of fairness here, the escort had to be taken
out immediately, without the slightest opportunity to alert their
command. His features hadn't registered at the time, but over
the following months they'd drifted more and more clearly into
view. A young man, barely her own age, splashed with pain
around the eyes and mouth, but mostly with surprise. Bang—
he was dead, end of story. Not that bad-looking, either. Maybe
not so awful a person as well.

She had no idea who he was, where he came from, what
had pushed him into space and then into the embrace of the
raiders. The same yearnings that drove her, she wondered,
to see what was beyond the horizon? Or just a job? Was
he looking for a quick buck, a few tours of slash-and-burn
before retiring to the good life? Did he leave anyone behind?
She knew everything about Morgan and somehow that made
what happened all right; with this lone trooper, it was her
imagination twisting the knife.

"Nicole," Maguire said, "had you known about the raider
families, would that have made a difference? Would you have
traded your lives, the Halyan't'a's and their ship, for them?"

"No." Her voice was so soft even she barely heard it. And
Maguire's, as she continued, hardly much louder.

"Well, then."

"Ben Ciari said I have a capacity to kill. The special
ruthlessness of command."

"And that isn't what you bargained for."

This time, Nicole's "no" was so quiet it was barely more
than thought.

"If I go out again," she went on, "sooner or later, it'll
happen again. I'll have to choose again. I don't know if I

can. No, that's not it. I don't want to discover *that* I can."
A bitter twist to her mouth. "I suppose I should be grateful
our mysterious software savant has taken that possibility out
of my hands."

nine

"FOR FIVE YEARS, Nicole," Maguire said with a bitter anger that was made all the more intense by her tight control, "those people operated throughout the Belt and we didn't have a clue there was even a problem out there! If it weren't for Morgan's obsession with General Canfield, we probably wouldn't know to this day!"

She'd presented Nicole with a copy of her master case file, the same as she would one of her own deputies, and they'd gone through it together, entry by painstaking entry, until they were so bleary-eyed the very words stopped making sense. It was Maguire who suggested a workout before bed, clearing time for them in the gym.

They stood at the main entrance, with the room stretching before them, a featureless cube some twenty meters to a side that had originally been intended as a maintenance bay. Projecting out from the walls, at a variety of lengths and angles, were a maze of metal bars, forming a surrealist jungle gym. You pulled yourself from one to the next, along a programmed path that would ultimately bring you back to where you started, sort of like combining a slalom with show jumping. There were levels of difficulty, of course, with established times for each. Never a tournament or a prize. Everyone's level and time was logged and accessible; essentially, you measured yourself against your peers and that was that. Last time she was here, Nicole thought she'd done pretty well, but a glance at the terminal by the hatch told her she'd fallen something of a ways since.

Being at the heart of the station meant total weightlessness, which normally mandated all footwear to have Velcro gripsoles to anchor them to strips that ran at intervals along the bulkheads. The elimination of gravity took with it all but the most arbitrary concepts of "up" and "down," which meant as well that there was no such thing as a true "floor" or "ceiling." Any flat surface qualified, depending on what a person's orientation was at any given time. And could change with a move. So designers had to allow—at least in this section of the station—for all those planes being used. Here, though, the idea wasn't to stick, but to bounce. As hard and fast as possible. Which meant standard sneaks—in Nicole's case, borrowed, as was everything else she was wearing—plus shorts and a rugby shirt. Knee and elbow pads, fingerless gloves that were still more than a trifle too stiff for her taste, with a helmet she'd left floating by her head.

Maguire set up an expert run, and Nicole watched the appropriate bars light up. The whole path flared first, to give a sense of the route. Once the player started though, they'd only flash three bars ahead—to show where she was, where she was going next, and the one after that. The Maze was a test of skill and agility, that also forced you to think on the run and required a total awareness of your body's relationship to the space around it. Some of the clearances were uncomfortably tight, and more than a few people ended their runs through here wrapped painfully about a bar that had suddenly materialized—they swore, out of nowhere—right in front of them. Or they simply forgot the relationship of cause and effect, action and reaction, a sideswipe that on Earth would mean nothing throwing them just enough off-line that they missed the next junction and either totaled on another bar or bounced off the wall. Hence, the pads and helmet. Some serious velocity could be developed here, with equally serious consequences. That was the challenge and the fun. To push to the limit and emerge unscathed.

"Do you have the slightest *fucking* idea, Lieutenant, what that means?" Nicole caught so by surprise that she couldn't help staring at Maguire's language. The woman wasn't a prude, by any means, but she also prided herself on how she spoke, a reaction Nicole had heard to a childhood in the Brooklyn Public School System, where every other word was generally a curse. "Goddamn right, nobody'll talk. Under the circumstances, why the hell should they?

"All we have going for us out there—and by 'we,' I mean the Marshal Service, you blue suits, anybody who represents civil authority—is our rep. Yes, sometimes we go a little overboard on the melodrama, and kick ass a little harder than is absolutely necessary, because we operate on a frontier where backup is measured in days and weeks away, if it's even available. at all! One ship, Lieutenant, a team crew if it's lucky, more often than not a solo. Whose responsibility is to keep the peace. All by themselves!"

Nobody screws with the Marshals, that was an article of faith that Ciari had taught her. Because they made sure from the start that the cost would be prohibitive. They took care of their own, pure, simple, and absolute. Consequently, when they laid down the law—capital crime, domestic dispute, any and everything in between—people listened. The Marshals were trusted because they were the ones who came when there was trouble.

"But this . . ." And there was a long silence. "This strikes at the heart of all we're trying to build up here." Another pause. And Nicole could see how hard Maguire was trying to rein in her rage. That was the other thing you learned the moment you left the atmosphere: control. No careless movement, never *ever* go off half-cocked, regardless of the provocation. Yet for all the rational awareness of the realities in space, the principals involved were still human beings, and a billion years or more of evolution left the race with hard habits to break.

They'd spent a half hour stretching and warming up, but Nicole still felt too tight. She hoped it was nerves and that, once she started, things would calm down.

Flexing her fingers one last time, she crouched onto her heels and then launched herself for the first bar, a good ten meters distant. Second one was below and to the left, so she grabbed hold as she flew over it, letting momentum pull her into a forward somersault. Brought her legs into the bar as she came 'round, shoved off along the new vector, twisting her body in midair to allow for a better grip as she swung off the second for the third. Knew even as she did that speed and timing were off—just a hair, the merest fraction, but this was an environment where fractions made the difference. She didn't even bother setting up for the bar, but rolled her body into a ball to take the impact as best she could before shoving her way out of the Maze and back towards the doorway.

Just floated for a few minutes, catching her breath, accepting without surprise that her face was dripping with sweat and her shirt already wore huge stains.

"That stunk," she grumbled, taking the towel Maguire offered and using it to wipe herself as dry as she could manage. The Marshal didn't give her an argument. Then she gave arms and shoulders and legs a fair shake and took up her position once more.

"Turns out," Maguire went on, "there've been rumors all along. About how dangerous it was to strike a major claim."

"No one ever checked it out?"

An angry grimace that was partly shame. "Everything passed surface muster, each incident fit neatly into an appropriate box, where it was filed and forgotten.

"But the Belters, with them everything's personal. They saw friends, colleagues, whatever, bugging out, and it bothered 'em. Things would happen, and it bothered 'em. Us, we tagged their complaints to paranoia an' gave 'em back official platitudes.

"You see the cycle?" she asked. "We have nothing to go on, we figure nothing's there, we don't worry about it."

"But the Belters, they see something happening, only they can't figure quite what, but the folks they trust to answer their questions, resolve their doubts, allay their fears, don't."

Maguire nodded, set herself, leapt off on her own run through the Maze. Incredibly, to Nicole, continuing to talk as she went.

"So the perception takes root that maybe we're in on it, whatever 'it' is. So maybe we're not trusted quite so much. So maybe folks don't come to us as freely as they used to. And both sides drift further apart, spiraling tighter into their own spin-circles of misconception. Until they're locked into their role as victim and we become totally ineffectual."

"Why?" Nicole asked as Maguire landed within a meter of where she'd started. Not a perfect round, but she'd made it the whole way, which was the next best thing. "What's the point?"

"Perhaps the establishment of space as somebody's private preserve," was her reply. "Doesn't matter what the government says or does, they can't protect you. For all you know, they may be in on it. Technology being what it is, the realities of distance and transport being what they are, it's damned hard to protect yourself. Better maybe to bend with this prevailing wind and shift some allegiances. And all of a sudden, hey-presto, a very quiet de facto coup d'état. The de jure status quo doesn't change in the least, the legal structures all remain in place, but the realities underpinning them have just shifted fundamentally."

Nicole nodded. "Makes sense."

"If you're into horror stories. In my whole career, I have *never* seen anything so subtly sophisticated, yet so brutally simple. Even today, knowing all we do, *knowing* what they've done, there isn't a damn thing legally we can do about it. Because we can't prove one single, stinking, lousy, actionable offense. You weep for the families on the raiders' rock—I commend you for it, that makes you a decent soul—but there are other families involved and as a cop and a human being *I* can't help thinking your actions maybe balanced some necessary scales."

"So I can be just like them, only it's okay 'cause I'm one of the good guys?"

Maguire turned back towards Nicole with such violence that she should have gone cascading across the room, only she was such an experienced spacer that she was reflexively compensating for the move even as she made it.

"I suppose that answer depends," she said bitingly, slipping towards the hard-edged lilt of Belfast, the city of her birth, "on how long you plan to stay feeling shit-sorry for yourself."

Nicole took a deep breath. Didn't seem to help much. Even though she filled her lungs to capacity, she still had the sense that she was suffocating.

The computer never set up the same route twice. This cycle had three bars, close at hand and tight together; she swung through them one-handed, like a chimpanzee along a horizontal ladder, giving herself a sharp twist with the last to spin herself around so she could hook the back of her knees around the next bar, kicking forward as she flipped around to intensify the spin and position her for the next. But she didn't gain enough velocity and a final, desperate lunge only made matters worse as she careered into the wall hard enough to make an impact, even through her helmet. Without one, things would have been very messy.

She sniffed loudly, wiping her forearm across her nose, making a face at the sight of mingling sweat and blood. She could taste the salt, with its coppery undertone, on her lips. There was a mottled soreness on her thigh she knew would soon metamorphose into a monster bruise, but she hadn't a clue as to how it came there. Try as she might, she couldn't remember whacking anything with her leg.

"I'm sorry you're a part of this, Nicole," Maguire called from below and behind, "an' that's a fact. But like it or not, you're turning into a key player. You're short on experience, but you have good instincts and you learn faster than anyone I've seen this side of Ben Ciari."

"Which doesn't seem to have done me a whole helluva lot of good to date," she muttered, turning wearily baleful eyes on the Maze. Not like her at all. Oh, of a certainty she'd been beaten before; far more often than not, she failed to make a complete circuit. Hardly anyone did. But even at her worst, she'd never done this badly.

To run the Maze required a particular form of Zen, a Oneness of the physical instrument to the task to the moment, which she didn't have. There was a hesitancy to her movements, a conscious look to make sure she was going in the right direction—where necessity demanded that all that be done unconsciously. It didn't matter that the look was so quick it almost didn't register, the fact was she was taking it. Not because she needed to in order to make her decision, but to validate that decision. In a situation where she had to absolutely trust her instincts, she wasn't.

She was afraid.

"You're alive, woman, count that for something. How about considering the implications of that for a minute?"

"Just me, you said before. Not Hana or any of the others." And when Maguire nodded. "My parents, my family?"

"There's no indication thus far they're in any way at risk."

"Hardly a guarantee I can take to the bank."

"So do something about it."

"You've got nothing on the hijacks."

"There were no hijacks," Maguire told her. "In every instance, there was a legitimate transfer of title. A moderately capable lawyer could probably make a fair case that you callously and gratuitously caused the destruction of a totally legal operation."

"Comforting thought. Okay. Ships have owners. Cargoes have to belong to someone. Who were the titles transferred to?"

Her question got only a dismissive shrug for an answer. "We're still looking. Think of this as a Russian *Katrinka* doll—you know, the ones where you have a succession of dolls, hidden one within the other, getting smaller and smaller until you finally reach the teeny-tiny one in its heart. Only, in this case, each and every one of those dolls is hidden in its very own Chinese puzzle box. Maze piled upon maze. Shadow corporation enveloping shell company. Just when you think you're onto something, you discover the outfit's in long-ago liquidation with their records a tangled mess. Or it's been sold to someone else and the information's been lost in the shuffle. Or is now considered the proprietary property of some entity totally removed from the situation, in a locality beyond our jurisdiction, who has not the slightest interest in cooperating."

"If you can identify the backers, what then?"

"What then indeed? Good question."

"You can't touch them, can you?"

"We probably can't even secure an indictment, let alone a successful prosecution. There simply isn't a strong enough chain of evidence. We may know the truth, I doubt we'll ever be able to prove it."

"Then why am I a target?"

Maguire shook her head. "Serves no purpose, not even as a warning. As far as the incident itself went, you resolved the problem. You blew the living bejesus out of the base. On the surface, it's over and done with. The Wolfpack is history. Great victory for the forces of law and order. Cheers and commendations all 'round. A big medal for a certain Second Lieutenant. Certainly, there'll be aftereffects. For a while. We'll be a lot more meticulous about looking after the Belters, maybe they'll start being as open as they once were. But this was a long-view operation. The profits from the actual raids probably didn't do much more than cover expenses. The idea was to strike at the whole concept of free space. Of this being an open frontier.

"What?" she asked suddenly, seeing a change in Nicole's expression. But the young woman shook her head.

"It's nuts, forget about it."

"I'll be the judge of that, Lieutenant. What've you got?"

"Something I'm only just beginning to realize myself. About myself. Everyone keeps fixating on my being a Second Lieutenant, but that's not all I am anymore. Shavrin adopted me as her daughter. It isn't a figure of speech, or a pro forma gesture. I'm a part of her family." Unconsciously, as she spoke, Nicole let herself drift into the Maze, so that from more than one angle it looked like she was trapped; yet, at the same time, she had solid surfaces at every hand, allowing her—assuming she had the skill and courage to go for it—an extraordinary range and freedom of movement.

"Some country, maybe?" she hazarded, not totally trusting her own deductions. "But what would they have to gain, especially with President Russell pushing his One World Treaty?"

"My dear girl," Maguire chided with a decidedly unfunny laugh, "if there's anything to be learned from history, it's how passionately we humans cleave to our various tribes. Look how hard it's been keeping the boroughs of New York City together, much less the various elements of Yugoslavia, the Soviet Republics; hell, the United States itself. No one likes to yield sovereignty.

"And that isn't as farfetched a notion as you might think. Quite a few see Russell's proposal as no more than a ploy by the First and Second World to maintain its domination of the Third. The political equivalent in their eyes of the U.S. move into Saudi Arabia back in '90. The argument may be bogus to you and me"—she held up a hand to forestall Nicole's outraged protest—"but a plausible case can be made in its favor. Look around, Nicole, we got Americans and Soviets and Europeans and Japanese fully represented up here. How many from Africa, South America, the Middle East, South Asia? How much innate resentment remains because, even though there may be equal opportunity for all, the road up starts at Canaveral and Baikonur? And what about the price of that opportunity, the necessity to leave the old prejudices and inhibitions and cultural structures behind? D'you know how hard it is to find Mecca from seventy light-years out?

"On the other hand, who says we're necessarily talking about a country?"

"You have a better idea?"

"They're his ships, why not his space as well? You want historical precedent, take a look at the 'John Company.' The British East India Company. They did most of the initial exploitation of the subcontinent. Had their own military—army and navy—a state within a nation. Where better to procure space-going hardware than at the source? One thing we do keep a serious watch on is traffic. Everybody's supposed to be tagged and transpondered, logged into our central file. But if the vessel never gets registered in the first place, for all intents and purposes it doesn't exist. Sound familiar?"

And Nicole thought of Stu Hanneford's bike. Who knows, if he'd been tagged, he'd probably have been found the very night he disappeared. Might have made a difference.

She shook her head. "I see where you're going, I don't buy it. What's the motive?"

"Me, I'd say power."

"You don't think he has enough?"

"Young Lieutenant, I truly believe, where Manuel Cobri is concerned, there's no such concept as 'enough.' "

There was a *beep* from Maguire's kit bag, a portable transceiver, shielded to provide a secure com link. The news wasn't good, that was clear from the first. Her eyes grew the littlest bit hooded, her face losing all animation, reverting to a stoic, professional's mask.

"What's happened?" Nicole asked as Maguire closed the phone.

"Simone Deschanel is dead," in a voice like grating stone that spoke volumes about their friendship.

Nicole closed her eyes, and for some split seconds, no image of the other woman came to mind. So strange, how you meet someone, get to know them, imprint them into the patterns of memory, yet find vast, seemingly abyssal gaps when you suddenly try to call back their face. Or the sound of their voice. As though the act of dying had severed the bonds that kept them real inside your head and made them ghosts there as well as in reality, leaving you afraid—with varying degrees of desperation—you'll ever get them back. And compared to Maguire, Nicole hardly knew the woman. Yet the Marshal's face was the same as ever.

"How?"

"In the bedroom of your quarters, at Edwards."

"No."

"You're out of here." And Maguire reopened her phone, tapped in a call to Flight Control, putting a hold on the next available departure and claiming a seat.

"Just like that."

"If I had a bloody transporter, like on the videos, I'd beam you down." She gestured towards the gym door. "But this is the best I can do. Nicole," she flared when Nicole stubbornly stood her ground, "we knew what had been tried on the Moon, we thought we covered *every* eventuality, and still Simone got nailed. We cannot afford the slightest risk up here, it's too dangerous and those bastards—who*ever* they are—are too damn good."

Nicole had no argument.

"Flight's at Bay Three, a British Airways Scram to London Heathrow."

"I'm not exactly dressed for international travel." She was in fact a moderate mess, still flushed from her workout, cooling sweat making her chilly, complete with goose bumps, painfully conscious of how her bloody nose must look.

"Tough. Go. Wait for me at the boarding access."

They went out the door together, Nicole kicking off the sill into the corridor beyond, shooting diagonally across to the far wall, using the textured soles of her sneaks to increase her speed and send her up towards what was officially considered the "ceiling." Her hope being that she could race over the heads of anyone who happened to get in her way. And for the most part, that was how things went—except for one poor soul who found himself on a collision course with her as she hurtled around a corner, scything through the air at full extension, her hands using a stanchion as a pivot. She simply let go, sliding sideways like a propellor, yanking all her limbs together into a cannonball that missed him by a whisker, then popping them out again in time to flatten against the opposite vertical. Pushed off with toes, aided by the padded buckskin palms of her gloves, was almost out of sight by the time the man recovered wits enough to yell his protest.

She made record time, but had barely begun catching her breath when Maguire caught up with her.

"You can use the Scram's washroom for your face, I'm afraid the rest'll have to wait until you're back on home ground. The transfer connections home are as tight as we can make them. As for clothes," she handed over the carryall, with the ghost of a smile that reminded Nicole of Kymri. And suddenly she felt glad she didn't have Maguire after her. For *any* reason. "Call this a wild splash of inspiration."

Inside was the black flight suit of a United States Marshal, folded so the silver badge emblazoned on the left breast showed.

Nicole looked up questioningly, got a curt nod in return.

"It's exactly what it looks like," Maguire said. "Effective immediately, and for the next twenty-four hours—extensible at my discretion for the duration of this investigation—you are hereby appointed a Deputy United States Marshal, with all the rights, privileges, responsibilities, and most especially authority that go with it.' None, however"—again, that surprising, disconcerting smile, very small, mostly to herself, as though Maguire was enjoying some private joke—"of the pay. At that grade, your equivalent rank's a Major. But do us both a favor and don't throw any weight around unless it's absolutely necessary. Come the dawn, you'll probably be back at the bottom of the ladder. If you should need the clout, though," she added, "it's there."

"You can do this?"

Added to that smile, a mocking tilt of the head. "Up here, absolutely. Though I may be stretching the point extending my authority to the surface."

"What gives, Al, why the 'Cinderella' treatment? I mean, I'm not a trained investigator."

"You're all I've got. There's no one else—down there, anyway—whom I trust, Nicole." She dialed Sutherland Mission Control, told them the British high-flyer was released to launch.

Moments later, over the station loudspeaker system, they heard, "Attention please, British Airways Flight Zero-One to London Heathrow is now cleared for departure. All passengers and personnel should be aboard. The access airlocks will cycle in ten minutes."

"What am I supposed to be looking for?"

"Answers."

"To who killed Simone?"

"Officially, that has yet to be determined."

"What does that mean?"

"She's dead. That they know. All else is open to question. And interpretation. Everything sent me from Edwards, which is I presume everything they have thus far is on file"—she motioned her chin towards Nicole's bag—"in there. Review it on your flights."

"And then?"

"I don't know, Nicole. I'm flying blind, same as Judith Canfield did when she took the first Cobri starship into warp. Didn't know what would happen along the way, or what she'd find at the other end. But she went. Now it's my turn. And yours. We need to find out what happened. We need to push, hard and fast. As near as we can determine, the sniper sequences on the Moon were resident programs, they'd been in place awhile; the only reason you tripped the one you did was because you hadn't been on Luna since the *Wanderer* flight, except for a flash visit when our Embassy left for the Hal homeworld and then after your recertification exams, which was when you almost got bagged. This is a fresh kill, if indeed it is a kill. Maybe we can turn up something, maybe the killer wasn't as thorough this time at covering his tracks.

"You said it yourself, Nicole, most *countries* can't mount the kind of effort that Wolfpack base represented, and only one private firm: Cobri, Associates. Could be I'm paranoid, there's no reason to assume it's the old man; may well be a loose cannon in his organization who's pulled off the greatest con job in history. But whoever's behind this possesses capabilities that have to be respected. So either prove to me my fears are groundless—and yes, Lieutenant, they *are* fears, I am scared and so should you be—or give me something to act on.

"You want a goal, aside from simple survival, consider the fundamental integrity of the Frontier. This is my turf, *our* turf," and for emphasis she hammered a fist against the wall. "We're dreamers here, Nicole, that's why we come. Lord, why else live in holes in the ground or glorified tin cans? Where there's no such thing as a breath of fresh air? We're trying to build a decent way of life. Someone's doing

their miserable best to destroy it. That, I will not allow. And
if those wings you earned mean anything, young Lieutenant,
neither will you."

"I'll do my best."

"I need results, Nicole. Until then, we're hamstrung."

"And I'm on death row."

"Very likely," the Marshal said flatly, "as is anyone close
to you."

London was muted grey-greens, cool colors to go with the
cool afternoon air—not that she had much chance to sample
it, as she was bundled from one spaceplane to another, with
barely time for feet to touch solid ground before she was
skyborne once again. Seven hours, door to door—Sutherland
to southern California—with the longest single stretch being
at the end, waiting on the ramp at LAX for clearance to make
the eighty-minute flight to Edwards. Only forty-odd minutes
less than the time it took to return from Sutherland, or fly the
seven thousand miles from London to Los Angeles.

Eight-hour time difference, teatime there being predawn
twilight on the high desert. On any normal day, she'd be
finishing her stretches before collecting Kymri for their morning run. The cold was bitter and she was thankful for the
flight jacket Maguire had included with the uniform. She felt
strange, and wondered how she looked to everyone else, in
black from neck to toe, with the Marshal's crest on one shoulder, the DaVinci Headquarters patch on the other, plus her
badge. She'd thought about ditching it for a proper uniform—
didn't matter that all her clothes were in her quarters, currently sealed behind bright yellow-and-black security tape,
she could get what she needed from her locker at the South
Field Complex. Only she wasn't given the chance. A car
pulled up as the plane turned off onto the taxiway and she
was ushered out while the engines were still running, the car
speeding away before she'd barely had time to settle herself.

Colonel Sallinger was there, of course. Along with bods she
didn't know, presumably from Intelligence and the Military
Police. Some civilians, too, who she assumed were FBI and
Secret Service. Plus a minor but formidable contingent of uni-
formed Air Police to secure the street from the idly curious.
Of which, given the hour, there were none.

She reported to Sallinger, but he waved aside her salute before it was halfway complete.

"You don't work for me today, Nicole, no need for the courtesies."

"Not my choice, boss," she said. "No offense, but I'd rather be back in my blues."

"Mañana, Cinderella. I'm only sorry the occasion isn't a ball." He shook his head. "Not what we had in mind at all."

"I scanned the initial reports, sir. The Halyan't'a called this in?" A nod. "Did they know about my absence?"

"You'll have to ask them. But they weren't supposed to, my orders were quite specific on that score. At this end, it was you and me and Special Agent Deschanel; on Sutherland, Marshal Maguire. On the Moon, General Canfield." Which made sense, given the General's dual responsibilities as Commander in Chief of the Air Force's Space Command and NASA's Director of Manned Spaceflight. "That's it. Nobody else."

"Except the President." She thought of it as a small bit of humor, an attempt to ease the mood, but the words came out with an unconscious edge that brought Sallinger's head around sharply, and she realized with a shock that she'd meant them seriously.

"How do I handle this, sir," she asked with quiet desperation, flash-glancing down the line of hard-faced men and women.

"Ms. Shea," Sallinger replied, with just enough emphasis on the "Ms." to get her attention, "you bossed a multibillion-dollar spacecraft, how'd you handle that?"

"Just like flying a new plane, *huh*?"

"Precisely. So don't obsess about auguring in." *Or*, she thought, *it'll become a self-fulfilling prophecy*. "Just don't do it."

She strode over to the Base Provost Marshal, a bluff-bodied bruiser who topped her by half a head and dwarfed her bodily. He was a "mustang," starting his career well before she was born as an enlisted man, winning a battlefield commission during a vicious firefight in the Saudi desert. They'd met a few times early on after her assignment to Edwards, to coordinate security for the Hal, and she'd been struck—then as now—by how much he and Maguire seemed to be cut from the same mold. There was no warmth in his greeting, but not outright dismissal, either; he was taking her as she was, at least to start. Where she went from here was her lookout.

"Colonel Rachiim."

"Ms. Shea." Same mode of address Colonel Sallinger used, and she had to admire how neatly that straddled the gulf between her temporary status and the permanent one she'd revert to later on.

She cocked head and eyebrows slightly, silently prompting a status report. And the Provost, resting massive hands on hips, pivoted towards the front of the house.

"Decedent initially tagged as Nicole Shea, Second Lieutenant, United States Air Force. Upon direct physical examination, it became obvious the decedent was not the aforementioned Lieutenant Shea. Colonel Sallinger provided the correct identification, of Simone Deschanel, Special Agent of the United States Secret Service, attached to the presidential security detail."

"You keep saying 'decedent,' here and in the report."

"There's no empiric evidence of foul play. Autopsy has established the cause of death as myocardial infarction, a massive heart attack."

"Is there a natural etiology to support that?"

"Depends on what the hell you just meant?"

"She have a cardiac history? High blood pressure, genetic predisposition, arterial blockage, that sort of thing?"

He pivoted to face her. "She was on the President's detail, cleared for off-world. Those operatives go through the functional equivalent of a NASA first-class astronaut's medical every year. Agent Deschanel had her 'annual' immediately prior to the President's recent Lunar visit, which was directly prior to your posting here."

"I gather then, she was in good shape."

"Superb. Doesn't mean anything. Sometimes it happens."

"The house bio-monitors. If she was in such acute distress, there should have been an alarm."

"They appear to have been disabled."

"That doesn't seem suspicious to you, Colonel?"

"From the inside, Ms. Shea. Evidently, Agent Deschanel did the job herself. As a matter of fact, we don't have *any* real-time live surveillance recordings, because that would have jeopardized the integrity of *your* mission. Colonel Sallinger ordered your quarters taken off-line. It was logged as 'routine maintenance.' I wasn't informed until after the fact. Well after the fact. When I was standing over that poor woman's body."

"I'm sorry."

"So am I. And no, Ms. Shea, I'm not blaming you. Lieutenants follow orders, same as Colonels, it's just the Colonels are supposed to know a lot better. Fortunately, however," he added, "the surveillance video was dumped directly into the house's own memory. We're still scanning but all indications are that Agent Deschanel went to bed and simply died in her sleep."

"No offense, sir, but that doesn't mean dick."

"Howzzat?"

"An attempt was made on my life on the Moon."

"I know."

"Then you should also know that the hitter penetrated presumably fail-safe secure computer networks and used them to do his dirty work. He executed lethal modifications to environmental systems while perpetuating the fiction to the core monitors that everything was fine."

"You're suggesting the same here, that this was murder?"

"Yes. You can pull every data stream in the house, it'll only tell you what the killer wants you to know."

"A plausible scenario. Only this isn't the Moon, and she wasn't in a sealed physical environment. The bedroom window was open—and yes, we scoured the yard for any sign of an intruder, totally no joy—and there's not even a hint of residual atmospheric toxins. And the fact remains, she wasn't asphyxiated. She had a heart attack."

"Poison in the food?"

"Not there, not in the water. Scanned the video system, on the off chance she was watching a movie that scared her to death, nothing there, either. No external contact of any kind, from the moment she entered 'til the time my people kicked in the door. No outgoing calls, no answer of any incoming. Eleven in your buffer, mostly from the Cobri girl, Amelia. Concentrated in a two-hour window. She was eager as hell to get in touch. Along the way she figured you were home but not picking up, got pretty upset about it."

"Anyone spoken to her?"

"Not yet. Officially, that's still you in there. We're not treating this lightly or casually, Ms. Shea, but we need tangible evidence to pursue it as a homicide. I got no hunch here, an' yours don't count for much."

"You know Al Maguire?"

"Child, why d'you think we're talking? Wearing that uniform don't mean shit to me on my post. I respect you in this because I respect Al. But even she isn't sure. Hell, Shea, *you* aren't sure."

"The house is sealed?"

"Totally isolated. We physically pulled every external link right after we found the body. Why?"

"If the Hal hadn't called, would anyone have known anything was wrong?"

He crooked an eyebrow, then shook his head. "Colonel Sallinger and she had some sort of commo code," he said. "He'd call in on a random schedule and if she didn't give the proper response, that'd mean trouble. As I recall, there were some distractions through the evening. Nothing major, but they all seemed to require his intervention."

"So he was out of position."

"Seems like. Although a case could be made for coincidence."

"Be nice to be sure," she suggested gently.

"That it would." And he called over a uniformed investigator to turn her thought into an order.

"You want to go inside?" he asked.

"Not yet." And wondered how much of her answer was just plain fear. Simply because the trap had sprung once didn't mean it wasn't ready to try again. "I'll talk to the Halyan't'a first."

"Be my guest. Kymri was the soul of cooperation, but who's to tell with those folks? He could be lying through his teeth and I'd never know it."

"Same applies in reverse, Colonel."

"Maybe. Me, I'm in the habit of giving the guy across the table a tad more credit than he's due."

"You'll keep me informed if anything new pops."

He gave her a curt nod. "And you, likewise."

Their door was open, all three Hal waiting just inside, as she strode up their path. Their manner was as casual and overtly relaxed as ever, but she noted a faint, upstanding brush of fur down the back of each neck.

"We greet with joy," Kymri said formally as he ushered her across the threshold, "the finding that you have yet to transition from this corporeal plane."

"For myself, I could wish for happier circumstances," Nicole replied, matching his manner and bearing as best she could, feeling as always that she was falling far short. "Although I do appreciate the thought."

"Different uniform," he noted.

"Only for the day."

"It makes you an enforcer of the law."

"A Marshal, yes. You called in the alarm."

"Tscadi alerted me."

"To what?"

He growled something to the big engineer, the words too fast and slurred by accents for Nicole to properly follow, and she cursed the fact that she was learning the classical Hal language and not its colloquial variants. Same problem as trying to learn mainstream English and then trying to cope with the extremes of South Brooklyn or the Louisiana bayou. You come away with the knowledge of things as they should be, rather than what they really are.

"She is not precisely certain," he said. "Something on the order of what you would call . . ." and he spoke now to the CyberCrystal artifact on the living-room table, which replied—after a search of its memory paths—in its dulcimer tones: "A hunch."

"You have them?" Nicole asked Kymri.

"There are far more levels to awareness than simply the conscious mind, Shea-Pilot. A mark of sentience is the ability to take an intuitive leap, based somewhile on data you are not even aware you possess. Tscadi sensed"—the faintest of pauses for emphasis—"a wrongness. And acted upon it. Regrettably, not in time to save the lady serving as your stalking horse."

"Colonel Sallinger and Marshal Maguire thought they'd covered every eventuality. And I've been here at Edwards, wide open, for months now. Nothing had happened. I guess the sneaking assumption was nothing would."

"A false one."

"But why? What provoked it? The fact that I went haring off to Sutherland? If that's the case, why wasn't a strike made at *me*?! The attack came through the house, that has to be because the killer was certain I'd be there. Which means he couldn't have known I was away."

"Unless the intent was to strike at you through your friend."

She shook her head. "Where's the sense in that? Kymri, only a total fool pisses off the Secret Service. They're a proud group of people, they won't rest 'til they get the person responsible."

"Unless the perpetrator is certain that is impossible."

A ruefully mocking grin. "You're just full of hope and good cheer."

"You are at risk, Shea-Pilot. And part of my charge is to ensure your safety."

She faced him. "Says who?"

"The authority *I*—and mine—answer to."

"Just how far does that go?"

"As far as my discretion deems needful."

"Surveillance?" A nod. "A network independent of the base monitors?" She couldn't help the chill iron that layered her voice.

"Of course."

She reacted with a growl from the back-base of her throat, something she'd picked up from Shavrin without realizing until much later just how extreme a profanity it was. In the beginning, sheer poor pronunciation saved her, but the first time she got it right—during Rehab actually, when her wonky leg refused to behave and five months of frustration and fatigue took the opportunity to catch up with a vengeance—she stopped conversation all around her. From the Hal present had come nervous chuckles; from the humans, outright gasps at a noise that sounded more appropriate to a Tarzan film.

Kymri didn't bat an eye, though Tscadi laughed in outright appreciation and Matai humphed scandalized disapproval.

"Hunch?" she challenged, shifting a basilisk glare from Kymri to Tscadi.

"Knew you, it was not," came back from her in Hal, spoken slowly for Nicole's benefit, "from the start. Comprehension of the need for stealth. But at dawning, when mediscans indicated extreme distress, beheld no alternative."

"No warning? No physical anomalies?" Nicole started the questions in English, shifted in midstream to Hal, too impatient to wait for Kymri's translation.

"None, Shea-Pilot. She was alive"—a shrug—"and then was not."

"No chance," this to Matai, "that your system could have been corrupted? That you could have been picking up false images?"

The Hal cyberneticist looked insulted a moment, then responded with a vehement negative.

"The consensus on the outside," Nicole said quietly, looking through the window towards the crowd on her sidewalk, "is that she died of purely natural causes."

"A conclusion not without some plausibility," Kymri replied dryly.

"I wish I could believe that."

_____ **ten** _____

THE FIRST THING she noticed, entering her house, was the clutter. Wasn't very much, some items of clothing cast over the back of the couch and on the floor, a slew of papers and data disks strewn across a table, the kind of semiorganized mess made by someone used to living on the run. But it made Nicole uncomfortable nonetheless, and she had to resist the urge to pick them up and put them away.

She cracked the seal of her teapak and took a genteel sip, doing a slow pirouette in the center of the room, taking stock of what she could see from there. Pretty much the same as when she'd left it, a few days before. Reached up with her free hand to rub vigorously at the hair behind her skull, wishing she had the slightest idea what to look for, furious with Al Maguire for dumping this on her.

Not my area of expertise, Marshal, she thought, *Hana's the police procedural nut; she'd love this, probably spot a ton of clues right off!* Hana was one of the few people Nicole found it easy to talk with; really the only one left, now that Paul DaCuhna was dead. And she took a longer sip of tea, hugging herself as best she could, longing for her best friend's presence, the smart-ass remark that'd take the edge off the

diciest situation, the sounding board Nicole trusted enough to
bounce the silliest ideas and notions off of. She felt alone and
lonely, and desperately afraid all of a sudden that she and Hana
would never see each other again.

The door opened and she turned to see Matai follow her into
the house. Before Nicole could voice a question, the Hal
explained her presence in slow, careful phrases, making it as
easy as possible for Nicole to comprehend.

"It is my understanding," she said in Hal, "my specialty
may be of use." One of the suggestions broached by the
investigators had been to summon Alex Cobri to take apart
the house computer. Nicole was emphatic in her opposition,
drawing a raised eyebrow and an "O" of astonishment from
Arsenio Rachiim at this use of her new authority. Colonel
Sallinger backed her, and then smoothed the ruffled feathers
that resulted. *Doomed*, Nicole thought with irreverent self-
absorption; *my career—hah, what a joke* that's *become—is
well and truly doomed*. But where he wouldn't budge was his
decision that she not go in alone. More discussion resulted
in his reluctant approval of Kymri's suggestion that Matai
accompany her. Made sense, actually, she'd been working
side by side with Alex since the Hal's arrival and was more
familiar with Terrestrial computers than most; among her own
kind, according to Kymri, she was near top of the list.

She gave the room a disdainful glance, smiling shyly as she
caught Nicole looking at her. Evidently, she had the same
feelings about clutter.

"The Provost Marshal mentioned messages in my phone
buffer," Nicole told her, thankful that Matai's comprehension of
English was better than her ability to speak it. Her throat was raw
enough from the processed air she'd been breathing on her multiple flights, coupled with the sheer exhaustion of what had turned
into close to three full days of intense physical activity. Some
catnaps were staving off the inevitable but she knew she was
running on empty and the crash was simply a matter of will.

She called for a playback. And as she prowled about the
room, Amelia Cobri's face appeared on the VideoWall.

"Nicole, it's Amy," she said, "heard that you were back."

"Neat trick," Nicole noted, "since according to the date/time
stamp, I must have only just landed from San Diego." Nothing sinister in that. A short-wave radio tuned to the arrivals
frequency would have picked up her communications with the

Tower. More likely, though, some contact of Amy's in the Tower or traffic control probably phoned with the information. "I was hoping you and I could get together tonight," she was saying, "so like, call me as soon as you get in, okay?"

The young girl's face appeared again, the time-tag indicating all of fifteen minutes later: "Takin' your time putting your baby to bed, *huh*, Nicole? I guess something that old, especially when you've put so much work into it yourself, must be worth pampering." Except that Nicole saw something in the girl's eyes that belied the compliment, a blankness that indicated the words may only be words, that she really didn't understand how anyone could care so much, especially about some inanimate piece of machinery. "Alex is like that with his boat."

"Maybe you should follow our example, kiddo," Nicole said, unaware she was speaking aloud what she'd meant to be a thought, "try building something with your own two hands. Little sweat, some pain and blood, give you a whole different perspective."

"So look," Amy finished, "call me, okay, soon as you get in. It's important."

"What's important, kiddo? Too late for the concert. And not a word from Alex."

Five minutes later: "Nicole, I hate to be a bug, call me back, okay, we really need to talk."

"About what?"

And five minutes after that, a little snidely: "Must've been a fun little trip, *huh*, the way Alex blew by, all on his lonesome. Anybody else could say he didn't get any. Lucky for you, Alex doesn't know what that means. Maybe lucky for him, too, means never having to live with disappointment. Catty, aren't I?" Conspiratorial little grin, not at all nice, in a way that little sisters seem to have patented. Turning serious with her next line, "Nicole, you're making this too hard, it's no fun talking to a fuzzed screen, I thought we were buddies, please call me back, as soon as you get in."

Next was Colonel Sallinger, his first check-in. Then, Amelia. "I know you're there, Nicole." Her tone was sharper, blending anger and hurt enough to make it abundantly clear that Nicole was about to step over some line, with consequences to match, and Nicole couldn't help a reflexive, rhetorical response. "Who the hell does that child think she is?!"

"C'mon, this isn't funny, all you have to do is pick up the

phone. Talk to me, willya, stop acting like a flatline, I'm not kidding, it's really important, Nicole, c'mon, *please*!"

Five more messages, all Amelia, and, as Colonel Rachiim had said, increasingly terse and paradoxically more agitated. Until the very end, when the expression on Amy's face was so flat and cold she might have been a computer-generated image herself.

"I'll have to see the kid," she said quietly, aware that the words were being picked up both by the Provost Marshal's ScanTeam and Kymri's. She sank down on the couch, resting her face in her hands as exhaustion came crashing in on her, her body heavy as though she were pulling five times her weight in G's, so much so the smallest movement was an effort and the most natural thing in the world her slow sideways collapse onto the couch. *A few minutes, another nap*, she told herself; *won't be fine, won't be anywhere near my peak, but I'll be functional.*

She closed her eyes, opened them . . .

. . . and stretched full length on the bunk, extending herself as far as she could go, feeling—both with her body and her ears—the rush of water sliding past the hull. They were making good time, a smooth passage, the dawn of another day with the trade winds full at their back, pushing them westward across the Pacific. The better part of a week since departing Catalina, the better part of a thousand kilometers beneath their keel.

Casting about for something to wear, she came up with a T-shirt of Alex's and a pair of jogging shorts she'd found during their last frantic race through the pier-front shops and boutiques. Not her usual style at all, too daringly tight a cut and way too garishly much color. But then the same could be said for what she was doing. Probably mean a court-martial when the Air Force caught up with her—frowning, as the military is wont to do, on officers who go Absent Without Leave—but she didn't really care. Alex would take care of things. And her. She liked that.

She took time for a quick glance over the boat before giving him a smile that couldn't possibly show how she felt, offering him a mug of steaming coffee before tucking herself in the cockpit beside him. The sun was behind them, just clear of the horizon, its warmth just beginning to counter the nighttime chill. As she settled herself, a wayward toss of spray hit her full across the body, plastering her clothes to her skin, and she struck a poor parody of a bathing beauty pose that made Alex spill his coffee with laughter. On impulse, she reversed position and stripped off her shirt, letting the sunlight fall on her bare breasts. She hooked one foot on the rail, the other braced on the deck, legs spread invitingly wide. She still wore the shorts, but the material was so sheer—especially soaked through as it was—she might as well have been naked.

But then he was standing over her, and she closed her eyes and bit her lower lip as some fingers stroked lightly across a nipple. A groan then, as he moved them down her flank, across her belly, teasingly following the elastic band of her shorts. She didn't want to wait, he refused to be hurried, she wanted to scream and thought of killing him. And then she squealed as his mouth closed over her crotch and he exhaled, the moist warmth of his breath seemingly reaching deep inside her. Her teeth were chattering as she grabbed him by the hair over the ears and pulled him tight against her, wrapping her legs behind his shoulders to lock him in place. He kissed and sucked and nipped and she went dizzy with desire, wanting more but also not wanting this to end. The cords of her neck stood out as she arched her back, whimpering with sensations that couldn't be distinguished between pleasure or pain. It was more than she could stand, and she pulled his head hard enough to hurt to bring his face to hers, so she could kiss him on the mouth.

The sun was directly behind him, so Nicole had her eyes mostly closed, Alex no more than a silhouette seen beneath lowered lids. And then, his body was stretched out full length on hers, his mouth on hers, his tongue teasing responses from hers. Only now it felt wrong and she struggled to push him away, wriggle herself free, her eyes opening wide in shock and disbelief and no little horror as Charles Russell pulled away, smiling as a Great White does when its killer jaws close about some unsuspecting prey. The President kept moving away, as Nicole tried to find voice enough to call for Alex and demand an explanation, and the sun flashed blindingly bright in Nicole's eyes . . .

. . . and she twisted her head, blinking fast to clear the dazzle-flashes from her vision, furious that her shades hadn't done their job to cut down the glare. Automatic quick-check of the sky around, as best she could given the cumbersome mass of her crash helmet, thankful to find her wingman on station twenty meters off her left wing.

"God's-Eye," she snapped, and an aerial panorama of the sector flashed into three-dimensional being before her. Terrain wasn't a critical factor, they were too high, almost at the top of the blue, though still well within their equipment's performance envelope. Nothing else showed, friendly or hostile. But that wasn't the assurance it sounded. Stealth technology—the infernally artful blending of form and materials to create an airframe that gave radar fits—had progressed to the level where most state-of-the-art fighters had become functionally invisible to the electronic eye. Between jammers and active defense pods, the missile had become less and less effective as a weapon, especially from long-range. Which, in a weird—but for the pilots, wonderful—sort of way, brought the art of aerial combat full circle, back pretty much to the way it had been in the First and Second World Wars. You sought out the enemy—as much with your eyes, now as then—you tangled with him up-close and personal, and did your level best to punch him into the ground. The gun had once more become the weapon of choice. Because it couldn't be blocked, and it couldn't be jammed.

She was flying the *Mustang Deuce,* the modern namesake of the ace World War II dogfighter and touted by its manufacturer as its functional equivalent. Pilots knew better. It was a wicked-looking bird and if specs were anything to go by, a holy terror. But there was a world of difference between paper predictions and the reality of aerial combat. What worked fine in computer models and wind-tunnel simulations didn't quite follow through on the production aircraft. But commitments had been made, procurement contracts issued, the full force of Charles Russell's presidential prestige placed behind the project (because he desperately needed the votes of the men and women who'd be put to work building it), and so the Mustang went on-line. Didn't matter that the company had oversold and overcommitted, that the designer's imagination had nothing whatsoever in common with the manufacturer's capabilities, because at every step of the line, when objections were raised, Russell either ignored or discredited them. What emerged at the end was a hodgepodge of compromised improvisations and a brute that had become the quintessential JOATAMON—Jack-Of-All-Trades-And-Master-Of-None—a plane that was reputed to be more dangerous to its pilots than any enemy they were likely to face.

She switched her "God's-Eye" view to a tactical presentation—the heads-up display in front of her filling with all the critical data of her aircraft: course, speed, fuel state, stores list, and weapons status. She was lying in the cockpit at about a forty-five-degree angle, to better enable her to withstand the stresses of high-acceleration maneuvering, primary controls concentrated on a pair of sidestick yokes, one on a panel by her right knee, the other by her left. The main panel had a half-dozen analog dials clustered off in the corner; otherwise, the space was taken up by a quartet of video display screens, each capable of presenting any aspect of aircraft operations, far more comprehensively than the mechanical instruments they'd replaced. She had a veritable wealth of information at her fingertips, far more than she usually needed and she feared far more than was good for her in a fight. This was the Catch-22 of modern combat: Take time to keep track of everything coming at you off your glass panel, you got your ass cooked; yet miss anything, and you ended the same. The trick—which only a very few of the very best mastered—was to achieve a Zen state, where the data was assimilated directly to the back-brain. You were never consciously aware of the input, you were too busy hurling the aircraft through the sky in ridiculous gyrations at even more ridiculous speeds, yet whenever the data was needed, there it was in your head.

Another flash from above, as something broke the smooth pattern of the sunlight, barely a moment to register the hostile's presence—much less cry a warning—before a short-range air-to-air punched its way into Hana's cockpit and her plane became instant history. Nicole never saw the explosion, her reaction came with the realization of an attack, hands and feet moving to throw her Mustang into a downward twist, to reverse course after the hostile. It had come from above and ahead, in a diving attack; this was designed to put her on its tail. At this range, even Super-Stealth configurations couldn't avoid detection, but the hostile had jammers to pick up the slack, spreading its return across her screen in a smear of static. She tapped her thumb on the left-hand yoke, tagging the hostile with infrared, homing on his engine exhaust—which was fine so long as she remained behind him—muttering a curse as she caught a glimpse of the aircraft, painted in an air-superiority scheme of mottled blue and grey that made it that much harder to distinguish against the horizon haze. She opened the throttle on the downslope of her own dive, grunting as she pulled up after her foe, gravity crushing her into her padded chair, the bladders of her pressure suit filling with air, tightening around her legs and abdomen, forcing the blood into her upper torso and head.

Tried for a missile lock, no tone, no joy, too much separation to even think about gunfire. Quick, instinctive visual check of her six—a look over her shoulder above and behind—to make sure the sonofabitch hadn't come with friends.

Her attacker—an air-superiority fighter, code-named Stiletto—feinted right, then pitched left into a barrel roll, popping flaps and spoilers to chop his speed and force her to overshoot, to put him on her tail. But she rolled out the other way, a flipover that hit her like a punch to the belly, throwing her plane to the brink of stall and spin as she reversed direction, shooting past him and away before he could set up a shot, hauling back on the stick to burn for altitude, plumes of visible condensation pouring off the fuselage strakes as her nose came up to vertical, taking the calculated risk of lighting up her backside by going to afterburner for the few seconds it would take to gain the height advantage. If the Stiletto had been facing the right direction, a heat seeker would've ended things right then and there. But by the time he'd hauled himself around, she was cresting off her climb, nose-on to him, engines cycled back to a less prominent signature.

A shrill tone in her ears, the Stiletto tagging her with his targeting radar, screens confirming what her eyes were already telling her as two missiles flew off his wings. Seconds later, he was past her, turning even as she did. Her own countermeasures systems coped—she hoped, she prayed—with the missiles.

She saw him turning in the distance, pushing hard to the left, and she quickly pulled back on her stick, rolling away

from the direction of his turn, inverting herself at the peak
of her climb, and flipping into a shallow dive that brought
her straight across the radius of the circle he was forming.
Before she got close though, he flipped the other way and
they began a scissors, she and the Stiletto sashaying back and
forth across the sky, as though winding a ribbon through the
air, each trying to reverse position and tuck in tight enough
behind the other to get off a fatal shot. With two evenly
matched planes and pilots, one-on-one, the usual result was
a stalemate. But he could pull a turn tighter and faster than
she, each cut of the scissors forced her to push a little harder
to come out on his tail, and then keep him from getting
on hers.

She was breathing in hoarse animal gasps, the constant
compression of her bellyband G-belt making her feel like she
was being broken in half, and she knew that if she survived
the dogfight, in the morning she'd be lucky to move, much
less get up. After only a few minutes, each breath sent sharp
spikes of pain up the center of her chest. A glance at the
display told her they were maneuvering at the top end of
the operational window, nothing less than seven G's and
more than a few twists that pushed ten, each one of those
giving her an effective body weight of over half a ton. If it
got any worse, she'd have no choice but to break off. Her
only consolation was that the pilot of the Stiletto had to be
feeling the same.

The Stiletto popped a BackShot, a rear-firing micro-missile,
at the same time taking their scissors vertical, express to the
desert below. She had the option of breaking off. Stay level
while he dove and firewall the throttle. By the time he could
even begin to respond to her maneuver, she'd be so far gone
there'd be no point to continuing the engagement. But he
owed her for Hana. She knew she was making a mistake,
operating on balls rather than brains, and didn't care.

Computer raised some warnings. As they moved into thicker,
heavier air, the potential for serious acrobatics increased, but
so did the risk. The Stiletto's electronics had to be telling him
the same but it also seemed to bother him even less than
her. He was actually accelerating, and she risked a longer
look at his aircraft's specs on the basement display to see
if he had that kind of margin in his performance envelope.
She knew she didn't in hers. Starting to regret the impulse

that had pushed her after him. They'd lost so much altitude that should she decide now to cut and run, his own higher max speed would cancel her head start. He would catch her, with ease.

"Son of a *bitch*," she snarled, wondering what she could have been thinking of. If thinking at all.

Ground scan offered up a canyon, and he ducked into it on afterburner, the overpressure of his wake as he passed triggering small rockslides. Following was like diving into a rapids; the plane bucked around her, bubbling and rolling and skidding across every flight dimension—vertical and horizontal—as she fought for control, all thought of the dogfight banished by the overriding necessity of keeping from crashing, alarms flashing from every screen, the infernally serene voice of the computer warning her that she was stressing the plane beyond its design maximums. It was like an arcade video, one impossible situation after another, flashing at her out of nowhere, except that only hazarded a dollar token; here, she bet her life.

She saw an opening, knew he'd be waiting—it was too perfect a setup—saw no other alternative that offered even a ghost of a chance. Well, not quite true. A sidebar pass off to the right, very narrow, very nasty, something she could handle if she was totally in tune with herself and her aircraft, that would blind her from sight and scan long and far enough either to make a break or come up behind him to continue the engagement on more equal terms. But the very fact that she had to make the choice, a conscious decision, meant she didn't dare. And she nudged her Mustang over the crest of the ridge, terrain-following radar allowing her maybe ten meters clearance tops, hoping ground clutter would mask her.

He didn't even bother with his toys, just bounced her all of twenty meters above her canopy, at full military power, transitioning Mach as he ripped by, generating a shock wave that hammered her out of the sky before she even knew she'd been hit. As instantaneous as such a thing could be, she registered the shadow of his passing—Bastard, she thought incredulously, you're inverted!—streaking past her upside down, and in that terrible moment she realized just how badly she'd been suckered because even though the aircraft was full size, there was nobody in the cockpit, this was nothing but a drone, the man she'd been fighting hadn't been anywhere near here, never at risk in the slightest, she'd wasted herself for nothing—and then . . . .

... the ground was in her face. Aches from top to toe as she tried to regain her feet, settled for rolling over onto her back. Darkness overhead, too much haze to see any stars, the air soft and sultry, with a clinging warmth that made her want to close her eyes and sleep her life away.

But instead, she tucked her legs underneath her and pushed, a wobbly rise to her feet, sighing with slight exasperation at the genius who'd mandated spike-heeled boots for women's flight uniforms. Not to mention the leather suits themselves. Jaunty they may be—head-turners both on recruiting posters and anytime a pilot made an entrance—but not always the most practical of attire. The night was still, the only sounds coming from up the path a ways, surprisingly lively, a jazz combo mixing guitar, piano, and sax.

She made her way cautiously on the uneven terrain, in a sort of bent-leg, crooked-back, old-lady posture, until she reached the building where she heard the jazz combo playing.

Inside was all smoke and shadows, the kind of place where everything is suggested and the imagination is free to run riot. Turn on some decent lights, come back during daylight, there'd be not the slightest hint of magic. What seemed elegant would become tawdry and cheap, making you feel like a fool for having fallen under its spell. Hardly anyone present, which seemed strange considering how good the band was, especially Alex, downstage front, playing his sax like he was making love. The hollow-faced *maître d'* offered Nicole her own choice of seating with an airy wave of the hand and a predatory smile that made her stumble, he really couldn't care less, they were all meat to him, and she wondered how she could ever have thought that Charles Russell was a handsome man.

She moved as close to the stage as possible without straying into the spotlight. She liked the dark, a fighter pilot's instinctive need to see without being seen, because what mattered in a fight was getting in the first shot and making it count. If you staged the ambush, you dictated the dynamics of the engagement and that edge was generally what made the difference between coming home and not.

She took her tequila neat, the whole glass at once, with a lick of salt and lime for chasers, closing her eyes and sucking in her cheeks as the liquor burned through her. Then, a satisfied exhalation and a slow smile as she realized the sax player's eyes were on her, his body twisted ever so slightly her way, the tone and temper of his song changing as he shifted gears to something more haunting and evocative. And she realized that what she'd heard coming in had been an invitation, a siren's call that she had willingly, unknowingly answered.

Hana Murai sauntered across the room and Nicole smiled, offered a wave, the slightest of questions furrowing her brow—after all, wasn't Hana supposed to be in deep space, months from planet-fall—but eyes full of appreciation of how well her best friend looked, snug in dark crimson silk with a dangerous slit up the side seam of her skirt to show off her legs to best advantage. Only Hana looked right past her, to another table, another woman, Grace Kinsella.

Nicole didn't understand why that bothered her, drained another tequila to settle her thoughts a little more so she could puzzle things out. Wondered too late if she'd lost her capacity for the drink and was overreacting because she was drunk? But why react at all, it was no big deal who Hana spoke with—or, for that matter, slept with, that facet of her life was none of Nicole's business—did that mean their friendship was affected?

Russell was looking at her, taunting her, and she knew that whatever she decided would be for his pleasure.

The music made the decision for her, pulling her out of her seat, and she sidled sideways between the tables until she stood before the sax player. Alex was sitting, and her high heels combined with the low height of the stage put them pretty much on eye level. He played to her and for her— eyes meeting hers under his lowered lids, full of a passion nothing would deny—and she responded with a relaxed, devil-may-care abandon that matched him, move for note.

And then it was over.

She smiled, gloriously flushed, wanting him more than she'd desired anything in her life. Even, she realized, awed at the casual ease of this inner treachery, more than her slot as an astronaut.

Not even a smile in return. Alex capped the mouthpiece of his sax and tucked the instrument in its case, taking a proffered bottle of beer from the piano man and toasting the others in the combo before draining half. His gaze flashed over the darkened space, a perfunctory checkup wherein she scored about the same as the furniture around her. There was no emotion on his face anymore, as though some inner switch had been thrown, with one persona active while he played and another for the rest of his life. The stage was one world, and the audience another, and the two had nothing in common.

He stepped past her, gathering Hana and Grace from their table and moving off through the door, Russell offering them a bow and Nicole a look of sated triumph. She'd given him a show worth the watching.

She shook her head, she felt wrapped in slimy cushions, a clumsy sponge rubber doll unable to move unless something bounced into her. She looked around the club, matching its empty silence with the hollowness of shame growing inside herself, fixing a bleary focus on the bar and deciding to treat herself to a virgin bottle of Gold and see how much of it would be needed to sign her out.

But even as she took a first step, she heard a scream from outside, a deep-voiced bellow of defiance that spiraled almost immediately into a falsetto ululation. She sprang for the door, shoving tables and chairs aside as they tumbled into her path, finally bursting out onto the porch.

To see bodies, recognizable only by the ragged strips of cloth that were the remnants of what the three of them had been wearing. Before now, Nicole had never understood the full meaning of the term "savaged." But this was "savaged," if ever a word had meaning, and savagery besides.

The swinging doors banged, the *maître d'* looming behind her, taking in the carnage with a glance, looking from it to Nicole with an air of eager expectation, as though his show had just taken some delightfully unexpected turn and he couldn't wait for what would happen next. Revulsion made her stagger backward, almost losing her balance on the steps, catching herself at last on ground so soaked with blood and gore that her boots made squishy noises with each step. And Russell laughed.

Rage blazed white-hot in her breast, her own face twisting into a roar, hands hooking as though to extend claws, dropping into a slight crouch that would launch her at that hateful creature, desiring nothing so much as the crack of his bones, coupled with a shriek of terror to match those he'd aroused in so many others. She leapt . . .

. . . and dove into the pool, surfacing on the move, a fast, steady crawl to the far end and back, building with each circuit to a blistering pace that was near Olympic time to match the Olympic dimensions of the course. Six laps and then she called it quits, levering herself out of the water and to her feet in one easy motion that bespoke a perfect physical condition her years hadn't even begun to touch.

As she emerged, a ShimmerField activated automatically an arm's length from her, presenting a holographic projection of herself, as seen by the ScanCams scattered about the room. Much better than a simple mirror, this was her identical twin in every superficial respect, capable of being projected to any location on the estate. Indeed, more than once she'd used it as her own stand-in, when she wasn't feeling well or simply didn't want to cope or, as often happened on social occasions, found it necessary to be in seemingly dozens of places at once. Long ago, she'd started building a repertoire of files in the primary data base that allowed for creative interaction with the event. All she had to do was set the program in motion and it would do the rest.

Wet and naked, she picked a comb off her table and swept her hair straight back from her brow. She wore it longer these days, since she no longer flew as a pilot out of the atmosphere. No grey yet, and not for a good long time to come, the water accented the darker tones, turning it a much deeper black, with only the barest hint of russet. The planes of her face were softer, more overtly feminine, as was her body. The bone structure was there, but the bones themselves were no longer as easy to see. Not much as cosmetic surgery went but well worth the inconvenience and the price. Perhaps it was a function of growing older, or of the dramatic change in her life, but when she looked at flats or holos of herself from the old days, it seemed very much like a stranger. Like trying to relate to being a kid or a teenager, that was a phase she'd gone through, put gladly behind her with surprisingly few regrets.

(So why the dampness in her eyes, a voice seemed to whisper in her head, a flash flood of tearing, wiped hurriedly away before they could spill free?)

She looked around sharply, shifting ever so slightly onto the balls of her feet in an instinctive combat reflex she hadn't used since those old days as she pivoted through a full three-sixty, without a clue of what she was searching for, only that it had triggered cues in her that had lain dormant for ages.

The pool—indeed, this whole wing of the house—had been inspired by Louis Comfort Tiffany's mansion, Laurelton. Manuel had seen the exhibit at the Met, back in '90, and fallen under the spell of those few remnants of the master artisan's stained-glass work. He'd spent a small fortune gathering the finest private collection of *favrile* glass in the world, and a significantly larger one financing a master artisan's studio, in the process bringing about a minor renaissance in the decorating arts. High ceiling and open architecture, meant to convey as vast and airy a sense of space as possible, a room that bespoke quiet but all-embracing elegance and a sense of taste that was very much its own.

She heard voices from the next room, Alex's loudest of all, with that edge to it that meant he'd just scored his breakfast hit of Dust. And her mouth twitched, twisted, set into an expression far more appropriate to the Nicole of old than what she'd become, as she remembered waking in the middle of the night, pitched from her bunk so violently she'd gashed her face across her right eye and cheek—and a finger absently traced the line of the scar, or rather where it had been before her surgery—scrambling up the companionway to find the boat in the heart of a nightmare storm, with Alex laughing hysterically at the wheel, babbling about matching his skill against the raw power of the elements.

He'd Dusted, of course, jazzed himself to the limits with the RNA patterns of a 'round-the-world champion yachtsman, taking on the storm when she thought they'd agreed to steer well clear of it. When all was done, his crash was as extreme as the high. The Forty was in little better shape, dismasted, taking water, com systems so much expensive junk, well off the shipping routes and weeks travel from anywhere. She'd been taking inventory of their survival equipment, against the inevitable transfer to a life raft, when a big private Sikorsky rolled in from the horizon to gather them up and sweep them home. There'd been no need to call for help, Manuel Cobri already knew they were in trouble. The moment they left Coronado, and it became clear they weren't coming back, he simply piggybacked an EyeSpy program on as many commercial and military surveillance satellites as proved necessary to keep them under pretty much constant watch. Alex had never forgiven him; Nicole had been very much impressed.

On a table lay a single rose, a small card in Manuel's crabbed handwriting wishing her Happy Birthday, and beside it a necklace and earrings of such exquisite beauty they took her breath away. Custom-made and one of a kind, she recognized the design, from one of Studio Cobri's off-world protégés, easily worth more than she could have made in an entire Air Force career.

Again, the sense of another presence and she called to the ScanCams for a status, to be told she was all alone.

She pulled on a robe, then—impulsively thinking to surprise Manuel (she couldn't care less about Alex, and hadn't for years)—reached for the necklace.

It was gone, the earrings as well, and in their place a choker of raw, almost elemental passion, silver splashed around an oval gem that vaguely resembled a ruby, but whose color seemed to come from some mysterious source in the heart of the crystal, a rich glow that helped give the *fireheart* its name. It was Hal, found only on s'N'dare, and then so rarely that each discovery was front-page news. To possess one was a minor miracle; to be given one as a gift, a gesture of incomparable respect. This had come from Shavrin, after her return home. She'd never worn it—hadn't dared at first, then it hadn't seemed appropriate as relations with the Halyan't'a had started breaking down, following Charles Russell's assassination. His Treaty had died with him and the world had balkanized, all the various countries and factions—public and private, civil and military—jockeying for the best possible bargaining position with the Hal. Who themselves had simply taken two steps back, to wait for the dust to settle, before making any new moves.

She hadn't seen Shavrin since their last parting on the Moon, before she'd been grounded. Nor Ben Ciari, either. Nor anyone else from that life, it was a book she'd closed and filed away, forgotten intentionally until this morning. And she wasn't happy at the reminder.

The choker was a perfect fit and as magnificent a complement to her features. No, not quite, she had to concede that, examining the still-naked ShimmerField image of herself. It had been meant for the woman she had been, the baby warrior, following the path blazed by the likes of Canfield and Ciari.

Not the woman she'd become, willingly bound to Cobri.

And she thought of Robert Frost's poem about the paths not taken, and shook her head angrily, as though the sudden, violent motion would catch these annoying demons of conscience and memory by surprise and cast them from her skull.

Her long, rangy stride took her quickly into the next room, her eyes glazing at the sight of Alex and another ShimmerField of her, switching selection by selection through the latest in trendoid designer leathers. He liked things short and tight and borderline scandalous and the giggles coming from the couch beside him told her his companion was of the same opinion. A sales rep—equally cute, dressed to show her shop's wares to best advantage—stood attentively by, along with an entire stockroom on racks. Anyone else, they'd simply go to the store. For the Cobris, the store always came to the house.

When they found something that caught their fancy, the woman by Alex's side got to her feet and the sales rep helped her try it on. She was naked to start with, barely out of her teens, and made no secret of her attraction for the sales rep, who didn't know how to respond. This was a professional call, she considered herself a professional woman, presenting herself to a client who could wipe out her entire establishment with little more than chump change.

And Nicole felt her insides pull tight as she watched a seventeen-year-old replicant of herself push the other woman into a corner. She started forward, determined to put a stop to this, but Alex was a beat ahead of her, muttering something with a languid wave of the hand to call the child-Nicole off. The sales rep turned partially away, trying to regain her composure, while the child-Nicole straddled Alex's legs, rucking the micro-skirt up to her hips as she ground them against his crotch.

"Why do you watch?" Amelia asked.

"I still can't believe it."

"He's happy"—a dismissive shrug—"and you're free of him. The ideal solution."

"Amy, that's *me* down there."

"A simulacrum," her father said quietly.

"You make it sound like an object. Clone or not, that's a real being."

"Who bears a superficial resemblance to you, Nicole, but who in reality is no more *'you'* than these ShimmerField replications. I must say," the old man continued, with grudging admiration, "access to their optical technology is one of the few incontestable benefits of our encounter with the Halyan't'a."

"We could have shared so much more."

She relaxed against him, couldn't help herself, there was something about Manuel Cobri's natural strength that reduced her own to putty. He touched her neck with his lips, right at the junction where it joined the shoulder, tension creating the smallest of hollows for the kiss that sent tingles all the way to her toes.

"Is that why you wear their necklace?" he asked.

"I found it out, I thought it was your desire."

He shook his head. "The clone is a limited variant on your template, Nicole," he said, "configured along attributes that specifically appeal to my son." The way he said the word "son," he might as well have been referring to the family pet, one that was affectionally tolerated but which ultimately had proved a lasting disappointment. "But by the same token, much the same happens to all of us in so-called 'real life.' You are not the woman you thought you'd be, in part because of your association with me."

"That was my free choice. You manipulated the clone's genetic structure to make her the way she is."

"She's happy, she'll always be happy. She's doing what she was born to do."

"And I walked away from what I was."

"To twist an old phrase, my dear—better to rule in Heaven than slave in Hell."

"Easy to say when you're the boss."

"Nothing lasts forever," he said with a chuckle. And she looked suddenly from father to daughter, struck by the same ever-assessing gaze, the turn to the mouth as though they

were party to the ultimate cosmic joke that no one else
would ever get, and she found herself tumbling back through
the scrap file of her memory, one image in particular flying up
into her face, ghostly winds keeping it enticingly, infuriatingly
out of reach as she grabbed for it, the night of the Halyan't'a
reception, her conversation with Manuel.

"Son of a bitch," she breathed, amazed that it had taken
her so long to make the connection when the evidence
was going down on Alex on the sofa, the poor sales rep
looking around anxiously for someone to give her leave to
go, desperately afraid she'd be called on to join in.

"A perfect description for my brother," said Amelia, offering
Nicole the same look of command she found so irresistible in
Manuel. And, to the older woman's surprise, striking a similar
chord.

She turned away, clutching arms about herself, taking some
big strides, stopping in her tracks, as much without a clue of
where to go, what to do, as the sales rep on the level below.
Lost and trapped. Her head was pounding and she put the
heels of her hands to her eyes, wondering why she was
bothering, better by far to let it explode, embrace oblivion
and be done with this. And she laughed, more cackle really,
spiced with an edge of hysteria, because Manuel could simply
use the cell samples he had on file to build himself a newer,
more amenable version. As he himself had told her, so long,
long ago: "Keep trying 'til you get it right."

The air around her seemed to be changing, colors growing
brighter, the differentiation between them—and lights and
shadows as well—growing sharper. The very sunlight seemed
alive, full of glittery sparkles. She tucked her hands into the
sleeves of her robe, absently scratching at skin that was
becoming unbearably itchy, gasping in surprise at the sharp
touch of her nails, and then disbelief when she pulled them
free and found them looking more like claws. The hair on
her forearms was growing thicker before her eyes, a sleek,
rich pelt of russet fur—slightly thicker but much finer to the
touch than its human counterpart, covering her from head to
toe—streaked with dramatic indigo patterns. She could tell
from the weight on her scalp that her hair had grown longer,
thickening into a noble mane. Humanoid still, human—in any
Terrestrial sense of the term—no longer. Hal in form, as she'd
seen herself during the *chn'chywa* ceremony with Matai. And

more so in mind than she could remember being.

A cry caught her attention, the sight of her teenage self her eye, and blind fury sent her hurling across the room, landing on the back of the couch and stiff-arming the clone off Alex's idiot-grinning body. The girl yiped as she bounced on her backside, upset rather than afraid, not even aware she was in danger as Nicole's claws swept back and forth across her face, turning it into a bloody ruin in the same instant she claimed the clone's life. Casting the body aside, the taste of blood making her insatiable for more, she rounded on Alex— to find him sitting with open arms and open pants, the grin on his face a pale reflection of what she'd seen in Manuel and Amelia, everything about him no more than a flawed copy of those two originals. And deep within his eyes, belying the dumb-show facade he put on for the world and most especially his family, the awareness of what he was and how he'd been shortchanged, a sick despair that yearned for nothing so much as release. Her hand twitched, eager to grant his wish, Hal emotions pushing her to him even as her mind—the part of her that too late was grabbing desperate hold of her humanity—tried to hold herself back, and she sprang . . .

. . . crashing to her knees, baring teeth as fiery bands cinched tight around her breast, barely able to pull in a breath, letting it out almost immediately as a hoarse animal cry that toppled her forehead to the dirt, as though she was prostrating herself in prayer. She panted, exhaustion leaving her on the edge of consciousness, wanting more than anything to collapse, something inside her refusing to allow it. She'd never known such pain in her head, couldn't help the tears or the whimpers that complemented them; this was agony that made even the act of thinking unendurable, much less the slightest move. She had nothing in memory to equate it to, and precious little in imagination, this was all-encompassing, all-devouring, eagerly consuming every facet of her being.

Gingerly, she pushed herself up, to take stock of her surroundings. She was on dirt, in the midst of a vast flatness that stretched to darkness on each side of her, with a strangely forlorn splash of lights up ahead. The air was bitter, but her jacket offered some protection. Fumbling a little, she zipped it closed, brushing fingertips lightly across the raised silver

badge emblazoned on its left breast. She was wearing her Marshal's uniform. She hazarded a glance over her shoulder and
way off in the distance saw the sprawling, fun-fair light show
of the North Field ramp. There seemed to be a lot of activity,
scarlet strobe flashes marking the speedy progress of security
vehicles through the still and silent base. They were clearly
looking for someone and the thought struck her idly, *Is it me?*

The pain was easing, allowing her slightly fuller breaths, so
that she no longer felt quite like she was suffocating. She figured she'd try for her feet, but when she placed her right hand
down as a brace, she realized to her amazement that she was
holding a gun. Standard side arm, a Beretta 9mm automatic,
and she could tell from the weight—even though she broke
open the clip for confirmation—that it was fully loaded. A
round had been chambered. It was double-action, so all she
needed do to fire was snap off the safety and pull the trigger.

She couldn't remember how she got here, but that was
hardly surprising since her head seemed jumble-crammed with
images and memories that made not the slightest lick of sense.
A dogfight between a Stiletto and herself in a Mustang-Deuce?
The Stiletto was Alex's pet project, the combat drone that
nearly knocked her down the day she arrived at Edwards, and
the Mustang-Deuce had been the first and brightest triumph of
Charles Russell's first term, when the President won his spurs—
at least with the professional flying officers—by coming down
to Edwards and talking to the test pilots directly about this
much-touted weapons system, hearing firsthand their complaints and then acting on them by canceling the project.

And the rest? Layer upon layer, a porous sandwich of memory
whose bits all leaked together, one running into another, blurring
and losing precise definition even as they seemed to fix themselves permanently onto her psychic landscape, like weeds in
the somewhat rambly garden of her Self.

"Were they real?" she asked herself aloud, just to hear the
sound of her voice, a sensation that took her out of mind and
thoughts.

And she thrilled at the sensation of Manuel Cobri's arms,
only the face that went with the gesture was Amelia's, and
Nicole's features sagged as though she'd been punched at both
the feelings born of those memories and their intensity. But
if dreams, something imposed on her, was this an extension
of them, another fantasy? And she looked down at her hand,

pulling up the sleeve to bare the arm, making sure her own skin was underneath and not Halyan't'a fur. If illusion—"Has to be," she raged, "*has* to be!"—it was the best she'd ever experienced, bar none, a seamless imposition of the "what if" reality on an order she suspected surpassed that of the Halyan't'a holography system she'd experienced on *Range Guide*. And if *that* was the case, she couldn't trust anything— not the environment around her, not her instincts, not her very thoughts. Everything was subject to manipulation, even the fact that she was sitting here, in the middle of the desert, analyzing the mess.

She stood swaying at the crest of an infinitely self-perpetuating Moebius Loop, about to send herself 'round and 'round the roller-coaster course forever, trying in vain to find a way loose from this logic trap. For all she knew, that was what was intended of her. Better, regardless of risk, to take physical action.

Standing was an adventure that paled beside the taking of her first step. Actually, the step was an outgrowth of the stand, since she started toppling the moment she went fully vertical and automatically thrust out a leg to catch herself, then the other leg to keep on going. Her muscles were weak and ropy, doing their work mostly out of habit and that under vehement protest. She did a sloppy pivot, throwing a glance towards her street—way off in the distance, eyes too tired, head too achy to focus the details—before continuing on to the South Field Complex. The only answer that made sense was that she'd run the whole way. Until, in fact, she'd dropped.

Most of her voluntary bodily systems weren't operating anywhere near par, she wasn't even aware of the taxi light until she ran into it, hammering her left hip into the stanchion and pitching full length on the concrete, losing her gun as she fell. Injury added to insult, since she came up with a bloody nose and lip, but at least—paradoxically—the fall slightly cleared her muzzy-headedness.

The only reason for her being here was Alex. It wasn't simply where he worked; he spent more time here than at home. But what did that mean, her rushing over? Did she mean to offer help or do him harm? And if help, against what?

Too many questions, no way to get her answers on the ramp.

The hangar was darker inside than the night without, impossibly huge yet filled nonetheless with the sleek, powerful shapes of the Hal and NASA shuttles. Nicole made her way through the door and flattened against the wall, thankful for the black uniform that helped make her a shadow within shadows. All seemed peaceful, just as it should be. That only made her all the more nervous.

Alex's labs were out the far exit, but she knew she couldn't cross the floor without making noise. There was too much equipment, too little illumination, she was sure to run into something. She had no real choice but to take the long way 'round, and use the corridors where the security lamps would light her way.

But as she turned to go, the decision was made for her by a sharp cry—echoing in memory with the shrieks she'd heard outside the bar—and she cast caution to the winds. Now, her fatigue actually worked in her favor, limiting her speed and allowing her a few split seconds to evade any obstacle. It wasn't pretty but she managed to make the crossing with only a couple of collisions, and those only minor sideswipes, bulling her way through the door, shoulder as battering ram, gun held ready in a two-handed shooter's grip. The hall was empty, but sounds of a fierce struggle came from around a corner—as she'd feared, Cobri's lab.

"Alex," she bellowed, surprising herself with the force of her cry, bursting through his door ready to shoot, praying it wouldn't have to be at him, only to have the quandary taken out of her hands along with the gun as a muscular shape slammed into her, bouncing her hard off the wall. She lost her footing, which fortunately dropped her beneath the follow-up blow, and kicked clumsily forward in a tackle to try to bring her assailant down. She might as well have been trying to wrestle a tank; the muscles beneath her grasp were like corded iron, their speed and power defied description. A forearm like a sledgehammer came down on her back, breaking her grip, and this time there was no evading the knee that added a black eye to her bloody nose and left her sprawled and logy in a corner.

Another shape reared up from the chaos, a baseball bat connecting with Nicole's foe. It had to have hurt, had to have done damage, Nicole herself couldn't help wincing in sympathetic pain of a blow that certainly would have shattered her own bones. But the smaller, blockier shape simply rolled with the impact, sideswiping a fist that had much the same effect on the figure with the bat. Nicole caught a glimpse of him as he was spun away, Alex Cobri, looking a lot better than he had any right to given the ferocity and raw strength of his assailant.

That attacker went after him, and Nicole attempted a flying tackle, only to be plucked off the other's back and body-slammed down onto a table, an elbow punching into her solar plexus to drive every pascal of air from her lungs and leave her diaphragm momentarily paralyzed, terrified that she would never again draw another breath.

In all the confusion, someone came up with her gun and its muzzle flash blinded her, the raw sound of its discharge bursting in her ears as the trigger was pulled again and again, bullets spraying through the room, until the fifteen-shell clip was empty. She thought she heard a cry but she was hanging on to the rags and tatters of an awareness that was shredding in her grasp, so much so she had no idea whether or not the cry was even hers. All she wanted was to breathe, nothing else mattered, nothing else was possible. There was an eerie unreality to the silence as the echo of the shots faded, in no small measure because she was mostly deaf, every sound coming from the bottom of some infinite well. She tried to call out, but her voice remained locked in her head, her mouth working like a fish's yanked into the air, wondering where the life-sustaining water had gone.

Oxygen starvation was painting violent smears of red across her vision, events around her happening in a sort of strobo-scopic stop motion. She registered Alex—recognition that it was Alex with the gun, thankful to see him okay—looming like a Brobdingnagian giant over her, only to have him some-how instantaneously transport himself to the far side of the room. Belatedly, it dawned on her that he was leaving. The shock had begun to wear off, the tightness easing around her belly, and she used her first breath to tell him to stop, not to go—such a wasted effort, considering she barely heard the words herself, hadn't a hope of reaching him—tried as well to catch him, rolling herself off the edge of the table, letting loose a heartfelt "OW" as she crashed to the floor. She pushed as hard as she could, pitted the full force of her will—all her stubborn strength—against a body that simply wasn't up to the demands. And could only watch in helpless frustration as the door closed behind him.

· eleven

KYMRI'S FACE SWAM hazily into view.

"Haejmin cas'c!tai!" she cried in Hal, the words flowing in a fast cascade, "Miserable, lying, deceitful *bastard*!"

"Lieutenant," Sallinger now, backed by Arsenio Rachiim, in no mood to put up with the slightest back-flare from anyone.

She shoved herself to her feet, fury allowing her to ignore her body's myriad, insistent complaints, facing off against the Hal Commander, who returned her outrage with an almost preternatural calm.

"I had my orders, Shavrin's-Child," he explained quietly in his own language.

"Is that an explanation," she snapped, "or an excuse?"

"Lieutenant!"

She looked to Sallinger, eyes focusing ever so slightly, as though seeing him for the first time.

"I believe, Colonel," she said in English, and had to work some saliva into her mouth and then swallow, to ease the rawness left in her throat by her Hal outburst. "We may have been deliberately misled."

"Tell me."

"Kymri was identified as the Hal Speaker among his team. I think it was someone else, their cyber tech, Matai."

"Kymri?"

"Regrettably, Sallinger-Commander . . ."

"God *damn* it!" And Sallinger rounded on the Provost Marshal. "Rachiim, I want the room cleared."

"Colonel, my people—!"

, "Your investigation can wait. You stay, the rest out, *now!*"

And when the order had been obeyed—leaving only Nicole, Kymri, Sallinger, and Rachiim in the moderate ruin of Alex Cobri's lab—he fixed Nicole with a look she'd never seen from him before. That reminded her of what he'd been before turning to the Flight Test Center, an ace pilot who was equally at home dog-fighting in the highest reaches of the stratosphere or killing tanks down on the deck, with combat commands in both fields. A man who'd spent the first ten years of his Air Force career pretty much constantly at war.

"You have the floor, Lieutenant."

"To be honest, Colonel, I haven't the faintest idea of how I know. I'm not altogether sure what I'm doing here. It was day, I was in my quarters—the living room, I think—and then it was the middle of the night and I'm flap-doodling across the ramp out there, packing my side arm."

"You and Matai sat on your couch for the better part of seven hours," Arsenio Rachiim said. "Asleep. Your orders, Ms. Shea, were that we wait and watch what develops. You were under constant remote scan; at the slightest hint of trouble, we were ready to go in and get you. Our assessment was, there was minimal risk.

"Along around sunset, you crossed into your bedroom and picked up a necklace from your dresser, which you then proceeded to put on." Her hand went to her throat and, sure enough, found the familiar shape of the *fireheart* choker. She hadn't realized it was there. "Then you lay on the bed."

"That's it?"

"At twenty-thirteen hours, Matai made a break, smashing her way through the French doors leading out to your rear patio. Units responded, encountered the, *uhm*, lady in what they described as a berserker frenzy. Attempts to restrain her failed and she escaped towards the dry lake. Pursuit was initiated, unsuccessfully. By the time someone thought to check on you . . ."

"I was long gone, too. With a side arm."

She looked sideways towards Kymri, glaring at him under

lowered, slitted lids, flying now almost totally on instinct, evaluating thoughts and words only as they flashed free. "Let me guess," she hazarded, "your team's coming to Edwards is only marginally related to the shuttle program, am I right?" She turned back towards Sallinger. "We were dueling one morning—Kymri's insistence, akin to shadowboxing, a means of keeping his combat instincts honed—he implied knowledge of the attempt made on my life on the Moon. Even before, now that I think of it, we realized ourselves one had been made."

"The precise phrase, Sallinger-Commander," Kymri said calmly, "was that 'questions have been raised.' Which they were. Which I am told aided Maguire-Marshal in her inquiries."

"Sir, there's more," Nicole pressed on, ignoring the hurts that were beginning to make their presence felt. "He said, 'Concern has been expressed.' When I tried to tell him that wasn't necessary, he told me I didn't understand. 'You are of Shavrin's House,' he said, 'bonded by Oath and Blood.' And finally, that the Hal look after their own."

"He's Shavrin's Deputy Commander, Lieutenant, that makes sense."

"Colonel, don't you see? Command structures among the Hal are familial in nature. Units like *Range Guide* function almost as extended families. When I accepted Shavrin's adoption of me"—*Christ Almighty*, she thought, *if I'd only kept my mouth shut*—"I joined that family."

"So they're looking out for you. Just as we're doing."

"She adopted me as her daughter. God, I wish I'd realized what this might mean at the start." Her inner voice counterpointing futilely, *Cut some slack, girl, how could you be expected to?* "As far as the Hal are concerned—and especially the crew of *Range Guide*—I'm the next best thing to Shavrin herself, with the same claim, if not to their obedience, then to their loyalty."

"Kymri?" Sallinger asked.

"Truth, my friend."

"I'm not sure anymore those are terms with much meaning between us. Truth or friendship."

"Our dual brief was to explore the feasibility of merging our shuttle programs, and to protect Shea-Pilot. Of those two, the second had, and has, absolute priority. We did not inform you because we did not know then whom to trust. And because, quite frankly, this was considered *our* business. Affairs of crew do not go beyond the hull."

"She's not your 'crew.' She's *human*, dammit!"

"*Ahhh*, Sallinger-Commander, but what is defined by the term? Among ourselves, we of the People are what you call 'human.' And this"—he lightly tapped a claw-tip against the major gem of the *fireheart* necklace—"is but an external representation of what lies here." And the same finger touched her breastbone, over her heart.

"Still doesn't explain what happened," Rachiim rumbled in annoyance, "there or here."

"It was Matai then, in here?"

"We're hoping, Ms. Shea, you can tell us."

"Someone was here, fighting Alex tooth and claw." She shook her head in mingled wonderment-dismay at how naturally the Hal phrase fell from her lips, even in her native tongue.

"Ferociously strong, knew how to fight, no weapons that I could see. By the same token, though, I only got a decent look at Alex. Fighter was pretty tough, shrugged off a direct hit from a baseball bat."

"There were reports of shots."

She nodded. "My side arm. I lost it in the struggle, Alex popped the whole box, fifteen rounds, as fast as he could pull the trigger. I don't think he had a clue of a target, he was just laying cover fire for his escape. I don't think he hit anything, either, except maybe the walls."

She hammered knuckles gently against her forehead, slumped with exhaustion but determined this time to hold her own.

"Nothing on your scans?" Nicole asked Rachiim.

"Totally clean all across the spectrum."

"No." She shook her head. "No. No. A carrier wave, something. Masked. Cloaked. *Damn*," she hissed, exasperation fast giving way to raw fury, "why can't I remember the details? Dreams, dammit, scenarios. Things were happening that were totally . . ." Her voice trailed off. "Virtually," she said, comprehension dawning. "Real."

"Virtually real," Sallinger echoed. "Virtual Reality?"

"In a house video system," Rachiim scoffed, "no way. And especially not one screened from detection."

"I'm sorry, Colonel," Nicole told him, "I've seen him work. There isn't a computer on this base he can't get in to and play like a virtuoso. He's got remote programming routines that can reconfigure an entire system without his having to lay a physical hand on it."

"That's right," Sallinger said quietly, extending Nicole's lines of thought, "he's cutting edge, isn't he?" He picked a component off one of the worktables. "I hardly ever see his requisitions, they mostly go through Cobri, Associates, but they were never for whole items. Only the pieces."

"Nothing ever satisfied him," Nicole said. "He always figured he could do better, so he built his own equipment. Hardware and software."

"I don't even want to consider the implications of this."

Sallinger rubbed his jaw, then slid his hand around to the back of his neck. "Not without something irrefutably substantial. Arsenio, go over the lab, Ms. Shea's quarters, and Mr. Cobri's. Determine whether or not a Virtual Reality generator has been piggybacked into her house systems. If possible, isolate its scenarios. Give me those answers, we'll proceed accordingly."

"Yes, sir."

"Be discreet. Impress that upon your investigators. No talk and no mistakes. We're not out on a limb here, it's a goddamn twig, about as dry as can be. I don't want to think about what's waiting if it breaks."

"Why not simply *ask* him, sir?"

Sallinger was about to snap a caustic reply, then realized Nicole's condition. "My apologies, Lieutenant. I forgot, you don't know what's happened. We'd love to ask him, and Matai. And we will. Assuming we find them."

Oh, Alex, she thought, *what have you done?* And then, unbidden and quite the surprise, bouncing in from the left field of her subconscious, *What's been done to you?*

"Lieutenant," Sallinger went on, "you're on call at Colonel Rachiim's convenience. Anyone else wants to query you about this situation—without exception, I don't care who they are or what kind of badge or authority they flash—you refer them to him. Other than that, you're back in a blue suit and working for me and Uncle Sugar."

"I'd like to help, boss. I'm still on the bull's-eye."

"This isn't the time or place for amateurs, no matter how well meaning or motivated or even gifted. Do your job, Nicole. Let Arsenio and his people—and Maguire and the Secret Service and

the FBI and I'm sure"—with a pointed glare towards Kymri—
"their Hal counterparts—do theirs. That's an order.

"In the meanwhile, I get to pass this mess on up the line.
They're going to just love it at the Pentagon. Not to mention
the White House. Find Matai, Arsenio," he said from the
doorway, "find Cobri. The sooner, the better."

"Colonel," Nicole called before he could leave, "I should
in all fairness tell you that it's Marshal Maguire's considered
opinion that I not be allowed out of the atmosphere. Given
the capability and reach of this assassin, she can't guarantee
the integrity of any system I interface with, whether under my
own identity or some facsimile. I think the last couple of days
have proved the same about systems Earthside."

"She tell you that?"

"In about so many words, sir. I'm sure she's making a
formal report through channels, to Dr. Elias and General Canfield. But if I'm working the XSR, that'll involve flying. I
don't know if that's safe."

"I appreciate your forthrightness, Lieutenant, but I'll be the
judge of that. For the present, you'll remain on flight status.
Kymri, would you please escort her over to the hospital, make
sure that she's all right, and then that she gets some rest.
Assuming the best, we'll put her back to proper work in the
morning."

As he finished speaking, Nicole fumbled in her pocket,
handing over a computer diskette in its carry case.

"The report you wanted, sir," she said, managing a moderately awful attempt to stand at attention, "uprated performance
comparisons on the test vehicles."

He made a face as he plucked it from her grasp, an expression
she couldn't read. Behind him, however, Arsenio Rachiim
barely stifled a guffaw.

"You're a smart ass, Shea," Sallinger growled.

"I do as I'm asked, sir, best I can."

The Colonel took her by the shoulders and gently but firmly
shoved her into Kymri's arms, telling him to "get her the hell
out of here."

"You could have told me," Nicole said hours later to Kymri
as she climbed the boarding ladder ahead of him and into the
Halyan't'a shuttle. It was as functional as its NASA counterpart, yet containing as well an element of sleek beauty and

comfort that was evident at first glance. The air held the faintest twist of spice that she'd smelled for the first time on the command deck of *Range Guide*, months—a lifetime—ago.

"There was no need for you to know. And"—a reluctant admission, responding to her expression of dismay—"we felt a better job could be done."

"So much, as they say, for that idea."

"You are angry."

"Because I feel helpless. Everyone wants to take care of me, and they end up wrapping me so tightly I can hardly breathe, much less make a move to save myself." She leaned stiffly against a bulkhead, wishing for a way to make herself comfortable. Hard to do when your body's become a patchwork quilt of bandages and bruises. Nothing was broken, no lasting damage—or so the attending medic in the base Emergency Room cheerily told her amid his gleefully thorough poking and prodding—merely a few days extraordinary inconvenience. Sallinger's enthusiasm notwithstanding, it would be the better part of a week before she'd be cleared for duty and almost the full month before being allowed to fly. The doc didn't see any real need for her to stay the night, although he wanted to see her again within the next couple of days. Her own quarters were out of the question, but when Kymri suggested she take refuge with the Hal she insisted on returning to the hangar instead.

"You sure we're safe here?" she asked, the deliberate humor in her voice masking an undertone that was completely serious.

"The internals are isolated," he replied, "the external interfaces—both data and power—shut down. If anywhere can be made so, this is it."

"Terrific. I feel safer already."

"Shall I rig one of the bunking spaces?"

"If you don't mind, I'd rather sit awhile up on the flight deck."

"As you wish."

"Kymri . . ."

"I am sorry your friend is dead, Shea-Pilot. But if she was killed, what better way than in defense of a comrade?"

"Yeah, we have the same saying. The comfort's as cold now as it was when it applied to Paolo DaCuhna."

"She will be avenged. As was he."

"You really think so?"

"You believe otherwise?"

"How the *hell* did you learn such good English?" she demanded in wonderment. "I mean, to con us all this time?" But even as she spoke, she saw him bemused by the colloquial reference. "Deceive, I guess, would be the closest analogy. Though it's a harsher word than I'd intend."

"The language, it was not so hard. The usage, the nuances, an altogether different proposition. But you are wrong, Shea-Pilot, deception is a most appropriate description. I break no claws over it. And given the circumstances, I suspect I would do much the same again. As for the rest, Matai and I were always linked by a two-way transceiver. She heard my conversations and could relay an instantaneous analysis, together with the best response."

"No one ever twigged, *er*, noticed."

"As your Provost Marshal told you, we are alien to your species. You have little way of knowing which gestures are pure idiosyncrasy and which are meaningful."

"That cuts both ways, I would hope."

"More so without a Speaker, yes. Because our bonds are, as you said, familial, much of our lives are defined by obligation. The duty that transcends the responsibilities of the work place. Obligation to ship, to Commander, to crew. A mutually all-embracing network that can be both strength and, regrettably, weakness."

He "shrugged," tagging the gesture with a dismayed rumble from deep in his chest prompted, Nicole suspected, by a look back over some unpleasant memories. "Because to live is to be, in ways small and large, fallible." A grin now, more in his eyes than on his lips. "What both our species would call being 'only human.' "

"I don't want your obligations, Kymri."

"Then stay on the ground. Use Cobri's toys to craft in fantasy what is beyond reality's grasp. Sit upstairs in my chair—which, by rights, is as much yours, for the work you have done and the skill you possess—and tell yourself you do the right thing. Accept that is as far as you will ever go. Return to your island, Nicole. You will want for nothing. For all you have done we would see to that, even were you not Shavrin's child."

"You're being hard, Kymri."

"The primary function of a First. Shavrin rules the ship, *I* run it."

There was a scent of anger about him, echoed by movements that came in quick, precise staccatos, instead of the usual sleek legato that was the Hal's hallmark. She remembered the pattern from *Range Guide*, just before the battle; he didn't want to be here, felt his proper place was in the field, hunting his missing crewmate. But for all the years of service shared with Matai, Nicole was more important. That should have made her feel proud; instead, completely the opposite. Because not so many layers down was a wary touch of fear.

"Speakers are genetically engineered to be sympatico with their subjects." He acknowledged her statement with a flare of the nostrils. "Was Matai configured for the shuttle program or for me?"

"Both."

"But I had priority."

"Yes."

"Using the genetic material you must have taken aboard *Range Guide*, when you tested me and Ben Ciari to see which of us could handle the metamorph virus?"

"Yes."

"So what does that mean exactly? I assume she was bred for the job, trained for it, that's how it works, yes?"

"She was of that heritage. An aspect of her Self resonated with yours. She could think like you, react like you. It gave us insight."

"Was the *chn'chywa* part of it?"

"A form of bonding. Of shifting that which was abstract and empiric onto a more primal and instinctively physical plane. Making it in a sense more real."

"Imprinting, we call it," amazed to hear her voice so calm even when inside she was shrieking like a banshee, blood turning to fire as it rushed from a heart beating far too fast.

"Something happened there," she said.

"The initial . . . image we had of you did not match what Matai perceived during the ceremony."

"I was damaged goods, *huh*?"

"Old wounds had not healed. A determination had to be made whether or not they ever would."

"What *right*—?"

"Shavrin's-Child," he rumbled, using what was for him the equivalent of Sallinger's command voice, stopping her tantrum stillborn, "more than our lives hang in the balance. Shavrin, on *instinct*, bequeathed you an honor granted none other among her family. At her house, you sit by her, before her hearth. Such"—and he groped for the proper word, hobbled by the need for an absolutely precise meaning in a language that had no appropriate analog—"recognition must only go to one who is worthy."

"And on the second look, I didn't fit the bill?"

He didn't understand and she decided not to bother explaining.

"So for all intents and purposes, Matai is me."

"A part of her."

"More than a part, I suspect." He was shaking his great head, in the gesture he'd picked up since his arrival. "Trust me in this, Kym, I know whereof I speak. It happened on *Range Guide*, to Ben. Remember, after your Speaker—the one who was supposed to waltz you through First Contact with us—got killed, you found yourselves forced to choose between me and Ben for a replacement. He got the nod because of the concern I'd prove so resonant to the virus that I'd never find my way back to being human again. Even so, over time, Ciari's human personality was almost completely subsumed. Towards the end, when we were in the firefight with the Wolfpack, on their base asteroid, he was Hal. I mean, he knew he was Ben Ciari and that he was a United States Marshal—he knew that he was Terran and human—it didn't matter. In every way that counted—thought processes, emotions, instincts—he was Hal."

"So?"

"Whatever happened in my house triggered a psychotic response in both of us. Simultaneously. Matai got all the attention because she's the more physically dynamic of the two of us. If I'd had her capabilities, I'd have hit Alex's lab same as her, matching stride for stride. Blow for blow. Except I collapsed on the way." She grimaced. "Perhaps that was what broke me loose from my trance state? Maybe she hasn't been so lucky."

"Plausible. That being the case, you might have some insight into her movements. I will inform Rachiim-Colonel."

"I'm not the key. It's whatever was done to us."

"Why weren't you killed," the Hal mused, "as Deschanel-Officer was?"

"I'm going upstairs, okay?"

Without another word, she turned her back on him, hauling herself up the short ladder to the flight deck and halfway into the left-hand seat before she realized what she was doing. She almost climbed right back out, then flopped the rest of the way with a snort that turned instantly into a sharp groan as various sore spots all over her registered their protests. Regardless of what any scrap of paper said, much less the bureaucrats behind it, this was where she belonged.

The field of vision was spectacular, far better than in any Terrestrial shuttle—albeit, at the moment, presenting a view only of the blank-featured wall of the hangar. The transparency reached from above her head to below the level of her seat, creating a panoramic vista that swept forward from behind her chair all the way around the flight deck and down the other side. The panel was the same basic mix of flatscreen displays and analog instruments, switches filling a control hump between the twin pilot seats and a ceiling panel over-head. Sidestick controllers as well, instead of the central yoke still favored at NASA.

She slumped deep into her seat, struggling to find even a marginally comfortable position. *Amazing*, she grumbled silently, *how two races so fundamentally similar in physique can't come up with compatible furniture; amazing*, she went on without a break, *to find two races so fundamentally similar period! Especially first time out the box.* She smiled now. *And Einstein said God doesn't play dice with the Universe, hah!*

She pulled her jacket tight around her, tucking her hands up under her armpits, as though her arms were a kind of seat belt, crossing her chest to lock her into place. Started playing a tune inside her head, lifting her legs to tap her feet on the panel in time to the phantom melody, staring away at nothing, unaware she was crying even as tears flowed freely down her cheeks.

The air lay hushed about her with supernal stillness, as though the world itself still slept. Sitting on her heels atop the tier of rock that marked the crest of the ridge, she had a superb view of the valley below. She knew she should be moving, but didn't really care. The moment was too special, too precious to cast aside. And in a way, fitting with her purpose here.

With easy grace, she straightened to her full height, a faint tremble rippling the soft fur of her body as it responded to the predawn chill. Wasn't that cold, but she was dressed more for day, sleeveless pullover tucked into shorts, a pair of well-worn running boots, sweatbands on wrists, kerchiefs around forehead and neck, her thick mane tied back into a rough braid. Wasn't as clean or fresh as when she'd started, but that was partly the point of the pilgrimage.

She shifted her pack, settling it more comfortably on her shoulders, placing hands at the base of her spine and rolling her shoulders back, in the same motion extending her arms full length, before reaching them upward to stretch her body the same way. Followed by a gusting sigh of relief as she relaxed back to normal. A moment's further pause to look and listen, savoring the hint of salt sea off the ocean, but it was still too early in the day for anything animal to be stirring. And then she kicked herself off the rock and on down the moderate slope, slit pupils dilated almost to a full circle in the grey predawn half-light, enabling her to pick her way around any obstacles.

It was the turning of the year, and the valley floor was simmering with muted color as the flowers began their final transition. Later in the morning, responding to the sun's light and warmth, that simmer would burst into glorious flame, a magnificent palette of reds and golds that the slightest breeze would send into rippling motion, creating the illusion that the ground itself was burning.

An age-old path ran across the valley and she picked up speed as she reached it, thankful she wouldn't have to disturb the natural order of the field. Smiling with the realization that she wasn't the first to come this way, nor to have such a response. A mist overlay the horizon, masking her destination against the last shadows of night. She pushed a bit harder, confident there was time but wanting to give herself as much of a cushion as possible. This wasn't necessary. Fewer of the community made the trek these days and those that did often went by air to the high places of their respective Houses. Her schedule was no less jammed, her responsibilities no less demanding, she could have rationalized such a decision herself with hardly any effort. But that defeated the whole purpose of coming.

When a friend dies—and especially when that friend is a comrade in arms—their memory should be honored. And that moment should have as much meaning as the life now lost.

The track led her to the base of the bluff, a hulking plug of primordial stone thrust up in the last spurt of mountain building—the same that had created the Haukon Chain farther along the coast, whose peaks gave the sunward horizon its jagged-toothed appearance—and there, it ended. She would have to make her own way to the top. Sadly, that posed no great challenge, for she'd made the same trip not so long ago. Although then, she'd come from the beach and she hadn't really been here in any corporeal sense, but in the Vision Chamber aboard *Range Guide*, the Memorial Mount no more than a holographic illusion generated by the starship's computers.

On that occasion, the full surviving complement of crew had been present. This would be done by her alone.

She attacked the slope with a wildly careless abandon, as though this was some sort of personal test, refusing to slow her pace even as the way grew increasingly steep. Until, with the horizon banded pale to herald the rising sun, she cleared the crest and reached the top. There was a breeze now, a rich mingling of the scents of land and sea, and off in the middle distance she could hear the faint coughs of *J!kst'nai* as they gathered for breakfast along the rock reef, the shrill skirl of birds overhead hoping for a dive-and-grab at whatever carrion remained, in happy disregard that their approach made them just as fair game for the amphibious predators. Farther out to sea, she saw a familiar spurt-sparkle of spray as a *Polidan* shook itself to the surface, trailing its huge tentacles lazily through the water, splashing them in a random sequence that made sense only to them.

She could only spare a glance at the sights, as she cast off her pack and strode to the Herald Chime. At the seaward end of the bluff stood a head-high cairn that had originally been the roughest hewn of stone, worn down over the ages into a smooth, wind-polished pillar. She took the mallet, sounded the chime once to announce her presence to the Spirits. Then, in a quick, economical sequence of moves, she stripped off her clothes, picked and pulled at her braid until her hair hung loose, proceeding as she did towards the cairn to stand finally facing it, an arm's length distant. She held her arms slightly out from her body, palms towards the cairn, as she offered her greeting and stated her purpose. A heartbeat's pause, and she reversed direction, bringing her arms up level with her shoulders, facing the sun just as it broke the line of the horizon, the first brilliant dot of light searing itself into her eyes and brain. And her head went back, lips baring teeth in a snarl more appropriate to the prairie hunters of her evolutionary ancestors than the technological sophisticates they'd become, and she cried the name of her fallen friend, offering a portion of her own self and spirit to stand by what remained of the other in memory.

The mood splintered with the sound of a pair of hands in a slow, sarcastic clap, and she spun into a combat crouch to find Alex Cobri perched atop the cairn, cross-legged like Alice's caterpillar.

"Very nice," he said with a tone that matched his physical attitude, bored and contemptuous, and she couldn't help the hackles that rose in fury along the line of her neck.

"You don't belong here," she said, the English words emerging stretched and twisted around a Hal tongue that found them awkwardly uncomfortable.

"And you do?" he countered. And she looked askance at him, because the voice itself didn't fit the man at all. Higher and sharper than she was used to hearing from him, with a more rounded European pronunciation to the vowels.

"What's that supposed to mean?"

"You want to play with Pussies, dear heart," he said, "you really should look the part." And tossed a cat collar to her feet. There was a long silver leash attached, the far end held in one of his hands.

With a hiss, she grabbed at the cord and pulled, hard as she could, wanting to see his face bleed when it hit the rock—but it was she who fell, and when her sight settled she found herself on all fours, hands and knees, the collar buckled snugly about her throat.

"So tell me," he said with a laugh, unfolding from his seat and sauntering towards her, reeling in the leash along the way to keep it taut, "what do you do for an encore?"

And her eyes popped wide, body spasming just this side of totally out of control as she fought free of the confining embrace of the chair, almost colliding with Kymri as he came up from below. At the sight of him, the faintest brush of his fingers as he reached out for her, she pitched herself back, uttering a soundless cry of pain as she struck the main instrument panel. Even recognizing—at last—where she was, who was with her, it still required a conscious effort not to flinch, or snarl defiance, when his hands went out to her again, to catch her firmly by the upper arms.

She was breathing so hard, she couldn't speak at first, lungs pumping fit to burst, and she wondered absurdly how she looked to him, since she was still trying to sort in her own mind whether she was human or Hal.

"You were sleeping," he said.

"Dreaming." So inadequate a word, and nightmare so banal an alternative, to describe what she'd just endured.

"What is wrong?" he demanded, mixing a little of the starship officer in with the concerned friend, offering his strength to bolster hers. She was looking around wildly, making scrabbling motions with her hands. *Like some trapped and helpless little mouse,* she thought disturbingly, *or a baby, desperately trying to make sense of its reality. Hell, simply trying to determine what reality itself* is!

"I was on s'N'dare," she said at last, "the Memorial Mount. I issued the Sunrise Call in Simone's name. Alex Cobri was there, he was laughing at me." Her voice trailed off, her own expression mostly disbelief, with an undertone that shifted violently between stark horror and an even more fierce, and growing, rage. "Only I don't think it was wholly Alex, the mannerisms were his but pushed to an extreme I've never seen from him, especially with me. And the voice . . .

"I was Hal," she said flatly in English, deliberately breaking her train of thought as she realized she'd been speaking that Alien language. "The same duality of being that occurred during the Memorial we held on *Range Guide.* And in the ceremony with Matai. How is that possible, Kymri?" An accusatory tone slipping in. "You gave the Speaker virus to Ben Ciari, I was left out of it, isn't that right?"

"You miss the obvious, Shea-Pilot," he replied smoothly. "Might not this be simply another manifestation of Cobri's Virtual Reality trap? That would explain his presence."

And, she thought, *his actions.*

"A flashback, you mean?" He cocked a head, blanking on the reference, as she did when she sought through her own mental vocabulary for the Hal equivalent. "A residue," she tried, "of the original imprinting. Buried deep—or maybe not so deep—in the subconscious, slips out when you least expect it. In response to some equally subconscious cue."

"A possibility."

"But how could he know so much?"

"Why should he need to? If he stages the basic scenario, you possess all the memory data required to complete the process. The strength of these illusions seems to be that they speak to some aspect of your personality, they strike a resonant chord that prompts you to participate willingly. So, within yourself, you do whatever is necessary to fully realize the tapestry he has laid out . . ."

"While at the same time, ignoring—rationalizing—any false notes that might disturb it."

He nodded, another quirk he'd adopted.

"So is this real? Or am I still sprawled on my couch or my bed or whatever, lost in Alex's funhouse?"

"Any answer is suspect. As is any action."

"Neat little trap. If I assume it's real, I make no attempt to break loose of the fantasy. I might as well be dead. Do the reverse, embrace it as Virtual when it isn't, figuring I can recycle myself out of any disaster, I could be in for a very fatal surprise. Son of a *bitch*!"

"Agreed."

"It was a nice dream," she said, gently but firmly pulling loose from his grip, turning to separate herself a couple of steps from him, all really that was possible on the flight deck, "until that twist at the end. Question is, could it happen again?"

"Possible."

"Anything we can do about it?"

"I am no PsiTech, Shea-Pilot." The Hal equivalent of a shrink. "The best among us—anywhere in near-Earth space— to fulfill such a function, especially where you specifically are concerned . . ."

"Was Matai."

"Hence her assignment as your primary watcher. Forgive me, but had you not woken yourself I would have done so. Your presence is required by the Rachiim-Colonel."

"News?"

"None. Which is why he wishes to speak with you. Neither a sign of Matai nor Cobri. Both have gone to ground most effectively."

"How can I help?"

"In terms of Cobri, I know not. Evidently, his sire has engaged private trackers who bear the brunt of the responsibility for him. Although Rachiim-Colonel is to be notified immediately upon their success."

"You don't sound too terribly confident."

"They are reputable individuals, so I am told, competent craftspeople in their profession—as are Rachiim-Colonel's subordinates. But their agenda is not his, nor their primary loyalty to him. As for Matai, I believe he hopes by seeking what you would do under similar circumstances, he might divine some sense of her intentions."

"Because she's so much me?" A nod. "You don't sound hopeful there, either."

"You are better than you know. And Matai . . ."

"If she weren't top line, she wouldn't be one of Shavrin's crew, yes?"

"Our Lady inspires excellence."

"What're you saying then, Matai isn't likely to be found?"

"Barring fate's fortune . . ."

"Which neither of us believe in, though we'll always take what we can get."

"She will reveal herself at a time and place of her own choosing."

"She's an Alien, Kymri."

"All the more challenge to overcome. By nature, Shea-Pilot, we are hunters, and warriors. We thrive on adversity. And every contest is played to win."

Three weeks passed in a flash. By the time Nicole realized time was passing, it was gone. At Manuel Cobri's request, Grace Kinsella had been slotted as his personal spaceplane pilot, an assignment only slightly less prestigious, and in career terms far more potentially beneficial, than getting the left seat on Air Force One. He showed at the base the day he made the decision, although officially it bore the imprimatur of the Air Force Chief of Staff and the Secretary of Defense, and was his usual charming self. So much so that Nicole was hard put to reconcile the man before her with the grasping megalomaniac portrayed by Al Maguire. He left a fair-sized slot on his calendar for her, but surprisingly talked not a bit about his children. It was a charming afternoon, and one of the finest high teas Nicole had ever eaten, topping the best served by the old London hotels and made all the more delightful because it was a picnic.

That night she dreamed of a house on a hill, with herself being pressed as a figure into a Tiffany *favrile* stained-glass window.

The details didn't last past breakfast, only a vague after-taste of disquiet that she chalked up to the stress of over-work. She was back on the job within a couple of days of the incident, simply because the press of business wouldn't allow her to stay away any longer. Kinsella's departure only increased the burden, and the pressure, bearing the brunt of the work on the Hal/NASA Integrated Shuttle. Which in turn was coming down to a decision to mate Terrestrial systems and power plants to a Hal lifting body. She and Kymri and Tscadi were together almost constantly—especially since Nicole had shifted out of her own quarters and into theirs, in hopes the Hal computer network established there would prove more than the assassin could crack. And when more senior officers at the Test Center grumbled about a Second Lieutenant shouldering that kind of responsibility, Sallinger simply pointed to the data streams and flow charts, eloquent proof that she was doing the job as well as anyone and better than most. Nicole didn't know about the gripes—save for the good-natured ones that came at her on the flight line or in the maintenance bays, when she was getting down and dirty with Ray Castaneda's grunts, tearing equipment apart to put it back together better—and wouldn't have cared if she had, she was having too much fun. Working harder than she had since the Moon and loving every minute.

It would have been a perfect existence, but for the shadow cast by Arsenio Rachiim. As Colonel Sallinger had predicted, there was indeed hell to pay, and the news rumbled up and down the chain of command—all the way to the Oval Office—like an avalanche, gathering power and awful momentum as it went, giving rise to more than a little speculation that Sallinger himself would pay for Simone's death (not to mention the subsequent fireworks) with his job. For all the melodramatic anticipation, however, the initial repercussions seemed eerily low-key. Very little changed, in fact, at least as far as the Flight Test Center itself was concerned. New faces working out of the Provost Marshal's office. Some very high-tech snoopers operating from their own secure complex out in the boonies. Heightened security around the Cobri compound. That was pretty much all.

Those first days Nicole seemed to live in Rachiim's office, engaged in a seemingly relaxed conversation with him and some federal bods that, in retrospect, she realized was the most intensive and sophisticated interrogation she'd ever undergone. It frightened her, really, how much information they were able to charm out of her, and how easily she gave it up to them.

Not that it was any use. Both Alex and Matai remained missing. One obvious line of investigation was the string of distractions that kept Sallinger occupied while Simone was being killed. Rachiim pursued it for all he was worth, but no link could be found between them, no common denominator. Each appeared perfectly plausible and aboveboard, both on the surface and as deep beneath as the Provost Marshal was able to dig. Until at last he had no choice but to give up.

Beyond answering Rachiim's questions, whenever he or his people thought of them, Nicole was strictly and specifically ordered not to get further involved. Truth to tell, she didn't mind all that much; she was still a long way from sorting out her feelings about Alex—hell, about all three Cobris— and what had happened and wanted no part of him until she had.

But when she saw Amy's name on the transport request for the next available flight to the East Coast, she couldn't resist. She was going that way herself, for her Wings Club speech and attendant festivities. No Cobri aircraft were on-station, which was the reason for the request for Air Force equipment, and a quiet word in Ray Castaneda's ear made sure that the only wings available were Nicole's.

She was just finishing the preflight when smallish footsteps on concrete alerted her to her passenger's arrival. Amy walked with her head high and back straight, striding across the ramp like she owned it—and given the state of Cobri finances compared to the fed, Nicole had to concede it probably wouldn't be too terribly long before she did—tucked snugly into a pressure suit that was a junior version of the one Nicole herself wore. Helmet in one hand, suitcase in the other, a face in the middle trying its best to lock into an expressionless mask.

"Good evening, Miss Cobri," Nicole greeted her cheerily, taking the case, Amy offering a split second's resistance before she let go—an instinctive impulse, Nicole recognized, never to give up anything that's yours; but was it a *kid's* impulse—and tucking it behind the crew seats, next to her own.

She did shake off Nicole's hand, refusing help up the boarding ladder, preferring to make the climb unaided, and Nicole
let Ray Castaneda—who was acting as Crew Chief—couple
her into her seat, while Nicole finished the "walk-around."

"You won't get away with this," Amy grumbled as Nicole
climbed into the left-hand seat.

"Put your gloves on, and your helmet, please," Nicole
replied, asking Ray to give an assist, Amy having
sense enough to not give him a hard time as he did. "You read me,
Amy?" she asked when he was done, checking the intercom
through her headset.

"Fine." Determined to be the sourest voice ever.

"Get away with what?"

"This." Amy waved an arm to indicate the cramped confines
of the cockpit.

Nicole's voice was the verbal equivalent of wide-eyed inno-
cence. "You asked for a lift."

"Pretty darn amazing, *huh*"—Amy clearly didn't buy it in
the slightest—"how all the executive transports came off the
line right after."

"Life's like that sometimes." *Surprise, little girl*—Nicole
grinned inside—*you don't have this base wired quite as tightly
as you thought*. "But if you'd rather, I'm sure transportation
can be arranged to LAX in time for a morning flight to New
York."

"I don't fly commercial."

"Wait for one of your own, then."

"I can't."

Nicole shrugged, and went back to her cockpit checklist,
while Ray came around to her side of the aircraft and hooked
her into place, securing her four-point restraints and plugging
atmosphere and com lines into her suit. Then it was Nicole's
turn for gloves and, once she'd removed and stowed the headset, helmet.

"Look on the bright side," she told Amy, "we'll be on the
ground in time for breakfast."

"Can we just go, please?"

Nicole held up her right hand, index finger extended, made
a spinning motion, Ray donning a pair of headphones—nicknamed "Mouse Ears," which covered and protected the entire
ear, an absolute essential working this close to high-performance

engines—and spoke through the attached mike to the rest of his crew.

The Corsair had self-start capability, and as soon as Ray confirmed that his people were clear, Nicole flicked switches in quick sequence, cycling main power—to give life to the Internals and Avionics—and then, once the Ignition Menu was on-screen, primed her fans and kicked them to life. She heard a modest *pop* from aft, felt the faintest of trembles through the sleek airframe, echoed in detail on the power-plant status display, clear indications that she had turnover, and the left-hand turbofan was beginning to spin. As soon as it was up to speed, she did the same with the starboard engine, and in less than a minute had both her engines idling happily in the green. Last set of checks, including her navigational entries in both the LORAN and autopilot, confirmed by Ray, before he gave her a farewell pat on the top of the helmet and descended to the ramp, proceeding out in front of the aircraft with a pair of red-lit wands to guide her off the ramp.

"Edwards Clearance, Corsair One-Niner," Nicole called after she braked at the ramp entrance, "ready to go as filed to New York. Final destination: Westchester County Airport, White Plains, New York."

"Corsair One-Niner, Edwards Clearance. Approved as filed. Contact Ground, one-one-niner-point-seven."

"Having fun, so far?" Nicole asked Amy as she followed the Tower's directions out to the active. When she heard no reply, she went on pleasantly, "Okay, there's no movie and you can't walk around, but the sandwiches are as gourmet as they get and we'll be there in a couple of hours, tops. Get home fast enough, you might even have time for a decent snooze before sunrise. Is that service, or what?"

"Only if you drop me at my door."

"Well, if you insist, I suppose I can always eject you as we fly over Staten Island."

"You *wouldn't*!"

Nicole grinned, as nicely as she could, looking all the way around to make sure Amy could see as she patted the girl on the knee. "No, I wouldn't," she said. "But if you want, I can drop you at Newark, that'd save you a little time."

"No big deal. Newark, White Plains, all pretty much the same to the helicopter."

They reached the runway and Nicole pivoted the Corsair into

position. This was a beast who was just as much a beauty, an aircraft that was as impressive to look at as it was a murderous delight to fly. Reminiscent of the old General Dynamics F-111 fighter-bomber—in that it had been designed for twin engines, side-by-side crew seating, and, most importantly, variable geometry "swing" wings—it was primarily an attack bomber that could function with surprising effectiveness as a dogfighter. With the wings rolled out to full extension, as they were now, the Corsair could fly at private aviation speeds right down to the deck, so low and slow that all it would take to land the plane would be the dropping of its landing gear and the faintest touch of flaps. Yet, those same wings faired back snug against the fuselage, creating a sleek, clean arrowhead shape, and its engines pushed to the line, it could better the speed of sound at functional altitudes that topped thirty thousand meters.

"Edwards Tower, Corsair One-Niner, in position and holding." Last item was to close and lock the canopy.

"Corsair, Edwards Tower, cleared for takeoff."

"One-Niner. All strapped in?" she said to Amy, getting a grunt in reply. "Snug as a bug?" she asked.

And got a look in return that said plainly, *just get on with it, okay?!*

"Close your faceplate," she told her, and did the same with her own.

Nicole settled herself in her seat, gave a last tug on her own straps to make sure they fit, then pressed hard with both feet on the brakes, all the way to the floor, at the same time advancing the twin throttles forward on their sidestick. No tremor anymore, as the tail vanes of the huge engines cycled to intensify and focus the thrust even as more and more power was applied. The shrill banshee shriek of the turbofans dropped a seeming score of octaves into a basso profundo rumble that shook the air like a barrage of massed assault cannons, the Corsair actively straining against its brakes, struggling to burst loose and fly. Still, Nicole refused to let go.

A press of a button on the throttles kicked in the afterburners, raw fuel injecting into the combustion chambers of both engines to generate even more thrust. The airframe started to groan in protest, Amy's helmet shifting as the head within looked back and forth, her hands making unconscious little scrabbling motions on her armrests. She didn't quite understand the noise, only that she didn't like it.

At last, Nicole released the brakes. This was a modification of the production run aircraft, fitted with a new set of engines that created a thrust-to-mass ratio comparable to that of the old F-15 Eagles; in essence, they produced greater thrust—even without afterburner—than the plane had weight. Which, under these circumstances, turned it into the functional equivalent of a rocket.

Almost before Amy could register that they were moving, they were off the ground, and then the child cried out as Nicole pulled back on her flight control sidestick and stood the Corsair on its tail. It was a stunt the Eagles made famous, being the only aircraft of their day that could take off from a standing start and go into an accelerating vertical climb without traveling any farther horizontally than the end of the runway. The Corsair had the same capability, its wings pulling back automatically to supersonic configuration, pulsed diamond cones of blue fire forming a double line against the darkness to mark its passage as Nicole sent it streaking for the heavens.

Suit bladders compensated for the G-forces, Nicole sparing a fast glance at her HUD for a medical update on Amy, allowing a small grin when she saw the kid was coping.

As they passed twenty kay, Nicole eased off on the throttle, and as they approached thirty, she swung the Corsair up and over onto its back, so that they were flying inverted, upside down. The same view the shuttle had from orbit. After making sure the verniers were active—this high into the stratosphere, normal control surfaces lost effective function, so this model of the Corsair was equipped with attitude control jets, same as any spacecraft, to take up the slack—she pivoted them back to normal, configuring the power plant for normal cruise (under tonight's conditions, 1500 kilometers per hour) and engaging the autopilot. Then, with the computers running the show and the entire status board registering nominal function, she indulged in an overhead stretch, finger-tapping a drum roll on the canopy above her.

"Pretty pleased with yourself, *huh*?" groused Amelia from the right seat.

Nicole shrugged good-humoredly. "Didn't break any records. But the old bus"—she gave the panel an appreciative pat—"didn't do too badly."

"You think it's fun, right, showing off like that."

"Gets the juices flowing, that's a fact."

"You're worse than boys with football."

"Maybe." The Moon was a little past one o'clock, rising above their line of flight, a shade shy of full. Clouds were bulking along the western slope of the Rockies and the light transformed them into a silver still-life, broken here and there by patches of absolute shadow, where the view was clear down to the ground. And if she looked hard, amid those random voids, there were the faintest splashes of light, from towns and the very occasional small city. Sometimes, from this height, on such a night, it was surprisingly easy to convince herself she was looking up and not down, that the darkness was that of outer space and the lights, stars.

Then, with a small sigh, she turned her eyes skyward, towards the real thing.

"Word is, this is as close now as you'll ever get."

"Yup," Nicole said.

"Doesn't bother you?"

Nicole decided that didn't deserve a response, and busied herself with a brief systems status review.

"Does it bother you?" she asked Amy eventually.

The girl tried to shrug, a wasted effort inside her bulky pressure suit, strapped tight into her seat.

"I don't understand," the girl said at last.

"What?"

"You. Him." Meaning Alex. "Well, him," and there was a color to those two words that told Nicole that Amy understood her big brother completely. "You, I don't understand," she said finally, a major concession that the girl herself seemed a trifle surprised to admit.

And after a while, when Nicole didn't offer a reply—because Amy was the kind of person who perceived any pause as a vacuum that had to be filled—she went on, "All you want to do is lock yourself in a box for the rest of your life, except"—the edge of a sneer slipping into her voice—"for the occasional day trip down to some rock or other, where all you're really doing is exchanging one box for another. I mean, think about it, Nicole. Three days to reach the Moon, a whole *year* to fly round-trip to Pluto—that was the profile of your *Wanderer* mission, right? And what are you doing along the way? Basically, you're in prison. Is that fun, or what?"

Nicole had to smile, because the girl—especially from her

perspective—had a point. More than once in training, and afterward, she found herself asking many of the same questions: Is this what she truly wanted out of life? Were the rewards, if any, worth the sacrifice? That was part of the training, encouraged—often demanded—by the teaching staff, particularly once she'd made the shift into NASA. They wanted people who wanted to be there, because no one else had even a chance of surviving.

Amy was still talking. "You can't go anywhere," she said disgustedly, "can't do much of anything. There's no walking out for a breath of fresh air, no such thing as fresh air. No more sailing, no more flying, only the occasional visits to the home folks, until you probably become as much an alien to them as the Pussies. You're giving up all the things that make being alive worth the effort, it doesn't make any sense."

"No," Nicole said softly, her transmitter deliberately turned off, "I suppose not."

There was a small flash on a subordinate display, alerting her to an incoming message, and when she shifted it center screen she saw it was a SIGMET—a significant meteorological notification.

"What's up?" Amy asked.

"Nothing to concern us, there's some heavy weather brewing at the Cape," meaning Cape Canaveral, midway down Florida's Atlantic coast, after a century still NASA's primary launch facility. "They're shutting down manned ops for the next forty-eight to seventy-two hours."

"But we'll be all right?" A new shading to her voice, the vaguest hint of anxiety.

"This high, there's nothing can touch us. And the approach forecast to White Plains looks to be about as good as they get. Clear sky, minimal wind, piece of cake."

Amy grunted.

"You don't sound relieved."

Another attempt at a shrug.

"How was the concert?"

"Hmnh?"

"The one you called me about, the other week."

"Oh. Didn't go."

"Sorry I missed it."

"Yeah." Which meant, *like hell, you did.*

"And the downhill? In all the confusion, I never got a chance to ask. And afterward, you weren't around."

"Papa got a little hyper, wanted me to stay close to home."

"And the race?"

"Bagged it."

"Too bad. Some other time perhaps."

"Like I told you, it was no big deal."

"Any word about Alex?"

"Ask your pal with the badge."

"Colonel Rachiim?"

"Maguire."

She didn't need to see Amy's face to guess the expression, the kid probably figured she'd just scored a major point, popping one of Nicole's bigger secrets.

"You don't like Alex much."

"What is this, twenty questions?"

"Wasn't a question, statement of fact."

"Sibling rivalry."

"Hardly. That contest, I think, ended the day you were born."

"Hey what?"

"Rivalry indicates competition for the same goal. Hard to compete when the game's already over."

"You're spinning air."

"Rambling, actually. Comes pretty naturally up here. Especially in the old days, when they made the trip at half the speed and half the altitude. And then there was Lindbergh. Thirty-eight hours, was it, New York to Paris? A Scram suborbital can do it in as many minutes. I went to Sutherland and back in as long a time."

"Progress," Amy said, the fidget in her voice echoing the one in her body (or at least as much of one as her restraints allowed her).

"You said some pretty nasty things in those messages."

"Truth hurts. And what are you anyway, my conscience?"

"You feel the need for one?"

"Puh-*lease*! That flaw is such a poser. Such a sophisticate." Her tone was an acid mix of amused contempt. "Use his criteria, *I'm* knowledgeable. Which isn't to say he hasn't ever *done* anything"—and now the contempt was leavened with a vicious mockery—"it all depends on how you define the operating terms."

"What are you talking about?"

"You've seen his toys. You couldn't drag him in here where I'm sitting if his life depended on it. But he's probably logged more vacuum hours than any hotshot SkyBoy at Edwards. Probably has more deep-space experience than most in NASA. Go anywhere, do anything, his little heart desires. All the thrills and chills, none of the danger. Or cost.

"And the lady's *always* satisfied."

"That's enough, Amy."

"But I haven't even scratched the surface!" An appreciative giggle at the taste of forbidden fruit. "In Virtual, he can do *anything*. And, for that matter, anyone. Gal, guy, grown-up, kid, on top, on the bottom, solo, multitude, nice, nasty, animal, imaginary. He has one program for centaurs. Keyed under *Fantasia*. He can play any role."

"He sails, Amy. That's no fantasy."

"You're the first time he's taken that boat out in over a year. Done TransPacs in Virtual, though. Even has a cycle where he goes through the heart of a killer typhoon."

Nicole remembered. "You don't hold with that?"

"I'm here, aren't I?"

"But you don't see the sense in going farther."

"Like you? Astronaut Annie, blazing her trail through the heavens. Not a chance."

"No curiosity?" And she thought of the last three weeks, immersed with Kymri and Tscadi in their lives, learning more about the Hal than she had from a year's worth of briefing packs and tapes. And remembered her grandfather talking about a trip he'd made to Israel when he was in college, on his way home after two months working a kibbutz, chatting with some tourists, a synagogue from New Jersey, telling him how three weeks was more than enough time to see any country. Which made him laugh because in the time he'd been there he figured he'd just gotten to the point where the locals were starting to trust him enough to accept him. And she thought about Amy's words of a few minutes ago, about her becoming an alien among her own kind.

"Curiosity like that is for people who've nothing better to do. Or who can't fit into society."

"Maybe both apply to me?"

"For all the good that'll do you anymore."

"Touché."

"I didn't mean to hurt." And Nicole, to her surprise, realized the girl meant exactly that. "You know, Daddy likes you."

"He's a charming man."

"Told me once, you were the only person he'd met outside the family could give me a run for my money, what d'you think of that?"

"What do you?"

"Still working on it." With no doubt, Nicole knew, as to who would eventually end up on top. "Was she a friend, Nicole, that Secret Service agent who died?"

"She was growing into one."

"Pretty tough. You must be upset."

"Simone knew the risks."

"That's cold."

"Not yet, but I'm getting there."

"And you figure that's a good thing?"

"You expect me to roll over and die, just because someone says so? This isn't play, Amy. It isn't one of Alex's Virtual games, nor the tag Kymri and I run all over the Edwards ridges."

"I know that, I don't need any lecture."

Nicole saw the young trooper again, in her mind's eye, back on the wolfpack asteroid the crossbow bolt punch into his back, the body twisting under the powerful impact, the light leaving his eyes. Saw a twisting, different vision, herself sitting sprawled against a bulkhead where she'd drifted, a football-sized hole from Morgan's rifle blaster burned through the center of her chest, a death so quick and clean you'd think from her expression she was ready to leap up and continue the fight. Heard the metallic shriek of Paolo DaCuhna's radio melting as the blast flare of an antimatter detonation instantaneously vaporized his spacecraft. Remembered the hollow sickness deep in her belly as she watched helplessly while Harry Macon's aircraft disintegrated before her eyes into a puff ball of ceramic sparkles cooked from within by the dull fury of the elongated fireball formed by its exploding fuel. His sheer velocity smeared flame and wreckage for hundreds of meters across the sky before they began their tumbling descent to the desert better than ten kilometers below. Saw Simone Deschanel crumpled on a bed, the light doused from her eyes by a horror that left no external mark.

It could have been me, Nicole thought, *and someday it will.* But only partly believed it.

"You going to that stupid party?"

"Reception." A slightly threadbare smile as she made the automatic correction. "It's why I'm here."

"To shill for NASA."

"They invested a lot to put me into the sky, this is part of the payback."

"They kicked you out, too, why should you owe them anything?"

"I wear the uniform, Amy."

"Better you than me."

"What's best for you, then?"

"Blow 'em off. I mean to, though that's why Daddy called for me."

For a moment, Nicole was thrown, until she twigged that Amy's remark had nothing to do with her question.

"Just like that. A full complement of military and NASA brass, plus State, plus U.N.—not to mention the President."

"You don't want to be there."

"You offering an alternative?"

"We already played that scene. I don't ask twice."

Excuse me all to hell, Nicole thought, but said, "No matter. It isn't as if I have a choice."

"You don't want to be there," Amy repeated quietly, with no more emphasis than before, almost like a looped recording.

"Why? Is something going to happen?" Nicole asked jokingly.

But that was the last the girl said, and a look at the displays showed Nicole that she'd switched off her intercom and gone to sleep. If there was an answer, Nicole would have to find out the hard way.

═══ twelve ═══

THE ENTRANCE TO the hotel was jammed worse than a mid-town subway platform at rush hour, people clamoring for transport while taxis and limos vied for curb space, defying the best efforts of cops and traffic marshals to keep even a semblance of order. A mob scene made all the worse by the departure of the President, Secret Service holding everyone else in place until he was into his own Cadillac and away to the gala reception downtown.

Parents in tow, Nicole bulled her way to the street and flashed an ID at the nearest uniform. On command, a car appeared, complete with an NYPD blue-and-white up front and an unmarked federal cruiser as backup. But before they could enter, a local news crew popped into their way, cor-respondent and camera in Nicole's face, demanding her com-ment. Nicole spased, canceling her instinctive reaction to deck the man, once more grateful as her mother slipped smoothly into frame, to announce, taking full advantage of the fact this was a live telecast: "Twins, you'd better not be watching this. But if you are, *go to bed!*" And with a gracious smile—as the news crew found themselves body-checked between city police and a couple of no-nonsense feds—shoved her daughter through the open car door. The moment the three of them were inside, the procession shot away down the avenue, using lights and sirens to clear their path.

"I *am* impressed," said Conal, rearranging himself a trifle more decorously from the tangle on the back seat caused by their precipitate departure. "You have friends in high places?"

Nicole fought to repress a giggle, thinking that she had them in *very* high places, depending on what perspective you viewed the Moon, or the Universe beyond. But also had to shake her head.

"This isn't exactly for me," she explained, tongue-tied as usual around her parents, "as *me* per se. It's, *uhm*, a reflection of my status among the Halyan't'a."

"Status?" her mother asked, and the look in her eye was one Nicole remembered too well from the days when Siobhan had been a hell-on-wheels newspaperwoman. *A word*, she could hear her say, in the tone that meant some poor sod (could be some journalistic target, could just as easily be her own children, Nicole as first-born heading the list, Siobhan never played favorites) was about to get royally skewered, *and a half*.

"Well, position might be a better term."

"How much better?"

"To be honest, Mom, I'm not quite sure. A lot of this, I sort of seem to be discovering as I go along."

"That's not like you."

Nicole made a small, moderately helpless gesture, hating the way parents always managed to make children feel like kids, no matter how old, no matter how supposedly mature. And she reflexively touched the *fireheart* necklace, snug against the stand-up collar of her dress uniform. She hadn't planned on wearing it or the pendant earring, or accepting any of the perks that had shown up unexpectedly on her doorstep, until a seriously stressed woman from State who'd come along with them patiently explained the facts of protocol, in a tone that brooked neither discussion nor argument. Yes, Nicole was a Second Lieutenant in the United States Air Force. But she was also—and the Hal had been quite specifically forthright in this matter—a Primary of Shavrin's House, which made her a Very Important Personage indeed, and they wanted her treated as such.

"Christ," Nicole had cried in frustration, "it wasn't my idea."

"I appreciate your discomfiture, Lieutenant," the woman said, "believe me, it's shared by not a few of us at State. No one really—outside perhaps the Halyan't'a themselves—understands the ramifications of your adoption. On the other hand, we'd be fools not to use it to our advantage. If honoring your special status earns us some points with them, so be it. We're more than happy to oblige and so, I might add, will you be. Very happy. Consider it an order. Will that make this ordeal easier to endure?"

"What would be easiest would be not to be here at all."

"Life is tough, Lieutenant. Just make sure not to lose your glass slippers at the ball."

The reception was on the topmost floors of the Millennial Tower, itself—since the turn of the century, hence the name—the tallest building in Manhattan and one of the top five in the world, under the auspices of the Wings Club. Constructed on the site of the old World Trade Center, it topped the old Twin Towers by another hundred fifty meters, with a view of New York and the surrounding metropolitan area that, on a clear day (or better yet a clear night), could steal the breath of even the most jaded sightseer.

Nicole had been there earlier today, in the Club itself, to give her speech to the annual meeting of the International Society of Astronauts and accept—on behalf of the *Wanderer* crew—their Gold Medal for the successful First Contact with the Halyan't'a. The room had been jammed and when the presenter—none other than Cullen Lucas himself, NASA's Chief Administrator since Lord knew when and chief architect of the American InterStellar exploration program—had stepped away, leaving her all alone at the podium, she hadn't been sure she could even talk, much less plow through her text.

Many of the faces before her were familiar, some of them had been pictures on the wall over her bed since junior high, when she'd crystallized her desire to become an astronaut. Others she knew by reputation. They were her peers, but only she felt in the most technical sense, the way a brand-new cub reporter for the *New York Guardian* might consider himself towards Siobhan just before she packed up her two Pulitzers and quit. And she found herself wishing her mother could be here, to give the speech for her. Or her father, with the dry courtroom eloquence for which he was justly known.

And then, stumble-tongued and desperate, certain that hours had passed since she was abandoned on-stage (when in reality it wasn't more than a few seconds, unnoticed by anyone in the room save her), she found herself thinking of the people who weren't there. Harry Macon for one, Paolo DaCuhna for another, each in their own way reduced to ashes and memories, each partly responsible for putting her where she stood. Judith Canfield on the Moon and Ben Ciari, incalculably farther away—and the pang she felt thinking of him stabbed all the deeper because it wasn't so much that she missed the man but that she was jealous of where he was, somewhere she was starting to believe she'd never be allowed to go—and without realizing she was speaking aloud, words came to her.

"There's no point, really," she said, "in telling you the technical aspects of the mission, or the Contact itself. The reports are all on file, firsthand recollections, after-the-fact, objective analyses—you name it, it's there. In quintuplicate." Small laugh from the audience, since everyone present had a working knowledge of the federal bureaucracy. "For you all to peruse at your leisure, those few of you that is who haven't already done so.

"I remember as a kid reading how Neil Armstrong described the *Eagle* landing on the Moon. One of the things that stayed most strongly with him was the smell. Like gunpowder, was how he put it. That cordite residue left over when you fire a cap pistol. And I remember coming back in after my first Lunar excursion, sure enough there it was.

"The same applies to our exploration of the Hal starship *Range Guide*. We'd been poking about the better part of an hour, and what struck us all was how much like one of our ships it was. And we weren't sure, any of us, whether that was a good thing or not, because we were all thinking, extrapolating how we might feel if the situation were reversed and we maybe found strangers nosying about the innards of our ship. And the fact is, we human beings have never been all that hospitable to others of our own kind.

"Then, at last, on their flight deck—what the naval bods in NASA insist on calling the 'bridge'—we found out." So many emotions, running riot, totally out of control as she pivoted on Ciari's cue to face the assembled Hal, yet even though she was scared beyond all comprehension of the word, there wasn't a tremor to her body, a quaver to her voice. Whatever happened wouldn't be because she made a mistake. "All they could see of us," she continued, "were four figures in pressure suits, features hidden behind gold anodized visors. All they could tell of us were pretty much what we'd deduced of them from the pictographs we'd seen: bilateral, bipedal creatures with a central torso. So I decided we'd be better off giving them a sense of what we really were. We'd been scanning the atmosphere since boarding, we knew it was compatible and, as far as the sensors could tell, safe to breathe. Of course, that guarantee wasn't much good against bugs outside the sensors' data field and violating suit integrity was as much a danger to the Hal as us. But we had to break the ice somehow and the fact was, we were running out of air and had nowhere else to go. We either made friends pretty damn quick or we were as dead as our murdered crewmates. So, I popped my helmet.

"For Armstrong, the resonance was powder. For me, cinnamon. The kind of high-country tang to the air up in the Grand Tetons, or maybe the most northern Scottish highlands when the heather's in bloom. There was a moment, when Shavrin and I stood face-to-face, that defines what happened there and, I think, I hope, our reason for being as astronauts and explorers. She reached out to me, touching my face with her fingertips. Now"—and this time the laugh came from her, a hollowly amused chuckle—"that may not seem a major big deal to those who think solely in terms of human nails. But the Hal evolved from a far more overtly predatory line. Their nails are more like claws, even though they've pretty much grown out of the use of them as such. So here stands this Alien— with all the resonances that implies, good, bad, indifferent— painting a touch-portrait of me with a hand that looks like it could tear my face right off without the slightest effort or trouble. Yet I trusted her, as she did me when I removed my helmet. We at least knew something of what to expect from their air; the Hal had no such guarantees about us. Yet the need to reach out, to make a positive contact, to bring our two species together, that outweighed the fears we both brought to that moment. That meeting.

"Here we are, as President Russell has said, with our own house so torn and divided it's a miracle we're still around to talk about it. For all our technology, all our supposed maturity, we as a species still find it so easy to hate—people of other colors, other religions, other tribes—and to exercise that hate with casual murder. Now, suddenly, we're asked to put all that aside. To face outward from this world that's our home to a galaxy we now know beyond all shadow of a doubt is inhabited. Both by those who are willing to be our friends and others who may well become our enemies. We're asked as a species to adopt the fundamental reality that those of us who work and live beyond our atmosphere accept as a matter of course. That in space, there's no such thing as color or race or creed or even sex; all you can tell from a standard suit is that we've got five extremities—four major, one minor—grouped around a central trunk. It doesn't matter where a person comes from, only what they do once they're out there. You have to be accepted because you have to be trusted, because that mutual interdependence is the only thing—the *only* thing—that keeps us alive.

"Now—far in advance of even the most wildly fanciful time-table and *far* before we're even remotely prepared—we're at a crossroads. Stay the way we are and hope to muddle through. Or perhaps change as a race. Truly evolve, at long last. Folks used to say that what marked test pilots and astronauts—what made the Yeagers and the Shepards and the Canfields different from the rest of us mere mortals—was that they, that *we,* ladies and gentlemen, possessed the 'Right Stuff.' Well, I submit that it's time to pull the rest of the world up to our level. To realize that Earth is just as much a spacecraft as anything you or I have flown, or are ever likely to fly. And that if we are to simply survive, much less prosper, in a Space where we are no longer alone, we *all* need to discover that 'Right Stuff' within ourselves. We need to embrace the change that's coming, no matter how terrified it makes us.

"In effect, the baby's on its feet. It can either start walking or forever stay close to the ground where it's nice and safe and spend the rest of its life in a crawl. The risk is that we'll fall. The reward, that once we walk, we can begin to run."

She was preaching to the converted, they gave her a standing ovation. And for the bulk of the afternoon, she ragged her throat raw fielding questions from every quarter, on every aspect of the mission, actually enjoying herself even though she was running mostly on autopilot, her mind months and miles removed, picking over the very things she'd been ordered by Arsenio Rachiim to leave alone. Listening to the conversations rippling around her, offering subtle guidance when needed, to

steer talk in the directions most useful to her, hoping to find
the answers Al Maguire needed.

Mostly, as she herself had known, it came down to personnel. Three countries in the world officially trained astronauts:
the United States, the Russian Soviet Republic, and Japan.
And only the first two actually built and operated spacecraft.
Partly a matter of expertise, mostly one of cost; no one else
could—or really wanted to (national pride for once giving way
to practicality)—afford it.

Yet somehow the Wolfpack Nicole destroyed had managed
to field a force of a dozen vessels and the support facilities
to sustain them. No country could do it, doubtful even for a
consortium such as the European NonFederation. No matter
how the equation was structured, it always resolved the same:
a force, an entity, with the fiscal resources of a country and
none of the physical restraints, analogous to the expatriate
government of Kuwait fifty-odd years back, driven from their
homeland yet still operating a worldwide financial empire they
used to tear the heart out of the Iraqi economy. Except that a
project like this would beggar even those legendary wizards.
Which left only one possibility, possessing the required capabilities, as Al Maguire had told her.

Cobri.

But suspecting wasn't knowing, no matter how blindingly
precise and seemingly inexorable the logic. And knowing
wasn't proof. And proof meant nothing when the exercise
of it meant going up against the man who carried humanity
to the stars.

"Do you ever relax?" Siobhan asked as they stepped onto the
Sky Terrace, with its window walls creating a matte-painting
panorama of the glittering city beyond.

Nicole offered a bemused shrug, with an expression to match.
"I'm relaxed," she said.

"You may think so, my dear," her mother said, compan-
ionably tucking her arm into the crook of Nicole's elbow
and pulling her gently close, "but I'd say you're as far from
it as can be. You know you never go anywhere anymore
without looking about the room. What's so funny?" Nicole
was chuckling.

"Think about it, Mom. Where I used to work, the rooms
keep in the air. Lose your seal, lose your air, you have to be
alert for the slightest anomaly."

"Always?"

And Nicole thought back over the weeks to the initial attempt on her life, that supposed "accident."

"You never know," she said, "when you're going to be bitten on the butt. Like the Boy Scouts, it's always best to 'be prepared.' "

"It must be hard, never allowing yourself to let your guard down."

You should know, Nicole thought, followed by a ruefully chiding: *Nasty, girl,* nasty; *it may be true but does she deserve that?* And covered herself, buying some time and space, by going to collect a round of drinks.

This was a totally different crowd from the afternoon, and considerably less sympathetic. As she made her way to and fro, she heard comments she'd have loved to respond to, about the Hal and Russell's policies, but she passed on by without a word, beyond the occasional "Excuse me," and "I beg your pardon." No one seemed to recognize her—all they saw was the uniform and the rank, which both instantly boxed her and dismissed her as some high-up's dogsbody, too inconsequential to be worth noticing—for which she was grateful. She was too busy thinking about what her mother had said and realizing she'd been a little too hasty in her offhand dismissal of it. Yes, every astronaut learned—and carried with them the rest of their life—a degree of extra alertness to their local environment, but how she was feeling, what she realized she'd been doing pretty much the whole day, was far more than that. This was something Ben Ciari had taught her, what he called a "hunting phase." She'd been on the balls of her feet—literally and figuratively—since landing this morning, body strung with a light tension that left it poised to move on command; in essence, she was ready for a fight.

And when she met her father's eyes, handing him his glass, she saw he'd recognized that in her, and her mother as well.

"You never liked crowds," Con noted casually, and Nicole shook her head as she sipped her seltzer, wishing it were tequila.

"You're the ones who thrive on center stage," she said. "I could never get past all the poses and attitudes people feel compelled to strike."

"Including yourself?"

She replied to her mother's gently pointed aside with a nod of the head and a raise of her glass.

"That's a stance, Nicole," Siobhan went on, "which betokens a certain intolerance. These aren't 'your' type of people, therefore they aren't worthy of your interest."

"That's not fair, Mother."

"You don't particularly like them."

"Some of them, there isn't that much *to* like."

"Granted. That's also no reason to automatically write them off."

"Who needs the grief?"

"Knowledge, young lady. How can you even begin to deal with the Halyan't'a"—and Nicole's eyes widened a fraction at her mother's perfect pronunciation—"when you can't deal with your own species? What are you going to do when you find yourself flying with someone who doesn't quite fit your standards of what is or is not acceptable?"

"I'm grounded, Mom. Chances are I'll never be allowed out even as a passenger. So neither figures to be much of an issue, okay?"

"Nicole, stop it, you're behaving like a child."

"What's the situation," her father interjected smoothly, as though the other conversation hadn't taken place, deliberately catching Nicole before she could storm away, "with you and the Cobris?"

Nicole shrugged. "I know Manuel and the two kids, I work with Alex, there's an alert out for him over an incident we had back at Edwards last month. About which," she added hurriedly, to forestall a question from her mother, "I'm not at liberty to speak. Why?"

"Had some calls, your mother, too," he said with a smile, "marginally discreet inquiries about a relationship between you and the boy."

"Christ, are you serious?"

"One of the advantages of the cloistered life," this from Siobhan, "it's so easy to remain blissfully oblivious of the outside world."

"Also one of the advantages of being a Cobri," Con again. "You don't want something printed, it isn't. Nobody has the resources to risk a serious fight."

Nicole rounded on him. "That's not true, I've seen lots of stories over the years."

"Yes and no," Siobhan said. "Manuel is no dummy, quite the opposite. The way to play the game is to preserve the illusion of openness. Raise no objection to the general run of articles—some pro, some con, some even tough as nails—but on some very specific topics let it be known without the slightest doubt that a breach of confidentiality will have the most severe repercussions. One case in particular, when he and his wife split, I think it was about a year after Alex's birth—and bear in mind, a quarter century ago he wasn't anywhere near the level of raw power and influence he possesses today—a London paper dug out what was reputed to be some very nasty gossip, complete with allegations of genetic engineering, possibly illicit nanotechnology. Story never ran. Within a year, two tops, the paper was history. Reporter who dug up the material just retired from a very cushy sinecure on the Cobri payroll."

"They bought him off?"

"Him, yes. The editor, yes. The paper's owner, prince to pauper in thirty months. I think his kids live on trash they scavenge from the Delhi Dumps."

"You're kidding."

"Apocryphal, but true. Even my alma mater, that paragon of truth—and I don't mean that anywhere near as nastily as it sounds, forgive me—the *Guardian*, has backed off on a couple of Cobri stories. It isn't that we don't run what we know, we don't even try to find out."

"Find out what? What's off-limits?"

"I've been thinking, while we talked. Not the old man's personal life—or rather, I should say, not his *public* personal life. I actually think he enjoys seeing himself in print squiring all these leggy, lissome creatures. And for all I know, gives them as good a time as I'm sure he gets. Interesting though, that not one of his companions has even gone public with an account of their time together. More interesting that not even the Asian or EuroScandal rags have made an offer for one. They'll take on the British Royals without a second thought, but not Manuel. His work and play, they're fair game. His private life, no. Not the kids', either. Which is what spared you, when you and Alex flew off to San Diego. Otherwise, you'd have been all over the networks gossip hour, plus tabloid front pages and magazine covers. Alex got you a free ride."

"Money talks, I guess. D'you know anything about that gossip, back when Alex was born, about his mother?"

"She won't talk, either. Whatever Manuel did to her, he made it worth her while."

"Out of the kindness of his heart, maybe?"

"He has no heart," Con said flatly, "and kindness is merely a means to an end, tactical or strategic as circumstances require."

"That's cold."

"I've dealt with him, on a professional basis. Nothing nasty, nothing brutal"—he shook his head—"just the clearest possible sense of a man who knows exactly what he wants and what he's prepared to do to achieve it. He analyzes a situation, and arrives at what he believes is a fair resolution, and executes it. And to give the devil his due, more often than not that settlement is quite equitable, he sees no need to actively cheat people. He also has virtually no comprehension of being refused. He'll give you his price, or his terms, or whatever—with some room to maneuver on the margins, for form's sake—and that's that. Take it, period. No 'leave it' involved. He simply will not take—hell, won't even conceive of—no for an answer."

Con smiled. "He got the usual description once of being a steel hand in a steel glove, but I thought then—and I'm convinced of it now—that misses the point. The remark always forgets he's got two hands. One's velvet, the other's a spiked mace."

"Absolute power."

"Corrupting absolutely, as Lord Acton said? I'm not sure. He's worked for what he's got, that tempers a person. He knows the value people place on things, which is why his first instinct is to pay a fair price. Try to bad-mouth him, though, or cross him on a deal, and you won't know what hit you . . ."

"Which is what," Siobhan interjected, "happened to the English publisher I mentioned. A most injudicious attempt at blackmail. He wanted the status that went with owning the *Times* and demanded Cobri's backing for the takeover."

"But got destroyed instead. You still haven't answered my question, Mom, about Alex's mother."

"No," Siobhan said flatly. "I haven't."

"What about Amy's?"

No response at all.

"The references are oblique, and few-and-far-between, but at least Alex's mom has some. About Amy, though"—Nicole shook her head—"not a word."

"With good reason." But what that was, Nicole never learned, because as Siobhan spoke, Nicole pivoted so violently she almost decked a passing waiter, her father catching the poor girl as she struggled not to lose her tray of glasses.

Nicole tried to fob off the incident with a wan smile of apology but at the same time her gaze was flashing about the room, taking in the space and the crowd in a sequence of distinct sectors, a moment for each, not knowing in the slightest what she was looking for, only that something had triggered alarms at the base of her brain.

"Nikki?" her father asked, touching her elbow to regain her attention.

She nodded acknowledgment but didn't spare him a glance until she was satisfied the room was clean.

"Sorry about that," was what she thought she said then, what she meant to say, and believed she had—until she saw totally dumbfounded expressions on both parents' faces.

"I beg your pardon," Siobhan said. "Nicole, why are you speaking Hal?"

"Don't be ridiculous," she started to say, then stopped, took a slow, deep, deliberate breath, and spoke the words again, this time making sure they were in English. "Son of a bitch," she breathed when she was finished.

"That was interesting," noted her father.

Nicole lay fingers across the crest of her forehead, over her left eye, as though trying to divine the state of her consciousness by simple touch, then slid them down to cover her mouth.

"How did I do that"—still in the same soft and wondering voice—"I mean, I know the language—a bit, anyway—but a reflex like that . . ."

"A residue perhaps," Con suggested, offering a drink, which she refused with a shake of the head, "from that genetic virus the Halyan't'a used on *Range Guide*?"

She shook her head more emphatically. "Dad, they never gave me the virus."

Without warning, that same flash struck again, a sense of wrongness, the world going fluid within and without, perspectives disorienting wildly so that she didn't recognize anything or anyone she was looking at. Coming back to herself to find her parents a reflexive couple of steps removed.

Nicole looked towards Siobhan, not trusting herself to speak. "You growled, Nicole," her mother said softly.

"Jesus," under her breath. Then, a little louder, "I've got to get out of here."

"Things can't be that serious."

"Mom, the President's coming. If I'm having some sort of"—she groped for an appropriate term, then hurried on without—"episodes, I can't afford to be in his vicinity. I've no guarantee they're benign, or they won't get worse."

"There's a Hal coming," Con said, before they could leave, "perhaps he can help?"

"Kymri!"

"Greetings, Shea-Pilot. I have yet to meet your parents. Whose presence does me honor."

"Our pleasure," Con responded with equal formality.

"We need to talk," Nicole said, taking him by the arm, "something's happening."

"As you wish."

"Away from here, as quickly as possible."

"That will be difficult. All means of accessing the ground from this and the neighboring levels above and below have been isolated by your President's security."

She looked around, hoping to spot another route out, only to find the massive-bodied form of Arsenio Rachiim—his standard blues at odds with the full dress court around him—bulling towards her. In that same sweep, she registered—belatedly—at least a half-dozen men and women, civilian attire belied by the purposefulness of their movements, taking stations around her, creating a subtle but effective separation between the group clustered about her and the rest of the reception.

"An explanation, Rachiim-Colonel," demanded Kymri, with the casual authority of one used to an immediate reply. The Edwards Provost Marshal—though far from home and technically way off his turf—responded with equal courtesy and equal confidence in his own authority.

"With all due respect, Commander," he replied, refusing to be pressed in the slightest, "this does not concern you."

"What concerns Shea-Pilot very much concerns me."

"Forgive me, sir, but that's a matter you'll have to take up with higher authority. I'm allowed no latitude in this, and to be frank I wouldn't take it if offered . . ."

"What the devil," Con started to protest, as outraged at Rachiim's ignoring him as by the situation itself.

"If you'll come with us, Lieutenant," Rachiim said to Nicole.

She nodded, quelling anything further from her father with a look and a small slashing gesture, begging silently to be allowed to handle this herself, thankful for the quick exit.

She wasn't taken far, just to a small office, moderately removed from the main reception hall.

"You've found something," she said as the door closed behind them.

"Techs have been taking apart your electronics," he began.

"I know, ever since Simone's death. And?"

"Thanks to Tscadi, we've been able to interface a linkage with some Halyan't'a systems. Their optics and visuals are a quantum leap beyond ours."

"I know that, too."

"Your whole house was in effect transformed into a Virtual Reality chamber. Transmissions were piggybacked over the internal wiring, creating an invasive, pervasive field effect."

"Jesus."

"Evidently the generator matrix resonated on a frequency that managed not only to be outside our sensor range but to reach directly into the subject's mind, without need of the usual mechanical interface, skinsnug and helmet. Anyone in the house would have been affected to a degree but you were most susceptible, because the system was custom-configured specifically for you."

She had to sit. "Alex," she began. "All the time we were working together," another false start. "It got to the point where I wore the skinsnug automatically. He said the more comprehensive the subject data base could be, in terms of how my total instrument worked, brain and body, the more effective the Virtual Reality he could generate."

"He wasn't lying. We've been trying to piece together the patterns that hit both you and Agent Deschanel."

"They're still stored?"

"Remember, your quarters have been physically off-line since that night. Whoever inserted the program had no means of removing it, short of physically entering the building and wiping it from an internal console."

"If my dreams lately have been any indication, I don't think I want to know what you found."

"As far as the scenarios themselves are concerned, that's probably for the best. Especially considering what we found at what we consider their source. That isn't important. What is, and this is critical, is that there was a subliminal text appended to the primary structure."

"Brainwashing?!"

"We're not sure, but we can't afford any chances."

"To do what?"

"As near as we can tell, assassinate the President."

"That's nuts."

"It's there, Shea, take my word for it. Built along the lines of an absolute imperative. A reflex action triggered by physical proximity. No conscious thought would be involved. You'd see Russell and, *bang*, it'd be all over, with you wondering what the hell had just happened."

"That *is* nuts." But even as she spoke, images popped like fireworks behind her eyes, of Russell on the boat, his being somehow personally responsible for saddling her with a death trap of a fighter, his turn as the DecoTrash maître d'.

"What?" Rachiim prompted. "Something rang a bell."

"An image. I was older, different somehow, remembering"— she looked up at the Provost Marshal—"President Russell's assassination."

"He's already on the way up, so we'll hold you here until he's safely inside, then bring you down to the street."

"And then?"

"Psychological evaluation at a secure facility. To determine how deep the conditioning goes and whether or not it can be eradicated."

"Better and better. You said you had a source."

"Something of a misnomer, he's actually our prime suspect. You can probably guess who."

"Alex?"

"I find it hard to believe myself, on the surface. But it fits his psych profile, not to mention his vehement opposition to President Russell's Halyan't'a policies. Underneath that American Prince facade, I'm sad to say, is one seriously sick puppy. Lieutenant," he cried suddenly, "what's wrong?"

She staggered half a step sideways, waving back a fed who'd lunged forward to help—his three fellows keeping their

distance and their hands on their weapons, making continually
sure they had a clean shot at her, not taking the slightest of
chances—going almost down to one knee before making a
clumsy recovery, all the while looking wildly about the small
office. She anchored herself by her hands to the edge of a desk,
then flattened her back to the wall behind, like someone with
vertigo frantically seeking some way of restoring the spinning-
top world around them to sanity. Her teeth were chattering
and she clenched her jaw tight to still them, shuddering harder
inside at the thought of how this must look to the Provost
Marshal and the feds, as though she'd gone totally off the
edge. And for all she knew, she had.

A pounding at the door nearly sent her leaping from her
skin, the sight of Kymri and her father when an agent cracked
it open didn't help. The Hal didn't bother with any niceties,
he simply pushed and the agent as suddenly found himself
flattened between door and wall, Rachiim frantically waving
the others' guns down as Kymri stalked over to her, Conal
Shea stepping in hot on his heels, with an expression of barely
controlled fury on his face.

"What is going on here, Colonel?" he demanded, putting
himself in Rachiim's face and daring the other man to do
something about it. Not at all daunted by the fact that Rachiim
was clearly, sorely tempted.

"That, sir, is none of your concern."

"This, *sir*, is my daughter. I am her attorney. If you are
engaged in any sort of official capacity, you'd better be prepared to execute it to the full letter of the law."

"We are well within our rights, Counselor, this is a national
security matter. By interfering, you leave yourself liable to
arrest."

"Shea-Pilot," Kymri called softly, his own face close to
her, Nicole painfully conscious of how awful she must look,
alternately flushed and pale, sheened with sweat that cooled
clammily as it formed.

"I cannot"—pause for breath—"focus." Aware even as she
spoke, no need to register the look of surprise from Kymri,
that it was Hal.

"Incredible," was his response. "That *Rts'lai* accent . . ."

A piece clinked into place. "How can I have an accent"—
still speaking Hal, but aware now of a lilt that tagged the
phrases—"other than my own?"

"True enough. Ciari-Speaker provided most of your lingua tapes, and his is what we consider Standard, an essentially neutered form of the Speech, common to all while favoring none. And my own words are of a more northern flavor. Matai's the BarRunner among us, a coastal clan, that's most like her Speech."

"Still doesn't answer the question. How is it I speak like her?"

Kymri shook his head, absently scratching the jaw whiskers below his right ear. "No reason I can think of, save the osmosis of long association."

"We weren't together that much. If anything, I should favor you."

"As Speaker, she was most attuned to you, which means by rights, she should echo your manner of speaking English. But the reverse . . ."

"Could a link have been established when we were both in Virtual? Perhaps through the system itself. It's an interactive process, the CyberSpace interface acts on the subject as much as he does upon it. Only Alex'd know for sure, but there might have been some blurring of the lines of demarcation between us, a piece of me going to Matai and vice versa, I dunno. But Rachiim said we both came out of it simultaneously, we moved as one. The system was keyed to me, *she* was genetically keyed to me, almost like we were twins. My God—Kymri, when I came back to myself that night, I'd just raced across the base to find Alex and kill him. Only Matai was there before me."

"Stands to reason, we're stronger and faster than you."

"That's not the point, don't make fun! She's Speaker because—as you just said—she resonates most closely to me, the way I think and feel and act. If that scenario was patterned to condition me to a specific course of action, she'd be just as vulnerable."

"Perhaps more so."

"The same way Ciari was overwhelmed by his configuration of the *Speaker* virus?"

"A possibility."

"Colonel," she called, "the President has to be warned."

"Of what, Lieutenant?" The Colonel was understandably perplexed, since Nicole and Kymri had been shifting arbitrarily back and forth between English and Hal.

"Rachiim-Marshal, there is a more pressing threat than any posed by Shea-Pilot. Possibly from one of the Hal present. My runaway cyber tech, Matai."

"Christ, that's all we need. Commander, there are almost two dozen of your people present!"

"Boss is on the floor, gentlemen," one of the agents announced, having gotten the word over his Com Link.

"Kymri," Nicole demanded, "could there be a link? Between her and me?"

"If your theory is correct, it is possible. An empathic resonance, such as exists between—what was the word you used?" He growled in Hal, she gave him the translation. "Between identical twins. Not a case of being aware of Matai in any real-time sense, nor she of you. But you think in sympatico patterns, following the same paths. What she would do, so would you. And you, she. Mostly in terms of unconscious, reflexive actions."

"The duality of Self I've been feeling. Could it be a part of me trying to behave like her, cross-circuiting with the rest of me?"

A nod.

"She's here. I'll stake my life on it."

"A description," from Rachiim, "for the Secret Service?"

"The differentiations are too subtle for your kind, what is the saying: we all look alike? And she does not wish to be seen."

"Up to us, then," from Nicole.

"The hell you say!" vehemently, from the senior fed, blocking the door.

"If I take a wrong step," Nicole said to Kymri, ignoring the other man.

"I pledge my life that you shall not." And he stiff-armed Rachiim full in the chest, sending him tumbling into the agent between them and the door, pitching both over a desk-side trash can and dropping them in a shower of toppled papers, he and Nicole on their way before either man even hit the floor.

Nicole didn't bother thinking, she simply presented the situation to her back-brain and let it run her where it pleased, trusting, praying those instincts would play her true. She weaved fast through the press, working the crowd as she would the open sea, letting the occasional body contact push her further on her way, aware of a growing ripple of agitation along the

periphery of crowd and perception as an alarm was flashed to
the security bods.

There was another stir up ahead, reminding her of a wave,
so small and inconsequential when noted far out to sea, building impressively as it crested towards shore and shallow
water. Russell, had to be, confirmed by the briefest glimpse
of him. One of those men who improved with age, hitting his
prime when most other men were long past theirs. Silver hair,
now mostly gone from the crown of his head—which served
to emphasize the strong shape of his skull—counterpointed
by a salt-and-pepper beard he'd grown on a camping trip his
first year as President and kept ever since, trimmed to define
the line of his jaw while masking the slightly sagging flesh
underneath.

He hadn't in fact wanted the presidency, had been more than
a little surprised when Bill Chen tapped him as running mate.
Nobody'd imagined that Chen's death twenty-five months later
would usher Russell into the Oval Office, or that he'd come
to like the job enough to run for it in his own right. Or that,
winning once, he'd go for a second term.

Would have been a shoo-in, too, if not for the Contact with
the Halyan't'a, and Russell's proposed One World Treaty that
came out of it.

As a cadet, Nicole had marched in Chen's inaugural parade,
and then at his funeral. The latter was something she didn't
want to go through again.

Where is she, Nicole thought, once more bitterly coming
up empty after a sweep of the crowd, *too many people, too
much space*, painfully conscious that time was almost gone,
expecting any second to feel the hands of the Secret Service
on her, dragging her back into custody, afraid as well that she
was as primed a trigger as Matai, needing only proximity with
the target to go off. *No*—she shook her head suddenly—*not
where is she, where would I be? How would I approach the
Man*? And she forced herself to come to a stop, becoming
a rock in this human current, letting the others sweep for a
moment around her, taking the time to settle herself, giving
her instincts the chance to lock in.

Blur of motion from the corner of her left eye, cries of
fright and panic as Kymri kicked into high gear straight for
Russell. In that same moment, Nicole found herself angling
off the other direction, to a point ahead of the presidential

party. Images strobed across Nicole's vision, the Hal lunging forward, slapping aside a Secret Service agent as he wrapped both arms around the startled President and tackled him down, simultaneously with a mahogany-furred arm coming up, a viciously ugly shape clutched in its hand, kicking ever so slightly from the recoil as she pulled the trigger, screams erupting now, one of the shells clipping Kymri's side, impact pitching him and Russell to the floor, the gun tracking towards its primary target.

By then, Nicole had slammed into Matai, body-checking her off her feet while making a grab for the gun arm. But Matai planted a foot to check her fall and swept that arm around with a strength that beggared description, so that Nicole found herself flying through the air, holding on for dear life, knowing that if she was thrown loose Matai would have a clear shot at her. She was in Matai's arms, the Hal with a hand to her throat, and Nicole thought that was the end. One sharp slash and Matai's finger-claws would savage both jugular vein and windpipe.

But the Hal didn't fight like a Hal, she hammered a rabbit punch to the small of Nicole's back and a heel to the back of her knee, pitching her onto her back. And the thought came absurdly to Nicole as she fell that, *she's fighting like I would!* And she responded in kind, grabbing the Hal's legs as she looked around for Russell, heaving herself across Matai's body as it hit the floor to sprawl across her gun arm and sink her teeth into the heel of her hand.

Matai cried out, but couldn't do much more with Nicole on top of her. Most importantly, though, she opened her hand, allowing Nicole to grab the gun and roll sloppily away, desperately fumbling with the weapon—trying to find grip and trigger and get the barrel pointed the right sodding way. The Hal was already coming for her as Nicole brought the gun up, ignoring the threat of the weapon and Nicole's cry of warning, hands going for Nicole's throat, fangs bared, as the gun bucked—seemingly of its own accord—the bullet making the Hal woman stagger in midair, before, all direction fled, she thumped down beside her. Nicole lashed out, free hand and feet pushing her across the slick-slippery floor in the same frantic motions that also shoved the fallen body away from her, gun staying leveled at the end of an arm that remained stubbornly, disconcertingly steady, finally allowing herself to

come to rest when there was a good two-meter separation
between them.

All the while, Matai didn't move.

She registered agents closing in on Matai's body, Rachiim's
massive hand closing gently on hers, his voice deep and reassur-
ing in her ears—she didn't register the words, wasn't even sure
he spoke any, it was the tone that mattered and the calm it spread
over her like a quilt—giving her leave to release the gun to him.
There was a wetness on her cheek and she reached up to wipe
it away, dimly registering—without the slightest surprise—that
it was blood, covering much of her left side, its harsh, coppery
taste in her mouth.

"Kymri," she said, as though expecting him to be right there
beside her. And when he didn't answer, called again, louder,
a voice that threatened to top the agitated hubbub swirling
through the room as the crowd was ushered away.

"He's hurt, Lieutenant," Rachiim replied. "Leave him to the
medics."

She nodded, that made sense, noting dispassionately that she
seemed to be in shock, and she wondered why, since she had
no recollection of being hurt.

"The President," she asked.

"Not a scratch."

"Good for him."

"Thanks to you two."

"Matai." That wasn't a question, but a call to the other
woman, accompanied by a gesture—reaching out to her, body
starting to shift so that it could crawl after—forestalled by
Rachiim's hands on her shoulders, holding her in place.

"You hit her square, Lieutenant," he said quietly. "There's
nothing you can do. She's dead."

thirteen

THE WOUND WAS nastier than it looked, but Kymri proved tougher, and by morning the hospital was allowing him—albeit reluctantly—the occasional visitor.

His Intensive Care cubicle was an eclectic mix of Terran medical technology and Hal, the hospital staff at turns unnerved and irresistibly intrigued by their Hal counterparts (who, in all fairness, were no less edgy, no less fascinated). He was bare to the waist, where the folded bedsheet began, telemetry leads scattered all across his torso, the fur around them shaved to allow for positive skin contact, with a far larger patch about the entry and exit wounds, mercifully covered now by bandages. The luster was lacking in his color, his breathing slow but shallow, the general consensus being that he was incredibly lucky. Also—this overheard by Nicole from the Hal staff— that he'd be back on his feet in comparatively short order.

There was another Hal present in the room, slim and slight of form, distinctively older than Kymri, wearing a Speaker's robes, with diplomatic sigils worked in precious metals and gems up by the right shoulder.

Kymri cracked his eyelids as Nicole stepped hesitantly through the doorway, and gusted a small breath, stretching lips over foreteeth in what she interpreted as a smile of greeting.

"I came to see," she said softly.

"I have been more impressive," was his reply, a basic strength to the words even though they could barely be heard.

"Hardly. You're the story of the morning, the Hal who saved the President."

"From another," came his counter, with a subvocal rumble of fury that set the monitors flickering and prompted looks of concern from the nurse's station outside, "who nearly killed him."

"Matai's being portrayed as an aberrancy, the same as we have among our own kind."

"Expedient. Understandable. But she does not deserve such dishonor."

"I'm sorry, Kymri." Nicole wanted to look away, to cast her gaze anywhere else, but she found she had to meet his eyes. "I," she began again, before letting her voice trail off helplessly.

"It had to be done."

"I didn't have to kill."

"I submit you did, Shea-Pilot, else you would not have done so."

"That's a neat rationale."

"It happens. Here. On *Range Guide*. The same."

"That's right, the same."

"And as there is no need for crucifying yourself for the one, so also for the other. Shea-Pilot, she would have killed you. And then your President."

"Intellectually, I understand—!"

"*Phauggh!* I was her Commander. We were sworn by oaths only fractionally less binding than those offered to Shavrin herself. Yet she fired at me without hesitation."

"It wasn't her fault, Kymri. It isn't fair she had to die for this."

"A truth."

"Those same newslines," the Speaker interrupted diplomatically, "speak of a suspect."

"Alex Cobri," Nicole said. "Nothing's quite official yet, everyone's treading as softly and carefully as possible, the public release is that he's wanted for 'questioning.' But the subtext is that he's their man. Once he's caught, I doubt he'll ever be let free, no matter how good his lawyers are."

"You have a question about that?" This from Kymri, a gleam of interest in his eyes.

"I don't know. To be honest, I'd have thought him smarter than this."

"Remember," the Speaker noted, "the conditioning strike was aimed at you."

"Except that it hit Simone Deschanel first, only she died from it." Now that the pieces had fallen pretty much all into place, it had become clear that had been the only way Simone could do her duty. She was sworn to protect the President, with her life if necessary, yet she was trapped in a Virtual sequence that was designed to create a presidential assassin. She couldn't break loose, but she couldn't allow herself to be so used. So she went for what must have seemed the only viable option. And somehow been killed. And in Virtual, as with aboriginal mysticism, the fate of the spirit became that of the flesh. "At a time when," Nicole continued, "as far as Alex knew, we might not have even been on base. I mean, if the man was plotting to turn me into an assassin at the same time he was actively romancing me aboard his boat— that, gentlemen, is cold."

"But is such coldness beyond his capacity?"

"Master Speaker, I haven't a clue. The spooks—the federal investigators—all believe this mode of attack is perfectly consistent with Alex's psyche profile."

"And you?"

"As I've often been reminded, Kymri, I'm just a Second Loot. I'll probably get another medal for last night, and maybe my pick of Earthside assignments, but that's as far as things go. They certainly don't guarantee that anyone'll listen to what I have to say. Assuming I *had* anything to say."

He twitched his lips, as if to say, *but you are not satisfied.* Which she answered with a tilt of the head, before wishing him well and taking her leave, pausing on the street front outside the ivory fortress of the medical center to muster her thoughts, taking temporary refuge in a simple stroll along the avenue, watching the rest of the world rush purposefully by.

There'd been a sea change over the last generation, as many of the high-rise towers of the late twentieth century had reached the end of their useful lifetimes, aided by a deliberate policy intended to downscale the city's skyline. Gradually, the low-rises were coming back, three-story brownstones (or

rather, their modern equivalents since those original materials
had become prohibitively expensive to quarry) mixing with
five-story apartment buildings, the idea being to restore as
much as possible the sense of community that had always
existed in the Outer Boroughs, and once upon a time even
here in Manhattan itself. There were still skyscrapers, the Mil-
lennium Tower foremost among them, but they were restricted
now to Midtown and the Financial District, which relieved the
oppression many had felt around the turn of the century, that
they were living at the bottom of some ever-deepening rat's
maze of canyons, with more and more people concentrating in
less and less space. Now, the pace remained as fast and furious
as ever, but somehow the pressure had grown less intense.

York Avenue, as ever, was a company street north of the
Queensboro Bridge—gearing up for its bicentennial amid per-
ennial predictions of its imminent collapse—defined and
dominated by the phalanx of world-class medical centers and
hospitals that lined the East River all the way to Spanish
Harlem. She'd put in some time of her own here not so long
ago, one more stop on her road back to the Frontier. And a
twinge of phantom pain deep inside her right thigh made her
limp slightly a half-dozen steps. A couple of times on her
way up to Seventy-second Street, a man would catch her eye
and offer a smile—flattering to part of her awareness that she
should be found attractive, never a decent consideration given
to the proposition that it might actually be so—and she would
respond on automatic, with a smile that never went beyond her
lips, totally at odds with eyes that were scanning a reality that
had nothing whatsoever to do with the street and people she
passed, a trio of faces rotating one after the other, over and
over in succession, like a visual mantra she chanted in hopes
of some miraculous revelation.

Her leg was still being a pain, so there wasn't much grace to
her stride as she dashed across the avenue to beat the crosstown
skimmer to its stop, something on the order of a running hop,
but the driver took pity on her and overruled the guidance
system, holding the bus long enough for her to clamber aboard.
At Fifth, she made a connection downtown, alighting after a
nominally sedate procession (some things never changed, primarily the inability of surface traffic to get around) at the main
reference library on Forty-second. For luck, as she climbed the
steps, she patted one of the guardian lions, just as she had as

a kid, wishing she had the time—not to mention chutzpah—
to swing herself on its back and ride the great stone beast.

She brought her own PortaComp, which interfaced with
ease into the library's primary database—that she could have
done from anywhere, and often had—but there was another
aspect that made the MRL invaluable. Its hard-copy archives.
Possibly the most complete collection outside of the Library
of Congress.

Both parents were long-time patrons. That, plus her mother's stature as a double Pulitzer winner, plus what Nicole discovered was her own not inconsiderable clout as one of those
who'd saved the President last night, got her dispensation to
stay past the six o'clock closing time. Although her somewhat
disreputable appearance got her a share of scandalized looks
from staff and patrons both. She'd had enough of uniforms for
a time—her formal suit ruined by Matai's blood—and dressed
instead purely for comfort, in a pair of knockabout jeans worn
through at the knees, plus a sleeveless top, with a sweater in
her carryall as protection from the library's air conditioning.

However, as the ancient tick-tock out in the hall began chim-
ing closer to twelve she realized she'd outstayed her welcome.
No matter really, she'd found pretty much all she'd looked for.
Amazingly easy, in fact, once she laid out the pieces of the
puzzle before her and started seeing where they might connect.
Manuel had taken his cue from Edgar Allan Poe and laid out
the most private—and potentially damaging—secret of his
life in plain sight, confident that, because of the reputation
and ground rules he'd spent a lifetime establishing, nobody
would look for it. Or would simply refuse to see what was
patently there.

One set of answers, not that they meant much. All they
provided was insight into Alex. Beyond that, they weren't
any help.

The first thing she did when she stepped out of the plane and
onto the Nantucket Memorial Airport tarmac was stand stock-
still and smell the sea. There was a stiff breeze blowing in off
the Atlantic—a crosswind that had made landing a particular
delight, demanding a level of skill rarely required in military
aircraft—chill and clean, accented with sea salt and the faintest
hint of a dawn that was barely three hours distant, making her
instantly hungry for a boat and the feel of spray on her face.

She shook that fantasy out of her skull most emphatically, time enough for such indulgences by daylight. Bed was called for at the moment, and even that remained a good half hour away—assuming, of course, her message had gotten through and the caretaker had left wheels in the airport lot.

The island was mostly asleep—hardly a surprise, given the hour—and hers was the only car on the road as she wound her way westward down Madaket Road to the hamlet of the same name right at the end. As she climbed the steps after fumbling for the key under the porch, she had to fight to stifle a yawn that bid fair to split her face in two. She figured, if she couldn't manage the door, she'd curl up on the porch; she was fairly certain by this point she hadn't a dog's chance of making her bed, but it wouldn't be the first time she'd collapsed on the couch.

The door squeaked open, first try, its noise drowned by a yawn that wouldn't be stopped. She dropped her gear as she stepped inside and was in midcollapse when a familiarly sarcastic voice announced, "About fucking time, Shea. I was beginning to think you'd *never* show!"

She let herself bounce off the couch and flipped sideways onto the floor, gritting her teeth as she jammed a shoulder, desperately wide awake now and wishing for a gun.

"What are you doing here, Alex?"

"That's obvious, sweetheart, waiting for you."

"Should I be flattered?"

"Quite frankly, my dear, I couldn't give a damn. I got troubles of my own. Or haven't you heard?"

"Lucky me, I was there."

"Each and every time. Quite a moment, I confess, having that Halyan't'a nut case burst in on me, hot and eager to rip my lungs out, with you right behind her, waving a gun."

"Seems to us, we had cause."

"So I've been discovering."

She tried to pinpoint his voice, somehow it seemed to be coming from all around her—and she wondered if he'd managed to tap into the stereo, except that all the system lights were out and the speakers still—finally deciding on upstairs, the sprawling second-floor living room.

"That, we have in common," she said, wriggling her legs up under her, to give her better, faster leverage to her feet, the thought suddenly striking her that she had no way of knowing whether or not he was armed. Not, of course, that the couch was any decent protection. There were handguns and shells on the market—legal and illegal—that would shoot with ease through the body of the whole house. "I've been making some discoveries of my own."

"You really do look awfully uncomfortable huddled on your knees like that, L'il Loot; you're free to get up, if you like, I won't bite." Her insides had turned to ice, head twisting 'round to scan the room behind and above her, searching—she knew in vain—for signs of EyeSpys or ScanCams. Or, worse, Alex himself lurking in a convenient shadow. But found not a sign of either.

"That better?" he asked as she groaned to her feet.

"Much, thanks."

"Don't mention it. Looks like I'm pretty well fucked, *huh*?"

She nodded. "Looks like. Feds figure they have motive— your hostility to Russell and his policies—means, the Virtual system back at Edwards and the effects it had on me and Simone Deschanel. And opportunity."

There was a pause, and she could almost see him shaking his head in disgust. "Gimme a break. As though I'd leave them this nice, neat package."

"It works for them, Alex. Arsenio Rachiim showed me the reports, there's enough there that's incontrovertibly legit to make the rest seem credible." And, saying that, she didn't bother editing the edge that slipped into her voice.

"I said you could stand, Nicole, not go wandering. Let's leave things the way they are for the moment, 'kay?"

"I keep forgetting, you're so much more comfortable when relationships are remote."

"It allows for a time-lag, the opportunity to think, passions to cool, rationality to reassert itself. When someone's face-to-face, things happen spontaneously; this lets everyone consider the consequences of such rashness."

"Sometimes, Alex, that spontaneity adds spice to life."

"Spare me the clichés, Nicole, I thought better of you. I also get the sense that you'd like very much to take a swing."

"At the very least. As I said, I saw Rachiim's report. He saw the actual tapes."

A longer pause. A chastened tone to Alex's voice when he spoke again, Nicole's mouth turning down in irritation that bordered on outright anger at her inability to pinpoint where he was. She had the sense of him moving about, but how could he be doing so without making the slightest sound? This was an old house, scattered full of creaky floorboards, there should be at least some noise.

"I never meant . . ." he started to say.

"They were pretty rude, Alex."

"Fantasies are."

"So leave 'em inside your head, where they belong. You had me playing scenarios *I've* never conceived of."

"I never meant any harm!"

"You killed Simone Deschanel!"

"I never killed *anyone!*"

"You tried to condition me to do your dirty work with Russell and damn near succeeded with Matai. Another life you owe, Alex."

"That wasn't me," he shrieked, Nicole taking advantage of the moment to sprint for the stairs, flattening herself into the shadows as she snaked her way up.

"Stop, Nicole," he said, far more calmly, and she did. "The house has nice security internals—not state-of-the-art but then I guess you don't get much call for it way out here, and the weather must dick up the electronics something fierce—it was no trouble at all patching into 'em. And piggybacking my own toys on top. Which *are* cutting edge."

"Stop playing games."

"When games are the only option, might as well enjoy to the max."

"Now who's spouting clichés."

"To be honest, I don't even know why I'm here."

"Because it's the last place anyone would look."

"Not quite, but close. Hadn't thought of that, really. I guess I thought it's a place you'd show at eventually. I guess I felt it was important for us to talk."

"I don't like talking to myself, Alex, which is what this feels like."

"Fine," he said, stepping into view at the far end of the hall. "Satisfied."

She straightened, and froze once more as the barrel of a very nasty-looking piece of work swung up to meet her.

"I'm not a great shot, outside of Virtual"—self-deprecating smile—"but this has a full-auto capability and explosive SeekerSlugs. You're a nice person, Nicole, and this is a

real nice house, I'd like to leave both the way I found
them, 'kay?"

"No problem. May I sit?"

"Please do, top of the stairs. But"—the gun stirred for
emphasis—"keep your hands in view.

"It's something you can do in Virtual," he went on,
"physicalize the imagination. Bring your dreams to life."

"We've had this conversation before. What happens when
you lose your taste for the real thing? You lock yourself into a
pattern of behavior, Alex, a way of looking at the world. How do
you cope when the world doesn't follow your script? Remember
what happened when we went sailing? You responded according
to your programmed preconceptions, which had nothing to do
with the conditions at hand. You can't reset and reboot and
start again. You're stuck with what is."

"You don't understand."

"I'm not even sure I want to. I'm flesh-and-blood, I'm a
person. Your Virtual scenarios took the form of me and made
it your pet BoyToy. That's bad enough. But then they tried
to do the same with *me*!"

"It wasn't," he was pleading, "my doing." Then he shook
his head, shoulders slumping. "But why should you believe?"
He sank down on his heels, back flat against the doorjamb.
"Should've said yes, Nicole, could've sailed after the sun, put
all of this behind us."

"You really believe that?"

"Maybe some illusions are easier to hold on to."

"And if not, what, make better ones?"

"Got to admit, it's a family trait. What are you looking
around for?"

"Just thinking about what you said, about having the house
wired."

"Afraid I'll play with your head?"

"It's been done before."

"It's your house," he scoffed, "you know better than me
how old it is. Place doesn't have a fraction of the potential
your Edwards quarters did."

"So you're saying it's safe."

"I can say anything I like, L'il Loot, you'll simply have to
trust me."

"Why send me out to kill you at the end?"

"Hmnh?"

"I still can't put many of the pieces together. The scenarios are like dreams, it's hard to tell what actually was from the bits you add on afterward, but we were always in conflict."

"Art mimics life. But think about it. With me dead, who's to stand in my defense? Lee Oswald and Jack Ruby all over again. The neat package gets even tidier."

"Doesn't seem so tidy to me."

"You're looking from the inside. Deschanel wasn't supposed to happen. Maybe you weren't supposed to happen? Maybe the Pussy was the focus all along? Slips out, slips back, I'm found dead, who's to see a link?"

"Plausible."

"And impossible to prove."

"I've been reading at the library."

"I know. I was following your search paths."

"You and who else?" *God, is there anything he can't tap into?*

"Did you a favor, cleaned up after you. Any snoops go looking, most they'll come up with is my tag."

"Thanks."

"No need to be nervous. There's nothing you could do with the information."

"Yeah, my mom told me that story, about the London paper."

"I've never seen my mother, you know that? She and Dad split right after I was born, but that part of things was no big deal, there was nothing really between them. Emotionally. What was called, in the bygone, a marriage of convenience. When I got old enough to ask, I was told Dad got custody and Mom wanted nothing to do with me. When I got old enough to go check things out for myself, I never got past the door. Goons had my pix and orders they weren't about to disobey. Managed to get her on the phone a couple of times, she hung right up. Went in overline through a data net, same thing. With her account changed the next morning. After which I stopped trying."

"That sucks."

"Not from her perspective. I was the offspring"—he grinned, without the slightest humor—"of a business collaboration. However she may have actually felt, she was being well paid to cut me off completely. Which, when you look back on it, has more than its share of irony. Once the Old Man saw his personal, private *mene mene tekel upsharin* on the wall—the moving finger having writ, moving on, unable to be recalled—he probably would have been better served to cut me loose and move on along alone. But he's the kind who hates giving up even more than losing. He tinkered in the womb, he tinkered more after. For all the good it did him. And me."

"Genetic engineering. Mostly venture capital investments in small, idiosyncratic nanotech firms; university grants funding pure research . . ."

"With codicils granting him exclusive access to any discoveries that fit the specified parameters."

"Is he that afraid of dying?"

Alex chuckled. "Not in the conventional sense. At least, I don't think. I suppose he's like any man who's built an empire. He wants it to go on. And the sad fact of history is that personal empires don't last. Maybe a generation, maybe two, but sooner or later, genetic entropy sets in. A person who grows up enveloped by a life of wealth and privilege has a totally skewed outlook from someone who doesn't, or the one in a billion who starts with nothing and builds from there. They take for granted things their father had to work and fight for."

"The arrogance of accomplishment versus the arrogance of position."

"Exactly. You ever feel that way with your mom?"

Nicole shook her head, giving the house a sweep of the eyes. "The stuff I did best, she couldn't compete in"—a half shrug of acknowledgment—"or perhaps chose not to, for my sake. And what she did best, I really wasn't interested in."

"So you opted out of the competition. Neat trick."

"No. It's just they defined the terms of competing along lines we could all live with. If a challenge came—and, okay, those kinds of challenges always come, that's part of growing up—they shunted it into arenas where we were all pretty much on an equal footing. When you sail or fly, it's the same sea and sky regardless. The folks' edge was that they were older, more experienced, but us kids were quicker off the mark and in some ways—because this was all new and we were scared stiff at first of screwing up—a lot more on the ball. And what we got, Alex, we earned. My flying lessons came out of weekends and after-school busting my ass at the airport."

"The problem with being labeled the best, right from the start, is living up to it. A four-oh score merely fulfills expectations. Anything less . . ."

"At least it's your score, Alex. The standard you establish for yourself."

"I wish. The problem you know with being a chip off the old block is that you always remain a chip. And the Old Man, the block. Worse, by far, when the chip turns out to be less than perfect."

"Is that what happened?"

"Pretty much. The danger of cutting-edge technology. The blade isn't necessarily as sharp—the material as cuttable—as you assume."

"He said, your father, that night at Edwards, when they threw the welcoming party for the Hal, he just sort of sidled over and started chatting me up, that you were a bit too much your mother's child."

"Bad genes. But if at first you don't succeed . . ."

" 'Keep trying 'til you get it right,' was what he told me. At the time, I couldn't figure the joke."

"You do, now?"

"I've been watching Amy."

"There is a resemblance."

"Alex, for Christ's sake, cut yourself loose. It isn't this mess with Russell that's going to destroy you, it's your father. That's all the man is, Alex, he's not God!"

"Isn't he, Nicole?" And the young man turned his head from where he sat to look her in the eye. "He made me what I am. And then made my sister better. Learned from his mistakes, same as he did turning Baumier's equations into a viable power system. All his assets, none of his flaws."

"Alex!" she cried, forgetting herself and rising from her seat.

"You're right, actually. I don't have any choice. I can't live with him anymore. Amy's young, Nicole, at least she's still got time to pull her own head together, without him twisting it the way he did mine."

"What are you going to do?"

"I'm glad you're here, you'll be out of it."

"I'm out of nothing. And you're a fool if you think you can end this by yourself."

"I have to try."

"You're just as much programmed as everyone else, don't you realize that? Alex, come down."

"Give myself up, throw myself on the tender mercy of the Court and probably spend the rest of my life locked in a silk-lined box somewhere?"

"Isn't that what you've been trying to do all your life?"

"It's my choice, Nicole, that's the difference. I can always pull the plug. This way, someone else's hand's forever on the switch, I'll be at their mercy, I won't have any control. No thank you, no thank you, no *thank* you!"

"Please." He hadn't seemed to notice as she'd gathered herself—slowly and progressively—to the top of the landing, trying to keep the dryness of her mouth from affecting her speech, eyes flicking from gun to his face and back again, remembering Matai's speed when she lunged and her own shocked disbelief as the gun had fired. Still wasn't sure whether to go slow or fast.

"It's a done deal, Nicole. Already set in motion. I won't stop it. And if you're stupid enough to try, I won't let you stop it, either. Cast it as an Oedipal squabble and leave it in the family, 'kay? That's best for everyone."

She moved, came up three paces short to find the gun aimed right at her head, Alex impossibly instantly on his feet before her, a transition so fast she could have sworn it hadn't really happened.

"I warned you," he said.

And pulled the trigger.

And shimmered under an intentional burst of static as he played with the visual gain.

"Son of a *bitch*," she screamed, swinging furiously for his head only to see her clenched fist fly right through the holographic projection.

"Nicole," he admonished gently, as though to a child, "*Nicole*. Did you really think I'd be here in person? Or anywhere anyone could get a decent line on me?"

She said nothing, merely glared at the image, trying to determine without actively looking where the receptors and projectors were stashed. And from there, the source. Had to be line-of-sight transmission, there was no other way to establish so coherent an image, even through cable.

"You can't kill him, Alex."

"The way I see it, he's killing himself. Mary Shelley, right?
Be seeing you, Nicole. Just no more this lifetime."

And he vanished.

She dashed through the living room beyond, out onto the
deck, grabbing a pair of binoculars on the way to sweep
the horizon, paling with the approaching sunrise—she hadn't
realized how long they'd talked—then scrambling up to the
peak of the roof for a search of the land. That nothing came
immediately to view meant even less. A boat could've been
far out to sea—although size played a role there, for too small
a craft would have meant a less stable image; anything else,
she should be able to see. Also, for land or sea projection,
there would have to be a receiving nexus, a fairly considerable
rectenna array to process the image, especially for a two-way
livetime link. But there was nothing on the house, or anywhere
near it.

She hunkered down on the roof, dangling the glasses between
her splayed knees. A plane was another possibility. Given sufficient altitude, and a clear shot, he could be broadcasting from
fifty kilometers distant and more. Made sense. That way, the
entire building could be used as the antenna, through its internal
wiring, with just the addition of some internal remotes to process
the signal in both directions. But where to get a plane loaded with
that kind of specialized equipment, much less operate it, with no
one being the wiser, when Alex's picture was plastered across
every newsline and video on the continent, if not the world?
At least the young man had that aspect of reality pegged—he
bore the Cobri name, but his father held the power. No one
would even think of defying Manuel to protect Alex, or help
him. No, whatever was planned, Alex was acting wholly on
his own.

Even as she thought that, she found her gaze rising upward,
mouth forming an "O" of astonishment as she found the one
place that fit every requirement. Which led to an equally mad
dash back into the house, one almost fatal misstep as she came
off the roof, a twisting, tumbling recovery that saved her from
any injury worse than the ankle that got jammed on landing
plus the usual assortment of bumps and bruises, no more than
she used to regularly acquire as a kid, the only problem being
that she was a long way from a kid's body and reflexes.
Scrambled for her PortaComp, called up a SkyChart, gave a
clenched fist "yes" of triumph when her query came up aces.

She was grabbing for the phone when it rang. She couldn't help flinching, holding back for two more rings while asking herself if this was Alex?

It was, to her amazement, Al Maguire.

"I know where Alex Cobri is," Nicole said, right off.

"This isn't a secure line," was the reply, "and there are more important concerns. How's the tide where you are?"

Nicole furrowed her brow in confusion. "Lowering, I think," she replied.

"Go down on the beach. There's a blue suit helo already en route from Otis"—meaning the Air Force base on Cape Cod, about sixty klicks distant—"it'll take you back to Westchester. Your Corsair's already being prepped, it'll be ready to go when you get there."

"Go where?"

"Edwards. You have emergency clearance to altitude and authorization to firewall, you're needed in the barn ASAP."

She took a breath, a trifle dizzy from the lack. "What's happened?"

"We have a Situation. We may need your help. No more questions, Nicole."

"I can hear the helo." One of the big Sikorsky Air-Sea Rescue brutes, beside which even the Edwards beasts looked small in comparison, kicking up an impressive spray as it banked in low over the waves, swinging sideways towards the house. "I'm gone."

And in less than five minutes—remembering at the last to lock the door and stash the key—she was.

fourteen

SHE ACHED IN more places than she knew she had and didn't even want to consider how she smelled—appearance had gone by the board on the other side of the continent, as hair and clothes were pummeled by the downwash of the Sikorsky's giant rotor blades. Maguire was as good as her word, the helo roared down Long Island Sound at full throttle, descending onto the federal ramp at Westchester in a military touchdown. There was nowhere really to change and from the way everyone was behaving, precious little time, so she simply shucked jeans and top and pulled on her flight suit, thankful she'd worn a camisole for once (giggling at the memory of the classic Gramma moment, where she'd been cautioned always to wear clean—and respectable—underwear, because you never knew what might happen and you always wanted to look your best for strangers).

Within ten minutes of touchdown, she was airborne, cleared to the Corsair's max of fifty kay, with a ninety-minute run slotted to the coast. She didn't inquire about what was up and nobody along the way felt obliged to enlighten her as she scattered shock diamonds out her tail and beat the sun to Edwards, leaving predawn half-flight for full darkness.

As she shambled into the Ready Room, Colonel Sallinger

shoved a steaming mug of black tea into her hand and she took a reflexive, incautious sip, wincing at the heat and the bitter, battery-acid taste.

"You functional?" she was asked.

"Do I have to be?" she responded in kind. The main board was lit, displaying a hemispherical schematic centered on the African continent, with a series of orbital tracks as well, each marked by its own individual color. Data columns off to the side flashed constantly changing numbers, which she twigged immediately as course, velocity, and altitude. Faces filled the secondary screens: Al Maguire up top, Grace Kinsella in the middle, a middle-aged civvie male below who rang a vague bell in Nicole's head as someone senior connected with the White House staff. Tscadi was present in the flesh, as was Sallinger, his Vice-Commander, and the State Department liaison. Belatedly, Nicole recognized the faces in two other screens: Judith Canfield and her Chief Astronaut, David Elias.

Nicole shot a nervous glance in Sallinger's direction, silently asking, "What?"

He leaned her way, offering a slightly less vicious mug of tea—cut more the way Nicole liked it, with a dollop of milk and sugar—and spoke fast and low in reply. "In a nutshell, young Master Cobri appears to have seized control of the guidance system of his father's spaceplane and locked it onto a collision course with Patriot Station."

"Which is where he is," Nicole said back to him.

Sallinger cocked an eyebrow.

"He was waiting for me at my folks' home on Nantucket. I thought he was there for real, it was a brilliant hologram." *And brilliantly staged*, she realized, keeping her far enough away and himself in a moderately shadowed corner so that she could never get a chance to spot that she was being conned. "I tried to tell Marshal Maguire when she called."

"That's only part of it. Patriot's internals have been activated. The orbit's no longer stable. We forecast twelve hours max before reentry. Any sort of violent collision between the spaceplane and the station can only make things worse."

"That stupid, pathetic son of a bitch," she breathed. And then, louder, "Twelve hours, that's a lifetime these days. More than enough time to launch a retrieval."

"The boy's been very busy. He's managed to infiltrate and

corrupt the master guidance links both on Earth and up on Sutherland. The numbers can't be trusted. The best anyone can figure to do is purge the entire system and reload from scratch. Even then, the software will have to be recalibrated and checked for glitches. There simply isn't enough time. Baikonur hasn't got anything in position for a tower launch and Canaveral's closed down because of the damned weather."

"The Japanese?"

"We're victims of our own damn success. The spaceplanes do the manned lifting so well that all the old launch centers have shifted almost exclusively to unmanned shots. There's no hardware they can get ready in time, nothing that can be diverted down the gravity well from the Moon."

"So what rocket scientist suggested the Hal shuttle as our ace in the hole?"

Sallinger sighed and shook his head, visibly impressed. "Very good, Lieutenant," he told her, "I was wondering how to break the news."

"I can't fly it."

"Under the circumstances, you're about the only one who can. Kymri's out of action; Grace as you can see is otherwise occupied; I submit it's you or no one."

"I submit in return, Colonel, I'm not qualified. For reasons that have nothing to do with my ability to fly the bloody thing. Besides, even if you use the Hal CyberNet, you'll have to interface with ours to input the raw intercept data. Alex is no fool—hell, he helped design the interface—they'll be corrupted same as ours were."

"The thought is to fly a manual intercept."

"You're crazy!" She spoke too loudly, words very few people—and especially Second Lieutenants—spoke to Bird Colonels, and heads turned across the room, plus a couple (allowing for the time-lag in Trans-Lunar communications) on-screen who reacted a few seconds after the fact.

"I beg your pardon, sir," she apologized, straightening as best she could to a semblance of attention, "I'm sorry."

"I know you're tired, Nicole. You're also looking to be the only option."

"I haven't slept in better than two days, Colonel."

"What d'you want from me, Lieutenant? I can't revoke the laws of physics. Whatever we say or do, Cobri's spaceplane's going to run smack into Patriot Station, and not terribly long after that, Patriot's going to come back down to Earth. Question is, does it reenter empty? And as importantly, in a state that can do serious damage on the ground? SkyLab had people scared, this one's ten times its size."

"What does Dr. Elias say?"

"With all due respect to his expertise and reputation, Lieutenant, he has input here solely as a courtesy. This is my shop, and near-Earth space my bailiwick."

"Yes, sir. Have I time to at least freshen up? A shower might make some difference."

"I'll take any edge I can get. You have a half hour, be back here ready to launch."

"We'll have to structure the launch window . . ."

"What d'you think we've been doing all evening? Go, woman, go, go-go-go." He made shooing motions with his hands to hurry her along.

It wasn't so much her eyelids that felt heavy, but the flesh atop her cheekbones, along the ridge they formed beneath her eyes, accompanied by a flatness of vision and expression and a perpetual tendency to yawn. She moved it seemed by reflex, trusting all the bits of her body to do what was expected of them with no more than the minimal prompting, painfully aware that if anything went wrong she probably wouldn't be able to catch herself. She took refuge in the locker room, pushing the shower as blisteringly hot as she could stand, scrubbing herself from top to toe, before grabbing the knotted rope above the Cool Pool, allowing herself a few moments hang time before dropping herself in. She actually cried out underwater, the stark contrast with the shower making it seem far icier than it actually was, surfacing amid a spluttering sequence of coughs that bent her double as she spat water from her throat. When she'd calmed a bit, she flopped her elbows over the lip of the pool and hung off the side, rolling first her shoulders, then the whole of her back, curving it convex, then concave, before lifting herself free with an upward, straightening thrust of the arms. Only they weren't interested tonight and gave out at the last instant and she flopped back into the water with a fair-sized splash.

Before trying again, she decided to take a little more of a soak, stretching full length off the pool's steps as mind and body slid back into focus. She was still exhausted but at least the effects would be held off until she let down her guard.

The wildest aspect about being so tired while remaining fully functional was the way her thoughts wildly free-associated, memories and images scatter-shooting through her head like freeway speedsters driving California Rules. No courtesy, no quarter, you see an opening, you go for it, make the other sod get out of the way, and never *ever* hit the brake. Fighter jock Heaven, where they played with cars the way they did their fighters. Nicole never found herself comfortable playing those games. She loved speed, and the skill that went hand in hand, she just never felt the perpetual need to prove it the way most other hotshots indulged in at the drop of the proverbial hat. Her way of counting professional *coup* had always been to do the job, any job asked of her, the best it could be done.

That was why being grounded hurt so much, it was the first time she herself had been found wanting. It wasn't a case of making a mistake, something apart from her that could actively be isolated and corrected, this was a flaw in Nicole herself. And where before, after she'd screwed up on her original simulator evaluation—which came as close as anything could to washing her right out of the astronaut program—she'd welcomed the second chance that allowed her to prove herself, now she wasn't so sure. She kept asking herself, would it have been better to quit that time? Chances were, Paolo would still be alive, and Cat Garcia and Chagay Shomron, and all the raiders who'd died on their asteroid. The trooper she'd shot in the back.

"Stop it," she said quietly to herself, suddenly tired of the rant. Wishing wouldn't change a thing and obsessing about it did nothing but make her miserable. Of course, there was a tremendously seductive luxury in that, it was an attitude that served Alex supremely well. And seeing him as the reflection in her mirror didn't sit well with Nicole.

She dunked herself a final time, then hauled herself up and went in search of a towel, still physically on autopilot, while her thoughts played cat-chases with each other: *Al Maguire saw the Cobris behind the Wolfpack Nicole had destroyed. Made sense. Assume that as the primary given. Primary suspects? Manuel? Same question now as before, why? He's got more power than almost anyone, what does he need with more? By the same token,* she sighed sadly, *why seek to perpetuate yourself with genetically engineered children?*

She shook her head. *Even allowing for his hand in the*

Wolfpack, that doesn't explain what's happened since. Business is business, the attacks on me were personal. And she had to chuckle, grimacing at her face in the washroom mirror and the witch-crone rat's nest of damp hair spiking all directions from her head, no matter what she tried it never behaved, and wondering if she wouldn't be better served simply cutting it off. The laugh, though, had nothing to do with her appearance, but with the suspicion that if Manuel wanted anything to happen to her—good or bad—there would be no mistake and no need for a second attempt. He was a ferociously precise man, like all engineers; if she was the target, she would be the target, there'd be no bystanders clipped on the sidelines.

Alex, then, prompting another chuckle and a rueful shake of the head. Fantasizing a hit was one thing, but actual, real-world execution? *No, what's needed is an amalgam of Alex's raw genius and Manuel's ruthlessness, coupled to a being who acts on impulse.* Who perhaps, in a fit of pique, sets in motion a killing scenario only to think better of it and call the victim—ostensibly her friend—to pull her to safety before it's too late.

And she remembered her father's words at the reception: "He's worked for what he's got, that tempers a person." But for someone with all the power and drive and passion and none of the leavening effects of experience . . .

"Amy," she breathed. Baby and brilliant, the person no one would suspect, for the same reason no one thought to look for Alex off the Earth. He traveled Virtual or not at all, an actual space shot was inconceivable.

She was a kid, and kids simply did not do these sorts of things. Only she wasn't a kid, not really, but her father in small, picking up where he was leaving off, testing her limits in the directions he wouldn't go. Pushing the outside of her envelope as all kids do, a totally natural evolution from setting up a network at Edwards to one that spanned the System. A perfectly natural attitude for one born to power to view the environment that gave her that power as her own private fiefdom. And like any kid, to stake that possession indelibly as her own.

Nicole got in the way. Nicole ruined things. Nicole had to pay. And she wondered how Amy had gotten Alex to set up the software scenario? If Alex had ever made the connection between what he'd done—because only he had that kind of expertise—and what had happened to her? But that was before they'd met, and Amy had come to actually like this woman she wanted hurt.

"Sundowner," she heard announced over the PA, the pilot call-sign Harry Macon had given her the day she'd arrived.

"Here," she acknowledged from the nearest WallCom.

"Your presence required in briefing."

"Five minutes."

She'd pulled one of her old flight suits from storage, emblazoned with the *Wanderer* mission patch over her left breast; over that went her leather flight jacket. She returned to the Ready Room with a minute to spare.

"Lieutenant," Sallinger called as she entered, nodding approval of the obvious improvement in her condition as she stood to attention and snapped a parade ground salute. "Welcome back to the land of the living."

"For as long as it lasts, boss."

"Or you do, *hmnh*? Fair enough. You had some valid points earlier, I won't order you to make this flight. Instead, I'm asking—do you feel yourself capable of handling this mission?"

There's the rub, she thought, the first answer coming to mind being, *I honestly haven't a clue*. And she turned towards the video wall, to Elias and Canfield above. But the words she heard came from Harry Macon, the pair of them sitting side by side in the XSR cockpit, Nicole looking pole-axed as he told her she'd be flying its first reentry with him. "Flying's like money," he said, popping a square of gum into his mouth, interrupting every few words with an attempt to blow a bubble, "if you have to ask how much a thing costs, you probably can't afford it. If you have to ask someone whether or not you're capable of flying, you probably aren't. Certainty is our stock in trade, young Lieutenant—that's where the arrogance comes from, can't be helped, we're only human—the measure of a great pilot is the ability to know which is which. *Knowing* you can do something, as opposed to telling yourself you can."

"Suppose you're wrong, skipper. Suppose I'm wrong."

"Then, kiddo"—*pop* went Macon's bubble and he made a face as he scraped goo off his mustache—"we'll both of us get our pictures on the Hotshots' wall."

"Yes, sir," she told Sallinger simply.

He nodded, the questioning quirk to his brow making Nicole wonder how long she'd zoned before answering. "You'll have two as crew," he said. "Tscadi will be systems monitor, I'll take the right seat."

She wasn't surprised.

"When do we go?"

"Soon as we're dressed."

Someone had fixed the pilot's seat since she'd last sat in it, modifying its configuration to better suit her back. On the central console, between her and Sallinger, was attached a PortaComp, hard-wired into the panel itself so its data could be displayed on the much larger built-in screens. Behind, at her engineer's station, Tscadi was running through the start-up checklist. It was a painfully laborious process, because each time the Hal spoke, Nicole had to spend crazed seconds hunting around her head for the proper response. The unconscious facility with the language that had come from the adrenaline rush of the assassination attempt had faded in the days since; she still possessed the knowledge, but she'd lost the automatic ease of using it. And though she'd executed the procedure scores of times in the simulator, this was her first live flight and she was determined to take the time to make sure she got things right. It was a decision arrived at without doubt or hesitation, one she knew she'd have made under the most ordinary and normal of circumstances. They wouldn't have this kind of opportunity once they lifted.

"Ascent profile established and enabled," Sallinger reported, "shall I lock it in?"

"Negative," she said, "display only. From ground-to-ground, this has to be a hands-on mission." Manual control, the whole trip. That way, there was no risk of any interference.

He nodded agreement, and with clearance granted from Mission Control—seconded by the Edwards Tower—the sun cracking the mountains behind them, the dawn air miserably still, Tscadi fired the mains.

To facilitate the launch, the shuttle had been towed out onto Rogers Dry Lake, with virtually the entire length of the landing bed stretched out before them. They started moving the moment the engines came to life—Nicole saw no sense in using the brakes to hold them in place with kilometers of room to play with; the idea was to get off the ground, not do so in a mad rush, and she wanted to use the opportunity to begin to get a feel for the craft—a leisurely start, initially slower than

a man could pedal on a bicycle. But with a "Go" cue from
Tscadi, Nicole moved the throttle sticks forward and the huge
vehicle began to seriously move. The aerodynamics of the Hal
design were every bit as impressive to fly as to watch, only
improved by the addition of the Terrestrial hydrogen-fueled
ramjets; with very little urging from the control stick, the
shuttle was airborne in less than three klicks, slicing easily
upward through the cool morning air. It was no Corsair—and,
in truth, no spaceplane, either—making much slower progress
out of the blue, but again this was time well spent by the crew
getting to know each other and the craft.

They flew the same basic profile as any spaceplane flight out
of Edwards, a climbing leg far out over the Pacific before course
was reversed for the final ascent into LEO, low Earth orbit.
The primary difference being that the spaceplanes had barely
an orbit's hang time to achieve rendezvous with Sutherland,
or any of the other LEO stations, before they'd have to return
to the surface; powerful as they were, they lacked the thrust
to achieve true escape velocity. This Hybrid Shuttle was a
different breed. Given the right enhancements, it was theo-
retically capable of high-orbital insertions, all the way out to
a geo-synchronous station. And with refueling, of traveling
anywhere in near-Earth space. Operating as easily from there
to the ground as the reverse.

"I scan an anomaly in number three main," Tscadi reported.

Nicole switched one of her screens to the appropriate display, noting the slight differences in pressure readings between
the four primary engines.

"Trouble?" she asked.

The Hal made a *hunhn* sound—a noise that was part sigh,
part groan with none of the meanings of either, indicative more
of her being caught up in a sequence of thoughts—and Nicole
wished she weren't strapped in so tight, or hamstrung by the
confining bulk of her pressure suit, so she could make her way
back to the engineer's station and get a physical sense of how
she felt.

"Unknown, at this point. There is a possibility this is an
aspect of the normal operating regime."

"Can I reduce thrust?"

"To do so will mandate a Mission Abort. We will be unable
to achieve the necessary orbit."

"Even assuming nothing's wrong," Sallinger said after Nicole had relayed Tscadi's information, "we won't have time to pull a turnaround. It's this or nothing."

"Edwards," Nicole said, "Sundowner Zero-One, proceeding as profiled." The shuttle was downlinked to the Test Center, with every aspect of the flight being relayed instantaneously to the ground for evaluation. So that regardless of what happened to them, the data provided by the mission would be used to help those who came afterward.

At turnaround, the air intakes cycled closed and the Rams kicked in as full rockets, the shuttle pulling into a steeper climb—though still far less intense an ascent than used by the first generation of vertical-launched shuttles—acceleration pressing the three of them deep into their chairs.

"Anomaly worsening," came Tscadi's supernally calm voice through Nicole's headphones.

"Balls," came far less calmly from Nicole as she tapped the keypad under her fingers—she had a full range of display controls built into the arms of her chair, hard by the sidesticks—to first recall the engine master display and then focus in on the offending thruster. There was indeed a pressure variance—she couldn't tell if it was because of a rough burn, an uneven consumption of fuel (which occasionally happened), or a possible flaw in one of the joints along the way, or worse of all a weakness in the combustion casing itself.

"Thirty-eight seconds to orbit," Sallinger said. *Might as well be thirty-eight years*, Nicole thought, scrolling through the PowerSystem menu, trying to find any additional data that would give her a better handle on what was wrong.

"Any thoughts, Tscadi," she called.

"Procedure says shut it down," Sallinger said.

"We do, boss, odds are we go down with it. We won't have the height to achieve a decent rendezvous."

"You want to do a *Challenger*, Lieutenant?"

"Tscadi," Nicole called again.

"Ten percent reduction on three," the Hal answered, "five percent increase on the others. Shift in angle of attack of three degrees. It will mean a longer run to target."

"It's a half hour we'll have to take. Okay, down on three, up the others."

And as the numbers settled down—but only marginally, and Nicole knew that if this had been a standard flight, they'd

already be on their way back to the barn—Sallinger made
the ritual announcement through clenched teeth, "Black sky."
They were in space.

"Sundowner, Edwards Mission Control."

"Roger, Edwards," Nicole replied, "go."

"We've noted the engineering telemetry. Recommend you
leave number three inactive for the duration of the flight, we
are unable to determine at this juncture the nature and extent of
the fault. We also have no predictions regarding future status."
The plan had been to treat the Hybrid's evaluation flights the
same way NASA did the original manned spaceflights; every
vehicle that was launched had a twin on the ground that duplicated the mission as closely as possible. Any condition aboard
the flight craft was duplicated as closely as possible with its
slave-linked counterpart, in hopes that a solution could more
easily be found to any fault. But this emergency had come
before the backup procedures had been fully implemented,
the only four working engines being the ones installed in
the Hybrid. Which left Ground with nothing to rely on but
computer models and simulations, which under the circumstances were less than nothing. Everyone was blazing new
trails. "Determination here is that you proceed on Mission
Commander's discretion."

She looked to Sallinger, because that was his hat.

"I defer to pilot's discretion," he said quietly, isolating the
intercom so that he spoke to her alone.

I don't want the goddamn responsibility, she screamed inside
her head. But said, in a voice that matched his for evenness of
tone, "We've come this far, boss."

He dipped his shoulders, the only way available to let her
see he was nodding agreement, and he relayed the decision to
the ground.

"Acknowledged, Sundowner," the controller said, "we have
further information. Telemetry relays from Cheyenne Mountain indicate that Target One has impacted with Target Two."

"Terrific," she said. And to Edwards, "Status?"

"Unknown, Sundowner. We had a full-spectrum LOS"—
loss of signal—"with Target One immediately prior to impact.
Consensus is this was not, repeat not, a natural occurrence."

"Alex cut 'em off," she said to Sallinger.

"Further, there are indications that Target Two has begun
to roll."

"Oh, *joy!*"

"We're currently determining the effect this will have on Target Two's orbital status, we'll relay to you as soon as we have something."

Nicole popped her belts and switched umbilicals to a walk-about air bottle, which she clipped to her left thigh.

"Mind the store, boss," she said to Sallinger with a soft clap on the shoulder, "be back in a flash." And pulled her way aft along the ceiling to Tscadi's station. The Hal suits were far sleeker than their Terrestrial counterparts, with more intrinsic strength—so that even a standard suit was the equivalent of midrange body armor—with less bulk. She reached past the Hal to call up a course display, then said, "I need a fifteen-second burn on one and four, to take us to about there."

"A higher orbit. But a slower approach velocity."

"It'll add a little more time to the intercept, but when we do catch him, we'll be coming up on the nightside terminator. The sun'll be at our back."

"And in the Cobri renegade's eyes."

"That's the idea. Can do?"

"Seventeen seconds would be better. Twelve-degree ascension, from here. Establish a shallow parabola, to allow Earth's own gravity to increase what you would call our delta-V."

"Go." Nicole started to turn away, then swung back to touch her helmet to Tscadi's, letting sound induction carry her voice to the Hal engineer, rather than the intercom. "Something more," she said quietly.

"Shea-Pilot?"

"Can you establish a full power approach to Patriot?"

Tscadi turned her face full towards Nicole, plainly doubting what she'd just heard, so Nicole repeated it.

"Number three is not dependable," the Hal said.

"Have to chance it. If he's armed, our only defense is surprise and maneuverability."

"Provided that surprise maneuver does not do us more harm than good."

Nicole grinned. "And Kymri said you had no sense of humor."

"Your pardon, Shea-Pilot, but a sense of humor is all that has kept me sane on this world of yours."

"One full orbit, we should be on him," she told Sallinger as she regained her seat.

"Ground isn't happy. Things are looking very tight from their perspective. They want to pop a boomer from Sutherland on the next circuit, to crack Patriot into as many small bits as possible to minimize the impact damage below."

"That's nice."

"If it comes to the crunch, Lieutenant, we're considered expendable."

"So what else is new?"

"There is something else."

"Sir?"

"How would you characterize the boy?"

"Alex? Very smart, very bitter, very good with toys. Give him a remote to play with, he's probably as good as it gets. Reality, though"—and she shrugged—"that's a whole other concept."

"He covered all the bases, except the Hybrid."

"No easy way to get at it?"

"On the ground. But he had to assume the attempt would be made, to use this to rescue his father. Manuel Cobri's too important to simply do nothing."

"So?"

"If you were him, Ms. Shea, what would you do?"

Thank God I'm not, she thought. "I'd have a gun," she said.

"Yeah, that's what I've been figuring, too."

"Can I try calling him?"

"We don't have line of sight, you'll have to bounce it off the ComSats."

"Patriot Station, Sundowner, do you copy, over?"

Silence.

"Alex, this is Nicole, you gonna be sulky to the end, or what?"

"Seems like," said Sallinger.

"Patriot Station, this is Sundowner, over."

"This is nothing to do with you, Nicole," came an answer finally, "go away."

"Hey, chum, even if I thought you were right, you've no call dragging Colonel Kinsella into your private scrap. Or the folks on the ground put at risk by this reentry."

"Just add it to the profile of the mad killer who almost wiped the President."

"This isn't funny, Alex."

"Keep coming, Nicole, you'll get added to the list. I don't want that, but I won't be stopped."

"There's no need, Alex, C'mon, man, cut yourself some slack. It doesn't have to be this way."

Again, silence.

"Alex!" Her voice was harsher, growing from deep in her gut, the kind of cry that would reach across a boat against the wind of a howling gale, booming loud in the confined space of her helmet.

"Stupid stupid *stupid*," she muttered over and over.

"You or him," Sallinger asked.

"Take your pick, it's probably a toss-up. Why the *hell* won't he listen?"

"Probably because he's scared he actually will."

"Excuse, Shea-Pilot," and Nicole started slightly as Tscadi loomed over her like a living wave, reaching past to tap a code into her Command Keypad. A new screen—previously blank—popped to life, the schematic diagram on its face replicated in a heads-up display floating ahead of her just inside the canopy. A targeting grid flanked by a weaponry status scheme.

"What the hell," Sallinger exclaimed.

"What is this?"

"What it appears to be, Shea-Pilot."

"This critter's armed?"

"There was no mention of this on any of the reports my office received." Sallinger wasn't bothering to hide his anger, he felt blindsided the same way he had when it was revealed that Matai was the Speaker and not Kymri.

"Because, Sallinger-Commander, there was no need. This is my own improvisation, an adaptation of the ranging-communication laser system. It will register to the Cobri-Child's sensors as a much more powerful beam of energy."

"He'll know it's a con when he sees nothing happen."

"Maybe, Colonel," Nicole said, "but for those first few seconds he's going to be scared stiff, especially with his internals going totally haywire." She was nodding, putting the pieces together on the fly. "And remember, he's never done this before, not for real. That's going to make a difference. Maybe a critical one."

"How do you mean?"

She let out a solid exhalation. "What I said, he's never done this before, for real. He's not acting through remotes, he's not sitting safe and secure in his Command Nest while his toys take the hits. His own ass is on the line."

"The man's on a path to commit certain suicide, Lieutenant."

"Doesn't mean he won't be scared, especially of elements that disrupt his program. He's a creature of habit, Colonel, his life is a carefully collected and nurtured network of patterns. He isn't good at handling the unexpected, especially when it's in his face. It hits at his control of the situation. Christ, boss, the whole family's nothing but control freaks. In Virtual, Alex defines reality, and that definition makes him safe. Same goes when he flies his remotes—they're simply extensions of his Virtual environment—the same applies here. Essentially, he's turned his dad's spaceplane into one of those remotes. But we're outside those operating parameters, we're beyond his control. Intellectually, he may know how to cope. Emotionally and physically though"—she shook her head—"I'm not sure he can."

"Suppose he comes at us with a remote?"

"Cobri-Child knows everything of our systems we have taught him," Tscadi said with a dangerous smile, "but that is not everything we know. He might surmise a great deal but there will be no certainty. This vehicle may lack aggressive weaponry, but it carries a full complement of electronics warfare systems. Any remote vehicle sent against us can be jammed."

"I hope you're right," Nicole said. "We're getting a flash from Sutherland; something's launching from Patriot."

"Missile?" Sallinger asked as Tscadi returned to her station and Nicole gave a tug on her shoulder harness to pull it snug about her.

"Too big." The Hybrid's computer was already analyzing the return, tapping into the PortaComp's memory for confirmation before reporting it as a Jeep. A general-purpose local ops spacecraft.

"Gunship," from Sallinger.

"Got to assume." The real question was whether it was a dedicated combat craft or something Alex managed to cobble together. *Wanderer* carried two, cram-jammed full of fire-and-forget missiles (nuclear capable if necessary) plus an antimissile laser plus, for close-in work when things got personally nasty, a rapid-fire Gatling gun that fired a mixture of armor-piercing depleted uranium slugs and explosive seeker shells. As they closed on Patriot, the Hybrid's own systems augmented the data relayed from Sutherland—a hundred klicks above them but almost a thousand down range, its far more powerful and extensive scanners limited by the distance and extreme angle—painting a picture that pretty much convinced Nicole what they faced wasn't the real thing. For which she was supremely grateful. Now it was simply a matter of determining what Alex had aboard and how best to keep from being killed by it.

They were racing along the downward arc of their parabola, positive delta-V giving them about a half-G acceleration, with the sun full at their back. Even with shades, Nicole figured Alex would have a hard time spotting them. Probably wouldn't even be trying, he'd be trusting his instruments.

"Live or remote, Tscadi," she called.

"I believe live, Shea-Pilot."

"He's coming out to meet us."

"Prime the motors," Nicole said.

"What," cried Sallinger.

"Hold on to your seats, folks," she said, priming the ignition sequence on her chair arm and firing all four mains as soon as the engineer gave her a green light. Instantly, she was hammered in the chest as the Hybrid went from zero to full launch thrust in a matter of seconds, hurled forward by the same amount of power it would use to burst free of the atmosphere below. And just as quickly, her helmet filled with the clang and whoop and honk of various alarms, all telling her what she already knew, that she was pushing the spacecraft dangerously close to its design tolerances, that she was risking a potentially catastrophic loss of course control, and most importantly, she was on a collision course with the Jeep, and Patriot beyond.

"What the devil," Sallinger again.

"I know what I'm doing, boss," she said. "Trust, me. Tscadi," she yelled, a reflex made unnecessary really by the fact that her mike would transmit the smallest whisper clear as could be, "disengage the flight control net, the damn computer's trying to take over!"

"The computer is merely responding to your attempt to operate the vehicle beyond its limitations."

"You and I both know the vehicle's limitations, Tscadi-Engineer, and we're nowhere near. And if this bloody machine shuts us down right now all we'll be is dust."

"You have full control, Shea-Pilot," but it was clear from the engineer's voice that while she bought Nicole's argument she didn't at all like it. Neither did Sallinger, who was already setting up a breakaway course that would swing them past the station and off the roof of the atmosphere. Be hell getting home, probability was they'd need an intercept from Sutherland with either fuel or a tow, but they'd survive.

"C'mon, Alex boy, now's the time to show your stuff"— Sallinger gaped at the ComBoard, then at Nicole beside him; she was transmitting—"gonna play us a little game of chicken."

"Lieutenant," he snapped, "I'm relieving you."

"I wouldn't do that, sir."

"Yield your stick. You're as crazy as he is."

"Quite possibly. Certainly as scared. He's fired."

A new telltale flashing its frantic warning, reticules on the HUD isolating a pair of brilliant flashes barely visible against the night-shadowed Earth, the display screen below pumping relevant schematics.

"Zero the mains," Nicole told Tscadi and the engines were as quickly shut down. "Leave them primed," she continued, "to refire on my mark, Max Launch."

"I have a redline warning on thruster three, Shea-Pilot."

"Push it anyway, we'll need all we've got." While Nicole was speaking both hands operated independently of each other, one locking the lasers on Alex's Jeep, the other twisting the handle on her sidestick, cycling it over to control of the attitude thrusters. Twin beams flashed from below the nose, their progress shown more clearly on the HUD and its slaved display screen as the laser's coherent light splashed violently across the other spacecraft. It was an impressively dramatic display, a most classic example of sound and fury signifying nothing, and she hoped she'd scared him shitless, because if they'd been the MainForce Pulse Rifles mounted aboard *Range Guide*, the Jeep would have been reduced to instant slag. At the same time, she ignited all the vertical thrusters banked along the Hybrid's belly, Sallinger crying out as the ship shuddered upward, rising with elephantine slowness above their flight path.

"Missiles still locked and closing," he reported when he found his voice, only to lose it again as quickly and completely as Nicole fired nose and tail in sequence, pitching the spacecraft literally end over end, ascribing a sweeping arc that took them high over the top of Cobri's Jeep and started them on an inverted path straight for Patriot.

"Tscadi," Nicole called.

"Countermeasures against the missiles effective. They lost our track and have detonated upon exhaustion of propellant. No active response from the hostile vehicle."

"Probably can't believe his eyes."

"That, Shea, makes two of us. He also probably figures we'll splatter ourselves all over Patriot and do his damn job for him."

"Have faith, Colonel. I need the thrust now, Tscadi-Engineer."

"As you command, Shea-Pilot." And the anger in her tone was leavened just a bit by grudging respect. "I also believe the hostile may have an operational failure of his scan systems. I can detect no active emanations."

"Break for us. If he's well and truly blind—even if only temporarily—he may not twig to what we've done 'til it's too late."

Again, they were pressed deep into their chairs, as the great engines applied braking thrust to slow their headlong descent. The Hybrid was shuddering violently, so much so that all the crew could do was to hold on—they dared not try to operate any of the controls, all they'd do was make a botch of it—until Tscadi's hoarse cry penetrated Nicole's aching, shaking consciousness.

"Number three, we are losing—!"

And there was a *bang* from behind of a kind Nicole remembered only too well—only the last such occasion had been the simulator run that had almost washed her out of the Astronaut Corps. Now, as then, her reactions were fast and sure: a grab for the garishly outlined EMERGENCY SHUTDOWN handle on the ceiling panel, a check to see how badly they were hurt, some fast and furious play with the attitude jets to keep the venting gas from the explosion from throwing them off their track. A swallow of sick relief as a glance at the displays told her things weren't as bad as they could have been. Tscadi had evidently started the shutdown from her panel a split second

before the combustion chamber ruptured, limiting the severity
of the blast and the extent of the damage. One motor was down
but the other three were still solid and the Hybrid itself was
still intact. With a word of warning, Tscadi pulled the plug
on the other engines and an air of relative calm returned to
the flight deck.

"I take it back," Sallinger said slowly, "you're insane."

And Nicole had to concede the nod. She wasn't really paying attention to the Colonel, though, she had her head back,
craning her neck and body—as much as she could in the
restrictive confines of her seat—for a better view out the top-
side windows.

In the confusion, their attitude had slipped so that in relation
to the Earth, their tail was up, their nose down. And of course,
the whole spacecraft was flying backward, and upside-down.

Close enough, it seemed, to touch, Patriot Station was drifting slowly past, right outside the windows. That view was
fortunately deceptive because even as they watched—Nicole
playing with the attitude thrusters to match velocities with the
derelict—the tinker-toy assemblage slipped past in a slow,
majestic roll, end over spoked end.

"It can't handle those stresses," Sallinger said.

Patriot was built outward from a central stalk, with docking modules at each end—the Cobri spaceplane mounted on
one. Radiating outward from a coupling just in-board of those
modules was a network of five spokes, linked halfway along
their length by transit tubes, allowing for passage from one to
the other without returning to the core, the spokes at one end
half the size of those at the other. The larger were the research
elements, the smaller reserved for power and maintenance.
The hub was where everyone lived. As time went on, the
station was designed to expand according to need, growing a
little like Topsy into a permanent habitat intended to support a
resident community and serve as the primary staging platform
for humanity's exploration of the Solar System. But it had
never gotten beyond that initial stage. And now, way ahead
of schedule, it was returning home.

Nicole made a clucking noise with her tongue. "Each rotation," she said, pointing at the station as it swept past, "the
longer arms catch the fringes of the upper atmosphere." Only
a comparatively few—and far between—molecules at this altitude but enough to create drag in an orbiting body, especially

once the station swept out into dayside where the Sun's radiance caused normal atmospheric expansion. "But the short arms don't," she continued, "so with each turn, the spin gets more skewed, the short side flipping over faster and faster. Nothing you'd really notice at first . . ."

"But before long," Sallinger picked up her thought, "a vicious enough torque to bend the hub in half."

"And then," Nicole finished, "won't things be a lovely, lovely mess. Tscadi, the hostile?"

"I do not think he perceives us, Shea-Pilot. His control is not steady."

"He's losing it a little."

"I don't blame him."

Nicole smiled. "We have time, boss, but only a little. Only one way to get what we came for."

"Someone has to go over there and bring them out, is that what you're saying?"

"Yes, sir."

"You?"

"Forgive me, Colonel, there's qualified and there's qualified. You're flying right seat because you pulled rank and I guess because you didn't trust me with anyone else—and for that I think I'm flattered—but that doesn't mean you can handle an EVA, especially into that zoo. Tscadi's needed to help get this baby home. That leaves me."

"As you say, Lieutenant, there's qualified . . ."

"You're the boss, sir."

"Did you know it would come to this when I asked you on the ground?"

"I don't really know anything anymore, sir."

"I hate these frigging suits, how the hell can you tell anything about anyone, it's like talking to them from another room, trying to shove your face through some stupid, small window."

"No argument, sir."

"Be quick, Shea."

"Like a bunny, boss."

The words were jaunty, and they stuck in her throat like spiked molasses, going down oh so slowly and ripping her to shreds along the way. She stood in the airlock, without even the security blanket of a Manned Maneuvering Unit— she couldn't risk the bulk or afford the time it would take to toss it off once she reached the station and pull it on again when it came time to leave—just a hand thruster and a backpack, with a spare bottle on her thigh. This was a freefall EVA, the station's spin made it impossible to establish a tether linking it with the Hybrid; she'd have to find Cobri and Kinsella— praying with all her heart they had suits because if they didn't they were royally screwed—tie the three of them together and push out the most convenient doorway in what she hoped was the right direction.

"Sundowner-Prime, Sundowner-Remote, how copy?"

"Five-by, Remote," Sallinger said as casually as if she were heading out for her morning jog. "No significant change of status of our hostile."

"Praise the Lord for small favors."

"You okay, Shea? I'm monitoring some spikes on your MedBoard."

I want to piss my pants, she thought, and had to force herself once more to stand stock-still and take a slow, steady series of breaths, a gentle sequence of in-out, in-out that shifted into a subvocalized hum whose tone and intensity built to an equally calm crescendo, her mind's eye flashing to the Nantucket shore with big combers thundering in from a storm that was raging far beyond the visible horizon, whose fury didn't touch the island in the slightest save through the water that surrounded it. *Be like the sea,* she told herself, *follow the rhythm, become the strength. Fear isn't important, it's what you do with it.*

"Lieutenant?"

"Yah, Colonel, sorry, my mind wandered."

"You were singing."

"Hope it wasn't too awful, sir."

"Don't quit your day job, Shea." His concern was evident, but so was the subtext that demanded a decision, either go or stay.

So she pushed out into space.

She floated at first, telling herself she was taking stock of the situation, evaluating the risks, seeking out the best approach. But she was scared. Filling her mind were images of destruction, the miscue that bounced her off the station hull, smashing her helmet or rupturing her suit. A body tumbling outward into the dark or the other direction, a candle burning oh so briefly, oh so bright as friction turned her into a falling torch.

An arm threw itself forward, seemingly of its own accord, creating enough force to pivot her slowly in a circle, back towards the beckoning hatch. That same arm could stop her with a touch, and then pull her back inside. She kept staring at the gloved fingers, waiting for all the arguments pro and con to marshal themselves inside her head, as though decisions there were made in a kind of psychic parliament, through rational debate and an orderly vote.

And in the time it took her to consider all that, and have a sad, self-mocking laugh at the absurdity of it all, she swung back 'round full circle the way she was originally going. And just as reflexively, found her other hand pulling the firing trigger of her thruster.

The actual approach turned out to be something of an anti-climax, or so she felt—Sallinger couldn't stop his heart from pounding as he watched, his own MedStats causing Tscadi more concern than Nicole's—the station's spin was comparatively slow and still more or less regular. She came in broadside to the hub, using a grappling gun to snag a solid hold and reel her in the last stretch. Once she made contact, the major thing was to keep her eyes fixed on the hull before her; without any external referents to add to the discomfort, it was easier to cope with the rotation. She crabbed her way partially around, then a fair distance along the hub until she came at last to a station airlock. To her delight, the conduits were still carrying power and it slid open at a touch of the command plate. Far too easily in fact, for a station that had supposedly been derelict most of her lifetime.

She had to pressurize the lock before continuing, which meant at least this element of the station was maintaining its environment. Her external receptors confirmed what her eyes read from all the flashing telltales once she was inside: that happy state wouldn't last much longer. Deep, anguished groans rippled the length of the hub cylinder, in time to a perceptible shimmy in the fabric of the hull. A crash to one side made her jump, as a cabinet—twisted too far out of position to hold anymore—exploded off its brackets, contents caroming off the opposite wall along every ballistically reflective trajectory calculable.

"Sundowner-Prime, do you copy?" she called.

"Raj, Remote," came Sallinger's welcome, immediate response.

"Sorry about this, but I'm lost. I figure my best bet's to check the plane itself, only I don't know which way to go."

"Which way you facing."

"*Uhhh*," disconcerting, to have to think about that. "Back to the hull wall I entered through, that of any use?"

"Affirmative. Relative vector zero-niner-zero, and a range of eighty-three meters."

"Oh, joy."

"That a problem?"

"Well, bits are shaking loose on the premises, makes for a lively stroll. Also, I suspect internal integrity ain't what it used to be. Wish I had a camera."

"Concur about station status, we're already marking atmosphere leaks. Say again, that last?"

"For something that's been abandoned twenty years, this hulk looks awfully good."

"Tidy ghosts, perhaps?"

"You've heard those stories, too?"

"Everyone who flies this way does, one time or other."

"Anybody ever check it out?"

"Believe so. Nothing ever came of it, that much I know."

"I wonder . . ."

"What?"

"Probably my paranoid imagination."

"What?"

"There's a fairly extensive antenna array. And its orbit keeps it pretty far removed from Sutherland."

"When Sutherland went up, Patriot was still active and military. The Pentagon didn't like the idea of anyone looking over their shoulders. The antagonistic track was at their insistence."

"So if there weren't ghosts at all but a live crew, who would really know?"

"Lieutenant, the place can be seen from the ground."

She yelped, as much in startlement as anything else, as another component came tumbling by, arms and treads scrabbling futilely for a hold as it bounced from surface to surface.

"How about housekeeping remotes?" she asked.

"If you see 'em, I guess they must be so, but to what end?"

"Relay ComStation? A way of passing messages back and forth without anyone knowing, much less eavesdropping. Tight-beam links to Patriot, held for a summons from the ground, and vice versa."

"Feasible."

"I wonder if this is how the Wolfpack got its marching orders? And passed news down again?"

"I hate to be a nudge, but you have more important concerns."

"I can see the boundary 'lock, I'm almost there."

There was gravity here, at the periphery of the spin, and she had to strain to lift the hatch, at the same time staying alert for any stray chunks of debris that decided to tumble her way. She couldn't latch it open, with the station's internal pressure dropping it would never release the locks on the outer door. The best bet was to push it as high as she could, then drop through the hatch and let it crash down behind her. She fell slower than she wanted and it far faster than expected, the door clipped her helmet and bounced her hard off the other wall, prompting a fair share of cries and curses and a fast, frantic check of her stats to determine the suit's integrity. It seemed to have held up better than she herself; from the soreness on her shoulders, she knew there'd be some spectacular bruises where the helmet's seal ring was hammered into her flesh, a fair price she decided compared to the alternative of a broken shoulder or collarbone.

She heaved the locking bar into place, grimly realizing she'd never get the door open again, even with power assist, then turned to the one at her feet. That was another effort, and this time she locked it open.

She was feeling hot and a bit light-headed, so much so she lost her balance reaching for the access port on the spaceplane's hatch and toppled in slow-motion right onto her face, lying upside down, tucked in a corner, laughing herself silly at the absurdity of the moment and giving serious consideration to staying where she was for a good, long, terribly well-deserved nap.

She shook her head, repeated the gesture as violently as she could manage, then scrabbled ineffectually at the locking lugs of her helmet, managing to snag one, then at last the other, pulling them both open and twisting off the helmet.

The air was thin and chill but infinitely better than the poison she'd been swallowing inside her suit, and in a minute or so she could feel her head begin to clear, aside from what threatened to be a jackhammer of an ache, spiking right across her temples. She wore a status display on her left forearm, a

look confirmed what she already knew, that somewhere along
the way her backpack had taken a major hit that cracked the
regulator. Instead of providing clean air, she was getting a
dangerously skewed mixture. Another look, at the offending
piece of equipment, told her she wasn't going to fix it, either.
Which left her baby bottle. Which held, max, a half hour. Less
with exertion.

She plugged it into her umbilical, but didn't turn it on, as she
took a deep breath—noting that even with the hatch supposedly
sealed the compartment was losing air—and once more locked
her helmet into place. She'd lost her aerials, too, putting her
out of touch with Sallinger.

Nothing for it, she told herself, *but to push on*. And pounded
on the spaceplane's hull before thumbing the access plate.
The hatch obligingly cycled wide, sealing itself gently and
automatically behind her as she descended inside. The wall-
mounted telltales told her there was good air and she cracked
her helmet as the inner door was opened manually by Grace
Kinsella.

Nicole offered a salute, which wasn't acknowledged much
less returned as the older woman turned back to the cabin and
announced, "The cavalry's here."

At least she's in a suit, Nicole thought, stepping over the
threshold and letting herself slide slowly along the cabin floor
until she could brace herself on the hull wall below. As was
Manuel Cobri, she saw when she came to rest.

"Good to see you, Ms. Shea," he said with more good cheer
than most under similar circumstances. And she thought he'd
probably have done well on the *Titanic*.

"Time to go," she told them both flatly.

"We can't disengage," Kinsella replied in the same tone,
"all our systems are down."

"My son was very thorough."

"Like father, sir . . ." and got a sharp look in return and an
internal reminder to leave well enough alone, the ice beneath
her feet was thin enough already.

"Patriot's in a runaway spin," Nicole told them.

"What do you think, Shea," Kinsella snapped, "we're completely dim in here? We *know* that!"

"The torque's growing more extreme with every rotation;
the longer we delay here, the greater the likelihood of the
station coming apart on top of us. Add to that the fact that

Alex is skating around in a modified Jeep gunship, with the Hal shuttle too tempting and easy a target to miss."

"What's your point, Lieutenant?"

"You've both got suits and portable bottles. We crack an outboard hatch and go walkabout." Kinsella was shaking her head. "The three of us on a tether," Nicole hurried on, trying to keep her voice calm even as her words picked up speed in time to the ever more vehement shakes of Kinsella's head, "pulled by my thruster. We get free, we stabilize, we make the crossing to the Hybrid."

"You're insane."

"I assume, Colonel, you have an alternative?"

"You said it yourself, the station's coming apart. When the docking module tears free, let the shuttle come to us. Our hull's solid, we have air."

"You could find yourselves dumped straight down into the atmosphere, Colonel," Nicole said incredulously. "And there's no guarantee your precious integrity will be maintained. I'd say pretty much the opposite. Yes, there's a risk following my lead, but I think it offers a better chance than staying put."

"In your experience, Lieutenant," Kinsella put a vicious twist to every word.

"Sarcasm notwithstanding, Colonel," she replied in a disconcertingly level voice, "yes. You're a visitor here, Colonel, a comparative short-timer. Compared to most I know on the Frontier, so am I. But that doesn't include you. Here and now, ma'am, I'm the best you've got. You don't want to listen, that's your privilege. Me, I'm outta here."

"The hell you say. You can't crack one of the emergency hatches without putting us all at risk."

"What's your problem, Colonel?" And even as Nicole spoke, the answer came as clear as sunlight between them, in the set to Kinsella's jaw and the unnatural tension along legs and body, as though she were trying to plant herself as deeply and securely as any ancient oak. *She's scared*, Nicole thought, amazed because she hadn't thought Kinsella capable of such an emotion, and even more amazed because she wasn't really surprised. *Good in the simulator*, she continued to herself, *possibly even good on the line—but only in those aspects that are most closely related to the life she knew, to flying a plane. The rest, though, that's totally beyond her.*

"Colonel," Cobri said softly, "I must agree with the Lieutenant. This is a superb vehicle but I, as well as anyone, know
its limitations. To stay here is to die here. If it is my time, I
would rather face it actively fighting for my life."

"You trust her judgment more than mine," Kinsella snarled
bitterly.

"She belongs here."

"And I don't."

The plane shuddered around them as a hollow boom echoed
from far along the station superstructure.

"Maybe we got lucky," Nicole said hurriedly, "maybe what
just broke loose is heading off the other direction." *Please*, she
prayed, *not towards the shuttle*. "If not, in maybe a minute or
so, all our arguments are going to be moot. If so, let's not push
that luck any further. I'm not here to score points, Colonel, just
bring you both home."

"You two go," Kinsella began, "I'll . . ."

And Nicole hammered her in the face.

It wasn't the neatest of punches. She'd been slipping closer
throughout their exchange, carefully planting feet, setting her
body, to give her maximum force with minimum cause to
alarm her target. Once along the way, she'd caught Cobri's
eye and seen he knew full well what she was about, and he
was quick enough to pull Kinsella's attention to him, giving
Nicole an extra moment. Her hand hurt like blazes—though
probably no less than Kinsella's jaw (no mean feat, tucking
the punch in over the helmet ring with enough force to cold
cock her first time)—and there would be a glorious bruise
come morning, they should all live so long. Felt good, though.
As far as Nicole was concerned, the Colonel had it coming.

"How shall we proceed, Lieutenant?" Cobri asked.

Firstly, Nicole checked their air, hers included, making
certain the bottles were full, their junctions and hoses in good
working order. Next came the helmets, locked with visors
open, to buy them as much free time as possible. Once they
went on the bottles, the clock was counting down. Then, the
tether, a double line binding Kinsella to Cobri and the pair of
them to her.

"Interesting," Cobri noted, as casually as he would the
weather.

"What?"

"Colonel Kinsella and I are securely bound, yet the line that connects us to you is fastened with a quick release buckle."

"There could be a situation where I'll need room to maneuver. I don't know how long Grace'll be out and if she wakes while we're in transit, she could panic."

"What is wrong with her?"

"Happens sometimes. You can deal with the environment until you have to step outside. Ready to go?"

"No."

Something in his tone brought her up to her full height, facing him at double arm's length along the plushly appointed cabin, designer corporate in elements of sleek, understated power.

"Perhaps it is my turn to be paranoid, but I cannot help wondering if your 'room to maneuver' carries a hidden meaning."

"Such as?"

"You have been exceptionally curious about aspects of my private life."

"I could say the same about your family."

"I have done you no harm, Lieutenant."

"In that, sir, you couldn't be more wrong. But I'm not going to argue about it now, we haven't the time, and quite frankly I haven't the interest. I'm here to get you and Grace home. *Safe*, sir. And if you don't believe that, then you haven't a clue about what living up here is all about."

"My apologies."

"Save 'em, sir. Talk is cheap. I'm going to bleed the atmosphere before blowing the hatch; that'll minimize any effect of an explosive decompression. One more thing, my coms are out, so there'll be no remote contact between us once we're sealed. Watch me, follow my hand signals. If I need to explain anything, I'll come close and touch helmets."

"I've worked in space, Lieutenant. I know the drill."

She closed Kinsella's and Cobri's visors, checking to make sure they were secure, opening the valve on their portable air bottles before repeating the procedure with herself. Her movements were sharp and tightly controlled but that had nothing to do with any innate proficiency, it was an extension of a fury that flash-flamed through her like burning magnesium, white-hot and all-consuming, filling her so full of energy it was all she could do not to haul off and punch her way

through the wall. Cobri's words had struck a nerve but the
rage didn't come from there, it was the realization that she was
tempted. That she was alone and they were amateurs and the
smallest mistake could end their lives. Indeed, they wouldn't
even know they were in trouble 'til they were dying. There'd
be pointed fingers and blame in her direction, but nothing that
could be proved. Her career would be ruined but there wasn't
that terribly much left of it anyway. All it required was a
betrayal of everything she believed in.

And she was tempted.

She gave herself an extra few seconds before firing the
explosive bolts on the rear hatch, the 'plane's internal atmosphere so close to vacuum that there was hardly a stir as the
few remaining scraps of air gusted outside, barely rippling
some loose gear floating past. She clipped a tether of her
own onto a fastener inside the hatch, then played out the line
as she swung herself onto the outer hull. Initial response, a
bad move, because the first thing she saw was the monstrous,
glowing dinner plate of the Earth filling the sky before her
as Patriot rolled through another rotation, her hands closing
reflexively as tightly as possible on her rope, throat filling
with the desperate, atavistic fear that if she let go, she'd
be thrown straight out of the sky and all the way down to
the ground. Then one extreme, absurd reaction gave way to
another, and she whooped with manic delight, terror mixing
with a wild-and-wooly excitement that gripped her just as fully
at this best of all conceivable roller-coaster rides.

She'd have ridden all the way around had not a tap on the
ankle brought her back to the mundane. Cobri's helmet was
poking up through the hatch, looking expectantly towards her
for a cue. She motioned for him to hold her line, the centrifugal
force of the spin immediately acting to pull the unconscious
Kinsella straight out from the hatch, to its limit, Cobri wincing
at the strain as he anchored himself with one hand and tried to
take up some of Kinsella's slack with the other.

Nicole touched helmets.

"Do we simply let go?" he asked.

"My hand thruster doesn't have the power or the fuel to
overcome our departure delta-V, and without my Coms, I
can't guarantee the Hybrid getting a decent fix on us. It'll
take some time, but the best route is back along the core to
the axis of the spin, then kick off laterally, perpendicular to

the line of flight." Basically, the same way she came in.

"I thought you said this wreck is coming apart around us." *The sonofabitch,* she thought in infuriated admiration, *is grinning. He's probably having the time of his bloody life!*

"See for yourself." The long spokes at their end of the stalk were already bending double, all the peripheral components—any add-ons that weren't part of the primary hull—being stripped and scatter-blown into the station's wake. And there were some ominous rips and gullies along the hub as well.

"Let's go," Nicole said. "And remember, never move without being sure you're secure."

That proved far easier said than done. She still had her grapple gun but she couldn't use it until they cleared the crest of the docking module and made what seemed like an eternally laborious passage around the base of one of the spokes— the metal actually thrumming beneath Nicole's gloved palm as another rotation dipped the far end of the tower into the uppermost reaches of the atmosphere, like dipping an oar into the water to slow a boat down. So far the basic speed was so high, and the length of oar being dipped so small and for so short a time, that the effect was almost inconsequential. But each repetition increased the effect and it wouldn't be terribly long before there were consequences to match. They didn't dare be present to see that. Worse, because of the nature of the movement, they were essentially climbing uphill.

There was nothing ahead anywhere near midpoint to anchor the grapple to, so she raised the sights a fraction and let fly for the opposite spoke. Ten meters out from her, the grapple's little solid-fuel charge ignited and the anchor vanished into the distance, drawn unerringly to its target by a microchip seeker. She couldn't see or feel the impact, but the grapple obligingly transmitted a CONTACT confirmation back along a fiber-optic thread imbedded in the heart of the cable to the gun itself, and an LED crystal that flickered from red to green.

She passed the line back to Cobri, who patted her shoulder to tell her he had a good hold, and—after a final check of Grace Kinsella to make sure she was okay—Nicole led the way along the hub.

The farther they went, the less the rotational effect of the spin and consequently the lesser the gravity. But it also seemed to them that they were spinning ever faster, which raised

another potential danger, that of disorientation sickness. Along
the way, she pointed out the fairy-tale teardrop of the Hybrid,
pacing their course at a cautious remove from the disintegrating station. Seeing the shuttle, though, reminded Nicole of
Alex and the Jeep—cut off from the outside as she'd been,
she'd lost track of him in her thoughts as well.

Suddenly, she was caught by a hand. The tug caught her at
an awkward moment and her feet went out from under her.
They'd been making their way along the leading edge of the
hub, the part that was moving in the direction of the spin, so
that inertia would press them into the hull beneath their feet (as
opposed to the trailing edge, where it would be trying its best
to pull them off). Down side was that every spin they had the
looming presence of the daylit Earth and the Sun beyond full in
their faces. But that same force now threatened to drag Nicole
around the curve of the hull, and once she passed midpoint—
if she couldn't find a secure handhold—yank her into open
space. She latched on to the nearest thing in reach, but it was
a broken stanchion with the shape of a broken bottle and all
she accomplished was to tear the surface layer of her glove—
almost giving herself a heart seizure in the process, certain the
moment she saw the leather-covered palm begin to rip that she
was doomed.

She felt a tug at the waist, her body swinging sideways
and then miraculously to a stop, a painful twist of her head
giving her a view of Manuel Cobri sitting atop the hub, with
feet braced and the tether in both hands. Seeing her look, he
pointed, and she crabbed around—pulling herself back towards
him in the process—to gasp in astonishment and horror at a
set of distant navigation lights. The Jeep, in what she quickly
recognized was a fast, sloppy copy of her own maneuver. Alex
was above the plane of flight established by the Hybrid and the
station, nose down towards the shuttle and inverted, describing
a great loop that would ideally drop him pretty much on top
of them. She saw a flash from his tail and knew he'd applied
braking thrust, but that glance alone was enough to tell her
he'd fired too soon. He had the idea, but not the instincts.
He'd flinched, probably figuring to err on the side of caution,
except that he'd done so from too extreme an attitude to do
him any good. The engines were driving him ahead—what
Nicole registered as "down"—without slowing his forward
momentum. A standard Jeep didn't have the thrust, or the

reserves, for this kind of stunt. If he'd fired max power, as he'd doubtless seen Nicole do, he had nothing more to call for. Still, he tried, she gave him credit for that. Swinging the Jeep through the final degrees of pitch with attitude thrusters, lining up his mains where they should have been from the start, slowing perceptibly even as they watched.

Too little, too late.

If he was trying for them, he was way off line, skimming close overhead—Nicole and his father both instinctively ducking—to carom off the hub itself before final backward impact with the spokes beyond. There was a silent flash as the remaining fuel in the engines let go, an explosion that sliced through the base of one of the spokes, toppling it on top of the Cobri spaceplane, half tearing the beautiful craft from its moorings and leaving what remained a broken tangle of debris, venting raw hydrogen in a flickering gaseous display.

Nicole unbuckled the hand thruster and shoved it into Cobri's grasp. "Take this," she said, forgetting that he couldn't hear her.

"What," he protested, touching his helmet to hers, "what are you doing?"

"Slow bursts, straight out from here, perpendicular to the station's line of flight." There were Mayday signalers clipped to the shoulder harness and she flipped on both Cobri's and Kinsella's; the strobes could be seen for klicks and along with them went a pulsing radio tone that could be used for an RDF lock. Indeed, an answering flash from the Hybrid's roof window told her the signals had been received. "They know you're coming, either Colonel Sallinger or the Hal engineer, Tscadi, will be out to meet you. You tell 'em from me, that's as far as they're to go, that's my direct order as Spacecraft Commander. Understood, Mr. Cobri? I make it back on my own or not at all."

"I don't understand."

"The tail end of the Jeep bore the brunt of the impact. The cabin looks fundamentally intact. I'm going back for him."

"That's suicide. Look at your gauges, girl, you have too little air. And without the thruster, how will you return to the shuttle?"

"I'll take my chances, and find a way. That's a standard configuration Jeep, there should be portable bottles in the emergency locker, and a hand thruster, too. I won't leave him."

And she broke contact, pulling the tether from his grasp and giving him a shoulder shove that sent him and Kinsella into a slow spiral off the hub. He gave her a last, long look before turning his back and—after a moment's fumbling—igniting the thruster. Only a fractional burst, an attempt to stabilize his movement and get himself pointed in a better direction. He was as good as he'd intimated, careful and methodical, taking the time to learn the tool before trusting himself to use it, and she knew he'd be fine.

The kid was another matter entirely. Not to mention her.

Once more down the hub, descending reversed, playing out the tether hand over hand, even more conscious of the station's increasingly violent disintegration. She was singing again, delighted in a way that she had no one to hear her, giving full voice—far more enthusiasm than accuracy, but what the hell—to her favorite rock 'n' roll. Breaking a lyric line every so often to call Alex's name, even though she knew he couldn't hear her.

As she neared the Jeep, she reconsidered her earlier spot evaluation, the small vehicle was a mess. The ceramic composite hull was warped and split along its entire length, with spiderweb fractures across the canopy. She wrapped a few loops around its partially deployed landing skid to secure her tether, then clambered awkwardly up the broken, bleeding hull to manhandle the emergency hatch.

The interior wasn't much better. The fire had flashed forward as well as aft, scorching everything it touched, and making Nicole wonder if this was a wasted trip. She hadn't looked at her bottle telltale since she started, she didn't need to, she knew she had nowhere near enough to do the job. If she was wrong about the emergency locker, this was as far as she went.

She sought it first—another automatic reaction, acknowledging that she could do far more once her own status was secure—and found what she was after, breathing a sigh of relief as she clutched the oxygen gently to her breast. Fate was indeed smiling today, because it held a thruster pack as well.

She was set.

Alex was in trouble.

He was still strapped into his chair. The fire had come and gone too quickly for any reaction. But the charring on his suit was surface effect, residue of combustion in the internal atmosphere around Alex, not of the suit itself. She thought he was fine, until she looked through his faceplate.

His eyes were wide, staring, mouth open and moving, the transparency fogged with the intensity of his breath as he spoke. He was looking right at her but didn't seem to register her presence, even when she shined a torch full in his eyes. Not a matter of physical blindness, but of perception. And she cursed her lack of a functioning radio.

She leaned forward touching her visor to his and immediately heard a hoarse, hurried mantra, repeated over and over. "Recycle," he was saying, "reset recycle reset recycle reset."

"Alex," she called, in the command voices she'd learned crewing sailboats as a kid, and refined on the parade quad at the Air Force Academy, a deep resonance that was guaranteed to get a person's attention, anytime, anywhere. Or so she'd believed.

Live and learn. He didn't bat an eye.

"Alex, it's Nicole. Listen to me. Your vessel's a wreck but you appear to be all right. It's a serious situation, but not critical. I'm getting you out of here, Alex, I'm taking you home. Just relax, okay, take things easy. Can you hear me, Alex, are you listening?"

She might as well have been talking to the planet outside. He kept chanting.

"Goddammit, Cobri, this isn't a Virtual scenario. It's *real*, do you hear, do you understand, you can die here. If you don't do as I say, you will *die* here!"

She didn't like his color, and scrambled along his arm for a look at his telltale. But here the fire had done some damage, scoring the display circuits so that they flashed only intermittent and untrustworthy data.

"Alex," she said, "stop panting. You're creating an imbalance inside your suit. There's enough air, I have an extra bottle for each of us. Slow, even, steady breaths, Alex, that's the ticket. You're pumping too much carbon dioxide into your helmet, the suit scrubbers can't handle the load. Alex, you're poisoning yourself, for Christ's sake, will you listen? Let yourself go. Alex!" She was yelling, tearing her own throat raw in her effort to reach him. She looked around frantically, for anything that could be established as a sealed environment, kicked over to the locker in hopes of finding a LifeBall—

officially tagged a Solo Survival Module, essentially a self-sealing, inflatable cocoon. Start losing atmosphere, pull the trigger, duck inside, and zip the sucker shut behind you. Came complete with larger versions of the suit beacons and was guaranteed good for twenty-four hours. Even if he didn't come out of his mantra, the greater internal volume would allow her time to haul him back to the shuttle before his air got critical.

Wasn't where it was supposed to be. But the locker had sprung with the crash, couple of the restraints broken, so she began searching along the nooks and crannies, threatening a profane mantra of her own until fingers brushed a package and she half collapsed with delight to find it intact and unmarked.

Touched helmets again with Alex, more reassurance that he was going to be okay, reaching up through the hatch—because there was no way an inflated ball would fit, especially occupied—to fasten the package with a triple tie and pull the lanyard, grinning exultantly as the silver sphere popped gloriously full before her eyes. She'd lose pressure when she tucked him in and raised his visor, but she could use one of the emergency bottles to make up the difference.

Speaking of which, getting close to the time when she should switch her own. She glanced down through the clear canopy, en route to the locker, when she saw Alex spasm suddenly against his restraints.

She was on him in a flash—a risky dive considering the floating trash and occasional jagged outcrops—found his mouth gaping, tongue protruding, hands flailing aimlessly about his chest. He was straining against the straps, as though under the impact of a massive electric shock, his expression changing as she watched to one of real pain.

"No," she screamed. "You miserable rock-fucking little toad, don't you do this to yourself, *no!*" She punched the locking junction of the restraints, pivoting him over her hip to throw him to the deck, raising her fisted hands in helpless frustration and a scream of anguish because the stupid son of a bitch was wearing a hard suit (*Of course*, some insanely anal part of her noted in passing, *considering how he feels about taking risks, what else would he wear but something that affords the absolute maximum of protection?*) and there was no possible way to administer CPR through a solid breastplate. The poisoning air and his panic had combined to throw him into a massive heart attack and there was nothing she could do about it.

The shuttle, she thought, *get him to an open environment, where we can crack him out of his shell and buy time enough—please oh please oh please—to boost for Sutherland. Minimal G's, a lot safer than reentry, and their zero-gravity ward is ideal for critical recovery.*

So she hauled him off the deck and towards the hatch, and the waiting LifeBall. But he grabbed her hard, bunching the front of her suit in his hand, fear bursting in her own eyes that he'd open her suit and take her with him. It wasn't an intentional act, though, just reflex, and she saw his mouth working, trying to speak.

She touched his faceplate with hers and heard the mantra replaced by a breathily groaned, "Oh."

"Alex," she said, "hold on, I'll get you home. I've got a LifeBall right here. A few stinking minutes"—the better side of thirty was what she meant—"you can do that for me, for yourself, c'mon, man, please!"

"I screwed up," he managed to say.

"Everybody does," she said, wriggling them out of the wreck, making a quick grab for a tether before they went too far and got tumbled over the side.

"Recycle," he said.

"No," she cried.

"Reset." He sounded confused, unable to comprehend why his toys weren't behaving. The tension was draining out of him, his grip loosening on her suit, the pain leaving his face.

"No," she roared.

But he was beyond hearing.

fifteen

THE BUTLER POINTED her towards the garage, where he said the old man was puttering with a pet car. There was a spectacular view off the terrace towards the harbor and the glistening Manhattan skyline beyond and she paused for a moment's enjoyment before proceeding on her way. It was a crisp day, the kind she loved, when she'd enjoy nothing more than to be in an old beloved Skye sweater and jeans, wandering the Nantucket shore. Or better yet, chasing currents through the sky in her sailplane. The air was mostly clear, swept by a freshening breeze off the ocean, with clouds in scattered ranks overhead like Brobdingnagian puffballs. So many things she'd rather be doing, so many places she'd rather be than here.

Over the years, Cobri had bought up most of Todt Hill—making, and she smiled without mirth, the homeowners offers they couldn't refuse—plowing under the houses and lots and restoring the land to a pristine state. Talk was that his ultimate goal was to purchase all of Staten Island, making it private property except for the Interstate running from the Verrazano Narrows to the Goethals Bridge. No one took him seriously—except perhaps the locals who'd be shunted aside—but no one could afford to put it past him, either.

Nicole figured it was a done thing. It may take a generation or two, but if that's what Cobri wanted, that's what would happen. Not a doubt in her mind.

Her heels made small clicks on the flagstones and she wondered at the impression she'd made on the butler. This suit was an absolute change from her normal clothes—charcoal wool jacket and knee-length skirt, over stockings that were slightly less dark and a white blouse that had been given to her by Tscadi. A gift originally brought by Matai, welcoming her in a sense to the family. The fabric looked like fine cotton, felt like silk, a wraparound design that swept up to a high collar while leaving an open neck. Under it, warm against her skin, she wore the *fireheart* choker. Her hair was swept straight back, almost severely, from her forehead and her eyes hidden behind a pair of tortoiseshell, shadow-lensed RayBan *Wayfarers*. And hanging from her right ear, the *fireheart* earring. When she'd come down to breakfast, even her mother had been stunned speechless. All through the flight in to LaGuardia, where a State Department limo had been waiting, she hadn't felt like herself. But that had been the idea.

The garage was the size of a fair-sized barn, home to a score of modern and vintage cars—some of which weren't even legal to run anymore on the open highway—with a workshop attached behind. Which was where the path from the back of the house was leading her.

She had to grin, she dressed to total power and Cobri threw her a curve by meeting her in a location where one misstep would have her sprawled on her elegant posterior in a puddle of oil.

"It's been a while, Lieutenant," he said, checking a natural impulse to offer his hand, giving her an appraising glance while he cleaned off the morning's grease and grime.

She stood her ground, framed in the doorway, with the afternoon light behind her, the strength of her body not muted in the slightest by her ensemble.

"Hardly that, sir," she replied neutrally, "it only seems so."

"You missed the funeral." *You planted him*, she thought, *without a second to waste.*

"I had other obligations." Namely, standing before a hastily convened Board of Inquiry, livelinked with Maguire and Canfield on the Moon and Kymri in the Hal Embassy in New York, who grilled her about every aspect of the rescue flight, taking her further back to the attempted assassination of President Russell. It wasn't a punitive investigation, that was made clear at the start, they just wanted to know *everything* that had happened. And she told them. What she saw, what she did, what she knew, what she surmised.

"You did your best for Alex, I know."

Do you? She stayed silhouetted against the sky, eyes behind shades, letting him squint to get a closer look. He wasn't used to stillness, it threatened his control and made him edgy.

"Quite frankly, I am amazed you went back."

"Why?"

"He tried to kill you."

"He was hurt, I wasn't about to abandon him." *And if you don't comprehend that, Old Man,* she thought, *you don't know anything.*

"D'you think he'd care so much for you?"

Actually, yes.

"He's your son."

"Who tried to kill me."

"So what d'you figure, let him go, that balances the scales, ties up the loose ends? Simply write him off the way you would a flawed investment?"

"He was a grown man, Lieutenant. Am I responsible for the decisions of his life?"

"You made the ones that mattered."

"What does that mean?"

"You gimmicked the boy in the womb, same as you're doing with these cars, to maximize performance."

"Such an accusation is, at best, in the poorest of taste. Some might consider it slanderous."

"Just two people making conversation, where's the harm in that?"

"Perhaps you'd be better served then, talking to yourself. I have better things to do."

He tried to walk past but she didn't give way, and he realized that to leave he'd have to push her aside. For a moment, he contemplated it and saw the slight, anticipatory smile that told him she was waiting for him to try.

" 'Too much of his mother,' that was what you told me," Nicole continued conversationally. "What, the package wasn't as advertised. Not quite perfection. Ain't Ma Nature a bitch, shame on her.

"How soon after he was born did you twig that he didn't measure up to specs?"

"Leave my house, Ms. Shea."

"When I'm ready. When I'm done. The boy was brilliant, and gifted. His only crime was that he wasn't you. Since when is that a capital offense?"

"How *dare* you!"

"Amazing. That's more raw emotion on his behalf than I'll bet you ever showed when he was alive—except maybe to his mom when the truth came out. All that work and you get a son with a bum heart, an arrhythmia condition that couldn't cope with extreme physical stress. He could live a normal life, he just wasn't perfect. And you never told him, did you? Amy knew, you knew, not him.

"But what the hell, you were already back at the drawing board, yes? 'If at first you don't succeed,' you said. 'That's why we have more than one.' But this time, no mistakes. A carbon copy, a little modified on the facade so no one would guess, but inside where it counts, you."

"Is there some purpose to this?" He'd turned back to his tools and she wondered if he'd throw something at her. "Other than perhaps the acquisition of your pound of flesh?"

"Call me Cassandra, here to deliver warnings that most likely won't be heeded. She isn't you, Manuel. Or rather, she's the untempered you. Raw, elemental, messy. Ungoverned and I suspect ungovernable."

He said nothing, and she had an image of some hulking cave bear cornered in its den.

"The Wolfpack I destroyed goes back five years, can you imagine? Amy's barely a teenager, yet while she was a kid she masterminded one of the deadliest criminal operations ever fronted in Mid-System."

"Prove it," he snapped.

"Ah, there's the rub. If evidence there was, it went up with the Wolfpack's asteroid base, or down with Patriot." Perhaps she shouldn't have brought Alex back to the Hybrid—he was dead, what did he care—and instead should have dived straight back inside to pull the core datapacks, assuming she could find them, assuming they weren't booby-trapped, assuming she could have gotten in and out safely.

But the missiles from Sutherland were already on their way, curving back along the station's orbital track, so that in effect they and Patriot were racing headlong towards each other, and the Hybrid had all of five minutes, tops, to pull clear.

"To be honest, I don't think anybody really wants to. To prove it, I mean." That had been made abundantly clear by the White House rep, in terms even Canfield wasn't prepared to buck. "Especially when Alex provides such a perfect patsy. But that won't change the truth."

"As if you know what such a thing even is!"

"Better I suspect than you. What, was this supposed to be some sort of rite of passage, a way of determining whether or not Amy could function in the big leagues? See, I don't buy the argument she could have handled this all by her lonesome. That you're the grand old entrepreneur who's gotten to the age and stage where he's content to leave the actual running of his company to others. If you didn't know, it's because you didn't want to. It still amounts to tacit, implicit approval."

"You're deranged."

"Then what are you worried about? I'm a young woman spouting nonsense."

"A young and foolish woman who'd best start treading very carefully, if she knows what's good for her."

"Interesting. I was thinking pretty much the same about an old and foolish man."

That struck a nerve and she knew they were at the line that, with Cobri, was never crossed.

"How do you tell a person no," she demanded, "when the very concept has no meaning? At least Alex played out his fantasies—good and bad—in the sanctity of his Virtual theater. They were shameful, but they were private. For Amy, that theater is whatever she can see. Alex—on a dare, I'll bet, your classic brother-sister thing; hell, I'll lay odds he even thought this was some sort of bonding between them— established the scenario for the Wolfpacks. The feds found the cassette—awfully conveniently—I've seen it, the thing's a masterpiece. But Amy made it reality. Phylogeny recapitulates ontogeny. Jean-Claude Baumier came up with the theoretical basis for an FTL drive, you made it work. What she takes from you, most completely, Cobri-Sire, is not the brilliance of creation—which is what Alex had, rest his poor, damned soul—but of manipulation. The difference is, your dream, your all-consuming passion, was to create this empire. Hers, like any kid, is to play."

He stood with his back close to the side wall, and its shelves of tools, and she wondered if he heard a word she said, or if he'd made himself as deaf as Alex had at the end. One hand was laid across his chest, while the other traced its middle finger along the outline of his mouth, from the philtrum outward, one way and then the other.

"You may be right," he said at last.

"Anything is possible."

"Are you determined, Lieutenant, to give not a centimeter?"

"Forgive me, Cobri-Sire, I should have mentioned earlier. That is not an appropriate term of address."

"I'm sorry. But I can't say I blame you. The bureaucracy has treated you shabbily." *Quite the opposite*, she thought, without a bit of it showing on her face, *and isn't it nice to discover there's something I know that you don't. But "bureaucracy"— NASA, Air Force, or otherwise—has nothing to do with what I said.*

"Have you considered a career in the private sector?" he asked her.

"Working for you?"

"I admire your directness. No false modesty, no fencing, no preliminaries, just cut straight to the heart of the matter. Yes, for me."

"I quit being a baby-sitter before high school."

His head came up and the bear image in her head bared its teeth.

"I wasn't aware . . ."

"Please," she cut him off in a tone of brusque dismissal, amazed that she could talk so to him, marveling that this was just like taking a new bird up for its first evaluation flight, full of the heady delight of breaking virgin territory tempered by the awareness that any mistake could well be fatal. Caring totally and yet not at all. "Whatever the job is called, we both—we all *three* of us," she added pointedly, "would know why I was here. Look in the mirror, Cobri-Sire, tell me how you'd react if Amy hired me to stand on your tail just when you were really starting to fly? See yourself, you know her."

"People do not talk this way to me."

"Or to her. The difference being, you mostly let it ride. She gets even."

"Do you want me to perhaps follow her example?"

Hers was a genuine smile, and all the more unnerving because of it.

"I was wondering," she said, reaching up at last to remove her glasses, "how quickly we'd get to this point."

"And what point is that?"

"The declaration of war."

"You flatter yourself, my girl. Assuming you're right, that 'war' as you put it would be over before it's begun."

"Some victories have a price, Cobri-Sire."

"You keep calling me that."

"It's the closest human approximation of the appropriate honorific."

"In Hal, you mean. I fail to see the need for such an affectation. Unless you're going native?" He tried a laugh to go with his joke, the one sounding as hollow as the other.

"I am Hal, as much as human," She said, her ignorance of the true implications of those words going hand in hand with her acceptance of them. "This marks me, Cobri-Sire"— and she touched the necklace—"as one of Shavrin's Prime. In essence, as much her child as any she physically bore. The Hal are a familial species, communities to them are an expanding network of extended families. An attack on me is an attack on her. An attack on mine is an attack on me." She had his full attention and the look on his face was one she'd give almost anything never to have had to see.

"Maybe you're right it's all coincidence. Maybe it's all paranoid theory carried to its wildest extreme. Set up Cobri, Associates as the modern equivalent of Britain's East India Company, a mercantile government parallel to the real thing, eventually superseding it. The assassination of a President championing rapprochement with our first extra terrestrial contact, by one of those very extra terrestrials—not a hope for any treaty, then. And probably not for the concept of a united world. Balkanized countries, with less and less access to and influence over a local space increasingly defined and dominated by Cobri or some shadow front holding. A potential competitor for Cobri StarSystems suddenly wiped from the board, because who'd risk dealing with these Aliens who had shot down their best friend on Earth? On the other hand, who better to deal with them than the man who's able to meet them on their own ground, our ships matched against theirs, our tech against theirs. Power implicit becomes power explicit becomes power absolute."

"Do you really believe that?"

"Alex had it all worked out. He loved role-playing games, remember; this was one where he wanted to see if he could beat you at yours. The original scenario didn't include the Hal, this was something he crafted to prove to you that he was worthy of being your son."

"I wasn't interested."

"I know. You rarely initiate events, you exploit the living hell out of them. Very Japanese. It was Amy who put it into motion. And Alex never realized, until I blew it wide open a year ago. I submit, Cobri-Sire, the scenario's still active. The kid's still growing."

"Help me stop her, then."

"She's *you*, do you still not understand? She is as you *made* her, in every sense of the word. Could you stop yourself?" Nicole shook her head. "I'm not here for you, Cobri-Sire. To be honest, I couldn't care less. Alex was the best thing you had going for you, and he, poor boy, was a joke.

"I tell you, any act against my people—*anything*—and we come for you."

" 'We'?"

"*We!* The Hal don't play by human rules and have no respect for some human niceties. Their beliefs are encompassed by the concept of *alach'n'yn*, blood price. They take it very seriously."

"I have no interest in you, Ms. Shea. Or your 'people.' "

"This isn't meant for you."

"I see. I understand. Is there anything else?"

"We're done."

"Then you will excuse me if I do not show you out. I believe you have your own transport."

She shook her head as she turned her back on him, donning her shades once more as she strode up the path to the house. Whatever she'd expected from this confrontation, she wasn't sure she'd gotten it. Certainly not any sense of satisfaction. She felt like she'd just bulled her way through the heart of a brute thunderstorm, or into the eye of a killer hurricane, as though she'd been pummelled across the back and shoulders, all the way down to the base of her spine. And she was thankful for the hotel suite waiting for her across the harbor in Manhattan, craving nothing more than to turn herself into a shriveled prune in its bathtub.

Frankenstein isn't the right image, though, she considered, thinking back to her conversation on Nantucket with Alex. *Better to think of God on his throne, staring in bemused despair at the handiwork of Lucifer, crafted oh so gloriously in His image only to betray Him.* She started to chuckle at the image of the Lord lamenting, *I made him what he is, how could I get things so wrong?* And then the chuckle died as she made the logical extension of the analogy. "Always assuming," she muttered aloud, "he got it wrong and this really *is* a mistake."

She was inside the house, taking her camel coat from the butler, slinging it over her shoulders and scooping up bag and gloves, when a voice rang out from high above.

"*You*," Amy cried, trying to match Nicole's roar only to have her voice splinter in her throat.

The staircase towered four stories overhead and Amy was right up at the top, almost indistinguishable from the skylight just above her head.

"You killed my brother," she cried. And Nicole had nothing to say to that. So she stood her ground and waited for what would come next.

"You killed my brother," the girl shrieked again from on highest, in that falsetto tone kids slip into when losing any semblance of control.

Nicole shook her head again, once, twice, a short and definite denial, turning across the broad foyer with the girl's voice ripping after her, spiraling ever higher into a hysterical rant. If she'd been in range, Nicole would have slapped her hard enough to leave a mark, but she wasn't about to chase Amy around her own house. The noise was climbing into impossible registers, the words slurring-blurring with every repetition. "You killed my brother. You killed my brother." The kind of rant that no empirical counter could deny. And Nicole wondered if the girl was really sorry, or if this public show of grief was some form of rationalized expiation. See how upset I am, see how much he meant to me, I couldn't possibly have been responsible.

"But you were," Nicole said softly, striking a military cadence

down the steps to her waiting car, at the last moment catching
sight of Manuel Cobri trudging up the drive, the Man of the
People, the Blue-Collar Billionaire, old clothes marked with
the grit of honest physical labor. *To each,* Nicole thought, *their
favorite illusion.*

United States of America
National Aeronautics & Space Administration
Department of Manned Spaceflight
Office of the Chief Astronaut

After reviewing the opinion of the Medical Evaluations Board, together with all other pertinent data, it is the judgment of this office that Second Lieutenant Nicole Shea, United States Air Force, is fit to hold an astronaut's rating and is therefore restored to Flight Status, effective immediately.

    (Signed)
    Michael Sallinger
    Commanding Officer
    Edwards Flight Test Center

    David Elias
    Chief Astronaut

    Judith Canfield
    Commanding General
    U.S.A.F. Space Command
    Director of Manned Spaceflight